# THE ADVENTURES OF COLONEL SELLERS

# THE ADVENTURES
## OF
# COLONEL SELLERS

## *by* MARK TWAIN

Being Mark Twain's share of THE GILDED AGE,
a novel which he wrote with Charles Dudley Warner. Now published separately for the first time and
comprising, in effect, a new work.

*Edited and with an introduction and notes by*

## CHARLES NEIDER

GARDEN CITY, NEW YORK

*Doubleday & Company, Inc.*

1965

Library of Congress Catalog Card Number 65–11053
Copyright © 1965 by Charles Neider
All Rights Reserved
Printed in the United States of America
First Edition

# ACKNOWLEDGMENTS

I wish to acknowledge my indebtedness for help of several kinds to the following persons and institutions: John Gordon and Mrs. Lola Szladits and the Berg Collection of the New York Public Library; Miss Marjorie Wynne and the Beinecke Library of Yale University; Miss Julie Hudson and the Firestone Library of Princeton University; Frederick Anderson and the library of the University of California, Berkeley; the Special Collections library of Columbia University; and the library of the New York Historical Society.

# CONTENTS

# A NOVELIST'S DEBUT

*by Charles Neider*

Of the two paragraphs which Mark Twain contributed to the preface of *The Gilded Age,* one, the last of the preface, was the following:

"One word more. This is—what it pretends to be—a joint production, in the conception of the story, the exposition of the characters, and in its literal composition. There is scarcely a chapter that does not bear the marks of the two writers of the book."

The paragraph was designed to reassure the subscription reader (the volume was meant to be sold by subscription only) that the product was not a hodge-podge, a mish-mash, a conflict of styles, settings and characterizations; that it was a sensible, reasonable, harmonious joint production. The paragraph was less than candid, for some of the chief characters, Colonel Sellers, Laura Hawkins and Washington Hawkins, were Mark Twain's sole creations, as was the backwoods Missouri setting, and more than fifty of the sixty-three chapters were written not by two hands but by one. If we are to believe Mark Twain's friend and official biographer, Albert Bigelow Paine, even the basic story was Mark Twain's alone. Mark Twain almost gave the game away when he said, "This is—what it pretends to be—." The idea of a thoroughly joint production was a dubious one, for it is difficult to see how two minds and two styles as different as those of Clemens and Charles Dudley Warner could be depended on to bring forth anything but dissonance.

If Mark Twain—perhaps guilelessly—misled the prospective reader, he did not mislead certain of his friends. Shortly after *The Gilded Age* was published he wrote to his friend Mrs. Fairbanks (February 25, 1874), "I think you don't like the Gilded Age,—but that's because you've been reading *Warner's* chapters. I wrote chapters 1, 2, 3, 4, 5, 6, 7, 8, 9, 10, 11, 24, 25, 27, 28, 30, 32, 33, 34, 36, 37, 42, 43, 45, first three or four pages of 49,—also chapters 51, 52, 53, 57, 59, 60, 61, 62 & portions of 35 & 56. You read *those*." Three days later he wrote to Dr. John Brown, "My dear friend—we are all delighted with your commendations of the Gilded Age—& the more so because some of our newspapers have set forth the opinion that *Warner* really wrote the book & I only added my name to the title-page in order to give it a large sale. It is a shameful charge to make. I wrote the first eleven chapters—every word & every line—Warner never retouched a sentence in them, I believe. I also wrote chapters 24, 25, 27, 28, 30, 32, 33, 34, 36, 37, 42, 45, 51, 52, 53, 57, 59, 60, 61, 62, & *portions* of 35, 49, & 56. So I wrote 32 of the 63 chapters *entirely*, & part of 3 others beside.

"The fearful financial panic hit the book heavily, for we published in the midst of it. But nevertheless in the 8 weeks that have now elapsed since the day we published, we have sold 40,000 copies—which gives £3,000 royalty to be divided between the authors. This is really the largest two-months' sale which any American book has ever achieved (unless one excepts the cheap edition of Uncle Tom's Cabin). The average price of our book is 16 shillings a copy—Uncle Tom was 2 shillings a copy. But for the panic our sale would have been doubled, I verily believe. I do not believe the sale will ultimately go over 100,000 copies."

In July 1874 Mark Twain noted in a copy of *The Gilded Age* for his friend William Seaver the chapters and parts of chapters which he had written. It is clear from the letters and the marked copy that the novel is not the joint production which Clemens claimed it to be in the preface. This judgment is supported by an examination of a substantial portion of the extant manuscript. I have not been able to discover in the manuscript anything which challenges Clemens's ascription of authorship in the two letters and in the Seaver copy. It is for this reason—

Clemens's authoritative statement of his contribution to the novel—that it is possible to publish his contribution separately. It is worth noting in passing that whereas in the letters to Mrs. Fairbanks and to Dr. Brown, Clemens claimed all of Chapter 53, in the Seaver copy he indicated a few brief passages by Warner in that chapter. There are other small differences between the Seaver copy and the letters. It is clear that the Seaver copy has a higher authority than the letters.

The Gilded Age has lived because of Mark Twain's share of it, although most readers did not and do not know which parts were his. It has lived because his genius is in it, at a youthful and vigorous stage. It has lived despite Warner's contribution. Mark Twain's share is immeasurably superior to Warner's—in style, gusto, humor, characterization, story. Warner provided characters of rather trifling importance, and a style which served chiefly to show how idiomatic and lithe Clemens's was. The novel's central character, Colonel Sellers, is one of the successful creations of American fiction. It was an error for Mark Twain to seek Warner's help. There can be little doubt that had he undertaken the work alone he would have produced a good novel and one which would have spared him from living under the cloud of joint authorship. As it happens, his share of The Gilded Age is the central share and the text is cohesive and extensive enough to be printed separately if certain sections by Warner are synopsized to carry the story along.

To the possible objection that Mark Twain's work ought not to be "tampered with," we can recall that Bernard DeVoto modernized the punctuation of a masterpiece, Huckleberry Finn, and inserted a chapter into it which Clemens never put into it. Yet nobody consigned DeVoto to hell for doing it. He was, by the way, literary editor of the Mark Twain Estate and the outstanding Mark Twain scholar at the time he did it. I have not changed one word of Mark Twain's text. My sole purpose has been to rescue his text, not to change it; to let the reader see as clearly as possible just what it was that Clemens put into The Gilded Age. Clemens himself set a kind of precedent by extracting his share of *The Gilded Age* when he made the play called *Colonel Sellers,* which was a great success, with John T. Raymond playing the colonel. The method I have used in synopsizing Warner, printing him in a denser type than Clemens, and bracketing him, follows Clemens's method when he lifted *Those Extraordinary Twins* out of *Pudd'nhead Wilson* and printed it separately, with portions synopsized and printed in smaller type than the main text.

I have discussed *The Gilded Age* elsewhere and would like to repeat what I have said there. For some time before he began *The Gilded Age* Clemens had considered writing a tale based on the visionary character of his mother's cousin, James Lampton, but, as his biographer later explained, he was "unwilling to undertake an extended work of fiction alone." One evening early in 1873, when Clemens and his wife were dinner hosts to the Charles Dudley Warners, their neighbors in Hartford, the husbands made some slighting remarks about the quality of the novels their wives were currently reading. To which the wives responded with a challenge: all right, then why didn't the husbands write a better novel and improve the public's taste? The challenge was accepted in a spirit of fun and the two men conferred about a plan. Clemens proposed the tale he had had in mind, which pleased Warner, and without much ado Clemens set to work and quickly completed the first eleven chapters of the novel, which he read aloud to Warner. Warner then wrote the next installment of chapters.

The husbands' criticism of contemporary novels was echoed later the same year by the *Saturday Review* in some comments which were reprinted by the New York *Daily Graphic* under the title "Modern Novels."

"Nobody can look upon the stream of fiction which is constantly poured forth upon the public without some doubts as to the intellectual habits which it fosters. Every day brings forth some new aspirant to the pulpit. If we could believe, which indeed would be a rather rash assumption, that they all succeed in obtaining some kind of hearing, we should be awe-struck by the revelation of the waste of human energy. It is bad enough that so many people should write such trash, that so many printers should waste so much paper in circulating it, and that so many critics should be doomed to give it at least a cursory glance. It would be still more lamentable if we could believe that a large class of readers derives its chief intellectual sustenance from these monotonous reproductions of old materials. How can standard literature—or, not to use a term which has unfortunately become associated with much that is wearisome, how can the thoughts of men who have really had something to say about the world—receive a due share of attention when swamped and overwhelmed in this torrent of vapid literature? Nobody, of course, would be puritanical enough to deny to hard-worked men and women the right of unbending their minds over innocent, if insipid, literature at odd moments. We cannot all fill up the interstices of our lives with metaphysical or scientific or historical researches. But certainly it is a natural impression that the habit of endless story-telling and endless story-reading is hardly likely to encourage strenuous thought. If not demoral-izing in the sense of actually encouraging vice, it is perhaps de-moralizing in the sense of softening the intellectual fibre. A man raised upon rice-pudding and water-gruel would not have strong bones and firm muscles; and a mind nourished by modern novels would hardly be fitted for vigorous intellectual labor. In spite of the outcry about sensationalism, the bulk of our novel litera-ture is dull and colorless enough in all conscience. The objection to it is not that it is vicious, but that it is enervating; and when Mr. Trollope was delivering an address to youths who had won prizes in some kind of intellectual competition, he would per-haps have spoken more to the purpose if, instead of proving that Dickens does not teach us to be misers and debauchees, he had shown under what conditions Dickens and other modern writers may be used for purposes of rational relaxation without crushing the loftier imaginative or reasoning faculties under a weight of commonplace moralizing and indolent representations of every-day life."

*The Gilded Age,* begun in February 1873 if we are to believe Albert Bigelow Paine, or in January if we are to trust a letter of April 7th by Warner, was completed in April. In the April 7th letter, written to Whitelaw Reid, Warner said, "Maybe it's a great piece of presumption, but Mark and I are writing a novel . . . No one here, except our wives, knows anything of it. We conceived the design early in the winter, but were not able to get seriously at work on it till some time in January . . . We have hatched the plot day by day, drawn out the characters, and written it so that we cannot exactly say which belongs to whom; though the different styles will show in the chapters." On the 16th of April Clemens wrote to Mrs. Fairbanks, "Ever since I arrived from England, several months ago, Chas. Dudley Warner & I have been belting away every day on a *partnership novel.* I have worked 6 days a week—good full days—& laid myself up, once. Have written many chapters twice, & some of them three times—have thrown away 300 clean pages of MS. & still there's havoc to be made when I enter on final polishing. Warner has been more fortunate—he won't lose 50 pages . . . Every night for many weeks, Livy & Susie Warner have collected in my study to hear Warner & me read our day's work; & they have done a power of criticizing, but have always been anxious to be on hand at the reading & find out what has been happening to the dramatis personae since the previous evening. They both pleaded so long & vigorously for Warner's heroine, that yesterday Warner agreed to spare her life & let her marry— he meant to kill her. I killed my heroine as dead as a mackerel yesterday (but Livy don't know it yet). . . ."

On April 26 Clemens wrote to his wife Livy, who was in Elmira for a brief visit, "I have finished trimming & revamping all my MS, & to-day we began the work of critically reading the book, line by line, & numbering the chapters & working them in together in their appropriate places. It is perfectly fascinating work. All of the first eleven chapters are mine, & when I came to read them right straight along without breaking, I got really interested; & when I got to Sellers' eye-water & his clock & his fireless stove & his turnip dinner, I could hardly read for laughing. The turnip dinner is powerful good—& is satisfactory now. . . . We both think this is going to be no slouch of a novel, as Solomon said to the Hebrew children."

*The Gilded Age* was published shortly before Christmas of 1873. Long afterwards Clemens recalled that he and Warner had worked alternately "in the superstition that we were writing one coherent yarn, when I suppose, as a matter of fact, we were writing two *in*coherent ones." In this casual, almost haphazard, way Mark Twain began his career as a major American novelist. When the book was published he was in England and was being sought out as the famous author of *The Innocents Abroad* and *Roughing It,* as well as of numerous sketches and stories. The novel appeared in England at about the same time that it appeared in America. On December 11 Mark Twain wrote a preface to the London edition, which he signed·

"In America nearly every man has his dream, his pet scheme, whereby he is to advance himself socially or pecuniarily. It is this all-pervading speculativeness which we have tried to illustrate in 'The Gilded Age.' It is a characteristic which is both bad and good, for both the individual and the nation. Good, because it allows neither to stand still, but drives both for ever on, toward some point or other which is ahead, not behind nor at one side. Bad, because the chosen point is often badly chosen, and then the individual is wrecked; the aggregation of such cases affects the nation, and so is bad for the nation. Still, it is a trait which it is of course better for a people to have and sometimes suffer from than to be without.

"We have also touched upon one 'sad feature, and it is one which we found little pleasure in handling. That is the shameful corruption which lately crept into our politics, and in a handful of years has spread until the pollution has affected some portion of every State and every Territory in the Union.

"But I have a great strong faith in a noble future for my

country. A vast majority of the people are straightforward and honest; and this late state of things is stirring them to action. If it would only keep on stirring them until it became the habit of their lives to attend to the politics of the country personally, and put only their very best men into positions of trust and authority! That day will come. ↙○

"Our improvement has already begun. Mr. Tweed (whom Great Britain furnished to us), after laughing at our laws and courts for a good while, has at last been sentenced to thirteen years' imprisonment, with hard labor. It is simply bliss to think of it. It will be at least two years before any governor will dare to pardon him out, too. A great New York judge, who continued a vile, a shameless career, season after season, defying the legislature and sneering at the newspapers, was brought low at last, stripped of his dignities, and by public sentence debarred from ever again holding any office of honor or profit in the State. Another such judge (furnished to us by Great Britain) had the grace to break his heart and die in the palace built with his robberies when he saw the same blow preparing for his own head and sure to fall upon it."

*The Gilded Age* is in many respects a *roman à clef* and it was widely recognized as such in contemporary reviews. The *New York World* wrote: "Senator Dilworthy will be as readily recognized as though his true name had been used. . . . So, too, the great Mr. Braham, New York's most successful criminal lawyer, is as palpable to the reader . . . as he is to the frequenters of our criminal courts." The *New York Evening Mail* wrote: "The murder trial in New York makes some hard hits, and Mr. Braham's speech will be easily identified. . . . The authors evidently meant, when they drew a character from life, that he should recognize himself. They have in some instances made sure of this by using the real name of the man intended, and in other cases the modifications made in the proper names of the persons described are so slight that nobody can mistake the originals. Thus we have Jeff Thompson, without any mask at all, as the engineer who of all others was the man to make a

preliminary survey for a railroad, it being the principal business
of the preliminary survey to make the road seem certain to pass
through every town, and intersect every big plantation, within
thirty miles of its probable route. We have Mr. Duff Brown
too, whom every Western man will recognize simply by substitut-
ing for Brown another color." The Boston *Saturday Evening
Gazette* noted that Senators Cameron and Nye might recognize themselves in the novel, as Senators Pomeroy and Harlan
surely would. The Gazette also noted that Credit Mobilier, Back
Pay, and other schemes and scandals were depicted with
"photographic accuracy." The Springfield, Mass., *Union* reported:
"The melancholy developments of political venality at Washington, last winter, with their exhibitions of religious hypocrisy and
general corruption, are, with slight changes in the names of the
parties concerned, fully shown up in a light mercilessly clear.
That 'Christian statesman,' Senator Pomeroy [of Kansas], is
one of the leading characters of the book. The character and
methods of the Washington female lobbyists are fully illustrated
in the career of Laura Hawkins. This lady finally kills her par-
amour, and her trial, acquittal and attempt to enter the lecture
field are worked up from the Laura Fair case [of San Fran-
cisco], and the emotional insanity farces for which New York
courtrooms have been famous. The reader of this book will
say, how astonishing, absurd and sensational are its transitions
and situations, and yet his memory will tell him that the most
startling developments of the story are but slightly veiled reproductions of events that have been in the newspapers within
a year."

*The Gilded Age* is a very spotty book, as we might expect it to
be. There are gross differences in style, tone and characterization,
due to the fact that two different hands were at work, showing
Mark Twain's broad strokes, earthy humor and backwoods setting together with Warner's deft, sophisticated touches, ur-
bane humor and in general urban setting. The novel is a mongrel
work. Warner was working on Clemens's terrain and was at a
disadvantage in any comparison with Clemens. On his own ter-

rain Warner was a good writer. He was especially good as an essayist. His *My Summer in a Garden* is pleasant reading. Some of his *Backlog Studies* is beautiful and well-sustained, and much sounder, more personal and more lyrical than *My Summer in a Garden*. Warner had a "refined" style but it was surprisingly uncluttered and supple. As far as the social theme of *The Gilded Age* was concerned, however, the two men worked harmoniously. Both were inspired by a profound skepticism regarding the course the nation was taking, and they produced a portrait of the feverish, overblown, corrupt Reconstruction period. The title of the novel is a superb epigraph on that time.

From the beginning Mark Twain had the good sense, the instinct, to rely on familiar materials. Squire Hawkins is in some respects modelled on his father; Washington Hawkins is modelled on his brother Orion; and Uncle Dan'l is apparently modelled on the real Uncle Dan'l of Clemens's boyhood, who later became the great figure Jim in *Huckleberry Finn*. The motif of the Tennessee Land is based on real events. The description of the steamboat race is based on Mark Twain's knowledge of the river, and the description of Washington society and of Congress is based on personal experience and observation.

Clemens's great ability to hear and write dialogue and dialect authentically are in obvious evidence in the novel. We rarely *see* characters in *The Gilded Age;* mostly we hear them. At times, however, Clemens's dialogue is embarrassingly melodramatic and naïve, especially when he is dealing in "psychological" moments. Like Hemingway, Clemens was a master of the external life and weak when he was dealing with the internal one, or with sensitive psychology. His, like Hemingway's, was essentially a man's world, and women are for the most part shadowy figures in it. The emotions of his characters are mostly primitive, even when their psychology is not supposed to be primitive. For the most part the characters of *The Gilded Age* are cartoons, entertaining at times but too often letting us reflect that they are not seriously concerned with the business of life and literature. Not unexpectedly, Clemens in this

first novel begins a habit of dropping footnotes to assure us
that he has a real reality in mind, that he is not merely writing
a fairy tale, a fable. Non-fiction seems more important to him,
and he assures us of the importance of his fiction by pointing
to its "real" origins.

We ought not to assume that whereas Clemens worked from
authentic materials Warner did not. Warner had once been a
practicing lawyer and it is partly for this reason that the
courtroom scenes are so well done. He had once been a railroad surveyor in Missouri and was familiar with the Missouri
setting and with surveying. Even the motif of inherited land was
not foreign to him. His father was a farmer in western Massachusetts and when he died virtually all that he left his widow
and sons was the some 200 acres he owned.

There was a third co-worker in this vineyard: J. Hammond
Trumbull, who supplied the chapter mottoes. He was reputed
to be the most learned man in Hartford of his time. Clemens,
a choice practitioner and connoisseur of swearing, claimed with
awe that Trumbull could swear in twenty-seven languages.

The critical reception of *The Gilded Age* was not, on the
whole, the kind that warms the cockles of an author's heart,
or of his two hearts, as in this instance. There was a good deal
of the usual uncritical praise in the small-town papers, and
there was praise here and there in the large cities, but the authors were disconcerted by the general view that the experiment
in joint authorship had failed. Clemens was gloomy, almost bitter, about the book's reception. Six years later he wrote to
Howells, "I am justified in being afraid of the general press,
because it killed the 'Gilded Age' before you had a chance to
point out that there were merits in that book. The sale ceased
almost *utterly* until the adverse criticisms were forgotten—then
began again, & has kept smoothly on." Perhaps Clemens was still
unaware that Howells had not much liked the book.

Down to near the close of his life Clemens remained sensitive about the critical reception of *The Gilded Age*. On Sep-

tember 27, 1907, his secretary, Isobel Lyon, wrote in her notebook that after dinner Clemens had been pacing his living room
in Dublin, New Hampshire, when she remarked that in reading *The Gilded Age* that afternoon she had been "impressed by
the fact that it was notably the work of two minds." Clemens
had then talked about the novel. In 1933 Miss Lyon, consulting
her notebook, recalled the gist of his remarks. "He said it
was probably the end of 1872, when he had been in Hartford
only a short time, that he suggested to Warner that they
write a novel together. He said he did it because he had a
fresh great reputation and he had a fear that he must not stand
alone; so *The Gilded Age* was written and published. The first
review of it in a Chicago paper was a hostile one. It said he was
living on his reputation, and getting some one else to do his
work. Mr. Clemens was in a serious mood; he went on to say
it was all a mistake; he thought it was for the best, but it made
discomfort all around, for Warner felt that the adverse criticism
was for him."

Miss Lyon seems to imply that the Chicago review was the first
review of the novel but her punctuation has the sentence
state that it was merely the first Chicago review. It is impossible
to know her precise meaning. Perhaps Clemens had in mind
the review in the Chicago *Tribune* of April 5, 1874, which was
by no means the first review of the book. On that day the *Tribune* quoted a comment from the St. Louis *Democrat*: "The
secret is out. It is confidently asserted that *The Gilded Age* is a
gigantic practical joke. It is declared that, wishing to test the
credulity of the public, these two notorious wits had the book
prepared by several obscure newspaper local reporters. The
covenant was solemnly made that the joke was to be kept a
profound secret till 300,000 copies of the work were sold . . ."
This comment does not exactly match Clemens's description
of it, or rather Miss Lyon's recollection of Clemens's description.
In 1907 Clemens had implied that he had been charged with
getting Warner to do his work for him, but the *Tribune,* if
that was the paper he had in mind, had charged both him and

Warner with getting others to do their work for them. Clemens's memory was notoriously unreliable at times, as can be illustrated in his recollections of the New York *Daily Graphic* review of *The Gilded Age*. When he was dictating a chapter of his autobiography in July 1906 he said:

"I believe that the trade of critic in literature, music and the drama is the most degraded of all trades and that it has no real value—certainly no large value. When Charles Dudley Warner and I were about to bring out *The Gilded Age* the editor of the *Daily Graphic* persuaded me to let him have an advance copy, he giving me his word of honor that no notice of it should appear in his paper until after the *Atlantic Monthly* notice should have appeared. This reptile published a review of the book within three days afterward. I could not really complain, because he had only given me his word of honor as security. I ought to have required of him something substantial. I believe his notice did not deal mainly with the merit of the book or the lack of it but with my moral attitude toward the public. It was charged that I had used my reputation to play a swindle upon the public—that Mr. Warner had written as much as half of the book and that I had used my name to float it and give it currency—a currency which it could not have acquired without my name—and that this conduct of mine was a grave fraud upon the people. The *Graphic* was not an authority upon any subject whatever. It had a sort of distinction in that it was the first and only illustrated daily newspaper that the world had seen; but it was without character, it was poorly and cheaply edited, its opinion of a book or of any other work of art was of no consequence. Everybody knew this, yet all the critics in America, one after the other, copied the *Graphic's* criticism, merely changing the phraseology, and left me under that charge of dishonest conduct. Even the great Chicago *Tribune,* the most important journal in the Middle West, was not able to invent anything fresh but adopted the view of the humble *Daily Graphic,* dishonesty charge and all. However, let it go. It is the will of God that we must have critics and missionaries and congressmen and humorists, and we must bear the burden."

The *Daily Graphic* review was entirely different from what Clemens recalled it to be. Inasmuch as it has not been reprinted, to my knowledge, I include it here.

" 'The Gilded Age' is the title of the long expected novel written by Mark Twain and Charles Dudley Warner, and published by the American Publishing Company of Hartford, Ct. It is many months since this book was announced, and from the reputation of its authors it was anticipated that the book would be one of remarkable interest and merit. It is necessary to say that these expectations have been signally disappointed. Regarded either as a novel or an exponent of the wit and humor of the two authors, 'The Gilded Age' is a failure. It is simply a rather incoherent series of sketches, from which the characteristic fun of Mr. Clemens and the subtle humor of Mr. Warner have been, for the most part, eliminated. The reader can hardly fail to adopt the only theory of the manner in which the book was written, which will account for its peculiarities. According to this theory, each of the authors wrote alternate chapters of the work without any previous consultation. They then met and pieced those chapters together so as to form a story with some degree of connection between its parts. This theory easily explains the reason why characters introduced in one part of the book abruptly vanish in another, and why men who at their first introduction to us possess certain characteristics entirely lose them a little later. It explains, in short, why the book is so fragmentary in its character, and fully accounts for the wonderful weakness of the plot. We are inclined to think that Mark Twain originally intended that the story should be made as incoherent and exasperating as possible, by way of a joke, but that he was finally overruled, and a book that would otherwise have been a capital burlesque was fashioned into a semblance of a serious novel. But what will chiefly disappoint the readers of 'The Gilded Age' is the lack of that abundance of humor which we had the right to anticipate. It is probable that Mr. Warner revised Mark Twain's chapters, and saying to himself, 'This man's humor is far too wild and coarse,' toned them down till they had lost the characteristic mark of their authorship. And similarly it is probable that Mark revised Mr. Warner's chapters, and calling the good 'gosh' of New England worship to witness that Warner's humor was far too delicate and subtle, translated it into a plainness of speech adapted to the comprehension of the dullest idiot. And so it has come to pass that the two most brilliant humorists in America—with the exception of 'John Paul'—have written a book in which we look almost in vain for the traces of either's pen. Nevertheless, it is obvious that neither could altogether smother the other in a book of so many octavo pages. There are here and there a few glimpses of Warner's wit, and occasionally we find one of Mark's paragraphs which the destroyer has not wholly tamed. There is also much legitimate satire in the book; and the characters of Senator Dilworthy, the 'Christian statesman'; of 'Brother Balaam,' the pious occupant of a berth in the Interior Department; and of Mr. Braham, the eminent criminal lawyer of this city, are admirably drawn. In isolated passages the book is frequently clever and amusing. It is as a whole that it will be recognized as a rather dreary failure. There are illustrations without number scattered through its pages, but they are fearfully and wonderfully bad. There is neither humor nor artistic merit in any one of them, and in a second edition they ought without any exception to be ruthlessly struck out."

It was a biting, snide, harsh review and it went overboard in stressing the novel's flaws and was ungenerous and unfair regarding its virtues, especially those contributed by Clemens, such as the characters of Sellers and Laura Hawkins and the Missouri setting. It verged on idiocy when it put Warner in Clemens's class as a humorist. Warner's vein of humor was small and somewhat thin and at times it was very uncertain; and he had turned out two or three slim volumes as compared with the large and powerful and broad-scaled *The Innocents Abroad* and *Roughing It*. Strictly speaking he was not even a humorist. Idiocy was capped by lunacy when the review set John Paul (Charles H.

Webb) above both Clemens and Warner. Clemens ought to have discounted the review by three-quarters, except for its strictures on the novel's illustrations. The illustrations were indeed bad, designed as they were for a subscription audience.

But intemperate though it was, the review was probably sincere, and it did not make the moral accusations against Clemens which the latter much later recalled that it had made. It did not set the style for reviews of the novel, and the Chicago *Tribune* did not echo it in essentials, "dishonesty charge and all." *The Gilded Age*—or part of it—was Clemens's first novel, and we can appreciate his sensitivity to the *Graphic's* hard approach, especially because we can imagine that he may have felt defensive about the idea of joint authorship once it was too late to abandon it. It may be true that the editor of the *Graphic* broke his word to Clemens that he would not print a review until after the *Atlantic* had printed one; I have no way of checking Clemens's memory in this detail. The *Atlantic* did not review the book, probably for the reason that William Dean Howells, the editor and an excellent and sympathetic reader of Mark Twain, had a mixed reaction to it. Howells read an advance copy at the end of 1873 and wrote to Warner: "Up to the time old Hawkins dies your novel is of the greatest promise—I read it with joy—but after that it fails to assimilate the crude material with which it is fed, and becomes a confirmed dyspeptic at last. Still it is always entertaining; and it kept me up till twelve last night, though I needed sleep. I was particularly sorry to have Sellers degenerate as he did, and none of the characters quite fulfill their early promise."

Clemens's strong reaction to the *Graphic* is an interesting one and suggests that there was more to his relationship with the paper than meets the eye. A study of the files of the *Graphic* illuminates the relationship. The *Graphic's* first issue was Tuesday, March 4, 1873. In the issue of March 12 there appeared a letter to the editor, headlined MARK TWAIN WANTS "THE DAILY GRAPHIC". It was dated Hartford, March 8. "If I enclosed a check to 'Publishers Graphic' the cashier might not consider it good commercial literature, but, perhaps, you won't mind taking the chances on it yourself. I would like to have the paper sent—six dollars' worth—to the lady who bore me, viz.: Mrs. Jane Clemens, Fredonia, N.Y. Very truly yours, Mark Twain. P. S. After all, it isn't worth while to bother you with this check. If it should prove worthless, it will occur to the publishers not to send the paper."

Two days later the *Graphic* printed a letter headed A LETTER FROM MARK TWAIN, prefacing it with, "The following letter from Mark Twain shows what our most eminent and popular humorist thinks of our enterprise." The letter was dated Hartford, March 13. ". . . It is a marvellous paper—and the strangest marvel is that it seems to keep on going, like a substantial reality, instead of flaming a moment and then fading out, like an enthusiast's distempered dream. Every day when the carrier leaves it at the door, I think that that one doubtless contains the obituary (illustrated), and that he will collect his money now and come no more; but it does not result so, and I am one who is not sorry. Indeed, the pictures grow finer and clearer and softer, which is a surprising thing, and must be as gratifying to you as it is to me, I should think. I hope you will be able to keep it going all the time, for I don't care much about reading (unless it be some tranquillizing tract or other), but I do like to look at pictures, and the illustrated weeklies do not come to me as often as I need them. And then there is another thing—a national matter. We thought we invented the steamboat: England claimed priority and flooded the world with testimony. We thought we invented the magnetic telegraph: England claimed priority again, and gave all the credit to her Wheatstone. We thought we invented Old Probabilities—and now she comes forward with her old 'original Jacobs' in that line, and says he died some years ago and left no successor. But I don't think she has ever invented an illustrated daily newspaper. I do believe we have 'got her' at last, as the clergy say. And if it is so, let us keep her reminded of it in a friendly way—and pretty constantly. Yours truly, Samuel L. Clemens."

It is clear from this letter that Clemens at one time admired the *Graphic*, and that the *Graphic* was proud to be admired by him and that it regarded him, as did most newspapers, as highly newsworthy. It is doubtful that Clemens at that time believed that the *Graphic* "was without character" or that it was "poorly and cheaply edited" or that "its opinion of a book or of any other work of art was of no consequence." The *Graphic* was well edited, was printed on good paper, was expertly illustrated, and provided a variety of news and opinion. Its tone was lively and skeptical and it was recognized at once as a remarkable innovation. It is possible that Clemens thought highly of the paper and that for this reason he was stung by its sharp review. If he believed in 1906 that the *Graphic's* opinion of a book was of no consequence, how is it that his memory told him that "all the critics in America, one after the other, copied the *Graphic's* criticism"? Mark Twain may have felt that the *Graphic* had let their promising new relationship down. On the other hand the *Graphic* may have honestly felt that Mark Twain had let the cause of American humor down in the joint authorship project.

It was to the *Graphic* that Mark Twain publicly revealed the joint project. Learning that he was preparing to visit England, the *Graphic* asked him for a farewell statement to America. Clemens responded with a long and characteristically droll letter, which he closed with: "During the last two months my next-door neighbor, Chas. Dudley Warner, has dropped his 'Back-Log Studies,' & he & I have written a bulky novel in partnership. He has worked up the fiction & I have hurled in the facts. I consider it one of the most astonishing novels that ever was written. Night after night I sit up reading it over & over again & crying. It will be published early in the fall, with plenty of pictures. Do you consider this an advertisement?—& if so, do you charge for such things, when a man is your friend & is an orphan?

"Drooping now, under the solemn peacefulness, the general stagnation, the profound lethargy that broods over the land, I am Yrs truly . . ." He wrote the letter April 17. The *Graphic* devoted more than a half of one of its large pages on April 22, reproducing Clemens's handwriting. The next day the *Graphic* printed a description of Mark Twain as an editor, which it copied from the *Globe,* a monthly magazine published in Buffalo, N.Y. The item described Clemens's habits in the offices of the Buffalo *Express.* Then there was a long silence, due perhaps to the fact that Clemens was out of the country. The silence was broken by the *Graphic's* review, which appeared at a time when Clemens was again in England.

On January 15, 1874, the *Graphic* reprinted a letter by Clemens, with the preface, "The London *Post* prints as 'a specimen of transatlantic puffery' this hit by Mark Twain at the custom the English have of insisting upon the presence of some person of rank at popular gatherings." The letter is perhaps worth reviving and preserving here as part of the record of Clemens's relationship with the *Graphic.*

"Now that my lecturing engagement is drawing to its close, I find that there is one attraction which I forgot to provide, and that is the attendance of some great member of the Government to give distinction to my entertainment. Strictly speaking, I did not really forget this or underrate its importance, but the truth was, I was afraid of it. I was afraid of it for the reason that those great personages have so many calls upon their time that they cannot well spare the time to sit out an entertainment, and I knew that if one of them were to leave his box and retire while I was lecturing it would seriously embarrass me. I find, however, that many people think I ought not to allow this lack to exist longer; therefore I feel compelled to reveal a thing which I had intended to keep a secret. I early applied to a party in the East End, who is in the same line of business as Madame Tussaud, and he agreed to lend me a couple of kings and some nobility, and he said that they would sit out my lecture, and not only sit it out, but that they wouldn't even leave the place when it was done, but would just stay where they were, perfectly infatuated, and wait for more. So I made a bargain with him at once, and was going to ask the newspapers to mention, in the usual column, that on such an evening His Majesty King Henry VIII would honor my entertainment with his presence, and that on such and such an evening His Majesty William the Conqueror would be present, and that on the succeeding evening Moses and Aaron would be there, and so on. I felt encouraged now; an attendance like that would make my entertainment all that could be desired, and besides I would not be embarrassed by their going away before my lecture was over. But now misfortune came. In attempting to move Henry VIII to my lecture hall the porter fell down stairs and utterly smashed him all to pieces; in the course of moving William the Conqueror something let go, and all the sawdust burst out of him, and he collapsed and withered away to nothing before my eyes. Then we collared some dukes, but they were so seedy and decayed that nobody would ever have believed in their rank, and so I gave them up, with almost a broken heart. In my trouble I had nothing in the world left to depend on now but just Moses and Aaron, and I confess to you that it was all I could do to keep the tears back when I came to examine those two images and found that that man, in his unapproachable ignorance, had been exhibiting in Whitechapel for Moses and Aaron what any educated person could see at a glance, by the ligature, were only the Siamese Twins. You see now, sir, that I have done all that a man could do to supply a complained of lack, and if I have failed I think I ought to be pitied, not blamed. I wish I could get a king just only for a little while, and I would take good care of him and send him home and pay for the cab myself."

On January 27, as if to buttress its opinion of *The Gilded Age*, the *Graphic* announced that the London *Athenaeum* had not praised the novel, and it quoted the final sentence of the *Athenaeum's* review: "We think it just possible that the authors, one or both, may have it in them to produce a story which we may read without fatigue and without constant jars to our taste, while it shall have no lack of humour; but we cannot say that in *The Gilded Age* they have reached this desirable consummation."

We can disagree with this judgment of *The Gilded Age* and

still sympathize with its tone of disappointment. Clemens's great gifts were obvious in *The Innocents Abroad* and in *Roughing It,* and they were sufficiently displayed to make *The Gilded Age* a remarkable first novel, despite Warner's material and chapters. But it is not surprising that the merits of the novel—Clemens's merits—should have been obscured when the novel appeared. The Warner material distracts; often, as in the interminable love-and-flowers relationship between Philip Sterling and Ruth Bolton, it detracts. Also distracting, no doubt, was the contemporary reader's frustration in not knowing who created and who wrote what, a frustration shared by most of today's readers. Furthermore, Mark Twain's gifts were not as well understood or appreciated then as they are now.

When we remove Warner's material and chapters we tighten and strengthen a novel that often wanders and drags, a novel that is too long for its content and treatment. And we allow Mark Twain to hold the stage alone. He holds it commandingly. His material has a good deal more "bite" than Warner's. The novel no longer has the conventional happy ending which Warner appended to it. Now the story is all of a piece, all of one tone and style, one kind of wit and humor and pathos and tragedy. In *The Adventures of Colonel Sellers,* with its wonderful chapters on backwoods and river life, and with its caustic portraits of Washington and congressional society, Mark Twain holds the stage richly, uniquely and sometimes brilliantly. Which should hardly suprise us at this late date.

*Princeton, New Jersey*

# A NOTE ON THE TEXT

I have omitted those parts of Warner's story which are not necessary to Clemens's story and I have synopsized the rest. This means that I have omitted the material dealing with Ruth Bolton, her parents, her father's relations with swindlers, the Montagues—in short all the material which was brought in because of Philip Sterling. As a result, Philip is now a minor character, which is all he ever was to Clemens, and Harry Brierly is more prominent than he was, and it can now be seen that he was more useful to Clemens. I have taken pains to retain Clemens's contributions wherever feasible, even when they were fragmentary and minute. But in two instances I have omitted them because they were written not as part of his own story but to further Warner's plot. I refer to the beginning of Chapter 49 (68 lines on pages 443–445 of the first edition of *The Gilded Age*, ending with "as soon as I put my eyes on it.") and to the whole of Chapter 62 (183 lines on pages 560–566 of the first edition of *The Gilded Age*), both dealing with Philip's efforts to find coal in Pennsylvania.

I have omitted the Preface, to which Clemens contributed the third and sixth paragraphs, comprising 12 lines in the first edition of *The Gilded Age*. And I have omitted the Appendix, which Clemens wrote and which made 9 lines in the first edition of *The Gilded Age*. I have omitted the Preface and the Appendix because they are neither necessary nor very relevant to *Colonel Sellers*. I have also omitted the chapter mottoes, which have made little sense to anyone at any time. They were supplied by J. Hammond Trumbull of Hartford and were introduced as a "gag," but the "gag" failed, even when in a later edition translations of the mottoes were supplied. I have changed the chapter numbers from Roman to Arabic to make them more readable. It was a printing convention of the time to use Roman numerals for chapters. Clemens used Arabic numbers in his manuscript of *The Gilded Age.*

Clemens's text is that of the first edition, first issue of *The Gilded Age.* For this reason Sellers is called *Eschol* Sellers, not *Beriah* Sellers, as he is called in later issues and editions of the novel. Clemens himself explained the change from Eschol to Beriah in a note to *The American Claimant,* dated 1891:

"The Colonel Mulberry Sellers here reintroduced to the public is the same person who appeared as *Eschol* Sellers in the first edition of the tale entitled *The Gilded Age,* years ago, and as *Beriah* Sellers in the subsequent editions of the same book, and finally as *Mulberry* Sellers in the drama played afterwards by John T. Raymond.

"The name was changed from Eschol to Beriah to accommodate an Eschol Sellers who rose up out of the vasty deeps of uncharted space and preferred his request—backed by threat of a libel suit—then went his way appeased, and came no more."

Clemens also explained the change in his autobiography (page 20 of my edition). He said that Warner had proposed a change of Sellers's Christian name. "Ten years before, in a remote corner of the West, he had come across a man named Eschol Sellers, and he thought that Eschol was just the right and fitting name for our Sellers, since it was odd and quaint and all that. I liked the idea but I said that that man might turn up and object. But Warner said it couldn't happen; that he was doubtless dead by this time and, be he dead or alive, we must have the name; it was exactly the right one and we couldn't do without it. So the change was made. Warner's man was a farmer in a cheap and humble way. When the book had been out a week, a college-bred gentleman of courtly manners and ducal upholstery arrived in Hartford in a sultry state of mind and with a libel suit in his eye, and *his* name was Eschol Sellers! He had never heard of the other one and had never been within a thousand miles of him. This damaged aristocrat's program was quite definite and business-like: the American Publishing Company must suppress the edition as far as printed and change the name back to Colonel Mulberry Sellers in the plates. Apparently there is nothing that cannot happen. Even the existence of two unrelated men wearing the impossible name of Eschol Sellers is a possible thing."

On this occasion Clemens was confused in reporting the real Eschol Sellers's demands. Mr. Sellers could not have requested that the name "Eschol Sellers" be changed "back" to "Mulberry Sellers," for there was nothing to change "back" to, inasmuch as "Eschol Sellers" appeared in the first issue of the first edition of the novel. Mr. Sellers no doubt requested that "Eschol" be changed to something else. It was changed to "Beriah," which has the same number of letters as "Eschol" and therefore caused a minimum of trouble.

C.N.

# THE ADVENTURES OF COLONEL SELLERS

## CHAPTER 1

June, 18—. Squire Hawkins sat upon the pyramid of large blocks, called the "stile," in front of his house, contemplating the morning.

The locality was Obedstown, East Tennessee. You would not know that Obedstown stood on the top of a mountain, for there was nothing about the landscape to indicate it—but it did: a mountain that stretched abroad over whole counties, and rose very gradually. The district was called the "Knobs of East Tennessee," and had a reputation like Nazareth, as far as turning out any good thing was concerned.

The Squire's house was a double log cabin, in a state of decay; two or three gaunt hounds lay asleep about the threshold, and lifted their heads sadly whenever Mrs. Hawkins or the children stepped in and out over their bodies. Rubbish was scattered about the grassless yard; a bench stood near the door with a tin wash basin on it and a pail of water and a gourd; a cat had begun to drink from the pail, but the exertion was overtaxing her energies, and she had stopped to rest. There was an ash-hopper by the fence, and an iron pot, for soft-soap-boiling, near it.

This dwelling constituted one-fifteenth of Obedstown; the other fourteen houses were scattered about among the tall pine trees and among the corn-fields in such a way that a man might stand in the midst of the city and not know but that he was in the country if he only depended on his eyes for information.

"Squire" Hawkins got his title from being postmaster of Obedstown—not that the title properly belonged to the office, but because in those regions the chief citizens always must have titles of some sort, and so the usual courtesy had been extended to Hawkins. The mail was monthly, and sometimes amounted to

as much as three or four letters at a single delivery. Even a
rush like this did not fill up the postmaster's whole month,
though, and therefore he "kept store" in the intervals.

The Squire was contemplating the morning. It was balmy and
tranquil, the vagrant breezes were laden with the odor of flowers, the murmur of bees was in the air, there was everywhere
that suggestion of repose that summer woodlands bring to the
senses, and the vague, pleasurable melancholy that such a time
and such surroundings inspire.

Presently the United States mail arrived, on horseback.
There was but one letter, and it was for the postmaster. The long-
legged youth who carried the mail tarried an hour to talk, for
there was no hurry; and in a little while the male population of
the village had assembled to help. As a general thing, they were
dressed in homespun "jeans," blue or yellow—there were no other
varieties of it; all wore one suspender and sometimes two—yarn
ones knitted at home,—some wore vests, but few wore coats.
Such coats and vests as did appear, however, were rather
picturesque than otherwise, for they were made of tolerably
fanciful patterns of *calico*—a fashion which prevails there to this
day among those of the community who have tastes above the
common level and are able to afford style. Every individual arrived with his hands in his pockets; a hand came out occasionally
for a purpose, but it always went back again after service; and if
it was the head that was served, just the cant that the dilapidated
straw hat got by being uplifted and rooted under, was retained
until the next call altered the inclination; many hats were present, but none were erect and no two were canted just alike. We
are speaking impartially of men, youths and boys. And we are
also speaking of these three estates when we say that every
individual was either chewing natural leaf tobacco prepared on
his own premises, or smoking the same in a corn-cob pipe. Few
of the men wore whiskers; none wore moustaches; some had a
thick jungle of hair under the chin and hiding the throat—the
only pattern recognized there as being the correct thing in

whiskers; but no part of any individual's face had seen a razor for a week.

These neighbors stood a few moments looking at the mail carrier reflectively while he talked; but fatigue soon began to show itself, and one after another they climbed up and occupied the top rail of the fence, hump-shouldered and grave, like a company of buzzards assembled for supper and listening for the death-rattle. Old Damrell said:

"Tha hain't no news 'bout the jedge, hit ain't likely?"

"Cain't tell for sartin; some thinks he's gwyne to be 'long toreckly, and some thinks 'e hain't. Russ Mosely he tole ole Hanks he mought git to Obeds tomorrer or nex' day he reckoned."

"Well, I wisht I knowed. I got a prime sow and pigs in the cote-house, and I hain't got no place for to put 'em. If the jedge is a gwyne to hold cote, I got to roust 'em out, I reckon. But tomorrer'll do, I 'spect."

The speaker bunched his thick lips together like the stem-end of a tomato and shot a bumble-bee dead that had lit on a weed seven feet away. One after another the several chewers expressed a charge of tobacco juice and delivered it at the deceased with steady aim and faultless accuracy.

"What's a stirrin', down 'bout the Forks?" continued Old Damrell.

"Well, I dunno, skasely. Ole Drake Higgins he's ben down to Shelby las' week. Tuck his crap down; couldn't git shet o' the most uv it; hit warn't no time for to sell, he say, so he fotch it back agin, 'lowin' to wait tell fall. Talks 'bout goin' to Mozouri—lots uv 'ems talkin' that-away down thar, Ole Higgins say. Cain't make a livin' here no mo', sich times as these. Si Higgins he's ben over to Kaintuck n' married a high-toned gal thar, outen the fust families, an' he's come back to the Forks with jist a hell's-mint o' whoop-jamboree notions, folks says. He's tuck an' fixed up the ole house like they does in Kaintuck, he say, an' tha's ben folks come cler from Turpentine for to see it. He's tuck an' gawmed it all over on the inside with plarsterin'."

"What's plarsterin'?"

"*I* dono. Hit's what *he* calls it. Ole Mam Higgins, she tole me. She say she warn't gwyne to hang out in no sich a dern hole like a hog. Says it's mud, or some sich kind o' nastness that sticks on n' kivers up everything. Plarsterin', Si calls it."

This marvel was discussed at considerable length; and almost with animation. But presently there was a dog-fight over in the neighborhood of the blacksmith shop, and the visitors slid off their perch like so many turtles and strode to the battle-field with an interest bordering on eagerness. The Squire remained, and read his letter. Then he sighed, and sat long in meditation. At intervals he said:

"Missouri. Missouri. Well, well, well, everything is so uncertain."

At last he said:

"I believe I'll do it.—A man will just rot, here. My house, my yard, everything around me, in fact, shows that I am becoming one of these cattle—and I used to be thrifty in other times."

He was not more than thirty-five, but he had a worn look that made him seem older. He left the stile, entered that part of his house which was the store, traded a quart of thick molasses for a coonskin and a cake of beeswax to an old dame in linsey-woolsey, put his letter away, and went into the kitchen. His wife was there, constructing some dried apple pies; a slovenly urchin of ten was dreaming over a rude weather-vane of his own contriving; his small sister, close upon four years of age, was sopping corn-bread in some gravy left in the bottom of a frying-pan and trying hard not to sop over a finger-mark that divided the pan through the middle—for the other side belonged to the brother, whose musings made him forget his stomach for the moment; a negro woman was busy cooking, at a vast fire-place. Shiftlessness and poverty reigned in the place.

"Nancy, I've made up my mind. The world is done with me, and perhaps I ought to be done with it. But no matter—I can wait. I am going to Missouri. I won't stay in this dead country and decay with it. I've had it on my mind some time. I'm going to sell out here for whatever I can get, and buy a wagon and team and put you and the children in it and start."

"Anywhere that suits you, suits me, Si. And the children can't be any worse off in Missouri than they are here, I reckon."

Motioning his wife to a private conference in their own room, Hawkins said: "No, they'll be better off. I've looked out for *them*, Nancy," and his face lighted. "Do you see these papers? Well, they are evidence that I have taken up Seventy-five Thousand Acres of Land in this county—think what an enormous fortune it will be some day! Why, Nancy, enormous don't express it—the word's too tame! I tell you, Nancy——"

"For goodness sake, Si——"

"Wait, Nancy, wait—let me finish—I've been secretly boiling and fuming with this grand inspiration for weeks, and I *must* talk or I'll burst! I haven't whispered to a soul—not a word—have had my *countenance* under lock and key, for fear it might drop something that would tell even these animals here how to discern the gold mine that's glaring under their noses. Now all that is necessary to hold this land and keep it in the family is to pay the trifling taxes on it yearly—five or ten dollars—the whole tract would not sell for over a third of a cent an acre now, but some day people will be glad to get it for twenty dollars, fifty dollars, a hundred dollars an acre! What should you say to" [here he dropped his voice to a whisper and looked anxiously around to see that there were no eavesdroppers,] "*a thousand dollars an acre!*

"Well you may open your eyes and stare! But it's so. You and I may not see the day, but *they'll* see it. Mind I tell you, they'll see it. Nancy, you've heard of steamboats, and may be you believed in them—of course you did. You've heard these cattle here scoff at them and call them lies and humbugs,—but they're not lies and humbugs, they're a reality and they're going to be a more wonderful thing some day than they are now. They're going to make a revolution in this world's affairs that will make men dizzy to contemplate. I've been watching—I've been watching while some people slept, and I know what's coming.

"Even you and I will see the day that steamboats will come up that little Turkey river to within twenty miles of this land of ours—and in high water they'll come right *to* it! And this is not all, Nancy—it isn't even half! There's a bigger wonder—the railroad! These worms here have never even heard of it—and when they do they'll not believe in it. But it's another fact. Coaches that fly over the ground twenty miles an hour—heavens and earth, think of that, Nancy! Twenty miles an hour. It makes a man's brain whirl. Some day, when you and I are in our graves, there'll be a railroad stretching hundreds of miles—all the way down from the cities of the Northern States to New Orleans— and its got to run within thirty miles of this land—may be even touch a corner of it. Well, do you know, they've quit burning wood in some places in the Eastern States? And what do you suppose they burn? Coal!" [He bent over and whispered again:] *"There's whole worlds of it on this land!* You know that black stuff that crops out of the bank of the branch?—well, that's it. You've taken it for rocks; so has every body here; and they've built little dams and such things with it. One man was going to build a chimney out of it. Nancy I expect I turned as white as a sheet! Why, it might have caught fire and told everything. I showed him it was too crumbly. Then he was going to build it of copper ore—splendid yellow forty-per-cent. ore! There's fortunes upon fortunes of copper ore on our land! It scared me to death, the idea of this fool starting a smelting furnace in his house without knowing it, and getting his dull eyes opened. And then he was going to build it of *iron* ore! There's mountains of iron ore here, Nancy—whole mountains of it. I wouldn't take any chances. I just stuck by him—I haunted him—I never let him alone till he built it of mud and sticks like all the rest of the chimneys in this dismal country. Pine forests, wheat land, corn land, iron, copper, coal—wait till the railroads come, and the steamboats! *We'll* never see the day, Nancy—never in the world—never, never, never, child. We've got to drag along, drag along, and eat crusts in toil and poverty, all hopeless and forlorn—but *they'll* ride in coaches, Nancy! They'll live like the princes of the earth; they'll be courted and worshiped; their names will be known from ocean to ocean! Ah, well-a-day! Will they ever come back here, on the railroad and the steamboat, and say 'This one little spot shall not be touched—this hovel shall be sacred—for here our father and our mother suffered for us, thought for us, laid the foundations of our future as solid as the hills!' "

"You are a great, good, noble soul, Si Hawkins, and I am an honored woman to be the wife of such a man"—and the tears stood in her eyes when she said it. "We *will* go to Missouri. You are out of your place, here, among these groping dumb creatures. We will find a higher place, where you can walk with your own kind, and be understood when you speak—not stared at as if you were talking some foreign tongue. I would go anywhere, anywhere in the wide world with you. I would rather my body should starve and die than your mind should hunger and wither away in this lonely land."

"Spoken like yourself, my child! But we'll not starve, Nancy. Far from it. I have a letter from Eschol Sellers—just came this day. A letter that—I'll read you a line from it!"

He flew out of the room. A shadow blurred the sunlight in Nancy's face—there was uneasiness in it, and disappointment. A procession of disturbing thoughts began to troop through her mind. Saying nothing aloud, she sat with her hands in her lap; now and then she clasped them, then unclasped them, then tapped the ends of the fingers together; sighed, nodded, smiled— occasionally paused, shook her head. This pantomime was the elocutionary expression of an unspoken soliloquy which had something of this shape:

"I was afraid of it—was afraid of it. Trying to make our fortune in Virginia, Eschol Sellers nearly ruined us—and we had to settle in Kentucky and start over again. Trying to make our fortune in Kentucky he crippled us again and we had to move here. Trying to make our fortune here, he brought us clear down to the ground, nearly. He's an honest soul, and means the very best in the world, but I'm afraid, I'm afraid he's too flighty. He has splendid ideas, and he'll divide his chances with his friends with a free hand, the good generous soul, but something does seem to always interfere and spoil everything. I never did think he was right well balanced. But I don't blame my husband, for I do think that when that man gets his head full of a new notion, he can out-talk a machine. He'll make anybody believe in that notion that'll listen to him ten minutes—why I do believe he would make a deaf and dumb man believe in it and get beside himself, if you only set him where he could see his eyes talk and watch his hands explain. What a head he has got! When he got up that idea there in Virginia of buying up whole loads of negroes in Delaware and Virginia and Tennessee, very quiet, having papers drawn to have them delivered at a place in Alabama and take them and pay for them, away yonder at a certain time, and then in the meantime get a law made stopping everybody from selling negroes to the south after a certain day— it was somehow that way—mercy how the man would have made money! Negroes would have gone up to four prices. But after he'd spent money and worked hard, and traveled hard, and had heaps of negroes all contracted for, and everything going along just right, he couldn't get the laws passed and down the whole thing tumbled. And there in Kentucky, when he raked up that old numskull that had been inventing away at a perpetual motion machine for twenty-two years, and Eschol Sellers saw at a glance where just one more little cog-wheel would settle the business, why I could see it as plain as day when he came in wild at midnight and hammered us out of bed and told the whole thing in a whisper with the doors bolted and the candle in an empty barrel. Oceans of money in it—anybody could see that. But it did cost a deal to buy the old numskull out—and then when they put the new cog-wheel in they'd overlooked something somewhere and it wasn't any use—the troublesome thing wouldn't go. That notion he got up here did look as handy as anything in the world; and how him and Si did sit up nights working at it with the curtains down and me watching to see if any neighbors were about. The man did honestly believe there was a fortune in that black gummy oil that stews out of the bank

Si says is coal; and he refined it himself till it was like water, nearly, and it *did* burn, there's no two ways about that; and I reckon he'd have been all right in Cincinnati with his lamp that he got made, that time he got a house full of rich speculators to see him exhibit, only in the middle of his speech it let go and almost blew the heads off the whole crowd. I haven't got over grieving for the money that cost, yet. I am sorry enough Eschol Sellers is in Missouri, now, but I was glad when he went. I wonder what his letter says. But of course it's cheerful; *he's* never down-hearted—never had any trouble in his life—didn't know it if he had. It's always sunrise with that man, and fine and blazing, at that—never gets noon, though—leaves off and rises again. Nobody can help liking the creature, he means so well—but I do dread to come across him again; he's bound to set us all crazy, of course. Well, there goes old widow Hopkins—it always takes her a week to buy a spool of thread and trade a hank of yarn. Maybe Si can come with the letter, now."

And he did:

"Widow Hopkins kept me—I haven't any patience with such tedious people. Now listen, Nancy—just listen at this:

"'Come right along to Missouri! Don't wait and worry about a good price but sell out for whatever you can get, and come along, or you might be too late. Throw away your traps, if necessary, and come empty-handed. You'll never regret it. It's the grandest country—the loveliest land—the purest atmosphere—I can't describe it; no pen can do it justice. And it's filling up, every day—people coming from everywhere. I've got the biggest scheme on earth—and I'll take you in; I'll take in every friend I've got that's ever stood by me, for there's enough for all, and to spare. Mum's the word—don't whisper —keep yourself to yourself. You'll see! Come!—rush!—hurry!—don't wait for anything!'

"It's the same old boy, Nancy, just the same old boy—ain't he?"

"Yes, I think there's a little of the old sound about his voice yet. I suppose you—you'll still go, Si?"

"Go! Well, I should think so, Nancy. It's all a chance, of course, and chances haven't been kind to us, I'll admit—but whatever comes, old wife, *they're* provided for. Thank God for that!"

"Amen," came low and earnestly.

And with an activity and a suddenness that bewildered Obedstown and almost took its breath away, the Hawkinses hurried through with their arrangements in four short months and flitted out into the great mysterious blank that lay beyond the Knobs of Tennessee.

## CHAPTER 2

Toward the close of the third day's journey the wayfarers were just beginning to think of camping, when they came upon a log cabin in the woods. Hawkins drew rein and entered the yard. A boy about ten years old was sitting in the cabin door with his face bowed in his hands. Hawkins approached, expecting his footfall to attract attention, but it did not. He halted a moment, and then said:

"Come, come, little chap, you mustn't be going to sleep before sundown."

With a tired expression the small face came up out of the hands,—a face down which tears were flowing.

"Ah, I'm sorry I spoke so, my boy. Tell me—is anything the matter?"

The boy signified with a scarcely perceptible gesture that the trouble was in the house, and made room for Hawkins to pass. Then he put his face in his hands again and rocked himself about as one suffering a grief that is too deep to find help in moan or groan or outcry. Hawkins stepped within. It was a poverty-stricken place. Six or eight middle-aged country people of both sexes were grouped about an object in the middle of the room; they were noiselessly busy and they talked in whispers when they spoke. Hawkins uncovered and approached. A coffin stood upon two backless chairs. These neighbors had just finished disposing the body of a woman in it—a woman with a careworn, gentle face that had more the look of sleep about it than of death. An old lady motioned toward the door and said to Hawkins in a whisper:

"His mother, po' thing. Died of the fever, last night. Tha warn't no sich thing as saving of her. But it's better for her—

better for her. Husband and the other two children died in the spring, and she hain't ever hilt up her head sence. She jest went around broken-hearted like, and never took no intrust in anything but Clay—that's the boy thar. She jest worshiped Clay— and Clay he worshiped her. They didn't 'pear to live at all, only when they was together, looking at each other, loving one another. She's ben sick three weeks; and if you believe me that child has worked, and kep' the run of the med'cin, and the times of giving it, and sot up nights and nussed her, and tried to keep up her sperits, the same as a grown-up person. And last night when she kep' a sinking and sinking, and turned away her head and didn't know him no mo', it was fitten to make a body's heart break to see him climb onto the bed and lay his cheek agin hern and call her so pitiful and she not answer. But bymeby she roused up, like, and looked around wild, and then she see him, and she made a great cry and snatched him to her breast and hilt him close and kissed him over and over agin; but it took the last po' strength she had, and so her eyelids begin to close down, and her arms sort o' drooped away and then we see she was gone, po' creetur. And Clay, he—Oh, the po' motherless thing— I cain't talk about it—I cain't bear to talk about it."

Clay had disappeared from the door; but he came in, now, and the neighbors reverently fell apart and made way for him. He leaned upon the open coffin and let his tears course silently. Then he put out his small hand and smoothed the hair and stroked the dead face lovingly. After a bit he brought his other hand up from behind him and laid three or four fresh wild flowers upon the breast, bent over and kissed the unresponsive lips time and time again, and then turned away and went out of the house without looking at any of the company. The old lady said to Hawkins:

"She always loved that kind o' flowers. He fetched 'em for her every morning, and she always kissed him. They was from away north somers—she kep' school when she fust come. Goodness knows what's to become o' that po' boy. No father, no mother, no kin folks of no kind. Nobody to go to, nobody that k'yers for him—and all of us is so put to it for to get along and families so large."

Hawkins understood. All eyes were turned inquiringly upon him. He said:

"Friends, I am not very well provided for, myself, but still I would not turn my back on a homeless orphan. If he will go with me I will give him a home, and loving regard—I will do for him as I would have another do for a child of my own in misfortune."

One after another the people stepped forward and wrung the stranger's hand with cordial good will, and their eyes looked all that their hands could not express or their lips speak.

"Said like a true man," said one.

"You was a stranger to me a minute ago, but you ain't now," said another.

"It's bread cast upon the waters—it'll return after many days," said the old lady whom we have heard speak before.

"You got to camp in my house as long as you hang out here," said one. "If tha hain't room for you and yourn my tribe'll turn out and camp in the hay loft."

A few minutes afterward, while the preparations for the funeral were being concluded, Mr. Hawkins arrived at his wagon leading his little waif by the hand, and told his wife all that had happened, and asked her if he had done right in giving to her and to himself this new care? She said:

"If you've done wrong, Si Hawkins, it's a wrong that will shine brighter at the judgment day than the rights that many a man has done before you. And there isn't any compliment you can pay me equal to doing a thing like this and finishing it up, just taking it for granted that I'll be willing to it. Willing? Come to me, you poor motherless boy, and let me take your grief and help you carry it."

When the child awoke in the morning, it was as if from a troubled dream. But slowly the confusion in his mind took form, and he remembered his great loss; the beloved form in the coffin;

his talk with a generous stranger who offered him a home; the funeral, where the stranger's wife held him by the hand at the grave, and cried with him and comforted him; and he remembered how this new mother tucked him in his bed in the neighboring farm house, and coaxed him to talk about his troubles, and then heard him say his prayers and kissed him good night, and left him with the soreness in his heart almost healed and his bruised spirit at rest.

And now the new mother came again, and helped him to dress, and combed his hair, and drew his mind away by degrees from the dismal yesterday, by telling him about the wonderful journey he was going to take and the strange things he was going to see. And after breakfast they two went alone to the grave, and his heart went out to his new friend and his untaught eloquence poured the praises of his buried idol into her ears without let or hindrance. Together they planted roses by the headboard and strewed wild flowers upon the grave; and then together they went away, hand in hand, and left the dead to the long sleep that heals all heart-aches and ends all sorrows.

## CHAPTER 3

Whatever the lagging dragging journey may have been to the rest of the emigrants, it was a wonder and delight to the children, a world of enchantment; and they believed it to be peopled with the mysterious dwarfs and giants and goblins that figured in the tales the negro slaves were in the habit of telling them nightly by the shuddering light of the kitchen fire.

At the end of nearly a week of travel, the party went into camp near a shabby village which was caving, house by house, into the hungry Mississippi. The river astonished the children beyond measure. Its mile-breadth of water seemed an ocean to them, in the shadowy twilight, and the vague riband of trees on the further shore, the verge of a continent which surely none but they had ever seen before.

"Uncle Dan'l" (colored,) aged 40; his wife, "Aunt Jinny," aged 30, "Young Miss" Emily Hawkins, "Young Mars" Washington Hawkins and "Young Mars" Clay, the new member of the family, ranged themselves on a log, after supper, and contemplated the marvelous river and discussed it. The moon rose and sailed aloft through a maze of shredded cloud-wreaths; the sombre river just perceptibly brightened under the veiled light; a deep silence pervaded the air and was emphasized, at intervals, rather than broken, by the hooting of an owl, the baying of a dog, or the muffled crash of a caving bank in the distance.

The little company assembled on the log were all children, (at least in simplicity and broad and comprehensive ignorance,) and the remarks they made about the river were in keeping with the character; and so awed were they by the grandeur and the solemnity of the scene before them, and by their belief that the air was filled with invisible spirits and that the faint zephyrs were caused by their passing wings, that all their talk took to itself a tinge of the supernatural, and their voices were subdued to a low and reverent tone. Suddenly Uncle Dan'l exclaimed:

"Chil'en, dah's sumfin a comin'!"

All crowded close together and every heart beat faster. Uncle Dan'l pointed down the river with his bony finger.

A deep coughing sound troubled the stillness, way toward a wooded cape that jutted into the stream a mile distant. All in an instant a fierce eye of fire shot out from behind the cape and sent a long brilliant pathway quivering athwart the dusky water. The coughing grew louder and louder, the glaring eye grew larger and still larger, glared wilder and still wilder. A huge shape developed itself out of the gloom, and from its tall duplicate horns dense volumes of smoke, starred and spangled with sparks, poured out and went tumbling away into the farther darkness. Nearer and nearer the thing came, till its long sides began to glow with spots of light which mirrored themselves in the river and attended the monster like a torchlight procession.

"What is it! Oh, what *is* it, Uncle Dan'l!"

With deep solemnity the answer came:

"It's de Almighty! Git down on yo' knees!"

It was not necessary to say it twice. They were all kneeling, in a moment. And then while the mysterious coughing rose stronger and stronger and the threatening glare reached farther and wider, the negro's voice lifted up its supplications:

"O Lord, we's ben mighty wicked, an' we knows dat we 'zerve to go to de bad place, but good Lord, deah Lord, we ain't ready yit, we ain't ready—let dese po' chil'en hab one mo' chance, jes' one mo' chance. Take de ole niggah if you's got to hab somebody.—Good Lord, good deah Lord, we don't know whah you's a gwyne to, we don't know who you's got yo' eye on, but we knows by de way you's a comin', we knows by de way you's a tiltin' along in yo' charyot o' fiah dat some po' sinner's a gwyne to ketch it. But good Lord, dese chil'en don't b'long heah, dey's f'm Obedstown whah dey don't know nuffin, an' you knows, yo' own sef, dat dey ain't 'sponsible. An' deah Lord, good Lord, it ain't like yo' mercy, it ain't like yo' pity, it ain't like yo' longsufferin' lovin'-kindness for to take dis kind o' 'vantage o' sich little chil'en as dese is when dey's so many ornery grown folks chuck full o' cussedness dat wants roastin' down dah. Oh, Lord, spah de little chil'en, don't tar de little chil'en away f'm dey frens, jes' let 'em off jes' dis once, and take it out'n de ole niggah. HEAH I IS, LORD, HEAH I IS! De ole niggah's ready, Lord, de ole——"

The flaming and churning steamer was right abreast the party, and not twenty steps away. The awful thunder of a mud-valve suddenly burst forth, drowning the prayer, and as suddenly Uncle Dan'l snatched a child under each arm and scoured into the woods with the rest of the pack at his heels. And then, ashamed of himself, he halted in the deep darkness and shouted, (but rather feebly:)

"Heah I is, Lord, heah I is!"

There was a moment of throbbing suspense, and then, to the surprise and the comfort of the party, it was plain that the august presence had gone by, for its dreadful noises were receding. Uncle Dan'l headed a cautious reconnoissance in the direction of the log. Sure enough "the Lord" was just turning a point a short distance up the river, and while they looked the lights winked out and the coughing diminished by degrees and presently ceased altogether.

"H'wsh! Well now dey's some folks says dey ain't no 'ficiency in prah. Dis chile would like to know whah we'd a ben now if it warn't fo' dat prah? Dat's it. Dat's it!"

"Uncle Dan'l, do you reckon it was the prayer that saved us?" said Clay.

"Does I reckon? Don't I know it! Whah was yo' eyes? Warn't de Lord jes' a comin' chow! chow! CHOW! an' a goin' on turrible— an' do de Lord carry on dat way 'dout dey's sumfin don't suit him? An' warn't he a lookin' right at dis gang heah, an' warn't he jes' a reachin' for 'em? An' d'you spec' he gwyne to let 'em off 'dout somebody ast him to do it? No indeedy!"

"Do you reckon he saw us, Uncle Dan'l?"

"De law sakes, chile, didn't I see him a lookin' at us?"

"Did you feel scared, Uncle Dan'l?"

"*No* sah! When a man is 'gaged in prah, he ain't 'fraid o' nuffin —dey can't nuffin tetch him."

"Well what did you run for?"

"Well, I—I—mars Clay, when a man is under de influence ob de sperit, he do-no what he's 'bout—no sah; dat man do-no what he's 'bout. You mout take an' tah de head off'n dat man an' he wouldn't scasely fine it out. Dah's de Hebrew chil'en dat went frough de fiah; dey was burnt considable—ob *coase* dey was; but *dey* didn't know nuffin 'bout it—heal right up agin; if dey'd ben gals dey'd missed dey long haah, (hair) maybe, but dey wouldn't felt de burn."

"*I* don't know but what they *were* girls. I think they were."

"Now mars Clay, you knows better'n dat. Sometimes a body can't tell whedder you's a sayin' what you means or whedder you's a sayin' what you don't mean, 'case you says 'em bofe de same way."

"But how should *I* know whether they were boys or girls?"

"Goodness sakes, mars Clay, don't de Good Book say? 'Sides, don't it call 'em de *he*-brew chil'en? If dey was gals wouldn't dey be de she-brew chil'en? Some people dat kin read don't 'pear to take no notice when dey *do* read."

"Well, Uncle Dan'l, I think that—— My! here comes another one up the river! There can't be *two!*"

"We gone dis time—we done gone dis time, sho'! Dey ain't two, mars Clay—dat's de same one. De Lord kin 'pear eberywhah in a second. Goodness, how de fiah and de smoke do belch up! Dat mean business, honey. He comin' now like he fo'got sumfin. Come 'long, chil'en, time you's gwyne to roos'. Go 'long wid you—ole Uncle Daniel gwyne out in de woods to rastle in prah—de ole niggah gwyne to do what he kin to sabe you agin."

He did go to the woods and pray; but he went so far that he doubted, himself, if the Lord heard him when He went by.

## CHAPTER 4

Early in the morning Squire Hawkins took passage in a small steamboat, with his family and his two slaves, and presently the bell rang, the stage-plank was hauled in, and the vessel proceeded up the river. The children and the slaves were not much more at ease after finding out that this monster was a creature of human contrivance than they were the night before when they thought it the Lord of heaven and earth. They started, in fright, every time the gauge-cocks sent out an angry hiss, and they quaked from head to foot when the mud-valves thundered. The shivering of the boat under the beating of the wheels was sheer misery to them.

But of course familiarity with these things soon took away their terrors, and then the voyage at once became a glorious adventure, a royal progress through the very heart and home of romance, a realization of their rosiest wonder-dreams. They sat by the hour in the shade of the pilot house on the hurricane deck and looked out over the curving expanses of the river sparkling in the sunlight. Sometimes the boat fought the midstream current, with a verdant world on either hand, and remote from both; sometimes she closed in under a point, where the dead water and the helping eddies were, and shaved the bank so closely that the decks were swept by the jungle of overhanging willows and littered with a spoil of leaves; departing from these "points" she regularly crossed the river every five miles, avoiding the "bight" of the great bends and thus escaping the strong current; sometimes she went out and skirted a high "bluff" sand-bar in the middle of the stream, and occasionally followed it up a little too far and touched upon the shoal water at its head—and then the intelligent craft refused to run herself

aground, but "smelt" the bar, and straightway the foamy streak
that streamed away from her bows vanished, a great foamless
wave rolled forward and passed her under way, and in this instant she leaned far over on her side, shied from the bar and
fled square away from the danger like a frightened thing—and
the pilot was lucky if he managed to "straighten her up" before
she drove her nose into the opposite bank; sometimes she approached a solid wall of tall trees as if she meant to break
through it, but all of a sudden a little crack would open just
enough to admit her, and away she would go plowing through
the "chute" with just barely room enough between the island
on one side and the main land on the other; in this sluggish
water she seemed to go like a racehorse; now and then small
log cabins appeared in little clearings, with the never-failing
frowsy women and girls in soiled and faded linsey-woolsey leaning in the doors or against wood-piles and rail fences, gazing
sleepily at the passing show; sometimes she found shoal water,
going out at the head of those "chutes" or crossing the river, and
then a deck-hand stood on the bow and hove the lead, while the
boat slowed down and moved cautiously; sometimes she stopped
a moment at a landing and took on some freight or a passenger
while a crowd of slouchy white men and negroes stood on the
bank and looked sleepily on with their hands in their pantaloons
pockets,—of course—for they never took them out except to
stretch, and when they did this they squirmed about and
reached their fists up into the air and lifted themselves on tip-
toe in an ecstasy of enjoyment.

When the sun went down it turned all the broad river to a
national banner laid in gleaming bars of gold and purple and
crimson; and in time these glories faded out in the twilight and
left the fairy archipelagoes reflecting their fringing foliage in the
steely mirror of the stream.

At night the boat forged on through the deep solitudes of the
river, hardly ever discovering a light to testify to a human presence—mile after mile and league after league the vast bends
were guarded by unbroken walls of forest that had never been

disturbed by the voice or the foot-fall of a man or felt the edge of his sacrilegious axe.

An hour after supper the moon came up, and Clay and Washington ascended to the hurricane deck to revel again in their new realm of enchantment. They ran races up and down the deck; climbed about the bell; made friends with the passenger-dogs chained under the life-boat; tried to make friends with a passenger-bear fastened to the vergè-staff but were not encouraged; "skinned the cat" on the hog-chains; in a word, exhausted the amusement-possibilities of the deck. Then they looked wistfully up at the pilot house, and finally, little by little, Clay ventured up there, followed diffidently by Washington. The pilot turned presently to "get his stern-marks," saw the lads and invited them in. Now their happiness was complete. This cosy little house, built entirely of glass and commanding a marvelous prospect in every direction, was a magician's throne to them and their enjoyment of the place was simply boundless.

They sat them down on a high bench and looked miles ahead and saw the wooded capes fold back and reveal the bends beyond; and they looked miles to the rear and saw the silvery highway diminish its breadth by degrees and close itself together in the distance. Presently the pilot said:

"By George, yonder comes the Amaranth!"

A spark appeared, close to the water, several miles down the river. The pilot took his glass and looked at it steadily for a moment, and said, chiefly to himself:

"It can't be the Blue Wing. She couldn't pick us up this way. It's the Amaranth, sure."

He bent over a speaking-tube and said:

"Who's on watch down there?"

A hollow, unhuman voice rumbled up through the tube in answer:

"*I* am. Second engineer."

"Good! You want to stir your stumps, now, Harry—the Amaranth's just turned the point—and she's just a-humping herself, too!"

The pilot took hold of a rope that stretched out forward, jerked it twice, and two mellow strokes of the big bell responded. A voice out on the deck shouted:

"Stand by, down there, with that labboard lead!"

"No, I don't want the lead," said the pilot, "I want *you*. Roust out the old man—tell him the Amaranth's coming. And go and call Jim—tell *him*."

"Aye-aye, sir!"

The "old man" was the captain—he is always called so, on steamboats and ships; "Jim" was the other pilot. Within two minutes both of these men were flying up the pilot-house stairway, three steps at a jump. Jim was in his shirt-sleeves, with his coat and vest on his arm. He said:

"I was just turning in. Where's the glass?"

He took it and looked.

"Don't appear to be any night-hawk on the jack-staff—it's the Amaranth, dead sure!"

The captain took a good long look, and only said:

"Damnation!"

George Davis, the pilot on watch, shouted to the night-watch-man on deck:

"How's she loaded?"

"Two inches by the head, sir."

" 'T ain't enough!"

The captain shouted, now:

"Call the mate. Tell him to call all hands and get a lot of that sugar forrard—put her ten inches by the head. Lively, now!"

"Aye-aye, sir!"

A riot of shouting and trampling floated up from below, presently, and the uneasy steering of the boat soon showed that she was getting "down by the head."

The three men in the pilot house began to talk in short, sharp sentences, low and earnestly. As their excitement rose, their voices went down. As fast as one of them put down the spy-glass another took it up—but always with a studied air of calmness. Each time the verdict was:

"She's a gaining!"

The captain spoke through the tube:

"What steam are you carrying?"

"A hundred and forty-two, sir! But she's getting hotter and hotter all the time."

The boat was straining and groaning and quivering like a monster in pain. Both pilots were at work now, one on each side of the wheel, with their coats and vests off, their bosoms and collars wide open and the perspiration flowing down their faces. They were holding the boat so close to the shore that the willows swept the guards almost from stem to stern.

"Stand by!" whispered George.

"All ready!" said Jim, under his breath.

"Let her come!"

The boat sprang away from the bank like a deer, and darted in a long diagonal toward the other shore. She closed in again and thrashed her fierce way along the willows as before. The captain put down the glass:

"Lord how she walks up on us! I do hate to be beat!"

"Jim," said George, looking straight ahead, watching the slightest yawing of the boat and promptly meeting it with the wheel, "how'll it do to try Murderer's Chute?"

"Well, it's—it's taking chances. How was the cotton-wood stump on the false point below Boardman's Island this morning?"

"Water just touching the roots."

"Well it's pretty close work. That gives six feet scant in the head of Murderer's Chute. We can just barely rub through if we hit it exactly right. But it's worth trying. *She* don't dare tackle it!"—meaning the Amaranth.

In another instant the Boreas plunged into what seemed a crooked creek, and the Amaranth's approaching lights were shut out in a moment. Not a whisper was uttered, now, but the three men stared ahead into the shadows and two of them spun the wheel back and forth with anxious watchfulness while the steamer tore along. The chute seemed to come to an end every fifty yards, but always opened out in time. Now the head of it was at hand. George tapped the big bell three times, two leads-men sprang to their posts, and in a moment their weird cries rose on the night air and were caught up and repeated by two men on the upper deck:

"No-o bottom!"

"De-e-p four!"

"Half three!"

"Quarter three!"

"Mark under wa-a-ter three!"

"Half twain!"

"Quarter twain!——"

Davis pulled a couple of ropes—there was a jingling of small bells far below, the boat's speed slackened, and the pent steam began to whistle and the gauge-cocks to scream:

"By the mark twain!"

"Quar-ter-*her*-er-*less* twain!"

"Eight *and* a half!"

"Eight feet!"

"Seven-ana-half!——"

Another jingling of little bells and the wheels ceased turning altogether. The whistling of the steam was something frightful, now—it almost drowned all other noises.

"Stand by to meet her!"

George had the wheel hard down and was standing on a spoke.

"All ready!"

The boat hesitated—seemed to hold her breath, as did the cap-tain and pilots—and then she began to fall away to starboard and every eye lighted:

"*Now* then!—meet her! meet her! Snatch her!"

The wheel flew to port so fast that the spokes blended into a spider-web—the swing of the boat subsided—she steadied her-self——

"Seven feet!"

"Sev—six and a *half!*"

"*Six* feet! Six f——"

Bang! She hit the bottom! George shouted through the tube:

"Spread her wide open! *Whale it at her!*"

Pow—wow—chow! The escape-pipes belched snowy pillars of steam aloft, the boat ground and surged and trembled—and slid over into——

"M-a-r-k twain!"

"Quarter-*her*——"

"Tap! tap! tap!" (to signify "Lay in the leads.")

And away she went, flying up the willow shore, with the whole silver sea of the Mississippi stretching abroad on every hand.

No Amaranth in sight!

"Ha-ha, boys, we took a couple of tricks that time!" said the captain.

And just at that moment a red glare appeared in the head of the chute and the Amaranth came springing after them!

"Well, I swear!"

"Jim, what *is* the meaning of that?"

"I'll tell you what's the meaning of it. That hail we had at Napoleon was Wash Hastings, wanting to come to Cairo and we didn't stop. He's in that pilot house, now, showing those mud turtles how to hunt for easy water."

"That's it! I thought it wasn't any slouch that was running that middle bar in Hog-eye Bend. If it's Wash Hastings—well, what he don't know about the river ain't worth knowing—a regular gold-leaf, kid-glove, diamond-breastpin pilot Wash Hastings is. We won't take any tricks off of *him*, old man!"

"I wish I'd a stopped for him, that's all."

The Amaranth was within three hundred yards of the Boreas, and still gaining. The "old man" spoke through the tube:

"What is she carrying now?"

"A hundred and sixty-five, sir!"

"How's your wood?"

"Pine all out—cypress half gone—eating up cotton-wood like pie!"

"Break into that rosin on the main deck—pile it in, the boat can pay for it!"

Soon the boat was plunging and quivering and screaming

more madly than ever. But the Amaranth's head was almost abreast the Boreas's stern:

"How's your steam, now, Harry?"

"Hundred and eighty-two, sir!"

"Break up the casks of bacon in the forrard hold! Pile it in! Levy on that turpentine in the fantail—drench every stick of wood with it!"

The boat was a moving earthquake by this time.

"How is she now?"

"A hundred and ninety-six and still a-swelling!—water below the middle gauge-cocks!—carrying every pound she can stand! —nigger roosting on the safety-valve!"

"Good! How's your draft?"

"Bully! Every time a nigger heaves a stick of wood into the furnace he goes out the chimney with it!"

The Amaranth drew steadily up till her jack-staff breasted the Boreas's wheel-house—climbed along inch by inch till her chimneys breasted it—crept along, further and further till the boats were wheel to wheel—and then they closed up with a heavy jolt and locked together tight and fast in the middle of the big river under the flooding moonlight! A roar and a hurrah went up from the crowded decks of both steamers—all hands rushed to the guards to look and shout and gesticulate—the weight careened the vessels over toward each other—officers flew hither and thither cursing and storming, trying to drive the people amidships—both captains were leaning over their railings shaking their fists, swearing and threatening—black volumes of smoke rolled up and canopied the scene, delivering a rain of sparks upon the vessels—two pistol shots rang out, and both captains dodged unhurt and the packed masses of passengers surged back and fell apart while the shrieks of women and children soared above the intolerable din——

And then there was a booming roar, a thundering crash, and the riddled Amaranth dropped loose from her hold and drifted helplessly away!

Instantly the fire-doors of the Boreas were thrown open and

the men began dashing buckets of water into the furnaces—for it would have been death and destruction to stop the engines with such a head of steam on.

As soon as possible the Boreas dropped down to the floating wreck and took off the dead, the wounded and the unhurt—at least all that could be got at, for the whole forward half of the boat was a shapeless ruin, with the great chimneys lying crossed on top of it, and underneath were a dozen victims imprisoned alive and wailing for help. While men with axes worked with might and main to free these poor fellows, the Boreas's boats went about, picking up stragglers from the river.

And now a new horror presented itself. The wreck took fire from the dismantled furnaces! Never did men work with a heartier will than did those stalwart braves with the axes. But it was of no use. The fire ate its way steadily, despising the bucket brigade that fought it. It scorched the clothes, it singed the hair of the axemen—it drove them back, foot by foot—inch by inch—they wavered, struck a final blow in the teeth of the enemy, and surrendered. And as they fell back they heard prisoned voices saying:

"Don't leave us! Don't desert us! Don't, don't do it!"

And one poor fellow said:

"I am Henry Worley, striker of the Amaranth! My mother lives in St. Louis. Tell her a lie for a poor devil's sake, please. Say I was killed in an instant and never knew what hurt me— though God knows I've neither scratch nor bruise this moment! It's hard to burn up in a coop like this with the whole wide world so near. Good-bye boys—we've all got to come to it at last, anyway!"

The Boreas stood away out of danger, and the ruined steamer went drifting down the stream an island of wreathing and climbing flame that vomited clouds of smoke from time to time, and glared more fiercely and sent its luminous tongues higher and higher after each emission. A shriek at intervals told of a captive that had met his doom. The wreck lodged upon a sand-bar, and when the Boreas turned the next point on her upward journey it was still burning with scarcely abated fury.

When the boys came down into the main saloon of the Boreas, they saw a pitiful sight and heard a world of pitiful sounds. Eleven poor creatures lay dead and forty more lay moaning, or pleading or screaming, while a score of Good Samaritans moved among them doing what they could to relieve their sufferings; bathing their skinless faces and bodies with linseed oil and lime water and covering the places with bulging masses of raw cotton that gave to every face and form a dreadful and unhuman aspect.

A little wee French midshipman of fourteen lay fearfully injured, but never uttered a sound till a physician of Memphis was about to dress his hurts. Then he said:

"Can I get well? You need not be afraid to tell me."

"No—I—I am afraid you can not."

"Then do not waste your time with me—help those that can get well."

"But———"

"Help those that can get well! It is not for me to be a girl. I carry the blood of eleven generations of soldiers in my veins!"

The physician—himself a man who had seen service in the navy in his time—touched his hat to this little hero, and passed on.

The head engineer of the Amaranth, a grand specimen of physical manhood, struggled to his feet a ghastly spectacle and strode toward his brother, the second engineer, who was unhurt. He said:

"You were on watch. You were boss. You would not listen to me when I begged you to reduce your steam. Take that!—take it to my wife and tell her it comes from me by the hand of my murderer! Take it—and take my curse with it to blister your heart a hundred years—and may you live so long!"

And he tore a ring from his finger, stripping flesh and skin with it, threw it down and fell dead!

But these things must not be dwelt upon. The Boreas landed

her dreadful cargo at the next large town and delivered it over to a multitude of eager hands and warm southern hearts—a cargo amounting by this time to 39 wounded persons and 22 dead bodies. And with these she delivered a list of 96 missing persons that had drowned or otherwise perished at the scene of the disaster.

A jury of inquest was impaneled, and after due deliberation and inquiry they returned the inevitable American verdict which has been so familiar to our ears all the days of our lives—"NO-BODY TO BLAME."*

* The incidents of the explosion are not invented. They happened just as they are told.—M.T.

## CHAPTER 5

When the Boreas backed away from the land to continue her voyage up the river, the Hawkinses were richer by twenty-four hours of experience in the contemplation of human suffering and in learning through honest hard work how to relieve it. And they were richer in another way also. In the early turmoil an hour after the explosion, a little black-eyed girl of five years, frightened and crying bitterly, was struggling through the throng in the Boreas' saloon calling her mother and father, but no one answered.—Something in the face of Mr. Hawkins attracted her and she came and looked up at him; was satisfied, and took refuge with him. He petted her, listened to her troubles, and said he would find her friends for her. Then he put her in a state-room with his children and told them to be kind to her (the adults of his party were all busy with the wounded) and straightway began his search.

It was fruitless. But all day he and his wife made inquiries, and hoped against hope. All that they could learn was that the child and her parents came on board at New Orleans, where they had just arrived in a vessel from Cuba; that they looked like people from the Atlantic States; that the family name was Van Brunt and the child's name Laura. This was all. The parents had not been seen since the explosion. The child's manners were those of a little lady, and her clothes were daintier and finer than any Mrs. Hawkins had ever seen before.

As the hours dragged on the child lost heart, and cried so piteously for her mother that it seemed to the Hawkinses that the moanings and the wailings of the mutilated men and women in the saloon did not so strain at their heart-strings as the sufferings of this little desolate creature. They tried hard to comfort her; and in trying, learned to love her; they could not help it, seeing how she clung to them and put her arms about their necks and found no solace but in their kind eyes and comforting words. There was a question in both their hearts—a question that rose up and asserted itself with more and more pertinacity as the hours wore on—but both hesitated to give it voice—both kept silence and waited. But a time came at last when the matter would bear delay no longer. The boat had landed, and the dead and the wounded were being conveyed to the shore. The tired child was asleep in the arms of Mrs. Hawkins. Mr. Hawkins came into their presence and stood without speaking. His eyes met his wife's; then both looked at the child—and as they looked it stirred in its sleep and nestled closer; an expression of contentment and peace settled upon its face that touched the mother-heart; and when the eyes of husband and wife met again, the question was asked and answered.

When the Boreas had journeyed some four hundred miles from the time the Hawkinses joined her, a long rank of steamboats was sighted, packed side by side at a wharf like sardines in a box, and above and beyond them rose the domes and steeples and general architectural confusion of a city—a city with an imposing umbrella of black smoke spread over it. This was St. Louis. The children of the Hawkins family were playing about the hurricane deck, and the father and mother were sitting in the lee of the pilot house essaying to keep order and not greatly grieved that they were not succeeding.

"They're worth all the trouble they are, Nancy."

"Yes, and more, Si."

"I believe you! You wouldn't sell one of them at a good round figure?"

"Not for all the money in the bank, Si."

"My own sentiments every time. It is true we are not rich—but still you are not sorry—you haven't any misgivings about the additions?"

"No. God will provide."

"Amen. And so you wouldn't even part with Clay? Or Laura!"

"Not for anything in the world. I love them just the same as I love my own. They pet me and spoil me even more than the others do, I think. I reckon we'll get along, Si."

"Oh yes, it will all come out right, old mother. I wouldn't be afraid to adopt a thousand children if I wanted to, for there's that Tennessee Land, you know—enough to make an army of them rich. A whole army, Nancy! You and I will never see the day, but these little chaps will. Indeed they will. One of these days it will be 'the rich Miss Emily Hawkins—and the wealthy Miss Laura Van Brunt Hawkins—and the Hon. George Washington Hawkins, millionaire—and Gov. Henry Clay Hawkins, millionaire!' That is the way the world will word it! Don't let's ever fret about the children, Nancy—never in the world. They're all right. Nancy, there's oceans and oceans of money in that land—mark my words!"

The children had stopped playing, for the moment, and drawn near to listen. Hawkins said:

"Washington, my boy, what will you do when you get to be one of the richest men in the world?"

"I don't know, father. Sometimes I think I'll have a balloon and go up in the air; and sometimes I think I'll have ever so many books; and sometimes I think I'll have ever so many weather-cocks and water-wheels; or have a machine like that one you and Colonel Sellers bought; and sometimes I think I'll have—well, somehow I don't know—somehow I ain't certain; maybe I'll get a steamboat first."

"The same old chap!—always just a little bit divided about things.—And what will *you* do when you get to be one of the richest men in the world, Clay?"

"I don't know, sir. My mother—my other mother that's gone away—she always told me to work along and not be much expecting to get rich, and then I wouldn't be disappointed if I didn't get rich. And so I reckon it's better for me to wait till I get rich, and then by that time maybe I'll know what I'll want—but I don't now, sir."

"Careful old head!—Governor Henry Clay Hawkins!—that's

what you'll be, Clay, one of these days. Wise old head! weighty old head! Go on, now, and play—all of you. It's a prime lot, Nancy, as the Obedstown folk say about their hogs."

A smaller steamboat received the Hawkinses and their fortunes, and bore them a hundred and thirty miles still higher up the Mississippi, and landed them at a little tumble-down village on the Missouri shore in the twilight of a mellow October day.

The next morning they harnessed up their team and for two days they wended slowly into the interior through almost roadless and uninhabited forest solitudes. And when for the last time they pitched their tents, metaphorically speaking, it was at the goal of their hopes, their new home.

By the muddy roadside stood a new log cabin, one story high —the store; clustered in the neighborhood were ten or twelve more cabins, some new, some old.

In the sad light of the departing day the place looked homeless enough. Two or three coatless young men sat in front of the store on a dry-goods box, and whittled it with their knives, kicked it with their vast boots, and shot tobacco juice at various marks. Several ragged negroes leaned comfortably against the posts of the awning and contemplated the arrival of the wayfarers with lazy curiosity. All these people presently managed to drag themselves to the vicinity of the Hawkins' wagon, and there they took up permanent positions, hands in pockets and resting on one leg; and thus anchored they proceeded to look and enjoy. Vagrant dogs came wagging around and making inquiries of Hawkins's dog, which were not satisfactory and they made war on him in concert. This would have interested the citizens but it was too many on one to amount to anything as a fight, and so they commanded the peace and the foreign dog furled his tail and took sanctuary under the wagon. Slatternly negro girls and women slouched along with pails deftly balanced on their heads, and joined the group and stared. Little half-dressed white boys, and little negro boys with nothing whatever on but towlinen shirts with a fine southern exposure, came from various directions and stood with their hands locked together behind them and aided in the inspection. The rest of the population were laying down their employments and getting ready to come, when a man burst through the assemblage and seized the new-comers by the hands in a frenzy of welcome, and exclaimed—indeed almost shouted:

"Well who *could* have believed it! Now is it you sure enough —turn around! hold up your heads! I want to look at you good! Well, well, well, it does seem most too good to be true, I de-clare! Lord, I'm so glad to see you! Does a body's whole soul good to look at you! Shake hands again! Keep *on* shaking hands! Goodness gracious alive. What *will* my wife say?—Oh yes in-deed, it's so!—married only last week—lovely, perfectly lovely creature, the noblest woman that ever—you'll like her, Nancy! Like her? Lord bless me you'll love her—you'll dote on her— you'll be twins! Well, well, well, let me look at you again! Same old—why bless my life it was only just this very morning that my wife says, 'Colonel'—she will call me Colonel spite of every-thing I can do—she says 'Colonel, something tells me somebody's coming!' and sure enough here you are, the last people on earth a body could have expected. Why she'll think she's a prophetess —and hanged if I don't think so too—and you know there ain't any country but what a prophet's an honor to, as the proverb says. Lord bless me—and here's the children, too! Washington, Emily, don't you know me? Come, give us a kiss. Won't I fix *you*, though!—ponies, cows, dogs, everything you can think of that'll delight a child's heart—and———. Why how's this? Little strang-ers? Well you won't be any strangers here, I can tell you. Bless your souls we'll make you think you never was at home before— 'deed and 'deed we will, *I* can tell you! Come, now, bundle right along with me. You can't glorify any hearth stone but mine in *this* camp, you know—can't eat anybody's bread but mine— can't do *any*thing but just make yourselves perfectly at home and comfortable, and spread yourselves out and *rest!* You hear *me!* Here—Jim, Tom, Pete, Jake, fly around! Take that team to my place—put the wagon in my lot—put the horses under the shed, and get out hay and oats and fill them up! Ain't any hay and oats? Well *get* some—have it charged to me—come, spin around, now! Now, Hawkins, the procession's ready; mark time, by the left flank, *for*ward—march!"

And the Colonel took the lead, with Laura astride his neck, and the newly-inspired and very grateful immigrants picked up their tired limbs with quite a spring in them and dropped into his wake.

Presently they were ranged about an old-time fire-place whose blazing logs sent out rather an unnecessary amount of heat, but that was no matter—supper was needed, and to have it, it had to be cooked. This apartment was the family bedroom, parlor, library and kitchen, all in one. The matronly little wife of the Colonel moved hither and thither and in and out with her pots and pans in her hands, happiness in her heart and a world of admiration of her husband in her eyes. And when at last she had spread the cloth and loaded it with hot corn bread, fried chickens, bacon, buttermilk, coffee, and all manner of country luxuries, Col. Sellers modified his harangue and for a moment throttled it down to the orthodox pitch for a blessing, and then instantly burst forth again as from a parenthesis and clattered on with might and main till every stomach in the party was laden with all it could carry. And when the new-comers ascended the ladder to their comfortable feather beds on the second floor—to wit, the garret—Mrs. Hawkins was obliged to say:

"Hang the fellow, I do believe he has gone wilder than ever, but still a body can't help liking him if they would—and what is more, they don't ever want to try when they see his eyes and hear him talk."

Within a week or two the Hawkinses were comfortably domiciled in a new log house, and were beginning to feel at home. The children were put to school; at least it was what passed for a school in those days: a place where tender young humanity devoted itself for eight or ten hours a day to learning incomprehensible rubbish by heart out of books and reciting it by rote, like parrots; so that a finished education consisted simply of a

permanent headache and the ability to read without stopping to
spell the words or take breath. Hawkins bought out the village
store for a song and proceeded to reap the profits, which
amounted to but little more than another song.

The wonderful speculation hinted at by Col. Sellers in his letter turned out to be the raising of mules for the southern market;
and really it promised very well. The young stock cost but a
trifle, the rearing but another trifle, and so Hawkins was easily
persuaded to embark his slender means in the enterprise and
turn over the keep and care of the animals to Sellers and Uncle
Dan'l.

All went well. Business prospered little by little. Hawkins even
built a new house, made it two full stories high and put a lightning rod on it. People came two or three miles to look at it. But
they knew that the rod attracted the lightning, and so they gave
the place a wide berth in a storm, for they were familiar with
marksmanship and doubted if the lightning could hit that small
stick at a distance of a mile and a half oftener than once in a
hundred and fifty times. Hawkins fitted out his house with
"store" furniture from St. Louis, and the fame of its magnificence
went abroad in the land. Even the parlor carpet was from St.
Louis—though the other rooms were clothed in the "rag" carpet-
ing of the country. Hawkins put up the first "paling" fence that
had ever adorned the village; and he did not stop there, but
whitewashed it. His oil-cloth window-curtains had noble pictures
on them of castles such as had never been seen anywhere in the
world but on window-curtains. Hawkins enjoyed the admiration
these prodigies compelled, but he always smiled to think how
poor and cheap they were, compared to what the Hawkins mansion would display in a future day after the Tennessee Land
should have borne its minted fruit. Even Washington observed,
once, that when the Tennessee Land was sold he would have a
"store" carpet in his and Clay's room like the one in the parlor.
This pleased Hawkins, but it troubled his wife. It did not seem
wise, to her, to put one's entire earthly trust in the Tennessee
Land and never think of doing any work.

Hawkins took a weekly Philadelphia newspaper and a semi-weekly St. Louis journal—almost the only papers that came to the village, though Godey's Lady's Book found a good market there and was regarded as the perfection of polite literature by some of the ablest critics in the place. Perhaps it is only fair to explain that we are writing of a bygone age—some twenty or thirty years ago. In the two newspapers referred to lay the secret of Hawkins's growing prosperity. They kept him informed of the condition of the crops south and east, and thus he knew which articles were likely to be in demand and which articles were likely to be unsalable, weeks and even months in advance of the simple folk about him. As the months went by he came to be regarded as a wonderfully lucky man. It did not occur to the citizens that brains were at the bottom of his luck.

His title of "Squire" came into vogue again, but only for a season; for, as his wealth and popularity augmented, that title, by imperceptible stages, grew up into "Judge;" indeed it bade fair to swell into "General" bye and bye. All strangers of consequence who visited the village gravitated to the Hawkins Mansion and became guests of the "Judge."

Hawkins had learned to like the people of his section very much. They were uncouth and not cultivated, and not particularly industrious; but they were honest and straightforward, and their virtuous ways commanded respect. Their patriotism was strong, their pride in the flag was of the old-fashioned pattern, their love of country amounted to idolatry. Whoever dragged the national honor in the dirt won their deathless hatred. They still cursed Benedict Arnold as if he were a personal friend who had broken faith but a week gone by.

## CHAPTER 6

We skip ten years and this history finds certain changes to record.

Judge Hawkins and Col. Sellers have made and lost two or three moderate fortunes in the meantime and are now pinched by poverty. Sellers has two pairs of twins and four extras. In Hawkins's family are six children of his own and two adopted ones. From time to time, as fortune smiled, the elder children got the benefit of it, spending the lucky seasons at excellent schools in St. Louis and the unlucky ones at home in the chafing discomfort of straightened circumstances.

[Neither the Hawkins children nor outsiders knew that Laura was not a Hawkins by blood. By twelve Laura was beginning to be a beauty but she did not realize it.]

When she tripped down the street on a summer's day with her dainty hands propped into the ribbon-broidered pockets of her apron, and elbows consequently more or less akimbo with her wide Leghorn hat flapping down and hiding her face one moment and blowing straight up against her forehead the next and making its revealment of fresh young beauty; with all her pretty girlish airs and graces in full play, and that sweet ignorance of care and that atmosphere of innocence and purity all about her that belong to her gracious time of life, indeed she was a vision to warm the coldest heart and bless and cheer the saddest.

["Willful, generous, forgiving, imperious, affectionate, improvident—bewitching, in short—was Laura at this period. . . . Laura had grown to be almost a woman in these few years . . . years which had seen Judge Hawkins pass through so many trials."]

When the judge's first bankruptcy came upon him, a homely human angel intruded upon him with an offer of $1,500 for the

Tennessee Land. Mrs. Hawkins said take it. It was a grievous temptation, but the judge withstood it. He said the land was for the children—he could not rob them of their future millions for so paltry a sum. When the second blight fell upon him, another angel appeared and offered $3,000 for the land. He was in such deep distress that he allowed his wife to persuade him to let the papers be drawn; but when his children came into his presence in their poor apparel, he felt like a traitor and refused to sign.

But now he was down again, and deeper in the mire than ever. He paced the floor all day, he scarcely slept at night. He blushed even to acknowledge it to himself, but treason was in his mind—he was meditating, at last, the sale of the land. Mrs. Hawkins stepped into the room. He had not spoken a word, but he felt as guilty as if she had caught him in some shameful act. She said:

"Si, I do not know what we are going to do. The children are not fit to be seen, their clothes are in such a state. But there's something more serious still.—There is scarcely a bite in the house to eat."

"Why, Nancy, go to Johnson———."

"Johnson indeed! You took that man's part when he hadn't a friend in the world, and you built him up and made him rich. And here's the result of it: He lives in our fine house, and we live in his miserable log cabin. He has hinted to our children that he would rather they wouldn't come about his yard to play with his children,—which I can bear, and bear easy enough, for they're not a sort we want to associate with much—but what I *can't* bear with any quietness at all, is his telling Franky our bill was running pretty high this morning when I sent him for some meal—and that was all he said, too—didn't give him the meal—turned off and went to talking with the Hargrave girls about some stuff they wanted to cheapen."

"Nancy, this is astounding!"

"And so it is, I warrant you. I've kept still, Si, as long as ever I could. Things have been getting worse and worse, and worse and worse, every single day; I don't go out of the house, I feel so down; but you had trouble enough, and I wouldn't say a word —and I wouldn't say a word now, only things have got so bad that I don't know what to do, nor where to turn." And she gave way and put her face in her hands and cried.

"Poor child, don't grieve so. I never thought that of Johnson. I am clear at my wit's end. I don't know what in the world to do. *Now* if somebody would come along and offer $3,000—Oh, if somebody only *would* come along and offer $3,000 for that Tennessee Land———"

"You'd sell it, Si?" said Mrs. Hawkins excitedly.

"Try me!"

Mrs. Hawkins was out of the room in a moment. Within a minute she was back again with a business-looking stranger, whom she seated, and then she took her leave again. Hawkins said to himself, "How can a man ever lose faith? When the blackest hour comes, Providence always comes with it—ah, this is the very timeliest help that ever poor harried devil had; if this blessed man offers but a thousand I'll embrace him like a brother!"

The stranger said:

"I am aware that you own 75,000 acres of land in East Tennessee, and without sacrificing your time, I will come to the point at once. I am agent of an iron manufacturing company, and they empower me to offer you ten thousand dollars for that land."

Hawkins's heart bounded within him. His whole frame was racked and wrenched with fettered hurrahs. His first impulse was to shout—"Done! and God bless the iron company, too!"

But a something flitted through his mind, and his opened lips uttered nothing. The enthusiasm faded away from his eyes, and the look of a man who is thinking took its place. Presently, in a hesitating, undecided way, he said:

"Well, I—it don't seem quite enough. That—that is a very valuable property—very valuable. It's brim full of iron ore, sir—brim full of it! And copper, coal,—everything—everything you can think of! Now, I'll tell you what I'll do. I'll reserve everything except the iron, and I'll sell them the iron property for $15,000 cash, I to go in with them and own an undivided interest of one-half the concern,—or the stock, as you may say. I'm out of business, and I'd just as soon help run the thing as not. Now how does that strike you?"

"Well, I am only an agent of these people, who are friends of mine, and I am not even paid for my services. To tell you the truth, I have tried to persuade them not to go into the thing; and I have come square out with their offer, without throwing out any feelers—and I did it in the hope that you would refuse. A man pretty much always refuses another man's first offer, no matter what it is. But I have performed my duty, and will take pleasure in telling them what you say."

He was about to rise. Hawkins said:

"Wait a bit."

Hawkins thought again. And the substance of his thought was: "This is a deep man; this is a very deep man; I don't like his candor; your ostentatiously candid business man's a deep fox— always a deep fox; this man's that iron company himself that's what *he* is; he wants that property, too; I am not so blind but I can see that; *he* don't want the company to go into this thing—O, that's very good; yes, that's very good indeed—stuff! he'll be back here to-morrow, sure, and take my offer; take it? I'll risk anything he is suffering to take it now; here—I must mind what I'm about. What has started this sudden excitement about iron? I wonder what *is* in the wind? just as sure as I'm alive this moment, there's something tremendous stirring in iron specula-tion" [here Hawkins got up and began to pace the floor with ex-cited eyes and with gesturing hands]—"something enormous going on in iron, without the shadow of a doubt, and here I sit mousing in the dark and never knowing anything about it; great heaven, what an escape I've made! this underhanded mercenary creature might have taken me up—and ruined me! but I *have* escaped, and I warrant me I'll not put my foot into—

He stopped and turned toward the stranger, saying:

"I have made you a proposition,—you have not accepted it,

and I desire that you will consider that I have made none. At the same time my conscience will not allow me to—. Please alter the figures I named to thirty thousand dollars, if you will, and let the proposition go to the company—I will stick to it if it breaks my heart!"

The stranger looked amused, and there was a pretty well defined touch of surprise in his expression, too, but Hawkins never noticed it. Indeed he scarcely noticed anything or knew what he was about. The man left; Hawkins flung himself into a chair; thought a few moments, then glanced around, looked frightened, sprang to the door——

"Too late—too late! He's gone! Fool that I am!—always a fool! Thirty thousand—ass that I am! Oh, *why* didn't I say fifty thousand!"

He plunged his hands into his hair and leaned his elbows on his knees, and fell to rocking himself back and forth in anguish. Mrs. Hawkins sprang in, beaming:

"Well, Si?"

"Oh, con-found the con-founded—con-*found* it, Nancy. I've gone and done it, now!"

"Done what, Si, for mercy's sake!"

"Done everything! *Ruined* everything!"

"Tell me, tell me, *tell* me! Don't keep a body in such suspense. Didn't he buy, after all? Didn't he make an offer?"

"Offer? He offered $10,000 for our land, and——"

"Thank the good Providence from the very bottom of my heart of hearts! What sort of ruin do you call that, Si!"

"Nancy, do you suppose I listened to such a preposterous proposition? No! Thank fortune I'm not a simpleton! I saw through the pretty scheme in a second. It's a vast iron speculation!—millions upon millions in it! But fool as I am I told him he could have half the iron property for thirty thousand—and if I only had him back here he couldn't touch it for a cent less than a quarter of a million!"

Mrs. Hawkins looked up white and despairing:

"You threw away this chance, you let this man go, and we in this awful trouble? You don't mean it, you *can't* mean it!"

"Throw it away? Catch me at it! Why woman, do you suppose that man don't know what he is about? Bless you, he'll be back fast enough to-morrow."

"Never, never, never. He never will come back. I don't know what is to become of us. I don't know what in the world is to become of us."

A shade of uneasiness came into Hawkins's face. He said:

"Why, Nancy, you—you can't believe what you are saying."

"Believe it, indeed? I *know* it, Si. And I know that we haven't a cent in the world, and we've sent ten thousand dollars a-begging."

"Nancy, you frighten me. Now could that man—is it possible that I—hanged if I don't believe I *have* missed a chance! Don't grieve, Nancy, don't grieve. I'll go right after him. I'll take—I'll take—what a fool I am!—I'll take anything he'll give!"

The next instant he left the house on a run. But the man was no longer in the town. Nobody knew where he belonged or whither he had gone. Hawkins came slowly back, watching wistfully but hopelessly for the stranger, and lowering his price steadily with his sinking heart. And when his foot finally pressed his own threshold, the value he held the entire Tennessee property at was five hundred dollars—two hundred down and the rest in three equal annual payments, without interest.

There was a sad gathering at the Hawkins' fireside the next night. All the children were present but Clay. Mr. Hawkins said:

"Washington, we seem to be hopelessly fallen, hopelessly involved. I am ready to give up. I do not know where to turn—I never have been down so low before, I never have seen things so dismal. There are many mouths to feed; Clay is at work; we must lose you, also, for a little while, my boy. But it will not be long—the Tennessee Land——"

He stopped, and was conscious of a blush. There was silence for a moment, and then Washington—now a lank, dreamy-eyed stripling between twenty-two and twenty-three years of age—said:

"If Col. Sellers would come for me, I would go and stay with him a while, till the Tennessee Land is sold. He has often wanted me to come, ever since he moved to Hawkeye."

"I'm afraid he can't well come for you, Washington. From what I can hear—not from *him* of course, but from others—he is not far from as bad off as we are—and his family is as large, too. He might find something for you to do, maybe, but you'd better try to get to him yourself, Washington—it's only thirty miles."

"But how can I, father? There's no stage or anything."

"And if there were, stages require money. A stage goes from Swansea, five miles from here. But it would be cheaper to walk."

"Father, they must know you there, and no doubt they would credit you in a moment, for a little stage ride like that. Couldn't you write and ask them?"

"Couldn't *you*, Washington—seeing it's you that wants the ride? And what do you think you'll do, Washington, when you get to Hawkeye? Finish your invention for making window-glass opaque?"

"No, sir, I have given that up. I almost knew I could do it, but it was so tedious and troublesome I quit it."

"I was afraid of it, my boy. Then I suppose you'll finish your plan of coloring hen's eggs by feeding a peculiar diet to the hen?"

"No, sir. I believe I have found out the stuff that will do it, but it kills the hen; so I have dropped that for the present, though I can take it up again some day when I learn how to manage the mixture better."

"Well, what have you got on hand—anything?"

"Yes, sir, three or four things. I think they are all good and can all be done, but they are tiresome, and besides they require money. But as soon as the land is sold——"

"Emily, were you about to say something?" said Hawkins.

"Yes, sir. If you are willing, I will go to St. Louis. That will make another mouth less to feed. Mrs. Buckner has always wanted me to come."

"But the money, child?"

"Why I think she would send it, if you would write her—and I know she would wait for her pay till——"

"Come, Laura, let's hear from you, my girl."

Emily and Laura were about the same age—between seventeen and eighteen. Emily was fair and pretty, girlish and diffident—blue eyes and light hair. Laura had a proud bearing and a somewhat mature look; she had fine, clean-cut features, her complexion was pure white and contrasted vividly with her black hair and eyes; she was not what one calls pretty—she was beautiful. She said:

"I will go to St. Louis, too, sir. I will find a way to get there. I will *make* a way. And I will find a way to help myself along, and do what I can to help the rest, too."

She spoke it like a princess. Mrs. Hawkins smiled proudly and kissed her, saying in a tone of fond reproof:

"So one of my girls is going to turn out and work for her living! It's like your pluck and spirit, child, but we will hope that we haven't got quite down to that, yet."

The girl's eyes beamed affection under her mother's caress. Then she straightened up, folded her white hands in her lap and became a splendid iceberg. Clay's dog put up his brown nose for a little attention, and got it. He retired under the table with an apologetic yelp, which did not affect the iceberg.

Judge Hawkins had written and asked Clay to return home and consult with him upon family affairs. He arrived the evening after this conversation, and the whole household gave him a rapturous welcome. He brought sadly needed help with him, consisting of the savings of a year and a half of work—nearly two hundred dollars in money.

It was a ray of sunshine which (to this easy household) was the earnest of a clearing sky.

Bright and early in the morning the family were astir, and all were busy preparing Washington for his journey—at least all but Washington himself, who sat apart, steeped in a reverie. When the time for his departure came, it was easy to see how fondly all loved him and how hard it was to let him go, notwithstanding they had often seen him go before, in his St. Louis schooling days. In the most matter-of-course way they had borne the burden of getting him ready for his trip, never seeming to think of *his* helping in the matter; in the same matter-of-course way Clay had hired a horse and cart; and now that the good-byes were ended he bundled Washington's baggage in and drove away with the exile.

At Swansea Clay paid his stage fare, stowed him away in the vehicle, and saw him off. Then he returned home and reported progress, like a committee of the whole.

Clay remained at home several days. He held many consultations with his mother upon the financial condition of the family, and talked once with his father upon the same subject, but only once. He found a change in that quarter which was distressing; years of fluctuating fortune had done their work; each reverse had weakened the father's spirit and impaired his energies; his last misfortune seemed to have left hope and ambition dead within him; he had no projects, formed no plans—evidently he was a vanquished man. He looked worn and tired. He inquired into Clay's affairs and prospects, and when he found that Clay was doing pretty well and was likely to do still better, it was plain that he resigned himself with easy facility to look to the son for a support; and he said, "Keep yourself informed of poor Washington's condition and movements, and help him along all you can, Clay."

The younger children, also, seemed relieved of all fears and distresses, and very ready and willing to look to Clay for a livelihood. Within three days a general tranquility and satisfaction reigned in the household. Clay's hundred and eighty or ninety dollars had worked a wonder. The family were as contented, now, and as free from care as they could have been with a fortune. It was well that Mrs. Hawkins held the purse—otherwise the treasure would have lasted but a very little while.

It took but a trifle to pay Hawkins's outstanding obligations, for he had always had a horror of debt.

When Clay bade his home good-bye and set out to return to the field of his labors, he was conscious that henceforth he was to have his father's family on his hands as pensioners; but he did not allow himself to chafe at the thought, for he reasoned that his father had dealt by him with a free hand and a loving one all his life, and now that hard fortune had broken his spirit it ought to be a pleasure, not a pain, to work for him. The younger children were born and educated dependents. They had never been taught to do anything for themselves, and it did not seem to occur to them to make an attempt now.

The girls would not have been permitted to work for a living under any circumstances whatever. It was a southern family, and of good blood; and for any person except Laura, either within or without the household, to have suggested such an idea would have brought upon the suggester the suspicion of being a lunatic.

## CHAPTER 7

Bearing Washington Hawkins and his fortunes, the stage-coach tore out of Swansea at a fearful gait, with horn tooting gaily and half the town admiring from doors and windows. But it did not tear any more after it got to the outskirts; it dragged along stupidly enough, then—till it came in sight of the next hamlet; and then the bugle tooted gaily again and again the vehicle went tearing by the houses. This sort of conduct marked every entry to a station and every exit from it; and so in those days children grew up with the idea that stage-coaches always tore and always tooted; but they also grew up with the idea that pirates went into action in their Sunday clothes, carrying the black flag in one hand and pistolling people with the other, merely because they were so represented in the pictures—but these illusions vanished when later years brought their disenchanting wisdom. They learned then that the stage-coach is but a poor, plodding, vulgar thing in the solitudes of the highway; and that the pirate is only a seedy, unfantastic "rough," when he is out of the pictures.

Toward evening, the stage-coach came thundering into Hawkeye with a perfectly triumphant ostentation—which was natural and proper, for Hawkeye was a pretty large town for interior Missouri. Washington, very stiff and tired and hungry, climbed out, and wondered how he was to proceed now. But his difficulty was quickly solved. Col. Sellers came down the street on a run and arrived panting for breath. He said:

"Lord bless you—I'm glad to see you, Washington—perfectly delighted to see you, my boy! I got your message. Been on the look-out for you. Heard the stage horn, but had a party I couldn't shake off—man that's got an enormous thing on hand—wants me to put some capital into it—and I tell you, my boy, I could do worse, I could do a deal worse. No, now, let that luggage alone; I'll fix that. Here, Jerry, got anything to do? All right—shoulder this plunder and follow me. Come along, Washington. Lord I'm glad to see you! Wife and the children are just perishing to look at you. Bless you, they won't know you, you've grown so. Folks all well, I suppose? That's good—glad to hear that. We're always going to run down and see them, but I'm into so many operations, and they're not things a man feels like trusting to other people, and so somehow we keep putting it off. Fortunes in them! Good gracious, it's the country to pile up wealth in! Here we are—here's where the Sellers dynasty hangs out. Dump it on the door-step, Jerry—the blackest niggro in the State, Washington, but got a good heart—mighty likely boy, is Jerry. And now I suppose you've got to have ten cents, Jerry. That's all right—when a man works for me—when a man—in the other pocket, I reckon—when a man—why, where the mischief *is* that portmonnaie!—when a—well now that's odd— Oh, now I remember, must have left it at the bank; and b'George I've left my check-book, too—Polly says I ought to have a nurse— well, no matter. Let me have a dime, Washington, if you've got— ah, thanks. Now clear out, Jerry, your complexion has brought on the twilight half an hour ahead of time. Pretty fair joke—pretty fair. Here he is, Polly! Washington's come, children!—come now, don't eat him up—finish him in the house. Welcome, my boy, to a mansion that is proud to shelter the son of the best man that walks on the ground. Si Hawkins has been a good friend to me, and I believe I can say that whenever I've had a chance to put him into a good thing I've done it, and done it pretty cheerfully, too. I put him into that sugar speculation—what a grand thing that was, if we hadn't 'held on too long!'"

True enough; but holding on too long had utterly ruined both of them; and the saddest part of it was, that they never had had so much money to lose before, for Sellers's sale of their mule crop that year in New Orleans had been a great financial success. If he had kept out of sugar and gone back home content to stick to mules it would have been a happy wisdom. As it was, he

managed to kill two birds with one stone—that is to say, he killed
the sugar speculation by holding for high rates till he had to sell
at the bottom figure, and that calamity killed the mule that laid
the golden egg—which is but a figurative expression and will be
so understood. Sellers had returned home cheerful but empty-
handed, and the mule business lapsed into other hands. The sale
of the Hawkins property by the Sheriff had followed, and the
Hawkins hearts been torn to see Uncle Dan'l and his wife pass
from the auction-block into the hands of a negro trader and de-
part for the remote South to be seen no more by the family. It
had seemed like seeing their own flesh and blood sold into ban-
ishment.

Washington was greatly pleased with the Sellers mansion. It
was a two-story-and-a-half brick, and much more stylish than any
of its neighbors. He was borne to the family sitting room in
triumph by the swarm of little Sellerses, the parents following
with their arms about each other's waists.

The whole family were poorly and cheaply dressed; and the
clothing, although neat and clean, showed many evidences of
having seen long service. The Colonel's "stovepipe" hat was napless and shiny with much polishing, but nevertheless it had an
almost convincing expression about it of having been just pur-
chased new. The rest of his clothing was napless and shiny, too,
but it had the air of being entirely satisfied with itself and
blandly sorry for other people's clothes. It was growing rather
dark in the house, and the evening air was chilly, too. Sellers
said:

"Lay off your overcoat, Washington, and draw up to the stove
and make yourself at home—just consider yourself under your
own shingles my boy—I'll have a fire going, in a jiffy. Light the
lamp, Polly, dear, and let's have things cheerful—just as glad to
see you, Washington, as if you'd been lost a century and we'd
found you again!"

By this time the Colonel was conveying a lighted match into
a poor little stove. Then he propped the stove door to its place
by leaning the poker against it, for the hinges had retired from

business. This door framed a small square of isinglass, which now warmed up with a faint glow. Mrs. Sellers lit a cheap, showy lamp, which dissipated a good deal of the gloom, and then everybody gathered into the light and took the stove into close companionship.

The children climbed all over Sellers, fondled him, petted him, and were lavishly petted in return. Out from this tugging, laughing, chattering disguise of legs and arms and little faces, the Colonel's voice worked its way and his tireless tongue ran blithely on without interruption; and the purring little wife, diligent with her knitting, sat near at hand and looked happy and proud and grateful; and she listened as one who listens to oracles and gospels and whose grateful soul is being refreshed with the bread of life. Bye and bye the children quieted down to listen; clustered about their father, and resting their elbows on his legs, they hung upon his words as if he were uttering the music of the spheres.

A dreary old hair-cloth sofa against the wall; a few damaged chairs; the small table the lamp stood on; the crippled stove—these things constituted the furniture of the room. There was no carpet on the floor; on the wall were occasional square-shaped interruptions of the general tint of the plaster which betrayed that there used to be pictures in the house—but there were none now. There were no mantel ornaments, unless one might bring himself to regard as an ornament a clock which never came within fifteen strokes of striking the right time, and whose hands always hitched together at twenty-two minutes past anything and traveled in company the rest of the way home.

"Remarkable clock!" said Sellers, and got up and wound it. "I've been offered—well, I wouldn't expect you to believe what I've been offered for that clock. Old Gov. Hager never sees me but he says, 'Come, now, Colonel, name your price—I *must* have that clock!' But my goodness I'd as soon think of selling my wife. As I was saying to——silence in the court, now, she's begun to strike! You can't talk against her—you have to just be patient and hold up till she's said her say. Ah—well, as I was saying, when—

she's beginning again! Nineteen, twenty, twenty-one, twenty-two, twen——ah, that's all.—Yes, as I was saying to old Judge——go it, old girl, don't mind me.—Now how is that?—isn't that a good, spirited tone? She can wake the dead! Sleep? Why you might as well try to sleep in a thunder-factory. Now just listen at that. She'll strike a hundred and fifty, now, without stopping,—you'll see. There ain't another clock like that in Christendom."

Washington hoped that this might be true, for the din was distracting—though the family, one and all, seemed filled with joy; and the more the clock "buckled down to her work" as the Colonel expressed it, and the more insupportable the clatter became, the more enchanted they all appeared to be. When there was silence, Mrs. Sellers lifted upon Washington a face that beamed with a childlike pride, and said:

"It belonged to his grandmother."

The look and the tone were a plain call for admiring surprise, and therefore Washington said—(it was the only thing that offered itself at the moment:)

"Indeed!"

"Yes, it did, didn't it, father!" exclaimed one of the twins. "She was my great-grandmother—and George's too; wasn't she, father! *You* never saw her, but Sis has seen her, when Sis was a baby—didn't you, Sis! Sis has seen her most a hundred times. She was awful deef—she's dead, now. Ain't she, father!"

All the children chimed in, now, with one general Babel of information about deceased—nobody offering to read the riot act or seeming to discountenance the insurrection or disapprove of it in any way—but the head twin drowned all the turmoil and held his own against the field:

"It's our clock, now—and it's got wheels inside of it, and a thing that flutters every time she strikes—don't it, father! Great-grandmother died before hardly any of us was born—she was an Old-School Baptist and had warts all over her—you ask father if she didn't. She had an uncle once that was bald-headed and used to have fits; he wasn't *our* uncle, I don't know what he was to us—some kin or another I reckon—father's seen him a thousand

times—hain't you, father! We used to have a calf that et apples
and just chawed up dishrags like nothing, and if you stay here
you'll see lots of funerals—won't he, Sis! Did you ever see a house
afire? *I* have! Once me and Jim Terry———"

But Sellers began to speak now, and the storm ceased. He
began to tell about an enormous speculation he was thinking of
embarking some capital in—a speculation which some London
bankers had been over to consult with him about—and soon he
was building glittering pyramids of coin, and Washington was
presently growing opulent under the magic of his eloquence. But
at the same time Washington was not able to ignore the cold
entirely. He was nearly as close to the stove as he could get,
and yet he could not persuade himself that he felt the slightest
heat, notwithstanding the isinglass door was still gently and
serenely glowing. He tried to get a trifle closer to the stove, and
the consequence was, he tripped the supporting poker and the
stove door tumbled to the floor. And then there was a revelation—there was nothing in the stove but a lighted tallow-candle!

The poor youth blushed and felt as if he must die with shame.
But the Colonel was only disconcerted for a moment—he
straightway found his voice again:

"A little idea of my own, Washington—one of the greatest
things in the world! You must write and tell your father about
it—don't forget that, now. I have been reading up some European
Scientific reports—friend of mine, Count Fugier, sent them to
me—sends me all sorts of things from Paris—he thinks the world
of me, Fugier does. Well, I saw that the Academy of France had
been testing the properties of heat, and they came to the con-
clusion that it was a non-conductor or something like that, and of
course its influence must necessarily be deadly in nervous organi-
zations with excitable temperaments, especially where there is
any tendency toward rheumatic affections. Bless you I saw in
a moment what was the matter with us, and says I, out goes
your fires!—no more slow torture and certain death for me, sir.
What you want is the *appearance* of heat, not the heat itself—
that's the idea. Well how to do it was the next thing. I just put

my head to work, pegged away a couple of days, and here you are! Rheumatism? Why a man can't any more start a case of rheumatism in this house than he can shake an opinion out of a mummy! Stove with a candle in it and a transparent door—that's it—it has been the salvation of this family. Don't you fail to write your father about it, Washington. And tell him the idea is mine— I'm no more conceited than most people, I reckon, but you know it is human nature for a man to want credit for a thing like that."

Washington said with his blue lips that he would, but he said in his secret heart that he would promote no such iniquity. He tried to believe in the healthfulness of the invention, and succeeded tolerably well; but after all he could not feel that good health in a frozen body was any real improvement on the rheumatism.

## CHAPTER 8

The supper at Col. Sellers's was not sumptuous, in the beginning, but it improved on acquaintance. That is to say, that what Washington regarded as first sight as mere lowly potatoes, presently became awe-inspiring agricultural productions that had been reared in some ducal garden beyond the sea, under the sacred eye of the duke himself, who had sent them to Sellers; the bread was from corn which could be grown in only one favored locality in the earth and only a favored few could get it; the Rio coffee, which at first seemed execrable to the taste, took to itself an improved flavor when Washington was told to drink it slowly and not hurry what should be a lingering luxury in order to be fully appreciated—it was from the private stores of a Brazilian nobleman with an unrememberable name. The Colonel's tongue was a magician's wand that turned dried apples into figs and water into wine as easily as it could change a hovel into a palace and present poverty into imminent future riches.

Washington slept in a cold bed in a carpetless room and woke up in a palace in the morning; at least the palace lingered during the moment that he was rubbing his eyes and getting his bearings—and then it disappeared and he recognized that the Colonel's inspiring talk had been influencing his dreams. Fatigue had made him sleep late; when he entered the sitting room he noticed that the old hair-cloth sofa was absent; when he sat down to breakfast the Colonel tossed six or seven dollars in bills on the table, counted them over, said he was a little short and must call upon his banker; then returned the bills to his wallet with the indifferent air of a man who is used to money. The breakfast was not an improvement upon the supper, but the Colonel talked it up and transformed it into an oriental feast. Bye and bye, he said:

"I intend to look out for you, Washington, my boy. I hunted
up a place for you yesterday, but I am not referring to that, now
—that is a mere livelihood—mere bread and butter; but when I
say I mean to look out for you I mean something very different.
I mean to put things in your way that will make a mere livelihood a trifling thing. I'll put you in a way to make more money
than you'll ever know what to do with. You'll be right here where
I can put my hand on you when anything turns up. I've got some
prodigious operations on foot; but I'm keeping quiet; mum's the
word; your old hand don't go around pow-wowing and letting
everybody see his k'yards and find out his little game. But all in
good time, Washington, all in good time. You'll see. Now there's
an operation in corn that looks well. Some New York men are
trying to get me to go into it—buy up all the growing crops and
just boss the market when they mature—ah I tell you it's a
great thing. And it only costs a trifle; two millions or two and a
half will do it. I haven't exactly promised yet—there's no hurry—
the more indifferent I seem, you know, the more anxious those
fellows will get. And then there is the hog speculation—that's
bigger still. We've got quiet men at work," [he was very impressive here,] "mousing around, to get propositions out of all
the farmers in the whole west and northwest for the hog crop,
and other agents quietly getting propositions and terms out of
all the manufactories—and don't you see, if we can get all the
hogs and all the slaughter houses into our hands on the dead
quiet—whew! it would take three ships to carry the money.—
I've looked into the thing—calculated all the chances for and all
the chances against, and though I shake my head and hesitate
and keep on thinking, apparently, I've got my mind made up
that if the thing can be done on a capital of six millions, that's
the horse to put up money on! Why Washington—but what's the
use of talking about it—any man can see that there's whole
Atlantic oceans of cash in it, gulfs and bays thrown in. But there's
a bigger thing than that, yet—a bigger———"

"Why Colonel, you can't want anything bigger!" said Washington, his eyes blazing. "Oh, I wish I could go into either of

those speculations—I only wish I had money—I wish I wasn't cramped and kept down and fettered with poverty, and such prodigious chances lying right here in sight! Oh, it is a fearful thing to be poor. But don't throw away those things—they are so splendid and I can see how sure they are. Don't throw them away for something still better and maybe fail in it! I wouldn't, Colonel. I would stick to these. I wish father were here and were his old self again—Oh, he never in his life had such chances as these are. Colonel, you *can't* improve on these—no man can improve on them!"

A sweet, compassionate smile played about the Colonel's features, and he leaned over the table with the air of a man who is "going to show you" and do it without the least trouble:

"Why Washington, my boy, these things are nothing. They *look* large—of course they look large to a novice, but to a man who has been all his life accustomed to large operations—shaw! They're well enough to while away an idle hour with, or furnish a bit of employment that will give a trifle of idle capital a chance to earn its bread while it is waiting for something to *do*, but—now just listen a moment—just let me give you an idea of what we old veterans of commerce call 'business.' Here's the Rothschild's proposition—this is between you and me, you understand———"

Washington nodded three or four times impatiently, and his glowing eyes said, "Yes, yes—hurry—I understand———"

"———for I wouldn't have it get out for a fortune. They want me to go in with them on the sly—agent was here two weeks ago about it—go in on the sly" [voice down to an impressive whisper, now,] "and buy up a hundred and thirteen wild cat banks in Ohio, Indiana, Kentucky, Illinois and Missouri—notes of these banks are at all sorts of discount now—average discount of the hundred and thirteen is forty-four per cent—buy them all up, you see, and then all of a sudden let the cat out of the bag! Whiz! the stock of every one of those wildcats would spin up to a tremendous premium before you could turn a handspring— profit on the speculation not a dollar less than forty millions!"

[An eloquent pause, while the marvelous vision settled into W.'s focus.] "Where's your hogs now! Why my dear innocent boy, we would just sit down on the front door-steps and peddle banks like lucifer matches!"

Washington finally got his breath and said:

"Oh, it is perfectly wonderful! Why couldn't these things have happened in father's day? And I—it's of no use—they simply lie before my face and mock me. There is nothing for me but to stand helpless and see other people reap the astonishing harvest."

"Never mind, Washington, don't you worry. I'll fix you. There's plenty of chances. How much money have you got?"

In the presence of so many millions, Washington could not keep from blushing when he had to confess that he had but eighteen dollars in the world.

"Well, all right—don't despair. Other people have been obliged to begin with less. I have a small idea that may develop into something for us both, all in good time. Keep your money close and add to it. I'll make it breed. I've been experimenting (to pass away the time,) on a little preparation for curing sore eyes—a kind of decoction nine-tenths water and the other tenth drugs that don't cost more than a dollar a barrel; I'm still experimenting; there's one ingredient wanted yet to perfect the thing, and somehow I can't just manage to hit upon the thing that's necessary, and I don't dare talk with a chemist, of course. But I'm progressing, and before many weeks I wager the country will ring with the fame of Eschol Sellers' Infallible Imperial Oriental Optic Liniment and Salvation for Sore Eyes— the Medical Wonder of the Age! Small bottles fifty cents, large ones a dollar. Average cost, five and seven cents for the two sizes. The first year sell, say, ten thousand bottles in Missouri, seven thousand in Iowa, three thousand in Arkansas, four thousand in Kentucky, six thousand in Illinois, and say twenty-five thousand in the rest of the country. Total, fifty-five thousand bottles; profit clear of all expenses, twenty thousand dollars at the very lowest calculation. All the capital needed is to manufacture the first two thousand bottles—say a hundred and fifty dollars—then the money would begin to flow in. The second year, sales would reach 200,000 bottles—clear profit, say, $75,000—and in the meantime the great factory would be building in St. Louis, to cost, say, $100,000. The third year we could easily sell 1,000,000 bottles in the United States and——"

"O, splendid!" said Washington. "Let's commence right away—let's——"

"——1,000,000 bottles in the United States—profit at least $350,000—and *then* it would begin to be time to turn our attention toward the *real* idea of the business."

"The *real* idea of it! Ain't $350,000 a year a pretty real——"

"Stuff! Why what an infant you are, Washington—what a guileless, short-sighted, easily-contented innocent you are, my poor little country-bred know-nothing! Would I go to all that trouble and bother for the poor crumbs a body might pick up in *this* country? Now do I look like a man who—does my history suggest that I am a man who deals in trifles, contents himself with the narrow horizon that hems in the common herd, sees no further than the end of his nose? Now *you* know that that is not me— couldn't *be* me. *You* ought to know that if I throw my time and abilities into a patent medicine, it's a patent medicine whose field of operations is the solid earth! its clients the swarming nations that inhabit it! Why what is the republic of America for an eye-water country? Lord bless you, it is nothing but a barren highway that you've got to cross to get *to* the true eye-water market! Why, Washington, in the oriental countries people swarm like the sands of the desert; every square mile of ground upholds its thousands upon thousands of struggling human creatures—and every separate and individual devil of them's got the ophthalmia! It's as natural to them as noses are—and sin. It's born with them, it stays with them, it's all that some of them have left when they die. Three years of introductory trade in the orient and what will be the result? Why, our headquarters would be in Constantinople and our hindquarters in Further India! Factories and warehouses in Cairo, Ispahan, Bagdad, Damascus, Jerusalem, Yedo, Peking, Bangkok, Delhi, Bombay and Calcutta! Annual income—well, God only knows how many millions and millions apiece!"

Washington was so dazed, so bewildered—his heart and his eyes had wandered so far away among the strange lands beyond the seas, and such avalanches of coin and currency had fluttered and jingled confusedly down before him, that he was now as one who has been whirling round and round for a time, and, stopping all at once, finds his surroundings still whirling and all objects a dancing chaos. However, little by little the Sellers family cooled down and crystalized into shape, and the poor room lost its glitter and resumed its poverty. Then the youth found his voice and begged Sellers to drop everything and hurry up the eye-water; and he got his eighteen dollars and tried to force it upon the Colonel—pleaded with him to take it—implored him to do it. But the Colonel would not; said he would not need the capital (in his native magnificent way he called that eighteen dollars Capital) till the eye-water was an accomplished fact. He made Washington easy in his mind, though, by promising that he would call for it just as soon as the invention was finished, and he added the glad tidings that nobody but just they two should be admitted to a share in the speculation.

When Washington left the breakfast table he could have worshiped that man. Washington was one of that kind of people whose hopes are in the very clouds one day and in the gutter the next. He walked on air, now. The Colonel was ready to take him around and introduce him to the employment he had found for him, but Washington begged for a few moments in which to write home; with his kind of people, to ride to-day's new interest to death and put off yesterday's till another time, is nature itself. He ran up stairs and wrote glowingly, enthusiastically, to his mother about the hogs and the corn, the banks and the eye-water—and added a few inconsequential millions to each project. And he said that people little dreamed what a man Col. Sellers was, and that the world would open its eyes when it found out. And he closed his letter thus:

"So make yourself perfectly easy, mother—in a little while you shall have everything you want, and more. I am not likely to stint *you* in anything, I fancy. This money will not be for me, alone, but for all of us. I want all to share alike; and there is going to be far more for each than one person can spend. Break it to father cautiously—you understand the need of that—break it to him cautiously, for he has had such cruel hard fortune, and.is so stricken by it that great good news might prostrate him more surely than even bad, for he is used to the bad but is grown sadly unaccustomed to the other. Tell Laura —tell all the children. And write to Clay about it if he is not with you yet. You may tell Clay that whatever I get he can freely share in—freely. He knows that that is true—there will be no need that I should swear to that to make him believe it. Good-bye—and mind what I say: Rest perfectly easy, one and all of you, for our troubles are nearly at an end."

Poor lad, he could not know that his mother would cry some loving, compassionate tears over his letter and put off the family with a synopsis of its contents which conveyed a deal of love to them but not much idea of his prospects or projects. And he never dreamed that such a joyful letter could sadden her and fill her night with sighs, and troubled thoughts, and bodings of the future, instead of filling it with peace and blessing it with restful sleep.

When the letter was done, Washington and the Colonel sallied forth, and as they walked along Washington learned what he was to be. He was to be a clerk in a real estate office. Instantly the fickle youth's dreams forsook the magic eye-water and flew back to the Tennessee Land. And the gorgeous possibilities of that great domain straightway began to occupy his imagination to such a degree that he could scarcely manage to keep even enough of his attention upon the Colonel's talk to retain the general run of what he was saying. He was glad it was a real estate office—he was a made man now, sure.

The Colonel said that General Boswell was a rich man and had a good and growing business; and that Washington's work would be light and he would get forty dollars a month and be boarded and lodged in the General's family—which was as good as ten dollars more; and even better, for he could not live as well even at the "City Hotel" as he would there, and yet the hotel charged fifteen dollars a month where a man had a good room.

General Boswell was in his office; a comfortable looking place, with plenty of outline maps hanging about the walls and in the windows, and a spectacled man was marking out another one on a long table. The office was in the principal street. The General received Washington with a kindly but reserved politeness. Washington rather liked his looks. He was about fifty years old, dignified, well preserved and well dressed. After the Colonel took his leave, the General talked a while with Washington—his talk consisting chiefly of instructions about the clerical duties of the place. He seemed satisfied as to Washington's ability to take care of the books, he was evidently a pretty fair theoretical book-keeper, and experience would soon harden theory into practice. By and by dinner-time came, and the two walked to the General's house; and now Washington noticed an instinct in himself that moved him to keep not in the General's rear, exactly, but yet not at his side—somehow the old gentleman's dignity and reserve did not inspire familiarity.

## CHAPTER 9

Washington dreamed his way along the street, his fancy flitting from grain to hogs, from hogs to banks, from banks to eye-water, from eye-water to Tennessee Land, and lingering but a feverish moment upon each of these fascinations. He was conscious of but one outward thing, to wit, the General, and he was really not vividly conscious of him.

Arrived at the finest dwelling in the town, they entered it and were at home. Washington was introduced to Mrs. Boswell, and his imagination was on the point of flitting into the vapory realms of speculation again, when a lovely girl of sixteen or seventeen came in. This vision swept Washington's mind clear of its chaos of glittering rubbish in an instant. Beauty had fascinated him before; many times he had been in love—even for weeks at a time with the same object—but his heart had never suffered so sudden and so fierce an assault as this, within his recollection.

Louise Boswell occupied his mind and drifted among his multiplication tables all the afternoon. He was constantly catching himself in a reverie—reveries made up of recalling how she looked when she first burst upon him; how her voice thrilled him when she first spoke; how charmed the very air seemed by her presence. Blissful as the afternoon was, delivered up to such a revel as this, it seemed an eternity, so impatient was he to see the girl again. Other afternoons like it followed. Washington plunged into this love affair as he plunged into everything else—upon impulse and without reflection. As the days went by it seemed plain that he was growing in favor with Louise,—not sweepingly so, but yet perceptibly, he fancied. His attentions to her troubled her father and mother a little, and they warned Louise, without stating particulars or making allusions to any special person, that a girl was sure to make a mistake who al-

lowed herself to marry anybody but a man who could support
her well.

Some instinct taught Washington that his present lack of
money would be an obstruction, though possibly not a bar, to
his hopes, and straightway his poverty became a torture to him
which cast all his former sufferings under that head into the
shade. He longed for riches now as he had never longed for
them before.

He had been once or twice to dine with Col. Sellers, and had
been discouraged to note that the Colonel's bill of fare was falling off both in quantity and quality—a sign, he feared, that
the lacking ingredient in the eye-water still remained undis-
covered—though Sellers always explained that these changes in
the family diet had been ordered by the doctor, or suggested by
some new scientific work the Colonel had stumbled upon. But
it always turned out that the lacking ingredient *was* still lacking—
though it always appeared, at the same time, that the Colonel
was right on its heels.

Every time the Colonel came into the real estate office Washington's heart bounded and his eyes lighted with hope, but
it always turned out that the Colonel was merely on the scent
of some vast, undefined landed speculation—although he was
customarily able to say that he was nearer to the all-necessary
ingredient than ever, and could almost name the hour when
success would dawn. And then Washington's heart would sink
again and a sigh would tell when it touched bottom.

About this time a letter came, saying that Judge Hawkins had
been ailing for a fortnight, and was now considered to be
seriously ill. It was thought best that Washington should come
home. The news filled him with grief, for he loved and honored
his father; the Boswells were touched by the youth's sorrow,
and even the General unbent and said encouraging things to
him.—There was balm in this; but when Louise bade him good-
bye, and shook his hand and said, "Don't be cast down—it will all
come out right—I *know* it will all come out right," it seemed
a blessed thing to be in misfortune, and the tears that welled

up to his eyes were the messengers of an adoring and a grateful heart; and when the girl saw them and answering tears came into her own eyes, Washington could hardly contain the excess of happiness that poured into the cavities of his breast that were so lately stored to the roof with grief.

All the way home he nursed his woe and exalted it. He pictured himself as *she* must be picturing him: a noble, struggling young spirit persecuted by misfortune, but bravely and patiently waiting in the shadow of a dread calamity and preparing to meet the blow as became one who was all too used to hard fortune and the pitiless buffetings of fate. These thoughts made him weep, and weep more broken-heartedly than ever; and he wished that she could see his sufferings *now*.

There was nothing significant in the fact that Louise, dreamy and distraught, stood at her bedroom bureau that night, scribbling "Washington" here and there over a sheet of paper. But there was something significant in the fact that she scratched the word out every time she wrote it; examined the erasure critically to see if anybody could guess at what the word had been; then buried it under a maze of obliterating lines; and finally, as if still unsatisfied, burned the paper.

When Washington reached home, he recognized at once how serious his father's case was. The darkened room, the labored breathing and occasional moanings of the patient, the tip-toeing of the attendants and their whispered consultations, were full of sad meaning. For three or four nights Mrs. Hawkins and Laura had been watching by the bedside; Clay had arrived, preceding Washington by one day, and he was now added to the corps of watchers. Mr. Hawkins would have none but these three, though neighborly assistance was offered by old friends. From this time forth three-hour watches were instituted, and day and night the watchers kept their vigils. By degrees Laura and her mother began to show wear, but neither of them would yield a minute of their tasks to Clay.—He ventured once to let the midnight hour pass without calling Laura, but he ventured no more; there was that about her rebuke when he tried to explain, that taught him that to let her sleep when she might be ministering to her father's needs, was to rob her of moments that were priceless in her eyes; he perceived that she regarded it as a privilege to watch, not a burden. And he had noticed, also, that when midnight struck, the patient turned his eyes toward the door, with an expectancy in them which presently grew into a longing but brightened into contentment as soon as the door opened and Laura appeared. And he did not need Laura's rebuke when he heard his father say:

"Clay is good, and you are tired, poor child; but I wanted you so."

"Clay is not good, father—he did not call me. I would not have treated *him* so. How could you do it, Clay?"

Clay begged forgiveness and promised not to break faith again; and as he betook him to his bed, he said to himself, "It's a steadfast little soul; whoever thinks he is doing the Duchess a kindness by intimating that she is not sufficient for any undertaking she puts her hand to, makes a mistake; and if I did not know it before, I know now that there are surer ways of pleasing her than by trying to lighten her labor when that labor consists in wearing herself out for the sake of a person she loves."

A week drifted by, and all the while the patient sank lower and lower. The night drew on that was to end all suspense. It was a wintry one. The darkness gathered, the snow was falling, the wind wailed plaintively about the house or shook it with fitful gusts. The doctor had paid his last visit and gone away with that dismal remark to the nearest friend of the family that he "believed there was nothing more that he could do"—a remark which is always overheard by some one it is not meant for and strikes a lingering half-conscious hope dead with a withering shock; the medicine phials had been removed from the bedside and put out of sight, and all things made orderly and meet for the solemn event that was impending; the patient, with closed eyes, lay scarcely breathing; the watchers sat by and wiped the gathering damps from his forehead while the silent

tears flowed down their faces; the deep hush was only interrupted by sobs from the children, grouped about the bed.

After a time,—it was toward midnight now—Mr. Hawkins
roused out of a doze, looked about him and was evidently trying to speak. Instantly Laura lifted his head and in a failing
voice he said, while something of the old light shone in his eyes:

"Wife—children—come nearer—nearer. The darkness grows.
Let me see you all, once more."

The group closed together at the bedside, and their tears and
sobs came now without restraint.

"I am leaving you in cruel poverty. I have been—so foolish—
so short-sighted. But courage! A better day is—is coming. Never
lose sight of the Tennessee Land! Be wary. There is wealth
stored up for you there—wealth that is boundless! The children
shall hold up their heads with the best in the land, yet. Where
are the papers?—Have you got the papers safe? Show them—
show them to me!"

Under his strong excitement his voice had gathered power and
his last sentences were spoken with scarcely a perceptible halt
or hindrance. With an effort he had raised himself almost without assistance to a sitting posture. But now the fire faded out of
his eyes and he fell back exhausted. The papers were brought
and held before him, and the answering smile that flitted across
his face showed that he was satisfied. He closed his eyes, and
the signs of approaching dissolution mutiplied rapidly. He lay
almost motionless for a little while, then suddenly partly raised
his head and looked about him as one who peers into a dim uncertain light. He muttered:

"Gone? No—I see you—still. It is—it is—over. But you are—
safe. Safe. The Ten———"

The voice died out in a whisper; the sentence was never
finished. The emaciated fingers began to pick at the coverlet, a
fatal sign. After a time there were no sounds but the cries of the
mourners within and the gusty turmoil of the wind without.
Laura had bent down and kissed her father's lips as the spirit
left the body; but she did not sob, or utter any ejaculation; her

tears flowed silently. Then she closed the dead eyes, and crossed the hands upon the breast; after a season, she kissed the forehead reverently, drew the sheet up over the face, and then walked apart and sat down with the look of one who is done with life and has no further interest in its joys and sorrows, its hopes or its ambitions. Clay buried his face in the coverlet of the bed; when the other children and the mother realized that death was indeed come at last, they threw themselves into each others' arms and gave way to a frenzy of grief.

## CHAPTER 10

Only two or three days had elapsed since the funeral, when something happened which was to change the drift of Laura's life somewhat, and influence in a greater or lesser degree the formation of her character.

Major Lackland had once been a man of note in the State—a man of extraordinary natural ability and as extraordinary learning. He had been universally trusted and honored in his day, but had finally fallen into misfortune; while serving his third term in Congress, and while upon the point of being elevated to the Senate—which was considered the summit of earthly aggrandizement in those days—he had yielded to temptation, when in distress for money wherewith to save his estate, and sold his vote. His crime was discovered, and his fall followed instantly. Nothing could reinstate him in the confidence of the people, his ruin was irretrievable—his disgrace complete. All doors were closed against him, all men avoided him. After years of skulking retirement and dissipation, death had relieved him of his troubles at last, and his funeral followed close upon that of Mr. Hawkins. He died as he had latterly lived—wholly alone and friendless. He had no relatives—or if he had they did not acknowledge him. The coroner's jury found certain memoranda upon his body and about the premises which revealed a fact not suspected by the villagers before—viz., that Laura was not the child of Mr. and Mrs. Hawkins.

The gossips were soon at work. They were but little hampered by the fact that the memoranda referred to betrayed nothing but the bare circumstance that Laura's real parents were unknown, and stopped there. So far from being hampered by this, the gossips seemed to gain all the more freedom from it. They supplied all the missing information themselves, they filled up all the blanks. The town soon teemed with histories of Laura's origin and secret history, no two versions precisely alike, but all elaborate, exhaustive, mysterious and interesting, and all agreeing in one vital particular—to wit, that there was a suspicious cloud about her birth, not to say a disreputable one.

Laura began to encounter cold looks, averted eyes and peculiar nods and gestures which perplexed her beyond measure; but presently the pervading gossip found its way to her, and she understood them then. Her pride was stung. She was astonished, and at first incredulous. She was about to ask her mother if there was any truth in these reports, but upon second thought held her peace. She soon gathered that Major Lackland's memoranda seemed to refer to letters which had passed between himself and Judge Hawkins. She shaped her course without difficulty the day that that hint reached her.

That night she sat in her room till all was still, and then she stole into the garret and began a search. She rummaged long among boxes of musty papers relating to business matters of no interest to her, but at last she found several bundles of letters. One bundle was marked "private," and in that she found what she wanted. She selected six or eight letters from the package and began to devour their contents, heedless of the cold.

By the dates, these letters were from five to seven years old. They were all from Major Lackland to Mr. Hawkins. The substance of them was, that some one in the east had been inquiring of Major Lackland about a lost child and its parents, and that it was conjectured that the child might be Laura.

Evidently some of the letters were missing, for the name of the inquirer was not mentioned; there was a casual reference to "this handsome-featured aristocratic gentleman," as if the reader and the writer were accustomed to speak of him and knew who was meant.

In one letter the Major said he agreed with Mr. Hawkins that the inquirer seemed not altogether on the wrong track; but he also agreed that it would be best to keep quiet until more convincing developments were forthcoming.

Another letter said that "the poor soul broke completely down when he saw Laura's picture, and declared it must be she."

Still another said:

"He seems entirely alone in the world, and his heart is so wrapped up in this thing that I believe that if it proved a false hope, it would kill him; I have persuaded him to wait a little while and go west when I go."

Another letter had this paragraph in it:

"He is better one day and worse the next, and is out of his mind a good deal of the time. Lately his case has developed a something which is a wonder to the hired nurses, but which will not be much of a marvel to you if you have read medical philosophy much. It is this: his lost memory returns to him when he is delirious, and goes away again when he is himself—just as old Canada Joe used to talk the French *patois* of his boyhood in the delirium of typhus fever, though he could not do it when his mind was clear. Now this poor gentleman's memory has always broken down before he reached the explosion of the steamer; he could only remember starting up the river with his wife and child, and he had an idea that there was a race, but he was not certain; he could not name the boat he was on; there was a dead blank of a month or more that supplied not an item to his recollection. It was not for me to assist him, of course. But now in his delirium *it all comes out:* the names of the boats, every incident of the explosion, and likewise the details of his astonishing escape— that is, up to where, just as a yawl-boat was approaching him (he was clinging to the starboard wheel of the burning wreck at the time), a falling timber struck him on the head. But I will write out his wonderful escape in full to-morrow or next day. Of course the physicians will not let me tell him now that our Laura is indeed his child—that must come later, when his health is thoroughly restored. His case is not considered dangerous at all; he will recover presently, the doctors say. But they insist that he must travel a little when he gets well—they recommend a short sea voyage, and they say he can be persuaded to try it if we continue to keep him in ignorance and promise to let him see L. as soon as he returns."

The letter that bore the latest date of all, contained this clause:

"It is the most unaccountable thing in the world; the mystery remains as impenetrable as ever; I have hunted high and low for him, and inquired of everybody, but in vain; all trace of him ends at that hotel in New York; I never have seen or heard of him since, up to this day; he could hardly have sailed, for his name does not appear upon the books of any shipping office in New York or Boston or Baltimore. How fortunate it seems, now, that we kept this thing to ourselves; Laura still has a father in you, and it is better for her that we drop this subject here forever."

That was all. Random remarks here and there, being pieced together gave Laura a vague impression of a man of fine presence, about forty-three or forty-five years of age, with dark hair and eyes, and a slight limp in his walk—it was not stated which leg was defective. And this indistinct shadow represented her father. She made an exhaustive search for the missing letters, but found none. They had probably been burned; and she doubted not that the ones she had ferreted out would have shared the same fate if Mr. Hawkins had not been a dreamer, void of method, whose mind was perhaps in a state of conflagration over some bright new speculation when he received them.

She sat long, with the letters in her lap, thinking—and unconsciously freezing. She felt like a lost person who has traveled down a long lane in good hope of escape, and, just as the night descends finds his progress barred by a bridgeless river whose further shore, if it has one, is lost in the darkness. If she could only have found these letters a month sooner! That was her thought. But now the dead had carried their secrets with them. A dreary melancholy settled down upon her. An undefined sense of injury crept into her heart. She grew very miserable.

She had just reached the romantic age—the age when there is a sad sweetness, a dismal comfort to a girl to find out that there is a mystery connected with her birth, which no other piece of good luck can afford. She had more than her rightful share of practical good sense, but still she was human; and to be human is to have one's little modicum of romance secreted

away in one's composition. One never ceases to make a hero of
one's self, (in private,) during life, but only alters the style of
his heroism from time to time as the drifting years belittle certain
gods of his admiration and raise up others in their stead that
seem greater.

The recent wearing days and nights of watching, and the
wasting grief that had possessed her, combined with the profound depression that naturally came with the reaction of idle-
ness, made Laura peculiarly susceptible at this time to romantic
impressions. She was a heroine, now, with a mysterious father
somewhere. She could not really tell whether she wanted to find
him and spoil it all or not; but still all the traditions of romance
pointed to the making the attempt as the usual and necessary
course to follow; therefore she would some day begin the search
when opportunity should offer.

Now a former thought struck her—she would speak to Mrs.
Hawkins. And naturally enough Mrs. Hawkins appeared on the
stage at that moment.

She said she knew all—she knew that Laura had discovered
the secret that Mr. Hawkins, the elder children, Col. Sellers and
herself had kept so long and so faithfully; and she cried and
said that now that troubles had begun they would never end;
her daughter's love would wean itself away from her and her
heart would break. Her grief so wrought upon Laura that the
girl almost forgot her own troubles for the moment in her com-
passion for her mother's distress. Finally Mrs. Hawkins said:

"Speak to me, child—do not forsake me. Forget all this miserable talk. Say I am your mother!—I have loved you so long, and
there is no other. I *am* your mother, in the sight of God, and
nothing shall ever take you from me!"

All barriers fell, before this appeal. Laura put her arms about
her mother's neck and said:

"You *are* my mother, and always shall be. We will be as we
have always been; and neither this foolish talk nor any other
thing shall part us or make us less to each other than we are this
hour."

There was no longer any sense of separation or estrangement between them. Indeed their love seemed more perfect now than it had ever been before. By and by they went down stairs and sat by the fire and talked long and earnestly about Laura's history and the letters. But it transpired that Mrs. Hawkins had never known of this correspondence between her husband and Major Lackland. With his usual consideration for his wife, Mr. Hawkins had shielded her from the worry the matter would have caused her.

Laura went to bed at last with a mind that had gained largely in tranquility and had lost correspondingly in morbid romantic exaltation. She was pensive, the next day, and subdued; but that was not matter for remark, for she did not differ from the mournful friends about her in that respect. Clay and Washington were the same loving and admiring brothers now that they had always been. The great secret was new to some of the younger children, but their love suffered no change under the wonderful revelation.

It is barely possible that things might have presently settled down into their old rut and the mystery have lost the bulk of its romantic sublimity in Laura's eyes, if the village gossips could have quieted down. But they could not quiet down and they did not. Day after day they called at the house, ostensibly upon visits of condolence, and they pumped away at the mother and the children without seeming to know that their questionings were in bad taste. They meant no harm—they only wanted to know. Villagers always want to know.

The family fought shy of the questionings, and of course that was high testimony—"if the Duchess was respectably born, why didn't they come out and prove it?—why did they stick to that poor thin story about picking her up out of a steamboat explosion?"

Under this ceaseless persecution, Laura's morbid self-communing was renewed. At night the day's contribution of detraction, innuendo and malicious conjecture would be canvassed in her mind, and then she would drift into a course of thinking. As her thoughts ran on, the indignant tears would spring to her eyes, and she would spit out fierce little ejaculations at intervals. But finally she would grow calmer and say some comforting disdainful thing—something like this:

"But who are they?—Animals! What are their opinions to me? Let them talk—I will not stoop to be affected by it. I could hate———. Nonsense—nobody I care for or in any way respect is changed toward me, I fancy."

She may have supposed she was thinking of many individuals, but it was not so—she was thinking of only one. And her heart warmed somewhat, too, the while. One day a friend overheard a conversation like this:—and naturally came and told her all about it:

"Ned, they say you don't go there any more. How is that?"

"Well, I don't; but I tell you it's not because I don't want to and it's not because I think it is any matter who her father was or who he wasn't, either; it's only on account of this talk, talk, talk. I think she is a fine girl every way, and so would you if you knew her as well as I do; but you know how it is when a girl once gets talked about—it's all up with her—the world won't ever let her alone, after that."

The only comment Laura made upon this revelation, was:

"Then it appears that if this trouble had not occurred I could have had the happiness of Mr. Ned Thurston's serious attentions. He is well favored in person, and well liked, too, I believe, and comes of one of the first families of the village. He is prosperous, too, I hear; has been a doctor a year, now, and has had two patients—no, three, I think; yes, it *was* three. I attended their funerals. Well, other people have hoped and been disappointed; I am not alone in that. I wish you could stay to dinner, Maria— we are going to have sausages; and besides, I wanted to talk to you about Hawkeye and make you promise to come and see us when we are settled there."

But Maria could not stay. She had come to mingle romantic tears with Laura's over the lover's defection and had found herself dealing with a heart that could not rise to an appreciation of affliction because its interest was all centred in sausages.

But as soon as Maria was gone, Laura stamped her expressive foot and said:

"The coward! Are all books lies? I thought he would fly to the front, and be brave and noble, and stand up for me against all the world, and defy my enemies, and wither these gossips with his scorn! Poor crawling thing, let him go. I *do* begin to despise this world!"

She lapsed into thought. Presently she said:

"If the time ever comes, and I get a chance, Oh, I'll——"

She could not find a word that was strong enough, perhaps. By and by she said:

"Well, I am glad of it—I'm glad of it. I never cared anything for him anyway!"

And then, with small consistency, she cried a little, and patted her foot more indignantly than ever.

## CHAPTER 11

Two months had gone by and the Hawkins family were domiciled in Hawkeye. Washington was at work in the real estate office again, and was alternately in Paradise or the other place just as it happened that Louise was gracious to him or seemingly indifferent—because indifference or preoccupation could mean nothing else than that she was thinking of some other young person. Col. Sellers had asked him several times, to dine with him, when he first returned to Hawkeye, but Washington, for no particular reason, had not accepted. No particular reason except one which he preferred to keep to himself—viz. that he could not bear to be away from Louise. It occurred to him, now, that the Colonel had not invited him lately—could he be offended? He resolved to go that very day, and give the Colonel a pleasant surprise. It was a good idea; especially as Louise had absented herself from breakfast that morning, and torn his heart; he would tear hers, now, and let her see how it felt.

The Sellers family were just starting to dinner when Washington burst upon them with his surprise. For an instant the Colonel looked nonplussed, and just a bit uncomfortable; and Mrs. Sellers looked actually distressed; but the next moment the head of the house was himself again, and exclaimed:

"All right, my boy, all right—always glad to see you—always glad to hear your voice and take you by the hand. Don't wait for special invitations—that's all nonsense among friends. Just come whenever you can, and come as often as you can—the oftener the better. You can't please us any better than that, Washington; the little woman will tell you so herself. We don't pretend to style. Plain folks, you know—plain folks. Just a plain family dinner, but such as it is, our friends are *always* welcome, I reckon you know that yourself, Washington. Run along, children, run along; Lafayette,* stand off the cat's tail, child, can't you see what you're doing?—Come, come, come, Roderick Dhu, it isn't nice for little boys to hang onto young gentlemen's coat tails—but never mind him, Washington, he's full of spirits and don't mean any harm. Children will be children, you know. Take the chair next to Mrs. Sellers, Washington—tut, tut, Marie Antoinette, let your brother have the fork if he wants it, you are bigger than he is."

Washington contemplated the banquet, and wondered if he were in his right mind. Was this the plain family dinner? And was it all present? It was soon apparent that this was indeed the dinner: it was all on the table: it consisted of abundance of clear, fresh water, and a basin of raw turnips—nothing more.

Washington stole a glance at Mrs. Sellers's face, and would have given the world, the next moment, if he could have spared her that. The poor woman's face was crimson, and the tears stood in her eyes. Washington did not know what to do. He wished he had never come there and spied out this cruel poverty and brought pain to that poor little lady's heart and shame to her cheek; but he was there, and there was no escape. Col. Sellers hitched back his coat sleeves airily from his wrists as who should say "*Now* for solid enjoyment!" seized a fork, flourished it and began to harpoon turnips and deposit them in the plates before him:

"Let me help you, Washington—Lafayette pass this plate to Washington—ah, well, well, my boy, things are looking pretty bright, now, *I* tell you. Speculation—my! the whole atmosphere's full of money. I wouldn't take three fortunes for one little operation I've got on hand now—have anything from the casters? No?

* In those old days the average man called his children after his most re-vered literary and historical idols; consequently there was hardly a family, at least in the West, but had a Washington in it—and also a Lafayette, a Franklin, and six or eight sounding names from Byron, Scott, and the Bible, if the offspring held out. To visit such a family, was to find one's self con-fronted by a congress made up of representatives of the imperial myths and the majestic dead of all the ages. There was something thrilling about it, to a stranger, not to say awe inspiring.—M.T.

Well, you're right, you're right. Some people like mustard with turnips, but—now there was Baron Poniatowski—Lord, but that man did know how to live!—true Russian you know, Russian to the back bone; I say to my wife, give me a Russian every time, for a table comrade. The Baron used to say, 'Take mustard, Sellers, try the mustard,—a man *can't* know what turnips are in perfection without mustard,' but I always said, 'No, Baron, I'm a plain man, and I want my food plain—none of your embellishments for Eschol Sellers—no made dishes for me!' And it's the best way—high living kills more than it cures in this world, you can rest assured of that.—Yes indeed, Washington, I've got one little operation on hand that—take some more water—help yourself, won't you?—help yourself, there's plenty of it.—You'll find it pretty good, I guess. How does that fruit strike you?"

Washington said he did not know that he had ever tasted better. He did not add that he detested turnips even when they were cooked—loathed them in their natural state. No, he kept this to himself, and praised the turnips to the peril of his soul.

"I thought you'd like them. Examine them—examine them—they'll bear it. See how perfectly firm and juicy they are—they can't start any like them in this part of the country, I can tell you. These are from New Jersey—I imported them myself. They cost like sin, too; but lord bless me, I go in for having the best of a thing, even if it does cost a little more—its the best economy, in the long run. These are the Early Malcolm—it's a turnip that can't be produced except in just one orchard, and the supply never is up to the demand. Take some more water, Washington—you can't drink too much water with fruit—all the doctors say that. The plague can't come where this article is, my boy!"

"Plague? What plague?"

"What plague, indeed? Why the Asiatic plague that nearly depopulated London a couple of centuries ago."

"But how does that concern us? There is no plague here, I reckon."

"Sh! I've let it out! Well, never mind—just keep it to yourself. Perhaps I oughtn't said anything, but its *bound* to come out sooner or later, so what is the odds? Old McDowells wouldn't like me to—to—bother it all, I'll just tell the whole thing and let it go. You see, I've been down to St. Louis, and I happened to run across old Dr. McDowells—thinks the world of me, does the doctor. He's a man that keeps himself to himself, and well he may, for he knows that he's got a reputation that covers the whole earth—he won't condescend to open himself out to many people, but lord bless you, he and I are just like brothers; he won't let me go to a hotel when I'm in the city—says I'm the only man that's company to him, and I don't know but there's some truth in it, too, because although I never like to glorify myself and make a great to-do over what I am or what I can do or what I know, I don't mind saying here among friends that I *am* better read up in most sciences, maybe, than the general run of professional men in these days. Well, the other day he let me into a little secret, strictly on the quiet, about this matter of the plague.

"You see it's booming right along in our direction—follows the Gulf Stream, you know, just as all those epidemics do,—and within three months it will be just waltzing through this land like a whirlwind! And whoever it touches can make his will and contract for the funeral. Well you can't *cure* it, you know, but you can prevent it. How? Turnips! that's it! Turnips and water! Nothing like it in the world, old McDowells says, just fill yourself up two or three times a day, and you can snap your fingers at the plague. Sh!—keep mum, but just you confine yourself to that diet and you're all right. I wouldn't have old McDowells know that I told about it for anything—he never would speak to me again. Take some more water, Washington—the more water you drink, the better. Here, let me give you some more of the turnips. No, no, no, now, I insist. There, now. Absorb those. They're mighty sustaining—brim full of nutriment—all the medical books say so. Just eat from four to seven good-sized turnips at a meal, and drink from a pint and a half to a quart of water, and then just sit around a couple of hours and let them ferment. You'll feel like a fighting cock next day."

Fifteen or twenty minutes later the Colonel's tongue was still chattering away—he had piled up several future fortunes out of several incipient "operations" which he had blundered into within the past week, and was now soaring along through some brilliant expectations born of late promising experiments upon the lacking ingredient of the eye-water. And at such a time Washington ought to have been a rapt and enthusiastic listener, but he was not, for two matters disturbed his mind and distracted his attention. One was, that he discovered, to his confusion and shame, that in allowing himself to be helped a second time to the turnips, he had robbed those hungry children. He had not needed the dreadful "fruit," and had not wanted it; and when he saw the pathetic sorrow in their faces when they asked for more and there was no more to give them, he hated himself for his stupidity and pitied the famishing young things with all his heart. The other matter that disturbed him was the dire inflation that had begun in his stomach. It grew and grew, it became more and more insupportable. Evidently the turnips were "fermenting." He forced himself to sit still as long as he could, but his anguish conquered him at last.

He rose in the midst of the Colonel's talk and excused himself on the plea of a previous engagement. The Colonel followed him to the door, promising over and over again that he would use his influence to get some of the Early Malcolms for him, and insisting that he should not be such a stranger but come and take potluck with him every chance he got. Washington was glad enough to get away and feel free again. He immediately bent his steps toward home.

In bed he passed an hour that threatened to turn his hair gray, and then a blessed calm settled down upon him that filled his heart with gratitude. Weak and languid, he made shift to turn himself about and seek rest and sleep; and as his soul hovered upon the brink of unconciousness, he heaved a long, deep sigh, and said to himself that in his heart he had cursed the Colonel's preventive of rheumatism, before, and now *let* the plague come if it must—he was done with preventives; if ever any man beguiled him with turnips and water again, let him die the death.

If he dreamed at all that night, no gossiping spirit disturbed his visions to whisper in his ear of certain matters just then in bud in the East, more than a thousand miles away, that after the lapse of a few years would develop influences which would profoundly affect the fate and fortunes of the Hawkins family.

## CHAPTER 12

[Philip Sterling was a New England young man who had been educated at Yale. He had brown hair, hazel eyes, was six feet tall and athletic. While waiting for a literary career to begin he was living with a classmate in a boarding house in New York. One morning the classmate, Henry Brierly, asked Philip how he would like to go to St. Jo, Missouri on a "big operation," together with some railroad men, engineers and contractors. The operation was to be a land and railroad speculation. Henry suggested that Philip go as an engineer, which was the way he himself was going. He said it did not matter that they knew nothing about engineering; they would pick up the details on the job. The two went down to Wall Street and had a talk with Henry's uncle, a "wily operator," and Philip was accepted for the venture. Early the next morning the two started on their way west.

Henry Brierly had blue eyes, a fresh complexion, silken whiskers, curly chestnut hair and was very handsome. He and Philip enjoyed the traveling party, which gave the impression that fortunes were about to be made with little trouble. Even Philip soon caught the fever. As for Harry, he habitually talked in six figures. In St. Louis Harry decided that he no longer cared to be an engineer. He would master the theory of engineering so he could check on the engineers. There were millions in the job and he was looking for the soft thing. He fooled his time away. One evening the two young men met Col. Sellers in the lobby of the Southern Hotel, where they were staying.]

The precipitating of this casual intercourse into the more substantial form of an acquaintanceship was the work of the gentleman himself, and occurred in this wise. Meeting the two friends in the lobby one evening, he asked them to give him the time, and added:

"Excuse me, gentlemen—strangers in St. Louis? Ah, yes—yes. From the East, perhaps? Ah, just so, just so. Eastern born myself—Virginia. Sellers is my name—Eschol Sellers. Ah—by the way—New York, did you say? That reminds me; just met some gentlemen from your State a week or two ago—very prominent gentlemen—in public life they are; you must know them, without doubt. Let me see—let me see. Curious those names have escaped me. I know they were from your State, because I remember afterward my old friend Governor Shackleby said to me—fine man, is the Governor—one of the finest men our country has produced—said he, 'Colonel, how did you like those New York gentlemen?—not many such men in the world, Colonel Sellers,' said the Governor—yes, it was New York he said—I remember it distinctly. I *can't* recall those names, somehow. But no matter. Stopping here, gentlemen—stopping at the Southern?"

In shaping their reply in their minds, the title "Mr." had a place in it; but when their turn had arrived to speak, the title "Colonel" came from their lips instead.

[The Colonel said that he himself stopped at the Planter's. He took Philip and Harry there and ordered whiskey and Havanas. He could not find any money in his pockets, so Philip paid the bill. When the young men had departed, Col. Sellers went to the distant part of the city where he was staying with a friend.

Philip and Harry were detained in St. Louis. Philip's money began to run low and Harry's ran out altogether, at which point Philip paid Harry's bills. Harry was happy-go-lucky and was liked by everyone. He told Col. Sellers that he was about to go out into the field with the engineer corps of the Salt Lick Pacific Extension, to which the Colonel responded with a speculation plan. With the help of a division engineer, Jeff Thompson, they would arrange to have the railroad run through Stone's Landing, even though the Landing was twenty miles off the straight line of the railroad. They would buy up land in the Landing and make a killing. The young men finally left St. Louis and started up river to the engineers' camp.

Hardly anyone in the party knew much about engineering, or needed to know. This was only a preliminary survey, the chief purpose of which was to excite interest and support by giving the impression that the railroad would strike every point within twenty or thirty miles of the real route. Stone's Landing was a muddy backwoods settlement and the party camped in the middle of it almost without knowing it was there. The Landing had a crooked little sluggish stream called Goose Run.

It was not long before Col. Sellers drove up in a wagon. The Colonel and Harry mapped out the proposed city of Napoleon, which was to be built on the site of Stone's Landing. There were various engineering difficulties in bringing a railroad in and out of that place but they were only trifles, in the Colonel's opinion. Harry and the Colonel went up to Hawkeye to complete their arrangements, which included a petition to Congress for the improvement of the navigation of the Columbus River, alias Goose Run.

We return to a time eight years after the death of Mr. Hawkins. Laura Hawkins was not a conventional woman. She had the fatal gifts of beauty and the power of fascination. She also had will, pride, courage, ambition and vanity. Those were difficult war-time days in Hawkeye. The Hawkins family waged a struggle with poverty while trying to keep up appearances. Laura read many books—novels, histories, biographies, travel books, poetry. During the war a Confederate officer, a Col. George Selby, was stationed in Hawkeye for a time, in command of the district. He was thirty, handsome, a graduate of the University of Virginia, a man of the world. Laura fell hopelessly in love with him. They were engaged to be married. Then the Colonel had to go away to the town of Harding. Finding that he had to stay there longer than he had expected, he urged Laura to join and marry him. She did as he wished. Three months passed. One morning Selby told her that he had been ordered to go south and must leave within two hours. When she said she would go with him he told her their romance was finished, that she had nothing to show for a legal marriage and that he already had a wife. Laura "fell senseless to the floor."

She returned to Hawkeye. Only Washington and his mother knew what had happened. The neighbors believed that the engagement with Selby had soured and that Laura had been in Harding to nurse Washington, who had been wounded. Laura was ill for a long time. When she recovered she was not much changed. "The lovely woman had a devil in her heart. That was all."

Harry was a hit in Hawkeye society. He became fascinated by Laura, and she delighted in toying with him. He hoped to possess her but she kept him off artfully. She had dreams of being rich and of having men at her feet. Harry thought she would flourish in a city like Washington and would be of great help in getting the Congressional appropriation through. When Philip made a brief visit to Hawkeye, Harry bragged about his conquest of Laura. Philip met her and saw that she was leading Harry a country dance.

Hawkeye had a great event: the visit of Senator Abner Dilworthy. Dilworthy was from a neighboring state. Although the Senator was the guest of his old friend, General Boswell, Col. Sellers gave the impression that it was he who chiefly welcomed the Senator to Hawkeye. The Senator was portly and large but not tall. He professed devotion to religion and to the education of the Negro in order to improve the latter's chances for the hereafter. The Senator had been a Unionist during the war. Col. Sellers assured him that the "niggro" was a "speculating race," lazy and impractical. The Colonel and Harry took him to Napoleon, where they revealed their speculation plan. The Senator favored it and favored the Congressional appropriation.

The Senator later met Washington Hawkins, liked him and proposed that he become his private secretary and the secretary of his committee. Washington eagerly accepted. Harry was furious because of the Senator's attentions to Laura and because she played up to the Senator. Harry finally left Hawkeye. The Senator left also, and eventually invited Laura to visit his family in Washington during the winter session of Congress. This was what she had hoped for.

Railroad-surveying and real-estate operations being at a standstill in Missouri in winter, Philip and Harry went East. When Harry spoke to his Wall Street uncle about the city which was going to rise on the site of Stone's Landing and about the Congressional appropriation for making Goose Run navigable, the uncle and his broker friends were not much interested in the new city but they did show interest in the appropriation. An appropriation, as Harry learned, was a tangible thing if you could get hold of it, regardless of what it was for. Harry went to Washington, where he was the guest of Senator Dilworthy. The Senator introduced the appropriation petition in the Senate. Meanwhile Philip, in New York, was working hard to master the science of engineering.]

## CHAPTER 13

The capital of the Great Republic was a new world to country-bred Washington Hawkins. St. Louis was a greater city, but its floating population did not hail from great distances, and so it had the general family aspect of the permanent population; but Washington gathered its people from the four winds of heaven, and so the manners, the faces and the fashions there, presented a variety that was infinite. Washington had never been in "society" in St. Louis, and he knew nothing of the ways of its wealthier citizens and had never inspected one of their dwellings. Consequently, everything in the nature of modern fashion and grandeur was a new and wonderful revelation to him.

Washington is an interesting city to any of us. It seems to become more and more interesting the oftener we visit it. Perhaps the reader has never been there? Very well. You arrive either at night, rather too late to do anything or see anything until morning, or you arrive so early in the morning that you consider it best to go to your hotel and sleep an hour or two while the sun bothers along over the Atlantic. You cannot well arrive at a pleasant intermediate hour, because the railway corporation that keeps the keys of the only door that leads into the town or out of it takes care of that. You arrive in tolerably good spirits, because it is only thirty-eight miles from Baltimore to the capital, and so you have only been insulted three times (provided you are not in a sleeping car—the average is higher, there): once when you renewed your ticket after stopping over in Baltimore, once when you were about to enter the "ladies' car" without knowing it *was* a lady's car, and once when you asked the conductor at what hour you would reach Washington.

You are assailed by a long rank of hackmen who shake their whips in your face as you step out upon the sidewalk; you enter what they regard as a "carriage," in the capital, and you wonder why they do not take it out of service and put it in the museum: we have few enough antiquities, and it is little to our credit that we make scarcely any effort to preserve the few we have. You reach your hotel, presently—and here let us draw the curtain of charity—because of course you have gone to the wrong one. You being a stranger, how could you do otherwise? There are a hundred and eighteen bad hotels, and only one good one. The most renowned and popular hotel of them all is perhaps the worst one known to history.

It is winter, and night. When you arrived, it was snowing. When you reached the hotel, it was sleeting. When you went to bed, it was raining. During the night it froze hard, and the wind blew some chimneys down. When you got up in the morning, it was foggy. When you finished your breakfast at ten o'clock and went out, the sunshine was brilliant, the weather balmy and delicious, and the mud and slush deep and all-pervading. You will like the climate—when you get used to it.

You naturally wish to view the city; so you take an umbrella, an overcoat, and a fan, and go forth. The prominent features you soon locate and get familiar with; first you glimpse the ornamental upper works of a long, snowy palace projecting above a grove of trees, and a tall, graceful white dome with a statue on it surmounting the palace and pleasantly contrasting with the back-ground of blue sky. That building is the capitol; gossips will tell you that by the original estimates it was to cost $12,000,-000, and that the government did come within $27,200,000 of building it for that sum.

You stand at the back of the capitol to treat yourself to a view, and it is a very noble one. You understand, the capitol stands upon the verge of a high piece of table land, a fine commanding position, and its front looks out over this noble situation for a city—but it don't see it, for the reason that when the capitol extension was decided upon, the property owners at once advanced their prices to such inhuman figures that the people went down and built the city in the muddy low marsh *behind* the temple of liberty; so now the lordly front of the building, with its imposing colonnades, its projecting, graceful wings, its picturesque groups of statuary, and its long terraced ranges of steps, flowing down in white marble waves to the ground, merely looks out upon a sorrowful little desert of cheap boarding houses.

So you observe, that you take your view from the back of the capitol. And yet not from the airy outlooks of the dome, by the way, because to get there you must pass through the great rotunda: and to do that, you would have to see the marvelous Historical Paintings that hang there, and the bas-reliefs—and what have you done that you should suffer thus? And besides, you might have to pass through the old part of the building, and you could not help seeing Mr. Lincoln, as petrified by a young lady artist for $10,000—and you might take his marble emancipation proclamation, which he holds out in his hand and contemplates, for a folded napkin; and you might conceive from his expression and his attitude, that he is finding fault with the washing. Which is not the case. Nobody knows what *is* the matter with him; but everybody feels for him. Well, you ought not to go into the dome any how, because it would be utterly impossible to go up there without seeing the frescoes in it—and why should you be interested in the delirium tremens of art?

The capitol is a very noble and a very beautiful building, both within and without, but you need not examine it now. Still, if you greatly prefer going into the dome, go. Now your general glance gives you picturesque stretches of gleaming water, on your left, with a sail here and there and a lunatic asylum on shore; over beyond the water, on a distant elevation, you see a squat yellow temple which your eye dwells upon lovingly through a blur of unmanly moisture, for it recalls your lost boyhood and the Parthenons done in molasses candy which made it blest and beautiful. Still in the distance, but on this side of the water and close to its edge, the Monument to the Father of his Country towers out of the mud—sacred soil is the customary term. It has the aspect of a factory chimney with the top broken off. The skeleton of a decaying scaffolding lingers about its summit, and tradition says that the spirit of Washington often comes down and sits on those rafters to enjoy this tribute of respect which the nation has reared as the symbol of its unappeasable gratitude. The Monument is to be finished, some day, and at that time our Washington will have risen still higher in the nation's veneration, and will be known as the Great-Great-Grandfather of his Country. The memorial Chimney stands in a quiet pastoral locality that is full of reposeful expression. With a glass you can see the cow-sheds about its base, and the contented sheep nimbling pebbles in the desert solitudes that surround it, and the tired pigs dozing in the holy calm of its protecting shadow.

Now you wrench your gaze loose and you look down in front of you and see the broad Pennsylvania Avenue stretching straight ahead for a mile or more till it brings up against the iron fence in front of a pillared granite pile, the Treasury building —an edifice that would command respect in any capital. The stores and hotels that wall in this broad avenue are mean, and cheap, and dingy, and are better left without comment. Beyond the Treasury is a fine large white barn, with wide unhandsome grounds about it. The President lives there. It is ugly enough outside, but that is nothing to what it is inside. Dreariness, flimsiness, bad taste reduced to mathematical completeness is what the inside offers to the eye, if it remains yet what it always has been.

The front and right hand views give you the city at large. It is a wide stretch of cheap little brick houses, with here and there a noble architectural pile lifting itself out of the midst—government buildings, these. If the thaw is still going on when you come down and go about town, you will wonder at the shortsightedness of the city fathers, when you come to inspect the streets, in that they do not dilute the mud a little more and use them for canals.

If you inquire around a little, you will find that there are more boarding houses to the square acre in Washington than there are in any other city in the land, perhaps. If you apply for a home in one of them, it will seem odd to you to have the landlady inspect you with a severe eye and then ask you if you are a member of Congress. Perhaps, just as a pleasantry, you will say yes. And then she will tell you that she is "full." Then you show her her advertisement in the morning paper, and there she stands, convicted and ashamed. She will try to blush, and it will be only polite in you to take the effort for the deed. She shows you her rooms, now, and lets you take one—but she makes you pay in advance for it. That is what you will get for pretending to be a member of Congress. If you had been content to be merely a private citizen, your trunk would have been sufficient security for your board. If you are curious and inquire into this thing, the chances are that your landlady will be ill-natured enough to say that the person and property of a Congressman are exempt from arrest or detention, and that with the tears in her eyes she has seen several of the people's representatives walk off to their several States and Territories carrying her unreceipted board bills in their pockets for keepsakes. And before you have been in Washington many weeks you will be mean enough to believe her, too.

Of course you contrive to see everything and find out everything. And one of the first and most startling things you find out is, that every individual you encounter in the City of Washington almost—and certainly every separate and distinct individual in the public employment, from the highest bureau chief, clear down to the maid who scrubs Department halls, the night watchmen of the public buildings and the darkey boy who purifies the Department spittoons—represents Political Influence. Unless you can get the ear of a Senator, or a Congressman, or a Chief of a Bureau or Department, and persuade him to use his "influence" in your behalf, you cannot get an employment of the most trivial nature in Washington. Mere merit, fitness and capability, are useless baggage to you without "influence." The population of Washington consists pretty much entirely of government employés and the people who board them. There are thousands of these employés, and they have gathered there from every corner of the Union and got their berths through the intercession (command is nearer the word) of the Senators and Representatives of their respective States. It would be an odd circumstance to see a girl get employment at three or four dollars a week in one of the great public cribs without any political grandee to back her, but merely because she was worthy, and competent, and a good citizen of a free country that "treats all persons alike." Washington would be mildly thunderstruck at such a thing as that. If you are a member of Congress, (no offence,) and one of your constituents who doesn't know anything, and does not want to go into the bother of learning something, and has no money, and no employment, and can't earn a living, comes besieging you for help, do you say, "Come, my friend, if your services were valuable you could get employment elsewhere—don't want you here?" Oh, no. You take him to a Department and say, "Here, give this person something to pass away the time at—and a salary"—and the thing is done. You throw him on his country. He is his country's child, let his country support him. There is something good and motherly about Washington, the grand old benevolent National Asylum for the Helpless.

The wages received by this great hive of employés are placed at the liberal figure meet and just for skilled and competent labor. Such of them as are immediately employed about the two Houses of Congress, are not only liberally paid also, but are remembered in the customary Extra Compensation bill which slides neatly through, annually, with the general grab that signalizes the last night of a session, and thus twenty per cent. is added to their wages, for—for fun, no doubt.

Washington Hawkins' new life was an unceasing delight to him. Senator Dilworthy lived sumptuously, and Washington's quarters were charming—gas; running water, hot and cold; bath-room, coal fires, rich carpets, beautiful pictures on the walls; books on religion, temperance, public charities and financial schemes; trim colored servants, dainty food—everything a body

could wish for. And as for stationery, there was no end to it;
the government furnished it; postage stamps were not needed—
the Senator's frank could convey a horse through the mails, if
necessary.

And then he saw such dazzling company. Renowned generals
and admirals who had seemed but colossal myths when he was
in the far west, went in and out before him or sat at the Senator's table, solidified into palpable flesh and blood; famous statesmen crossed his path daily; that once rare and awe-inspiring
being, a Congressman, was become a common spectacle—a spectacle so common, indeed, that he could contemplate it without
excitement, even without embarrassment; foreign ministers were
visible to the naked eye at happy intervals; he had looked upon
the President himself, and lived. And more, this world of enchantment teemed with speculation—the whole atmosphere was
thick with it—and that indeed was Washington Hawkins' native
air; none other refreshed his lungs so gratefully. He had found
paradise at last.

The more he saw of his chief the Senator, the more he honored him, and the more conspicuously the moral grandeur of
his character appeared to stand out. To possess the friendship
and the kindly interest of such a man, Washington said in a
letter to Louise, was a happy fortune for a young man whose
career had been so impeded and so clouded as his.

The weeks drifted by; Harry Brierly flirted, danced, added
lustre to the brilliant Senatorial receptions, and diligently
"buzzed" and "button-holed" Congressmen in the interest of
the Columbus River scheme; meantime Senator Dilworthy labored hard in the same interest—and in others of equal national
importance. Harry wrote frequently to Sellers, and always en-
couragingly; and from these letters it was easy to see that Harry
was a pet with all Washington, and was likely to carry the thing
through; that the assistance rendered him by "old Dilworthy"
was pretty fair—pretty fair; "and every little helps, you know,"
said Harry.

Washington wrote Sellers officially, now and then. In one of
his letters it appeared that whereas no member of the House

committee favored the scheme at first, there was now needed but one more vote to compass a majority report. Closing sentence:

"Providence seems to further our efforts.
"(Signed)    ABNER DILWORTHY, U. S. S.,
"per WASHINGTON HAWKINS, P. S."

At the end of a week, Washington was able to send the happy news,—officially, as usual,—that the needed vote had been added and the bill favorably reported from the Committee. Other letters recorded its perils in Committee of the whole, and by and by its victory, by just the skin of its teeth, on third reading and final passage. Then came letters telling of Mr. Dilworthy's struggles with a stubborn majority in his own Committee in the Senate; of how these gentlemen succumbed, one by one, till a majority was secured.

Then there was a hiatus. Washington watched every move on the board, and he was in a good position to do this, for he was clerk of this committee, and also one other. He received no salary as private secretary, but these two clerkships, procured by his benefactor, paid him an aggregate of twelve dollars a day, without counting the twenty per cent. extra compensation which would of course be voted to him on the last night of the session.

He saw the bill go into Committee of the whole and struggle for its life again, and finally worry through. In the fullness of time he noted its second reading, and by and by the day arrived when the grand ordeal came, and it was put upon its final passage. Washington listened with bated breath to the "Aye!" "No!" "No!" "Aye!" of the voters, for a few dread minutes, and then could bear the suspense no longer. He ran down from the gallery and hurried home to wait.

At the end of two or three hours the Senator arrived in the bosom of his family, and dinner was waiting. Washington sprang forward, with the eager question on his lips, and the Senator said:

"We may rejoice freely, now, my son—Providence has crowned our efforts with success."

## CHAPTER 14

Washington sent grand good news to Col. Sellers that night. To Louise he wrote:

"It is beautiful to hear him talk when his heart is full of thankfulness for some manifestation of the Divine favor. You shall know him, some day, my Louise, and knowing him you will honor him, as I do."

Harry wrote:

"I pulled it through, Colonel, but it was a tough job, there is no question about that. There was not a friend to the measure in the House committee when I began, and not a friend in the Senate committee except old Dil himself, but they were all fixed for a majority report when I hauled off my forces. Everybody here says you *can't* get a thing like this through Congress without buying committees for straight-out cash on delivery, but I think I've taught them a thing or two—if I could only make them believe it. When I tell the old residenters that this thing went through without buying a vote or making a promise, they say, 'That's rather too thin.' And when I say thin or not thin it's a fact, anyway, they say 'Come, now, but do you really believe that?' and when I say I don't believe anything about it, I *know* it, they smile and say, 'Well, you are pretty innocent, or pretty blind, one or the other—there's no getting around that.' Why they really do believe that votes *have* been bought—they do indeed. But let them keep on thinking so. I have found out that if a man knows how to talk to women, and has a little gift in the way of argument with men, he can afford to play for an appropriation against a money bag and give the money bag odds in the game. We've raked in $200,000 of Uncle Sam's money, say what they will—and there is more where this came from, when we want it, and I rather fancy I am the person that can go in and occupy it, too, if I do say it myself, that shouldn't, perhaps. I'll be with you within a week. Scare up all the men you can, and put them to work at once. When I get there I propose to make things hum."

The great news lifted Sellers into the clouds. He went to work on the instant. He flew hither and thither making contracts, engaging men, and steeping his soul in the ecstasies of business. He was the happiest man in Missouri. And Louise was the happiest woman; for presently came a letter from Washington which said:

"Rejoice with me, for the long agony is over! We have waited patiently and faithfully, all these years, and now at last the reward is at hand. A man is to pay our family $40,000 for the Tennessee Land! It is but a little sum compared to what we could get by waiting, but I do so long to see the day when I can call you my own, that I have said to myself, better take this and enjoy life in a humble way than wear out our best days in this miserable separation. Besides, I can put this money into operations here that will increase it a hundred fold, yes, a thousand fold, in a few months. The air is full of such chances, and I know our family would consent in a moment that I should put in their shares with mine. Without a doubt we shall be worth half a million dollars in a year from this time—I put it at the very lowest figure, because it is always best to be on the safe side—half a million at the very lowest calculation, and then your father will give his consent and we can marry at last. Oh, that will be a glorious day. Tell our friends the good news—I want all to share it."

And she did tell her father and mother, but they said, let it be kept still for the present. The careful father also told her to write Washington and warn him not to speculate with the money, but to wait a little and advise with one or two wise old heads. She did this. And she managed to keep the good news to herself, though it would seem that the most careless observer might have seen by her springing step and her radiant countenance that some fine piece of good fortune had descended upon her.

Harry joined the Colonel at Stone's Landing, and that dead place sprang into sudden life. A swarm of men were hard at work, and the dull air was filled with the cheery music of labor. Harry had been constituted engineer-in-general, and he threw the full strength of his powers into his work. He moved among his hirelings like a king. Authority seemed to invest him with a new splendor. Col. Sellers, as general superintendent of a great public enterprise, was all that a mere human being could be—and more. These two grandees went at their imposing "improvement" with the air of men who had been charged with the work of altering the foundations of the globe.

They turned their first attention to straightening the river just above the Landing, where it made a deep bend, and where the maps and plans showed that the process of straightening would not only shorten distance but increase the "fall." They started a cut-off canal across the peninsula formed by the bend, and such another tearing up of the earth and slopping around in the mud as followed the order to the men, had never been seen in that region before. There was such a panic among the turtles that at the end of six hours there was not one to be found within three miles of Stone's Landing. They took the young and the aged, the decrepit and the sick upon their backs and left for tide-water in disorderly procession, the tadpoles following and the bull-frogs bringing up the rear.

Saturday night came, but the men were obliged to wait, because the appropriation had not come. Harry said he had written to hurry up the money and it would be along presently. So the work continued, on Monday. Stone's Landing was making quite a stir in the vicinity, by this time. Sellers threw a lot or two on the market, "as a feeler," and they sold well. He re-clothed his family, laid in a good stock of provisions, and still had money left. He started a bank account, in a small way— and mentioned the deposit casually to friends; and to strangers, too; to everybody, in fact; but not as a new thing—on the contrary, as a matter of life-long standing. He could not keep from buying trifles every day that were not wholly necessary, it was such a gaudy thing to get out his bank-book and draw a check, instead of using his old customary formula, "Charge it." Harry sold a lot or two, also—and had a dinner party or two at Hawkeye and a general good time with the money. Both men held on pretty strenuously for the coming big prices, however.

At the end of a month things were looking bad. Harry had besieged the New York headquarters of the Columbus River Slack-Water Navigation Company with demands, then commands, and finally appeals, but to no purpose; the appropriation did not come; the letters were not even answered. The workmen were clamorous, now. The Colonel and Harry retired to consult.

"What's to be done?" said the Colonel.

"Hang'd if I know."

"Company say anything?"

"Not a word."

"You telegraphed yesterday?"

"Yes, and the day before, too."

"No answer?"

"None—confound them!"

Then there was a long pause. Finally both spoke at once:

"I've got it!"

"I've got it!"

"What's yours?" said Harry.

"Give the boys thirty-day orders on the Company for the back pay."

"That's it—that's my own idea to a dot. But then—but then——"

"Yes, I know," said the Colonel; "I know they can't wait for the orders to go to New York and be cashed, but what's the reason they can't get them discounted in Hawkeye?"

"Of course they can. That solves the difficulty. Everybody knows the appropriation's been made and the Company's perfectly good."

So the orders were given and the men appeased, though they grumbled a little at first. The orders went well enough for groceries and such things at a fair discount, and the work danced along gaily for a time. Two or three purchasers put up frame houses at the Landing and moved in, and of course a far-sighted but easy-going journeyman printer wandered along and started the "Napoleon Weekly Telegraph and Literary Repository"—a paper with a Latin motto from the Unabridged dictionary, and plenty of "fat" conversational tales and double-leaded poetry— all for two dollars a year, strictly in advance. Of course the merchants forwarded the orders at once to New York—and never heard of them again.

At the end of some weeks Harry's orders were a drug in the market—nobody would take them at any discount whatever. The second month closed with a riot.—Sellers was absent at the time, and Harry began an active absence himself with the mob at his heels. But being on horseback, he had the advantage. He did not tarry in Hawkeye, but went on, thus missing several appointments with creditors. He was far on his flight eastward, and well out of danger when the next morning dawned. He telegraphed the Colonel to go down and quiet the laborers—*he* was bound east for money—everything would be right in a week— tell the men so—tell them to rely on him and not be afraid.

Sellers found the mob quiet enough when he reached the Landing. They had gutted the Navigation office, then piled the beautiful engraved stock-books and things in the middle of the floor and enjoyed the bonfire while it lasted. They had a liking for the Colonel, but still they had some idea of hanging him, as a sort of make-shift that might answer, after a fashion, in place of more satisfactory game.

But they made the mistake of waiting to hear what he had to say first. Within fifteen minutes his tongue had done its work and they were all rich men.—He gave every one of them a lot in the suburbs of the city of Stone's Landing, within a mile and a half of the future post office and railway station, and they promised to resume work as soon as Harry got east and started the money along. Now things were blooming and pleasant again, but the men had no money, and nothing to live on. The Colonel divided with them the money he still had in bank—an act which had nothing surprising about it because he was generally ready to divide whatever he had with anybody that wanted it, and it was owing to this very trait that his family spent their days in poverty and at times were pinched with famine.

When the men's minds had cooled and Sellers was gone, they hated themselves for letting him beguile them with fine speeches, but it was too late, now—they agreed to hang him another time—such time as Providence should appoint.

## CHAPTER 15

It was a hard blow to poor Sellers to see the work on his darling enterprise stop, and the noise and bustle and confusion that had been such refreshment to his soul, sicken and die out. It was hard to come down to humdrum ordinary life again after being a General Superintendent and the most conspicuous man in the community. It was sad to see his name disappear from the newspapers; sadder still to see it resurrected at intervals, shorn of its aforetime gaudy gear of compliments and clothed only with rhetorical tar and feathers.

But his friends suffered more on his account than he did. He was a cork that could not be kept under the water many moments at a time.

He had to bolster up his wife's spirits every now and then. On one of these occasions he said:

"It's all right, my dear, all right; it will all come right in a little while. There's $200,000 coming, and that will set things booming again. Harry seems to be having some difficulty, but that's to be expected—you can't move these big operations to the tune of Fisher's Hornpipe, you know. But Harry will get it started along presently, and then you'll see! I expect the news every day now."

"But Eschol, you've *been* expecting it every day, all along, haven't you?"

"Well, yes; yes—I don't know but I have. But anyway, the longer it's delayed, the nearer it grows to the time when it will start—same as every day you live brings you nearer to—nearer—"

"The grave?"

"Well, no—not that exactly; but you can't understand these things, Polly dear—women haven't much head for business, you know. You make yourself perfectly comfortable, old lady, and you'll see how we'll trot this right along. Why bless you, *let* the appropriation lag, if it wants to—that's no great matter—there's a bigger thing than that."

"Bigger than $200,000, Eschol?"

"Bigger, child?—why, what's $200,000? Pocket money! Mere pocket money! Look at the railroad! Did you forget the railroad? It ain't many months till spring; it will be coming right along, and the railroad swimming right along behind it. Where'll it be by the middle of summer? Just stop and fancy a moment—just think a little—don't anything suggest itself? Bless your heart, you dear women live right in the present all the time—but a man, why a man lives——

"In the future, Eschol? But don't we live in the future most too much, Eschol? We do somehow seem to manage to live on next year's crop of corn and potatoes as a general thing while this year is still dragging along, but sometimes it's not a robust diet,—Eschol. But don't look that way, dear—don't mind what I say. I don't mean to fret, I don't mean to worry; and I *don't*, once a month, *do* I, dear? But when I get a little low and feel bad, I get a bit troubled and worrisome, but it don't mean anything in the world. It passes right away. I know you're doing all you can, and I don't want to seem repining and ungrateful—for I'm *not*, Eschol—you know I'm not, don't you?"

"Lord bless you, child, I know you are the very best little woman that ever lived—that ever lived on the whole face of the Earth! And I know that I would be a dog not to work for you and think for you and scheme for you with all my might. And I'll bring things all right yet, honey—cheer up and don't you fear. The railroad——"

"Oh, I *had* forgotten the railroad, dear, but when a body gets blue, a body forgets everything. Yes, the railroad—tell me about the railroad."

"Aha, my girl, don't you see? Things ain't so dark, are they? Now *I* didn't forget the railroad. Now just think for a moment—just figure up a little on the future dead moral certainties. For instance, call this waiter St. Louis.

"And we'll lay this fork (representing the railroad) from St. Louis to this potato, which is Slouchburg:

"Then with this carving knife we'll continue the railroad from Slouchburg to Doodleville, shown by the black pepper:

"Then we run along the—yes—the comb—to the tumbler—that's Brimstone:

"Thence by the pipe to Belshazzar, which is the salt-cellar:

"Thence to, to—that quill—Catfish—hand me the pincushion, Marie Antoinette:

"Thence right along these shears to this horse, Babylon:

"Then by the spoon to Bloody Run—thank you, the ink:

"Thence to Hail Columbia—snuffers, Polly, please—move that cup and saucer close up, that's Hail Columbia:

"Then—let me open my knife—to Hark-from-the-Tomb, where we'll put the candle-stick—only a little distance from Hail Columbia to Hark-from-the-Tomb—down-grade all the way.

"And there we strike Columbus River—pass me two or three skeins of thread to stand for the river; the sugar bowl will do for Hawkeye, and the rat trap for Stone's Landing—Napoleon, I mean—and you can see how much better Napoleon is located than Hawkeye. Now here you are with your railroad complete, and showing its continuation to Hallelujah and thence to Corruptionville.

"Now then—there you are! It's a beautiful road, beautiful. Jeff Thompson can out-engineer any civil engineer that ever sighted through an aneroid, or a theodolite, or whatever they call it —*he* calls it sometimes one and sometimes the other—just whichever levels off his sentence neatest, I reckon. But ain't it a ripping road, though? I tell you, it'll make a stir when it gets along. Just see what a country it goes through. There's your onions at Slouchburg—noblest onion country that graces God's footstool; and there's your turnip country all around Doodleville—bless my life, what fortunes are going to be made there when they get that contrivance perfected for extracting olive oil out of turnips—if there's any in them; and I reckon there is, because Congress had made an appropriation of money to test the thing, and they wouldn't have done that just on conjecture, of course. And now we come to the Brimstone region—cattle raised there till you can't rest—and corn, and all that sort of thing. Then you've got a little stretch along through Belshazzar that don't produce anything now—at least nothing but rocks—but irrigation will fetch it. Then from Catfish to Babylon it's a little swampy, but there's dead loads of peat down under there somewhere. Next is the Bloody Run and Hail Columbia country—tobacco enough can be raised there to support two such railroads. Next is the sassparilla region. I reckon there's enough of that truck along in there on the line of the pocketknife, from Hail Columbia to Hark-from-the-Tomb to fat up all the consumptives in all the hospitals from Halifax to the Holy Land. It just grows like weeds! I've got a little belt of sassparilla land in there just tucked away unobtrusively waiting for my little Universal Expectorant to get into shape in my head. And I'll fix that, you know. One of these days I'll have all the nations of the earth expecto—"

"But Eschol, dear—"

"Don't interrupt me, Polly—I don't want you to lose the run of the map—well, *take* your toy-horse, James Fitz-James, if you must have it—and run along with you. Here, now—the soap will do for Babylon. Let me see—where was I? Oh yes—now we run down to Stone's Lan—Napoleon—now we run down to Napoleon. Beautiful road. Look at that, now. Perfectly straight line—straight as the way to the grave. And see where it leaves Hawkeye—clear out in the cold, my dear, clear out in the cold. That town's as bound to die as—well if I owned it I'd get its obituary ready, now, and notify the mourners. Polly, mark my words—in three years from this, Hawkeye'll be a howling wilderness. You'll see. And just look at that river—noblest stream that meanders over the thirsty earth!—calmest, gentlest artery that refreshes her weary bosom! Railroad goes all over it and all through it—wades right along on stilts. Seventeen bridges in three miles and a half—forty-nine bridges from Hark-from-the-Tomb to

Stone's Landing altogether—forty-nine bridges, and culverts enough to culvert creation itself! Hadn't skeins of thread enough to represent them all—but you get an idea—perfect trestle-work of bridges for seventy-two miles. Jeff Thompson and I fixed all that, you know; he's to get the contracts and I'm to put them through on the divide. Just oceans of money in those bridges. It's the only part of the railroad I'm interested in,—down along the line—and it's all I want, too. It's enough, I should judge. Now here we are at Napoleon. Good enough country—plenty good enough—all it wants is population. That's all right—that will come. And it's no bad country *now* for calmness and solitude, I can tell you—though there's no money in that, of course. No money, but a man wants rest, a man wants peace—a man don't want to rip and tear around *all* the time. And here we go, now, just as straight as a string for Hallelujah—it's a beautiful angle—handsome up-grade all the way—and then away you go to Corruptionville, the gaudiest country for early carrots and cauliflowers that ever—good missionary field, too. There ain't such another missionary field outside the jungles of Central Africa. And patriotic?—why they named it after Congress itself. Oh, I warn you, my dear, there's a good time coming, and it'll be right along before you know what you're about, too. That railroad's fetching it. You see what it is as far as I've got, and if I had enough bottles and soap and boot-jacks and such things to carry it along to where it joins onto the Union Pacific, fourteen hundred miles from here, I should exhibit to you in that little internal improvement a spectacle of inconceivable sublimity. So, don't you see? We've got the railroad to fall back on; and in the meantime, what are we worrying about that $200,000 appropriation for? That's all right. I'd be willing to bet anything that the very next letter that comes from Harry will—"

The eldest boy entered just in the nick of time and brought a letter, warm from the post-office.

"Things *do* look bright, after all, Eschol. I'm sorry I was blue, but it did seem as if everything had been going against us for whole ages. Open the letter—open it quick, and let's know all about it before we stir out of our places. I am all in a fidget to know what it says."

The letter was opened, without any unnecessary delay.

## CHAPTER 16

Whatever may have been the language of Harry's letter to the Colonel, the information it conveyed was condensed or expanded, one or the other, from the following episode of his visit to New York:

He called, with official importance in his mien, at No.——, Wall street, where a great gilt sign betokened the presence of the head-quarters of the "Columbus River Slack-Water Navigation Company." He entered and gave a dressy porter his card, and was requested to wait a moment in a sort of ante-room. The porter returned in a minute, and asked whom he would like to see?

"The president of the company, of course."

"He is busy with some gentlemen, sir; says he will be done with them directly."

That a copper-plate card with "Engineer-in-Chief" on it should be received with such tranquility as this, annoyed Mr. Brierly not a little. But he had to submit. Indeed his annoyance had time to augment a good deal; for he was allowed to cool his heels a full half hour in the ante-room before those gentlemen emerged and he was ushered into the presence. He found a stately dignitary occupying a very official chair behind a long green morocco-covered table, in a room sumptuously carpeted and furnished, and well garnished with pictures.

"Good morning, sir; take a seat—take a seat."

"Thank you sir," said Harry, throwing as much chill into his manner as his ruffled dignity prompted.

"We perceive by your reports and the reports of the Chief Superintendent, that you have been making gratifying progress with the work.—We are all very much pleased."

"Indeed? We did not discover it from your letters—which we have not received; nor by the treatment our drafts have met with—which were not honored; nor by the reception of any part of the appropriation, no part of it having come to hand."

"Why, my dear Mr. Brierly, there must be some mistake. I am sure we wrote you and also Mr. Sellers, recently—when my clerk comes he will show copies—letters informing you of the ten per cent. assessment."

"Oh, certainly, we got *those* letters. But what we wanted was money to carry on the work—money to pay the men."

"Certainly, certainly—true enough—but we credited you both for a large part of your assessments—I am sure that was in our letters."

"Of course that was in—I remember that."

"Ah, very well then. Now we begin to understand each other."

"Well, I don't see that we do. There's two months' wages due the men, and——"

"How? Haven't you paid the men?"

"Paid them! How are we going to pay them when you don't honor our drafts?"

"Why, my *dear* sir, I cannot see how you can find any fault with us. I am sure we have acted in a perfectly straight forward business way. Now let us look at the thing a moment. You subscribed for 100 shares of the capital stock, at $1,000 a share, I believe?"

"Yes, sir, I did."

"And Mr. Sellers took a like amount?"

"Yes, sir."

"Very well. No concern can get along without money. We levied a ten per cent. assessment. It was the original understanding that you and Mr. Sellers were to have the positions you now hold, with salaries of $600 a month each, while in active service. You were duly elected to these places, and you accepted them. Am I right?"

"Certainly."

"Very well. You were given your instructions and put to work.

By your reports it appears that you have expended the sum of $9,640 upon the said work. Two months salary to you two officers amounts altogether to $2,400—about one-eighth of your ten per cent. assessment, you see; which leaves you in debt to the company for the other seven-eighths of the assessment—viz, something over $8,000 apiece. Now instead of requiring you to forward this aggregate of $16,000 or $17,000 to New York, the company voted unanimously to let you pay it over to the contractors, laborers from time to time, and give you credit on the books for it. And they did it without a murmur, too, for they were pleased with the progress you had made, and were glad to pay you that little compliment—and a very neat one it was, too, I am sure. The work you did fell short of $10,000, a trifle. Let me see—$9,640 from $20,000—salary $2,400 added—ah yes, the balance due the company from yourself and Mr. Sellers is $7,960, which I will take the responsibility of allowing to stand for the present, unless you prefer to draw a check now, and thus——"

"Confound it, do you mean to say that instead of the company owing us $2,400, we owe the company $7,960?"

"Well, yes."

"And that we owe the men and the contractors nearly ten thousand dollars besides?"

"Owe them! Oh bless my soul, you can't mean that you have not paid these people?"

"But I *do* mean it!"

The president rose and walked the floor like a man in bodily pain. His brows contracted, he put his hand up and clasped his forehead, and kept saying, "Oh, it is too bad, too bad, too bad! Oh, it is bound to be found out—nothing can prevent it—nothing!"

Then he threw himself into his chair and said:

"My dear Mr. Brierson, this is dreadful—perfectly dreadful. It will be found out. It is bound to tarnish the good name of the company; our credit will be seriously, most seriously impaired.

How could you be so thoughtless—the men ought to have been paid though it beggared us all!"

"They ought, ought they? Then why the devil—my name is not Bryerson, by the way—why the mischief didn't the compa—why what in the nation ever became of the appropriation? Where *is* that appropriation?—if a stockholder may make so bold as to ask."

"The appropriation?—that paltry $200,000, do you mean?"

"Of course—but I didn't know that $200,000 was so very paltry. Though I grant, of course, that it is not a large sum, strictly speaking. But where is it?"

"My dear sir, you surprise me. You surely cannot have had a large acquaintance with this sort of thing. Otherwise you would not have expected much of a result from a mere *initial* appropriation like that. It was never intended for anything but a mere nest egg for the future and *real* appropriations to cluster around."

"Indeed? Well, was it a myth, or was it a reality? Whatever become of it?"

"Why the matter is simple enough. A Congressional appropriation costs money. Just reflect, for instance. A majority of the House Committee, say $10,000 apiece—$40,000; a majority of the Senate Committee, the same each—say $40,000; a little extra to one or two chairmen of one or two such committees, say $10,000 each—$20,000; and there's $100,000 of the money gone, to begin with. Then, seven male lobbyists, at $3,000 each —$21,000; one female lobbyist, $10,000; a high moral Congressman or Senator here and there—the high moral ones cost more, because they give tone to a measure—say ten of these at $3,000 each, is $30,000; then a lot of small-fry country members who won't vote for anything whatever without pay—say twenty at $500 apiece, is $10,000; a lot of dinners to members—say $10,000 altogether; lot of jimcracks for Congressmen's wives and children —those go a long way—you can't spend too much money in that line—well, those things cost in a lump, say $10,000—along there somewhere;—and then comes your printed documents—your maps, your tinted engravings, your pamphlets, your illuminated show cards, your advertisements in a hundred and fifty papers at ever so much a line—because you've *got* to keep the papers all right or you are gone up, you know. Oh, my dear sir, printing bills are destruction itself. Ours, so far amount to—let me see—10; 52; 22; 13;—and then there's 11; 14; 33—well, never mind the details, the total in clean numbers foots up $118,254.42 thus far!"

"What!"

"Oh, yes indeed. Printing's no bagatelle, I can tell you. And then there's your contributions, as a company, to Chicago fires and Boston fires, and orphan asylums and all that sort of thing— head the list, you see, with the company's full name and a thousand dollars set opposite—great card, sir—one of the finest advertisements in the world—the preachers mention it in the pulpit when it's a religious charity—one of the happiest advertisements in the world is your benevolent donation. Ours have amounted to sixteen thousand dollars and some cents up to this time."

"Good heavens!"

"Oh, yes. Perhaps the biggest thing we've done in the advertising line was to get an officer of the U. S. government, of perfectly Himalayan official altitude, to write up our little internal improvement for a religious paper of enormous circulation—I tell you that makes our bonds go handsomely among the pious poor. Your religious paper is by far the best vehicle for a thing of this kind, because they'll 'lead' your article and put it right in the midst of the reading matter; and if it's got a few Scripture quotations in it, and some temperance platitudes and a bit of gush here and there about Sunday Schools, and a sentimental snuffle now and then about 'God's precious ones, the honest hard-handed poor,' it works the nation like a charm, my dear sir, and never a man suspects that it is an advertisement; but your secular paper sticks you right into the advertising columns and of course you don't take a trick. Give me a religious paper to advertise in, every time; and if you'll just look at their advertising pages, you'll observe that other people think a good deal as I do—especially people who have got little financial schemes to make everybody rich with. Of course I mean your great big metropolitan religious papers that know how to serve God and make money at the same time—that's your sort, sir, that's your sort—a religious paper that isn't run to make money is no use to *us*, sir, as an advertising medium—no use to anybody in our line of business. I guess our next best dodge was sending a pleasure trip of newspaper reporters out to Napoleon. Never paid them a cent; just filled them up with champagne and the fat of the land, put pen, ink and paper before them while they were red-hot, and bless your soul when you come to read their letters you'd have supposed they'd been to heaven. And if a sentimental squeamishness held one or two of them back from taking a less rosy view of Napoleon, our hospitalities tied his tongue, at least, and he said nothing at all and so did us no harm. Let me see—have I stated all the expenses I've been at? No, I was near forgetting one or two items. There's your official salaries—you can't get good men for nothing. Salaries cost pretty lively. And then there's your big high-sounding millionaire names stuck into your advertisements as stockholders—another card, that—and they *are* stockholders, too, but you have to *give* them the stock and non-assessable at that—so they're an expensive lot. Very, very expensive thing, take it all around, is a big internal improvement concern—but you see that yourself, Mr. Bryerman—you see that, yourself, sir."

"But look here. I think you are a little mistaken about it's ever having cost anything for Congressional votes. I happen to know something about that. I've let you say your say—now let me say mine. I don't wish to seem to throw any suspicion on anybody's statements, because we are all liable to be mistaken. But how would it strike you if I were to say that I was in Washington all the time this bill was pending?—and what if I added that *I* put the measure through myself? Yes, sir, I did that little thing. And moreover, I never paid a dollar for any man's vote and never promised one. There are some ways of doing a thing that are as good as others which other people don't happen to think about, or don't have the knack of succeeding in, if they do happen to think of them. My dear sir, I am obliged to knock some of your expenses in the head—for never a cent was paid a Congressman or Senator on the part of this Navigation Company.

The president smiled blandly, even sweetly, all through this harangue, and then said:

"Is that so?"

"Every word of it."

"Well it does seem to alter the complexion of things a little. You are acquainted with the members down there, of course, else you could not have worked to such advantage?"

"I know them all, sir. I know their wives, their children, their babies—I even made it a point to be on good terms with their lackeys. I know every Congressman well—even familiarly."

"Very good. Do you know any of their signatures? Do you know their handwriting?"

"Why I know their handwriting as well as I know my own—have had correspondence enough with them, I should think. And their signatures—why I can tell their initials, even."

The president went to a private safe, unlocked it and got out some letters and certain slips of paper. Then he said:

"Now here, for instance; do you believe that that is a genuine letter? Do you know this signature here?—and this one? Do you know who those initials represent—and are they forgeries?"

Harry was stupefied. There were things there that made his brain swim. Presently, at the bottom of one of the letters he saw a signature that restored his equilibrium; it even brought the sunshine of a smile to his face.

The president said:

"That name amuses you. You never suspected him?"

"Of course I ought to have suspected him, but I don't believe it ever really occurred to me. Well, well, well—how did you ever have the nerve to approach him, of all others?"

"Why my friend, we never think of accomplishing anything

without his help. He is our mainstay. But how do those letters strike you?"

"They strike me dumb! What a stone-blind idiot I have been!"

"Well, take it all around, I suppose you had a pleasant time in Washington," said the president, gathering up the letters; "of course you must have had. Very few men could go there and get a money bill through without buying a single—"

"Come, now, Mr. President, that's plenty of that! I take back everything I said on *that* head. I'm a wiser man to-day than I was yesterday, I can tell you."

"I think you are. In fact I am satisfied you are. But now I showed you these things in confidence, you understand. Mention facts as much as you want to, but don't mention *names* to *anybody*. I can depend on you for that, can't I?"

"Oh, of course. I understand the necessity of that. I will not betray the names. But to go back a bit, it begins to look as if you never saw any of that appropriation at all?"

"We saw nearly ten thousand dollars of it—and that was all. Several of us took turns at log-rolling in Washington, and if we had charged anything for that service, none of that $10,000 would ever have reached New York."

"If you hadn't levied the assessment you would have been in a close place I judge?"

"Close? Have you figured up the total of the disbursements I told you of?"

"No, I didn't think of that."

"Well, lets see:

| | |
|---|---:|
| Spent in Washington, say, . . | $191,000 |
| Printing, advertising, etc., say, . | 118,000 |
| Charity, say, . . | 16,000 |
| Total, . . | $325,000 |

"The money to do that with, comes from——

| | |
|---|---:|
| Appropriation, . . . | $200,000 |
| Ten per cent. assessment on capital of $1,000,000, . . . | 100,000 |
| Total, . . | $300,000 |

"Which leaves us in debt some $25,000 at this moment. Salaries of home officers are still going on; also printing and advertising. Next month will show a state of things!"

"And then—burst up, I suppose?"

"By no means. Levy another assessment."

"Oh, I see. That's dismal."

"By no means."

"Why isn't it? What's the road out?"

"Another appropriation, don't you see?"

"Bother the appropriations. They cost more than they come to."

"Not the next one. We'll call for half a million—get it and go for a million the very next month."

"Yes, but the cost of it!"

The president smiled, and patted his secret letters affectionately. He said:

"All these people are in the next Congress. We shan't have to pay them a cent. And what is more, they will work like beavers for us—perhaps it might be to their advantage."

Harry reflected profoundly a while. Then he said:

"We send many missionaries to lift up the benighted races of other lands. How much cheaper and better it would be if those people could only come here and drink of our civilization at its fountain head."

"I perfectly agree with you, Mr. Beverly. Must you go? Well, good morning. Look in, when you are passing; and whenever I can give you any information about our affairs and prospects, I shall be glad to do it."

Harry's letter was not a long one, but it contained at least the calamitous figures that came out in the above conversation. The Colonel found himself in a rather uncomfortable place—no $1,200 salary forthcoming; and himself held responsible for half of the $9,640 due the workmen, to say nothing of being in debt to the company to the extent of nearly $4,000. Polly's heart was nearly broken; the "blues" returned in fearful force, and she had to go out of the room to hide the tears that nothing could keep back now.

There was mourning in another quarter, too, for Louise had a letter. Washington had refused, at the last moment, to take $40,-000 for the Tennessee Land, and had demanded $150,000! So the trade fell through, and now Washington was wailing because he had been so foolish. But he wrote that his man might probably return to the city, soon, and then he meant to sell to him, sure, even if he had to take $10,000. Louise had a good cry—several of them, indeed—and the family charitably forebore to make any comments that would increase her grief.

Spring blossomed, summer came, dragged its hot weeks by, and the Colonel's spirits rose, day by day, for the railroad was making good progress. But by and by something happened. Hawkeye had always declined to subscribe anything toward the railway, imagining that her large business would be a sufficient compulsory influence; but now Hawkeye was frightened; and before Col. Sellers knew what he was about, Hawkeye, in a panic, had rushed to the front and subscribed such a sum that Napoleon's attractions suddenly sank into insignificance and the railroad concluded to follow a comparatively straight course instead of going miles out of its way to build up a metropolis in the muddy desert of Stone's Landing.

The thunderbolt fell. After all the Colonel's deep planning; after all his brain work and tongue work in drawing public attention to his pet project and enlisting interest in it; after all his faithful hard toil with his hands, and running hither and thither on his busy feet; after all his high hopes and splendid prophecies, the fates had turned their backs on him at last, and all in a moment his air-castles crumbled to ruins about him. Hawkeye rose from her fright triumphant and rejoicing, and down went Stone's Landing! One by one its meagre parcel of inhabitants packed up and moved away, as the summer waned and fall approached. Town lots were no longer salable, traffic ceased, a deadly lethargy fell upon the place once more, the "Weekly Telegraph" faded into an early grave, the wary tadpole returned from exile, the bull-frog resumed his ancient song, the tranquil turtle sunned his back upon bank and log and drowsed his grateful life away as in the old sweet days of yore.

## CHAPTER 17

Once more Louise had good news from her Washington—Senator Dilworthy was going to sell the Tennessee Land to the government! Louise told Laura in confidence. She had told her parents, too, and also several bosom friends; but all of these people had simply looked sad when they heard the news, except Laura. Laura's face suddenly brightened under it—only for an instant, it is true, but poor Louise was grateful for even that fleeting ray of encouragement. When next Laura was alone, she fell into a train of thought something like this:

"If the Senator has really taken hold of this matter, I may look for that invitation to his house at any moment. I am perishing to go! I do long to know whether I am only simply a large-sized pigmy among these pigmies here, who tumble over so easily when one strikes them, or whether I am really—." Her thoughts drifted into other channels, for a season. Then she continued:—"He said I could be useful in the great cause of philanthropy, and help in the blessed work of uplifting the poor and the ignorant, if he found it feasible to take hold of our Land. Well, that is neither here nor there; what I want, is to go to Washington and find out what I am. I want money, too; and if one may judge by what she hears, there are chances there for a—." For a fascinating woman, she was going to say, perhaps, but she did not.

Along in the fall the invitation came, sure enough. It came officially through brother Washington, the private secretary, who appended a postscript that was brimming with delight over the prospect of seeing the Duchess again. He said it would be happiness enough to look upon her face once more—it would be almost too much happiness when to it was added the fact that she would bring messages with her that were fresh from Louise's lips.

In Washington's letter were several important enclosures. For instance, there was the Senator's check for $2,000—"to buy suitable clothing in New York with!" It was a loan to be refunded when the Land was sold. Two thousand—this was fine indeed. Louise's father was called rich, but Laura doubted if Louise had ever had $400 worth of new clothing at one time in her life. With the check came two through tickets—good on the railroad from Hawkeye to Washington via New York—and they were "dead-head" tickets, too, which had been given to Senator Dilworthy by the railway companies. Senators and Representatives were paid thousands of dollars by the government for traveling expenses, but they always traveled "dead-head" both ways, and then did as any honorable, high-minded men would naturally do—declined to receive the mileage tendered them by the government. The Senator had plenty of railway passes, and could easily spare two to Laura—one for herself and one for a male escort. Washington suggested that she get some old friend of the family to come with her, and said the Senator would "dead-head" him home again as soon as he had grown tired of the sights of the capital. Laura thought the thing over. At first she was pleased with the idea, but presently she began to feel differently about it. Finally she said, "No, our staid, steady-going Hawkeye friends' notions and mine differ about some things—they respect me, now, and I respect them—better leave it so—I will go alone: I am not afraid to travel by myself." And so communing with herself, she left the house for an afternoon walk.

Almost at the door she met Col. Sellers. She told him about her invitation to Washington.

"Bless me!" said the Colonel. "I have about made up my mind to go there myself. You see we've got to get another appropriation through, and the Company want me to come east and put it through Congress. Harry's there, and he'll do what he can, of course; and Harry's a good fellow and always does the very best he knows how, but then he's young—rather young for some parts of such work, you know—and besides he talks too much, talks a good deal too much; and sometimes he appears to be a little bit visionary, too, I think—the worst thing in the world for a business man. A man like that always exposes his cards, sooner or later. This sort of thing wants an old, quiet, steady hand—wants an old cool head, you know, that knows men, through and through, and is used to large operations. I'm expecting my salary, and also some dividends from the company, and if they get along in time, I'll go along with you Laura—take you under my wing—you mustn't travel alone. Lord I wish I had the money right now.—But there'll be plenty soon—plenty."

Laura reasoned with herself that if the kindly, simple-hearted Colonel was going anyhow, what could she gain by traveling alone and throwing away his company? So she told him she accepted his offer gladly, gratefully. She said it would be the greatest of favors if he would go with her and protect her—not at his own expense as far as railway fares were concerned, of course; she could not expect him to put himself to so much trouble for her and pay his fare besides. But he wouldn't hear of her paying his fare—it would be only a pleasure to him to serve her. Laura insisted on furnishing the tickets; and finally, when argument failed, she said the tickets cost neither her nor any one else a cent—she had two of them—she needed but one—and if he would not take the other she would not go with him. That settled the matter. He took the ticket. Laura was glad that she had the check for new clothing, for she felt very certain of being able to get the Colonel to borrow a little of the money to pay hotel bills with, here and there.

She wrote Washington to look for her and Col. Sellers toward the end of November; and at about the time set the two travelers arrived safe in the capital of the nation, sure enough.

## CHAPTER 18

Washington's delight in his beautiful sister was measureless. He said that she had always been the queenliest creature in the land, but that she was only commonplace before, compared to what she was now, so extraordinary was the improvement wrought by rich fashionable attire.

"But your criticisms are too full of brotherly partiality to be depended on, Washington. Other people will judge differently."

"Indeed they won't. You'll see. There will never be a woman in Washington that can compare with you. You'll be famous within a fortnight, Laura. Everybody will want to know you. You wait—you'll see."

Laura wished in her heart that the prophecy might come true; and privately she even believed it might—for she had brought all the women whom she had seen since she left home under sharp inspection, and the result had not been unsatisfactory to her.

During a week or two Washington drove about the city every day with her and familiarized her with all of its salient features. She was beginning to feel very much at home with the town itself, and she was also fast acquiring ease with the distinguished people she met at the Dilworthy table, and losing what little of country timidity she had brought with her from Hawkeye. She noticed with secret pleasure the little start of admiration that always manifested itself in the faces of the guests when she entered the drawing-room arrayed in evening costume:—she took comforting note of the fact that these guests directed a very liberal share of their conversation toward her; she observed with surprise, that famous statesmen and soldiers did not talk like gods, as a general thing, but said rather commonplace things for the most part; and she was filled with gratification to discover that she, on the contrary, was making a good many shrewd speeches and now and then a really brilliant one, and furthermore, that they were beginning to be repeated in social circles about the town.

Congress began its sittings, and every day or two Washington escorted her to the galleries set apart for lady members of the households of Senators and Representatives. Here was a larger field and a wider competition, but still she saw that many eyes were uplifted toward her face, and that first one person and then another called a neighbor's attention to her; she was not too dull to perceive that the speeches of some of the younger statesmen were delivered about as much and perhaps more at her than to the presiding officer; and she was not sorry to see that the dapper young Senator from Iowa came at once and stood in the open space before the president's desk to exhibit his feet as soon as she entered the gallery, whereas she had early learned from common report that his usual custom was to prop them on his desk and enjoy them himself with a selfish disregard of other people's longings.

Invitations began to flow in upon her and soon she was fairly "in society." "The season" was now in full bloom, and the first select reception was at hand—that is to say, a reception confined to invited guests.

Senator Dilworthy had become well convinced, by this time, that his judgment of the country-bred Missouri girl had not deceived him—it was plain that she was going to be a peerless missionary in the field of labor he designed her for, and therefore it would be perfectly safe and likewise judicious to send her forth well panoplied for her work.—So he had added new and still richer costumes to her wardrobe, and assisted their attractions with costly jewelry—loans on the future land sale.

This first select reception took place at a cabinet minister's —or rather a cabinet secretary's—mansion. When Laura and the Senator arrived, about half past nine or ten in the evening, the place was already pretty well crowded, and the white-gloved negro servant at the door was still receiving streams of guests.—

The drawing-rooms were brilliant with gaslight, and as hot as ovens. The host and hostess stood just within the door of entrance; Laura was presented, and then she passed on into the maelstrom of be-jeweled and richly attired low-necked ladies and white-kid-gloved and steel pen-coated gentlemen—and wherever she moved she was followed by a buzz of admiration that was grateful to all her senses—so grateful, indeed, that her white face was tinged and its beauty heightened by a perceptible suffusion of color. She caught such remarks as, "Who is she?" "Superb woman!" "That is the new beauty from the west," etc., etc.

Whenever she halted, she was presently surrounded by Ministers, Generals, Congressmen, and all manner of aristocratic people. Introductions followed, and then the usual original question, "How do you like Washington, Miss Hawkins?" supplemented by that other usual original question, "Is this your first visit?"

These two exciting topics being exhausted, conversation generally drifted into calmer channels, only to be interrupted at frequent intervals by new introductions and new inquiries as to how Laura liked the capital and whether it was her first visit or not. And thus for an hour or more the Duchess moved through the crush in a rapture of happiness, for her doubts were dead and gone, now—she knew she could conquer here. A familiar face appeared in the midst of the multitude and Harry Brierly fought his difficult way to her side, his eyes shouting their gratification, so to speak:

"Oh, this *is* a happiness! Tell me, my dear Miss Hawkins—"

"Sh! I know what you are going to ask. I *do* like Washington —I like it ever so much!"

"No, but I was going to ask—"

"Yes, I am coming to it, coming to it as fast as I can. It *is* my first visit. I think you should know that yourself."

And straightway a wave of the crowd swept her beyond his reach.

"Now what can the girl mean? Of course she likes Washington —I'm not such a dummy as to have to ask her that. And as to its being her first visit, why hang it, she knows that I *knew* it was. Does she think I have turned idiot? Curious girl, anyway. But how they do swarm about her! She is the reigning belle of Washington after this night. She'll know five hundred of the heaviest guns in the town before this night's nonsense is over. And this isn't even the beginning. Just as I used to say—she'll be a card in the matter of—yes *sir!* She shall turn the men's heads and I'll turn the women's! What a team that will be in politics here. I wouldn't take a quarter of a million for what I can do in this present session—no indeed I wouldn't. Now, here—I don't altogether like this. That insignificant secretary of legation is—why, she's smiling on him as if he—and now on the Admiral! Now she's illuminating that stuffy Congressman from Massachusetts— vulgar ungrammatical shovel-maker—greasy knave of spades. I don't like this sort of thing. She doesn't appear to be much distressed about *me*—she hasn't looked this way once. All right, my bird of Paradise, if it suits you, go on. But I think I know your sex. *I'll* go to smiling around a little, too, and see what effect *that* will have on you."

And he did "smile around a little," and got as near to her as he could to watch the effect, but the scheme was a failure —he could not get her attention. She seemed wholly unconscious of him, and so he could not flirt with any spirit; he could only talk disjointedly; he could not keep his eyes on the charmers he talked to; he grew irritable, jealous, and very unhappy. He gave up his enterprise, leaned his shoulder against a fluted pilaster and pouted while he kept watch upon Laura's every movement. His other shoulder stole the bloom from many a lovely cheek that brushed him in the surging crush, but he noted it not. He was too busy cursing himself inwardly for being an egotistical imbecile. An hour ago he had thought to take this country lass under his protection and show her "life" and enjoy her wonder and delight—and here she was, immersed in the marvel up to her eyes, and just a trifle more at home in it than he was himself. And now his angry comments ran on again:

"Now she's sweetening old Brother Balaam; and he—well he is inviting her to the Congressional prayer-meeting, no doubt—better let old Dilworthy alone to see that she doesn't overlook that. And now its Splurge, of New York; and now its Batters of New Hampshire—and now the Vice President! Well I may as well adjourn. I've got enough."

But he hadn't. He got as far as the door—and then struggled back to take one more look, hating himself all the while for his weakness.

Toward midnight, when supper was announced, the crowd thronged to the supper room where a long table was decked out with what seemed a rare repast, but which consisted of things better calculated to feast the eye than the appetite. The ladies were soon seated in files along the wall, and in groups here and there, and the colored waiters filled the plates and glasses and the male guests moved hither and thither conveying them to the privileged sex.

Harry took an ice and stood up by the table with other gentlemen, and listened to the buzz of conversation while he ate.

From these remarks he learned a good deal about Laura that was news to him. For instance, that she was of a distinguished western family; that she was highly educated; that she was very rich and a great landed heiress; that she was not a professor of religion, and yet was a Christian in the truest and best sense of the word, for her whole heart was devoted to the accomplishment of a great and noble enterprise—none other than the sacrificing of her landed estates to the uplifting of the down-trodden negro and the turning of his erring feet into the way of light and righteousness. Harry observed that as soon as one listener had absorbed the story, he turned about and delivered it to his next neighbor and the latter individual straightway passed it on. And thus he saw it travel the round of the gentlemen and overflow rearward among the ladies. He could not trace it backward to its fountain head, and so he could not tell who it was that started it.

One thing annoyed Harry a great deal; and that was the reflection that he might have been in Washington days and days ago and thrown his fascinations about Laura with permanent effect while she was new and strange to the capital, instead of dawdling in Philadelphia to no purpose. He feared he had "missed a trick," as he expressed it.

He only found one little opportunity of speaking again with Laura before the evening's festivities ended, and then, for the first time in years, his airy self-complacency failed him, his tongue's easy confidence forsook it in a great measure, and he was conscious of an unheroic timidity. He was glad to get away and find a place where he could despise himself in private and try to grow his clipped plumes again.

When Laura reached home she was tired but exultant, and Senator Dilworthy was pleased and satisfied. He called Laura "my daughter," next morning, and gave her some "pin money," as he termed it, and she sent a hundred and fifty dollars of it to her mother and loaned a trifle to Col. Sellers. Then the Senator had a long private conference with Laura, and unfolded certain plans of his for the good of the country, and religion, and the poor, and temperance, and showed her how she could assist him in developing these worthy and noble enterprises.

## CHAPTER 19

Laura soon discovered that there were three distinct aristocracies in Washington. One of these, (nick-named the Antiques,) consisted of cultivated, high-bred old families who looked back with pride upon an ancestry that had been always great in the nation's councils and its wars from the birth of the republic downward. Into this select circle it was difficult to gain admission. No. 2 was the aristocracy of the middle ground—of which, more anon. No. 3 lay beyond; of it we will say a word here. We will call it the Aristocracy of the Parvenus—as, indeed, the general public did. Official position, no matter how obtained, entitled a man to a place in it, and carried his family with him, no matter whence they sprang. Great wealth gave a man a still higher and nobler place in it than did official position. If this wealth had been acquired by conspicuous ingenuity, with just a pleasant little spice of illegality about it, all the better. This aristocracy was "fast," and not averse to ostentation. The aristocracy of the Antiques ignored the aristocracy of the Parvenus; the Parvenus laughed at the Antiques, (and secretly envied them.)

There were certain important "society" customs which one in Laura's position needed to understand. For instance, when a lady of any prominence comes to one of our cities and takes up her residence, all the ladies of her grade favor her in turn with an initial call, giving their cards to the servant at the door by way of introduction. They come singly, sometimes; sometimes in couples;—and always in elaborate full dress. They talk two minutes and a quarter and then go. If the lady receiving the call desires a further acquaintance, she must return the visit within two weeks; to neglect it beyond that time means "let the matter drop." But if she does return the visit within two weeks, it then becomes the other party's privilege to continue the acquaintance or drop it. She signifies her willingness to continue it by calling again any time within twelve months; after that, if the parties go on calling upon each other once a year, in our large cities, that is sufficient, and the acquaintanceship holds good. The thing goes along smoothly, now. The annual visits are made and returned with peaceful regularity and bland satisfaction, although it is not necessary that the two ladies shall actually *see* each other oftener than once every few years. Their cards preserve the intimacy and keep the acquaintanceship intact.

For instance, Mrs. A. pays her annual visit, sits in her carriage and sends in her card with the lower right hand corner turned down, which signifies that she has "called in person;" Mrs. B. sends down word that she is "engaged" or "wishes to be excused"—or if she is a Parvenu and low-bred, she perhaps sends word that she is "not at home." Very good; Mrs. A. drives on happy and content. If Mrs. A.'s daughter marries, or a child is born to the family, Mrs. B. calls, sends in her card with the upper left hand corner turned down, and then goes along about her affairs—for that inverted corner means "Congratulations." If Mrs. B.'s husband falls down stairs and breaks his neck, Mrs. A. calls, leaves her card with the upper right hand corner turned down, and then takes her departure; this corner means "Condolence." It is very necessary to get the corners right, else one may unintentionally condole with a friend on a wedding or congratulate her upon a funeral. If either lady is about to leave the city, she goes to the other's house and leaves her card with "P. P. C." engraved under the name—which signifies, "Pay Parting Call." But enough of etiquette. Laura was early instructed in the mysteries of society life by a competent mentor, and thus was preserved from troublesome mistakes.

The first fashionable call she received from a member of the ancient nobility, otherwise the Antiques, was of a pattern with all she received from that limb of the aristocracy afterward. This call was paid by Mrs. Major-General Fulke-Fulkerson and daughter. They drove up at one in the afternoon in a rather antiquated vehicle with a faded coat of arms on the panels, an aged white-wooled negro coachman on the box and a younger darkey beside him—the footman. Both of these servants were dressed in dull brown livery that had seen considerable service.

The ladies entered the drawing-room in full character; that is to say, with Elizabethan stateliness on the part of the dowager, and an easy grace and dignity on the part of the young lady that had a nameless something about it that suggested conscious superiority. The dresses of both ladies were exceedingly rich, as to material, but as notably modest as to color and ornament. All parties having seated themselves, the dowager delivered herself of a remark that was not unusual in its form, and yet it came from her lips with the impressiveness of Scripture:

"The weather has been unpropitious of late, Miss Hawkins."

"It has indeed," said Laura. "The climate seems to be variable."

"It is its nature of old, here," said the daughter—stating it apparently as a fact, only, and by her manner waving aside all personal responsibility on account of it. "Is it not so, mamma?"

"Quite so, my child. Do you like winter, Miss Hawkins?" She said "like" as if she had an idea that its dictionary meaning was "approve of."

"Not as well as summer—though I think all seasons have their charms."

"It is a very just remark. The general held similar views. He considered snow in winter proper; sultriness in summer legitimate; frosts in the autumn the same, and rains in spring not objectionable. He was not an exacting man. And I call to mind now that he always admired thunder. You remember, child, your father always admired thunder?"

"He adored it."

"No doubt it reminded him of battle," said Laura.

"Yes, I think perhaps it did. He had a great respect for Nature. He often said there was something striking about the ocean. You remember his saying that, daughter?"

"Yes, often, mother. I remember it very well."

"And hurricanes. He took a great interest in hurricanes. And animals. Dogs, especially—hunting dogs. Also comets. I think we all have our predilections. I think it is this that gives variety to our tastes." Laura coincided with this view. "Do you find it hard and lonely to be so far from your home and friends, Miss Hawkins?"

"I do find it depressing sometimes, but then there is so much about me here that is novel and interesting that my days are made up more of sunshine than shadow."

"Washington is not a dull city in the season," said the young lady. "We have some very good society indeed, and one need not be at a loss for means to pass the time pleasantly. Are you fond of watering-places, Miss Hawkins?"

"I have really had no experience of them, but I have always felt a strong desire to see something of fashionable watering-place life."

"We of Washington are unfortunately situated in that respect," said the dowager. "It is a tedious distance to Newport. But there is no help for it."

Laura said to herself, "Long Branch and Cape May are nearer than Newport; doubtless these places are low; I'll feel my way a little and see." Then she said aloud:

"Why I thought that Long Branch—"

There was no need to "feel" any further—there was that in both faces before her which made that truth apparent. The dowager said:

"Nobody goes *there,* Miss Hawkins—at least only persons of no position in society. And the President." She added that with tranquility.

"Newport is damp, and cold, and windy and excessively disagreeable," said the daughter, "but it is very select. One cannot be fastidious about minor matters when one has no choice."

The visit had spun out nearly three minutes, now. Both ladies rose with grave dignity, conferred upon Laura a formal invitation to call, and then retired from the conference. Laura remained in the drawing-room and left them to pilot themselves out of the house—an inhospitable thing, it seemed to her, but then she was following her instructions. She stood, steeped in reverie, a while, and then she said:

"I think I could always enjoy icebergs—as scenery—but not as company."

Still, she knew these two people by reputation, and was aware that they were not icebergs when they were in their own waters and amid their legitimate surroundings, but on the contrary were people to be respected for their stainless characters and esteemed for their social virtues and their benevolent impulses. She thought it a pity that they had to be such changed and dreary creatures on occasions of state.

The first call Laura received from the other extremity of the Washington aristocracy followed close upon the heels of the one we have just been describing. The callers this time were the Hon. Mrs. Oliver Higgins, the Hon. Mrs. Patrique Oreillé (pronounced O-re*lay*,) Miss Bridget (pronounced Breezhay) Oreillé, Mrs. Peter Gashly, Miss Gashly, and Miss Emmeline Gashly.

The three carriages arrived at the same moment from different directions. They were new and wonderfully shiny, and the brasses on the harness were highly polished and bore complicated monograms. There were showy coats of arms, too, with Latin mottoes. The coachmen and footmen were clad in bright new livery, of striking colors, and they had black rosettes with shaving-brushes projecting above them, on the sides of their stove-pipe hats.

When the visitors swept into the drawing-room they filled the place with a suffocating sweetness procured at the perfumer's. Their costumes, as to architecture, were the latest fashion intensified; they were rainbow-hued; they were hung with jewels— chiefly diamonds. It would have been plain to any eye that it had cost something to upholster these women.

The Hon. Mrs. Oliver Higgins was the wife of a delegate from a distant territory—a gentleman who had kept the principal "saloon," and sold the best whiskey in the principal village in his wilderness, and so, of course, was recognized as the first man of his commonwealth and its fittest representative. He was a man of paramount influence at home, for he was public spirited, he was chief of the fire department, he had an admirable command of profane language, and had killed several "parties." His shirt fronts were always immaculate; his boots daintily polished, and no man could lift a foot and fire a dead shot at a stray speck of dirt on it with a white handkerchief with a finer grace than he; his watch chain weighed a pound; the gold in his finger ring was worth forty five dollars; he wore a diamond cluster-pin and he parted his hair behind. He had always been regarded as the most elegant gentleman in his territory, and it was conceded by all that no man thereabouts was anywhere near his equal in the telling of an obscene story except the venerable white-haired governor himself. The Hon. Higgins had not come to serve his country in Washington for nothing. The appropriation which he had engineered through Congress for the maintenance of the Indians in his Territory would have made all those savages rich if it had ever got to them.

The Hon. Mrs. Higgins was a picturesque woman, and a fluent talker, and she held a tolerably high station among the Parvenus. Her English was fair enough, as a general thing—though, being of New York origin, she had the fashion peculiar to many natives of that city of pronouncing saw and law as if they were spelt sawr and lawr.

Petroleum was the agent that had suddenly transformed the Gashlys from modest hard-working country village folk into "loud" aristocrats and ornaments of the city.

The Hon. Patrique Oreillé was a wealthy Frenchman from Cork. Not that he was wealthy when he first came from Cork, but just the reverse. When he first landed in New York with his wife, he had only halted at Castle Garden for a few minutes to receive and exhibit papers showing that he had resided in this country two years—and then he voted the democratic ticket and went up town to hunt a house. He found one and then went to work as assistant to an architect and builder, carrying a hod all day and studying politics evenings. Industry and economy soon enabled him to start a low rum shop in a foul locality, and this gave him political influence. In our country it is always our first care to see that our people have the opportunity of voting for their choice of men to represent and govern them—we do not permit our great officials to appoint the little officials. We prefer to have so tremendous a power as that in our own hands. We hold it safest to elect our judges and everybody else. In our cities, the ward meetings elect delegates to the nominating conventions and instruct them whom to nominate. The publicans and their retainers rule the ward meetings (for everybody else hates the worry of politics and stays at home); the delegates from the ward meetings organize as a nominating convention and make up a list of candidates—one convention offering a democratic and another a republican list of—incorruptibles; and then the great meek public come forward at the proper time and make unhampered choice and bless Heaven that they live in a free land where no form of despotism can ever intrude.

Patrick O'Riley (as his name then stood) created friends and influence very fast, for he was always on hand at the police courts to give straw bail for his customers or establish an *alibi* for them in case they had been beating anybody to death on his premises. Consequently he presently became a political leader, and was elected to a petty office under the city government. Out of a meager salary he soon saved money enough to open quite a stylish liquor saloon higher up town, with a faro bank attached and plenty of capital to conduct it with. This gave him fame and great respectability. The position of alderman was forced upon him, and it was just the same as presenting him a gold mine. He had fine horses and carriages, now, and closed up his whiskey mill.

By and by he became a large contractor for city work, and was a bosom friend of the great and good Wm. M. Weed himself, who had stolen $20,000,000 from the city and was a man so envied, so honored, so adored, indeed, that when the sheriff went to his office to arrest him as a felon, that sheriff blushed and apologized, and one of the illustrated papers made a picture of the scene and spoke of the matter in such a way as to show that the editor regretted that the offense of an arrest had been offered to so exalted a personage as Mr. Weed.

Mr. O'Riley furnished shingle nails to the new Court House at three thousand dollars a keg, and eighteen gross of 60-cent thermometers at fifteen hundred dollars a dozen; the controller and the board of audit passed the bills, and a mayor, who was simply ignorant but not criminal, signed them. When they were paid, Mr. O'Riley's admirers gave him a solitaire diamond pin of the size of a filbert, in imitation of the liberality of Mr. Weed's friends, and then Mr. O'Riley retired from active service and amused himself with buying real estate at enormous figures and holding it in other people's names. By and by the newspapers came out with exposures and called Weed and O'Riley "thieves," —whereupon the people rose as one man (voting repeatedly) and elected the two gentlemen to their proper theatre of action, the New York legislature. The newspapers clamored, and the courts proceeded to try the new legislators for their small irregularities. Our admirable jury system enabled the persecuted ex-officials to secure a jury of nine gentlemen from a neighboring asylum and three graduates from Sing-Sing, and presently they walked forth with characters vindicated. The legislature was called upon to spew them forth—a thing which the legislature declined to do. It was like asking children to repudiate their own father. It was a legislature of the modern pattern.

Being now wealthy and distinguished, Mr. O'Riley, still bearing the legislative "Hon." attached to his name (for titles never die in America, although we *do* take a republican pride in poking fun at such trifles), sailed for Europe with his family. They traveled all about, turning their noses up at every thing, and not finding it a difficult thing to do, either, because nature had originally given those features a cast in that direction; and finally they established themselves in Paris, that Paradise of Americans of their sort.—They staid there two years and learned to speak English with a foreign accent—not that it hadn't always had a foreign accent (which was indeed the case) but now the nature of it was changed. Finally they returned home and became ultra fashionables. They landed here as the Hon. Patrique Oreillé and family, and so are known unto this day.

Laura provided seats for her visitors and they immediately launched forth into a breezy, sparkling conversation with that easy confidence which is to be found only among persons accustomed to high life.

"I've been intending to call sooner, Miss Hawkins," said the Hon. Mrs. Oreillé, "but the weather's been *so* horrid.—How do you like Washington?"

Laura liked it very well indeed.

*Mrs. Gashly*—"Is it your first visit?"

Yes, it was her first.

*All*—"Indeed?"

*Mrs. Oreillé*—"I'm afraid you'll despise the weather, Miss Hawkins. It's perfectly awful. It always is. I tell Mr. Oreillé I can't and I won't put up with any such a climate. If we were obliged to do it, I wouldn't mind it; but we are *not* obliged to, and so I don't see the use of it. Sometimes it's real pitiful the way the children pine for Parry—don't look *so* sad, Bridget, *ma chère*— poor child, she can't hear Parry mentioned without getting the blues."

*Mrs. Gashly*—"Well I should think so, Mrs. Oreillé. A body *lives* in Paris, but a body only *stays* here. I dote on Paris; I'd druther scrimp along on ten thousand dollars a year there, than suffer and worry here on a real decent income."

*Miss Gashly*—"Well then I wish you'd take us back, mother; I'm sure *I* hate this stoopid country enough, even if it *is* our dear native land."

*Miss Emmeline Gashly*—"What, and leave poor Johnny Peterson behind?" [An airy general laugh applauded this sally].

*Miss Gashly*—"Sister, I should think you'd be ashamed of yourself!"

*Miss Emmeline*—"Oh, you needn't ruffle your feathers so. I was only joking. He don't mean anything by coming to the house every evening—only comes to see mother. Of course that's all!" [General laughter].

*Miss G. prettily confused*—"Emmeline, how *can* you!"

*Mrs G.*—"Let your sister alone, Emmeline.—I never saw such a tease!"

*Mrs. Oreillé*—"What lovely corals you have, Miss Hawkins! Just look at them, Bridget, dear. I've a great passion for corals— it's a pity they're getting a little common. I have some elegant ones—not as elegant as yours, though—but of course I don't wear them now."

*Laura*—"I suppose they are rather common, but still I have a great affection for these, because they were given to me by a dear old friend of our family named Murphy. He was a very charming man, but very eccentric. We always supposed he was an Irishman, but after he got rich he went abroad for a year or two, and when he came back you would have been amused to see how interested he was in a potato. He asked what it was! Now you know that when Providence shapes a mouth especially for the accommodation of a potato you can detect that fact at a glance when that mouth is in repose—foreign travel can never remove *that* sign. But he was a very delightful gentleman, and his little foible did not hurt him at all. We all have our shams—I suppose there is a sham somewhere about every individual, if we could manage to ferret it out. I would so like to go to France. I suppose our society here compares very favorably with French society does it not, Mrs. Oreillé?"

*Mrs. O.*—"Not by any means, Miss Hawkins! French society is much more elegant—much more so."

*Laura*—"I am sorry to hear that. I suppose ours has deteriorated of late."

*Mrs. O.*—"Very much indeed. There are people in society here that have really no more money to live on than what some of us pay for servant hire. Still I won't say but what some of them are very good people—and respectable, too."

*Laura*—"The old families seem to be holding themselves aloof, from what I hear. I suppose you seldom meet in society now, the people you used to be familiar with twelve or fifteen years ago?"

*Mrs. O.*—"Oh, no—hardly ever."

Mr. O'Riley kept his first rum-mill and protected his customers from the law in those days, and this turn of the conversation was rather uncomfortable to madame than otherwise.

*Hon. Mrs. Higgins*—"Is François' health good now, Mrs. Oreillé?"

*Mrs. O.*—(*Thankful for the intervention*)—"Not very. A body couldn't expect it. He was always delicate—especially his lungs—and this odious climate tells on him strong, now, after Parry, which is so mild."

*Mrs. H.*—"I should think so. Husband says Percy'll die if he don't have a change; and so I'm going to swap round a little and see what can be done. I saw a lady from Florida last week, and she recommended Key West. I told her Percy couldn't abide winds, as he was threatened with a pulmonary affection, and then she said try St. Augustine. It's an awful distance—ten or twelve hundred mile, they say—but then in a case of this kind a body can't stand back for trouble, you know."

*Mrs. O.*—"No, of course that's so. If François don't get better soon we've got to look out for some other place, or else Europe. We've thought some of the Hot Springs, but I don't know. It's a great responsibility and a body wants to go cautious. Is Hildebrand about again, Mrs. Gashly?"

*Mrs. G.*—"Yes, but that's about all. It was indigestion, you know, and it looks as if it was chronic. And you know I do dread dyspepsia. We've all been worried a good deal about him. The doctor recommended baked apple and spoiled meat, and I think it done him good. It's about the only thing that will stay on his stomach now-a-days. We have Dr. Shovel now. Who's your doctor, Mrs. Higgins?"

*Mrs. H.*—"Well, we had Dr. Spooner a good while, but he runs so much to emetics, which I think are weakening, that we changed off and took Dr. Leathers. We like him very much. He has a fine European reputation, too. The first thing he suggested for Percy was to have him taken out in the back yard for an airing, every afternoon, with nothing at all on."

*Mrs. O. and Mrs. G.*—"What!"

*Mrs. H.*—"As true as I'm sitting here. And it actually helped him for two or three days; it did indeed. But after that the doctor said it seemed to be too severe and so he has fell back on hot foot-baths at night and cold showers in the morning. But I don't think there can be any good sound help for him in such a climate as this. I believe we are going to lose him if we don't make a change."

*Mrs. O.*—"I suppose you heard of the fright we had two weeks ago last Saturday? No? Why that is strange—but come to remember, you've all been away to Richmond. François tumbled from the sky light in the second-story hall clean down to the first floor—"

*Everybody*—"Mercy!"

*Mrs. O.*—"Yes indeed—and broke two of his ribs—"

*Everybody*—"What!"

*Mrs. O.*—"Just as true as you live. First we thought he must be injured internally. It was fifteen minutes past 8 in the evening. Of course we were all distracted in a moment—everybody was flying everywhere, and nobody doing anything *worth* anything. By and by I flung out next door and dragged in Dr. Sprague, President of the Medical University—no time to go for our own doctor of course—and the minute he saw François he said, 'Send for your own physician, madam'—said it as cross as a bear, too, and turned right on his heel and cleared out without doing a thing!"

*Everybody*—"The mean, contemptible brute!"

*Mrs. O.*—"Well you may say it. I was nearly out of my wits by this time. But we hurried off the servants after our own doctor and telegraphed mother—she was in New York and rushed down on the first train; and when the doctor got there, lo and behold you he found François had broke one of his legs, too!"

*Everybody*—"Goodness!"

*Mrs. O.*—"Yes. So he set his leg and bandaged it up, and fixed his ribs and gave him a dose of something to quiet down his excitement and put him to sleep—poor thing he was trembling and frightened to death and it was pitiful to see him. We had him in my bed—Mr. Oreillé slept in the guest room and I laid down beside François—but not to sleep—bless you no. Bridget and I set up all night, and the doctor staid till two in the morning, bless his old heart.—When mother got there she was so used up with anxiety that she had to go to bed and have the doctor; but when she found that François was not in immediate danger she rallied, and by night she was able to take a watch herself. Well for three days and nights we three never left that bedside only to take an hour's nap at a time. And then the doctor said François was out of danger and if ever there was a thankful set, in this world, it was us."

Laura's respect for these women had augmented during this conversation, naturally enough; affection and devotion are qualities that are able to adorn and render beautiful a character that is otherwise unattractive, and even repulsive.

*Mrs. Gashly*—"I do believe I should a died if I had been in your place, Mrs. Oreillé. The time Hildebrand was so low with the pneumonia Emmeline and me were all alone with him most of the time and we never took a minute's sleep for as much as two days and nights. It was at Newport and we wouldn't trust hired nurses. One afternoon he had a fit, and jumped up and run out on the portico of the hotel with nothing in the world on and the wind a blowing like ice and we after him scared to death; and when the ladies and gentlemen saw that he had a fit, every lady scattered for her room and not a gentleman lifted his hand to help, the wretches! Well after that his life hung by a thread for as much as ten days, and the minute he was out of danger Emmeline and me just went to bed sick and worn out. *I* never want to pass through such a time again. Poor dear François—which leg did he break, Mrs. Oreillé?"

*Mrs. O.*—"It was his right hand hind leg. Jump down, François dear, and show the ladies what a cruel limp you've got yet."

François demurred, but being coaxed and delivered gently upon the floor, he performed very satisfactorily, with his "right hand hind leg" in the air. All were affected—even Laura—but hers was an affection of the stomach. The country-bred girl had not suspected that the little whining ten-ounce black and tan reptile, clad in a red embroidered pigmy blanket and reposing in Mrs. Oreillé's lap all through the visit was the individual whose sufferings had been stirring the dormant generosities of her nature. She said:

"Poor little creature! You might have lost him!"

*Mrs. O.*—"O pray don't mention it, Miss Hawkins—it gives me such a turn!"

*Laura*—"And Hildebrand and Percy—are they—are they like this one?"

*Mrs. G.*—"No, Hilly has considerable Skye blood in him, I believe."

*Mrs. H.*—"Percy's the same, only he is two months and ten days older and has his ears cropped.—His father, Martin Farquhar Tupper, was sickly, and died young, but he was the sweetest disposition.—His mother had heart disease but was very gentle and resigned, and a wonderful ratter."*

So carried away had the visitors become by their interest attaching to this discussion of family matters, that their stay had been prolonged to a very improper and unfashionable length; but they suddenly recollected themselves now and took their departure.

Laura's scorn was boundless. The more she thought of these people and their extraordinary talk, the more offensive they seemed to her; and yet she confessed that if one must choose between the two extreme aristocracies it might be best, on the whole, looking at things from a strictly business point of view, to herd with the Parvenus; she was in Washington solely to compass a certain matter and to do it at any cost, and these people might be useful to her, while it was plain that her purposes and

---

* As impossible and exasperating as this conversation may sound to a person who is not an idiot, it is scarcely in any respect an exaggeration of one which one of us actually listened to in an American drawing room—otherwise we could not venture to put such a chapter into a book which professes to deal with social possibilities.—M.T.

her schemes for pushing them would not find favor in the eyes of the Antiques. If it came to choice—and it might come to that, sooner or later—she believed she could come to a decision without much difficulty or many pangs.

But the best aristocracy of the three Washington castes, and really the most powerful, by far, was that of the Middle Ground. It was made up of the families of public men from nearly every state in the Union—men who held positions in both the executive and legislative branches of the government, and whose characters had been for years blemishless, both at home and at the capital. These gentlemen and their households were unostentatious people; they were educated and refined; they troubled themselves but little about the two other orders of nobility, but moved serenely in their wide orbit, confident in their own strength and well aware of the potency of their influence. They had no troublesome appearances to keep up, no rivalries which they cared to distress themselves about, no jealousies to fret over. They could afford to mind their own affairs and leave other combinations to do the same or do otherwise, just as they chose. They were people who were beyond reproach, and that was sufficient.

Senator Dilworthy never came into collision with any of these factions. He labored for them all and with them all. He said that all men were brethren and all were entitled to the honest unselfish help and countenance of a Christian laborer in the public vineyard.

Laura concluded, after reflection, to let circumstances determine the course it might be best for her to pursue as regarded the several aristocracies.

Now it might occur to the reader that perhaps Laura had been somewhat rudely suggestive in her remarks to Mrs. Oreillé when the subject of corals was under discussion, but it did not occur to Laura herself. She was not a person of exaggerated refinement; indeed the society and the influences that had formed her character had not been of a nature calculated to make her so; she thought that "give and take was fair play," and that to parry an offensive thrust with a sarcasm was a neat and legitimate thing to do. She sometimes talked to people in a way which some ladies would consider actually shocking; but Laura rather prided herself upon some of her exploits of that character. We are sorry we cannot make her a faultless heroine; but we cannot, for the reason that she was human.

She considered herself a superior conversationist. Long ago, when the possibility had first been brought before her mind that some day she might move in Washington society, she had recognized the fact that practiced conversational powers would be a necessary weapon in that field; she had also recognized the fact that since her dealings there must be mainly with men, and men whom she supposed to be exceptionally cultivated and able, she would need heavier shot in her magazine than mere brilliant "society" nothings; whereupon she had at once entered upon a tireless and elaborate course of reading, and had never since ceased to devote every unoccupied moment to this sort of preparation. Having now acquired a happy smattering of various information, she used it with good effect—she passed for a singularly well informed woman in Washington. The quality of her literary tastes had necessarily undergone constant improvement under this regimen, and as necessarily, also, the quality of her language had improved, though it cannot be denied that now and then her former condition of life betrayed itself in just perceptible inelegancies of expression and lapses of grammar.

## CHAPTER 20

When Laura had been in Washington three months, she was still the same person, in one respect, that she was when she first arrived there—that is to say, she still bore the name of Laura Hawkins. Otherwise she was perceptibly changed.—

She had arrived in a state of grievous uncertainty as to what manner of woman she was, physically and intellectually, as compared with eastern women; she was well satisfied, now, that her beauty was confessed, her mind a grade above the average, and her powers of fascination rather extraordinary. So she was at ease upon those points. When she arrived, she was possessed of habits of economy and not possessed of money; now she dressed elaborately, gave but little thought to the cost of things, and was very well fortified financially.—She kept her mother and Washington freely supplied with money, and did the same by Col. Sellers—who always insisted upon giving his note for loans—with interest; he was rigid upon that; she *must* take interest; and one of the Colonel's greatest satisfactions was to go over his accounts and note what a handsome sum this accruing interest amounted to, and what a comfortable though modest support it would yield Laura in case reverses should overtake her. In truth he could not help feeling that he was an efficient shield for her against poverty; and so, if her expensive ways ever troubled him for a brief moment, he presently dismissed the thought and said to himself, "Let her go on—even if she loses everything she is still safe—this interest will always afford her a good easy income."

Laura was on excellent terms with a great many members of Congress, and there was an undercurrent of suspicion in some quarters that she was one of that detested class known as "lobbyists;" but what belle could escape slander in such a city? Fair-minded people declined to condemn her on mere suspicion, and so the injurious talk made no very damaging headway. She was very gay, now, and very celebrated, and she might well expect to be assailed by many kinds of gossip. She was growing used to celebrity, and could already sit calm and seemingly unconscious, under the fire of fifty lorgnettes in a theatre, or even overhear the low voice "That's she!" as she passed along the street without betraying annoyance.

The whole air was full of a vague vast scheme which was to eventuate in filling Laura's pockets with millions of money; some had one idea of the scheme, and some another, but nobody had any exact knowledge upon the subject. All that any one felt sure about, was that Laura's landed estates were princely in value and extent, and that the government was anxious to get hold of them for public purposes, and that Laura was willing to make the sale but not at all anxious about the matter and not at all in a hurry. It was whispered that Senator Dilworthy was a stumbling block in the way of an immediate sale, because he was resolved that the government should not have the lands except with the understanding that they should be devoted to the uplifting of the negro race; Laura did not care what they were devoted to, it was said, (a world of very different gossip to the contrary notwithstanding,) but there were several other heirs and they would be guided entirely by the Senator's wishes; and finally, many people averred that while it would be easy to sell the lands to the government for the benefit of the negro, by resorting to the usual methods of influencing votes, Senator Dilworthy was unwilling to have so noble a charity sullied by any taint of corruption—he was resolved that not a vote should be bought. Nobody could get anything definite from Laura about these matters, and so gossip had to feed itself chiefly upon guesses. But the effect of it all was, that Laura was considered to be very wealthy and likely to be vastly more so in a little while. Consequently she was much courted and as much envied. Her wealth attracted many suitors. Perhaps they came to worship her riches, but they remained to worship her. Some of the noblest men of the time succumbed to her fascinations. She frowned upon no lover when he made his first advances, but by and by when he was hopelessly enthralled, he learned from her own lips that she had formed a resolution never to marry. Then he would go away hating and cursing the whole sex, and she would calmly add his scalp to her string, while she mused upon the bitter day that Col. Selby trampled her love and her pride in the dust. In time it came to be said that her way was paved with broken hearts.

Poor Washington gradually woke up to the fact that he too was an intellectual marvel as well as his gifted sister. He could not conceive how it had come about (it did not occur to him that the gossip about his family's great wealth had anything to do with it). He could not account for it by any process of reasoning, and was simply obliged to accept the fact and give up trying to solve the riddle. He found himself dragged into society and courted, wondered at and envied very much as if he were one of those foreign barbers who flit over here now and then with a self-conferred title of nobility and marry some rich fool's absurd daughter. Sometimes at a dinner party or a reception he would find himself the centre of interest, and feel unutterably uncomfortable in the discovery. Being obliged to say something, he would mine his brain and put in a blast and when the smoke and flying debris had cleared away the result would be what seemed to him but a poor little intellectual clod of dirt or two, and then he would be astonished to see everybody as lost in admiration as if he had brought up a ton or two of virgin gold. Every remark he made delighted his hearers and compelled their applause; he overheard people say he was exceedingly bright—they were chiefly mammas and marriageable young ladies. He found that some of his good things were being repeated about the town. Whenever he heard of an instance of this kind, he would keep that particular remark in mind and analyze it at home in private. At first he could not see that the remark was anything better than a parrot might originate; but by and by he began to feel that perhaps he underrated his powers; and after that he used to analyze his good things with a deal of comfort, and find in them a brilliancy which would have been

unapparent to him in earlier days—and then he would make a
note of that good thing and say it again the first time he found
himself in a new company. Presently he had saved up quite a
repertoire of brilliancies; and after that he confined himself to
repeating these and ceased to originate any more, lest he might
injure his reputation by an unlucky effort.

He was constantly having young ladies thrust upon his notice
at receptions, or left upon his hands at parties, and in time he
began to feel that he was being deliberately persecuted in this
way; and after that he could not enjoy society because of his
constant dread of these female ambushes and surprises. He was
distressed to find that nearly every time he showed a young lady
a polite attention he was straightway reported to be engaged to
her; and as some of these reports got into the newspapers
occasionally, he had to keep writing to Louise that they were
lies and she must believe in him and not mind them or allow
them to grieve her.

Washington was as much in the dark as anybody with regard
to the great wealth that was hovering in the air and seemingly
on the point of tumbling into the family pocket. Laura would
give him no satisfaction. All she would say, was:

"Wait. Be patient. You will see."

"But will it be soon, Laura?"

"It will not be very long, I think."

"But what makes you think so?"

"I have reasons—and good ones. Just wait, and be patient."

"But is it going to be as much as people say it is?"

"What do they say it is?"

"Oh, ever so much. Millions!"

"Yes, it will be a great sum."

"But *how* great, Laura? Will it be millions?"

"Yes, you may call it that. Yes, it *will* be millions. There, now—
does that satisfy you?"

"Splendid! I can wait. I can wait patiently—ever so patiently.
Once I was near selling the land for twenty thousand dollars;
once for thirty thousand dollars; once after that for seven thou-

sand dollars; and once for forty thousand dollars—but something always told me not to do it. What a fool I would have been to sell it for such a beggarly trifle! It *is* the land that's to bring the money, isn't it Laura? You can tell me that much, can't you?"

"Yes, I don't mind saying that much. It *is* the land. But mind—don't ever hint that you got it from me. Don't mention me in the matter at all, Washington."

"All right—I won't. Millions! Isn't it splendid! I mean to look around for a building lot; a lot with fine ornamental shrubbery and all that sort of thing. I will do it to-day. And I might as well see an architect, too, and get him to go to work at a plan for a house. I don't intend to spare any expense; I mean to have the noblest house that money can build." Then after a pause—he did not notice Laura's smiles—"Laura, would you lay the main hall in encaustic tiles, or just in fancy patterns of hard wood?"

Laura laughed a good old-fashioned laugh that had more of her former natural self about it than any sound that had issued from her mouth in many weeks. She said:

"*You* don't change, Washington. You still begin to squander a fortune right and left the instant you hear of it in the distance; you never wait till the foremost dollar of it arrives within a hundred miles of you,"—and she kissed her brother good-bye and left him weltering in his dreams, so to speak.

He got up and walked the floor feverishly during two hours; and when he sat down he had married Louise, built a house, reared a family, married them off, spent upwards of eight hundred thousand dollars on mere luxuries, and died worth twelve millions.

## CHAPTER 21

[Laura had a meeting with Senator Dilworthy, whom she called "uncle." He liked to be called "uncle" by this beautiful woman. They discussed the progress of their petition. Laura was keeping a record of those members of Congress who were for and those who were against the petition. Laura said:]

"Oh, I saw Senator Balloon."

"He will help us, I suppose? Balloon is a whole-hearted fellow. I can't *help* loving that man, for all his drollery and waggishness. He puts on an air of levity sometimes, but there aint a man in the senate knows the scriptures as he does. He did not make any objections?"

"Not exactly, he said—shall I tell you what he said?" asked Laura glancing furtively at him.

"Certainly."

"He said he had no doubt it was a good thing; if Senator Dilworthy was in it, it would pay to look into it."

The Senator laughed, but rather feebly, and said, "Balloon is always full of his jokes."

"I explained it to him. He said it was all right, he only wanted a word with you," continued Laura. "He is a handsome old gentleman, and he is gallant for an old man."

"My daughter," said the Senator, with a grave look, "I trust there was nothing free in his manner?"

"Free?" repeated Laura, with indignation in her face. "With *me!*"

"There, there, child. I meant nothing, Balloon talks a little freely sometimes, with men. But he is right at heart. His term expires next year and I fear we shall lose him."

"He seemed to be packing the day I was there. His rooms were full of dry goods boxes, into which his servant was crowding all manner of old clothes and stuff. I suppose he will paint 'Pub. Docs.' on them and frank them home. That's good economy, isn't it?"

"Yes, yes, but child, all Congressmen do that. It may not be strictly honest, indeed it is not unless he had some public documents mixed in with the clothes."

"It's a funny world. Good-bye, uncle. I'm going to see that chairman."

And humming a cheery opera air, she departed to her room to dress for going out. Before she did that, however, she took out her note book and was soon deep in its contents, marking, dashing, erasing, figuring, and talking to herself.

"Free! I wonder what Dilworthy *does* think of me anyway? One . . . two . . . eight . . . seventeen . . . twenty-one, . . . 'm'm . . . it takes a heap for a majority. Wouldn't Dilworthy open his eyes if he knew some of the things Balloon *did* say to me. There . . . . Hopperson's influence ought to count twenty . . . . the sanctimonious old curmudgeon. Son-in-law . . . . sinecure in the negro institution. . . . . That about gauges *him*. . . . . The three committeemen . . . . sons-in-law. Nothing like a son-in-law here in Washington . . . . or a brother-in-law . . . . And everybody has 'em. . . . . Let's see . . . . sixty-one . . . . with places; . . . . twenty-five . . . persuaded—it is getting on; . . . . we'll have two-thirds of Congress in time. . . . . Dilworthy must surely know I understand him. Uncle Dilworthy . . . . Uncle Balloon! . . . Tells very amusing stories . . . . when ladies are not present . . . . I should think so. . . . 'm . . . 'm. Eighty-five. . . .There. I must find that chairman. Queer . . . . Buckstone acts. . . . . Seemed to be in love. . . . . I was *sure* of it. He promised to come here . . . . and he hasn't. . . . Strange. *Very* strange. . . . I must chance to meet him to-day."

[After the meeting Laura went out, hoping to run into Mr. Buckstone, the chairman of the House Committee on Benevolent Appropriations, whose vote she wished to secure. Thinking that she was perhaps too early for Mr. Buckstone, she decided to drop in at a book store near his house. Laura knew many of the young men of Newspaper Row, who one day, when Col. Sellers came in, were talking about Balloon and the dry goods box packing story. One of the young men told the Colonel about it, and then went on with a serious air:]

"Colonel, if you register a letter, it means that it is of value, doesn't it? And if you pay fifteen cents for registering it, the government will have to take extra care of it and even pay you back its full value if it is lost. Isn't that so?"

"Yes. I suppose it's so."

"Well Senator Balloon put fifteen cents worth of stamps on each of those seven huge boxes of old clothes, and shipped that ton of second-hand rubbish, old boots and pantaloons and what not through the mails as registered matter! It was an ingenious thing and it had a genuine touch of humor about it, too. I think there is more real talent among our public men of to-day than there was among those of old times—a far more fertile fancy, a much happier ingenuity. Now, Colonel, can you picture Jefferson, or Washington or John Adams franking their wardrobes through the mails and adding the facetious idea of making the government responsible for the cargo for the sum of one dollar and five cents? Statesmen were dull creatures in those days. I have a much greater admiration for Senator Balloon."

"Yes, Balloon is a man of parts, there is no denying it."

"I think so. He is spoken of for the post of Minister to China, or Austria, and I hope will be appointed. What we want abroad is good examples of the national character. John Jay and Benjamin Franklin were well enough in their day, but the nation has made progress since then. Balloon is a man we know and can depend on to be true to—himself."

"Yes, and Balloon has had a good deal of public experience. He is an old friend of mine. He was governor of one of the territories a while, and was very satisfactory."

"Indeed he was. He was ex-officio Indian agent, too. Many a man would have taken the Indian appropriation and devoted the money to feeding and clothing the helpless savages, whose land had been taken from them by the white man in the interests of civilization; but Balloon knew their needs better. He built a government saw-mill on the reservation with the money, and the lumber sold for enormous prices—a relative of his did all the work free of charge—that is to say he charged nothing more than the lumber would bring."

"But the poor Injuns—not that I care much for Injuns—what did he do for them?"

"Gave them the outside slabs to fence in the reservation with. Governor Balloon was nothing less than a father to the poor Indians. But Balloon is not alone, we have many truly noble statesmen in our country's service like Balloon. The Senate is full of them. Don't you think so Colonel?"

"Well, I dunno. I honor my country's public servants as much as any one can. I meet them, Sir, every day, and the more I see of them the more I esteem them and the more grateful I am that our institutions give us the opportunity of securing their services. Few lands are so blest."

"That is true, Colonel. To be sure you can buy now and then a Senator or a Representative; but they do not know it is wrong, and so they are not ashamed of it. They are gentle, and confiding and childlike, and in my opinion these are qualities that ennoble them far more than any amount of sinful sagacity could. I quite agree with you, Col. Sellers."

"Well"—hesitated the Colonel—"I am afraid some of them do buy their seats—yes, I am afraid they do—but as Senator Dilworthy himself said to me, it is sinful,—it is very wrong—it is shameful; Heaven protect *me* from such a charge. That is what Dilworthy said. And yet when you come to look at it you cannot deny that we would have to go without the services of some of our ablest men, sir, if the country were opposed to—to—bribery. It is a harsh term. I do not like to use it."

The Colonel interrupted himself at this point to meet an engagement with the Austrian minister, and took his leave with his usual courtly bow.

## CHAPTER 22

In due time Laura alighted at the book store, and began to look at the titles of the handsome array of books on the counter. A dapper clerk of perhaps nineteen or twenty years, with hair accurately parted and surprisingly slick, came bustling up and leaned over with a pretty smile and an affable—

"Can I—was there any particular book you wished to see?"

"Have you Taine's England?"

"Beg pardon?"

"Taine's Notes on England."

The young gentleman scratched the side of his nose with a cedar pencil which he took down from its bracket on the side of his head, and reflected a moment:

"Ah—I see," [with a bright smile]—"Train, you mean—not Taine. George Francis Train. No, ma'm we—"

"I mean *Taine*—if I may take the liberty."

The clerk reflected again—then:

"Taine . . . . Taine . . . . Is it hymns?"

"No, it isn't hymns. It is a volume that is making a deal of talk just now, and is very widely known—except among parties who sell it."

The clerk glanced at her face to see if a sarcasm might not lurk somewhere in that obscure speech, but the gentle simplicity of the beautiful eyes that met his, banished that suspicion. He went away and conferred with the proprietor. Both appeared to be nonplussed. They thought and talked, and talked and thought by turns. Then both came forward and the proprietor said:

"Is it an American book, ma'm?"

"No, it is an American reprint of an English translation."

"Oh! Yes—yes—I remember, now. We are expecting it every day. It isn't out yet."

"I think you must be mistaken, because you advertised it a week ago."

"Why no—can that be so?"

"Yes, I am sure of it. And besides, here is the book itself, on the counter."

She bought it and the proprietor retired from the field. Then she asked the clerk for the Autocrat of the Breakfast Table—and was pained to see the admiration her beauty had inspired in him fade out of his face. He said with cold dignity, that cook books were somewhat out of their line, but he would order it if she desired it. She said, no, never mind. Then she fell to conning the titles again, finding a delight in the inspection of the Hawthornes, the Longfellows, the Tennysons, and other favorites of her idle hours. Meantime the clerk's eyes were busy, and no doubt his admiration was returning again—or may be he was only gauging her probable literary tastes by some sagacious system of admeasurement only known to his guild. Now he began to "assist" her in making a selection; but his efforts met with no success—indeed they only annoyed her and unpleasantly interrupted her meditations. Presently, while she was holding a copy of "Venetian Life" in her hand and running over a familiar passage here and there, the clerk said, briskly, snatching up a paper-covered volume and striking the counter a smart blow with it to dislodge the dust:

"Now here is a work that we've sold a lot of. Everybody that's read it likes it"—and he intruded it under her nose; "it's a book that I can recommend—'The Pirate's Doom, or the Last of the Buccaneers.' I think it's one of the best things that's come out this season."

Laura pushed it gently aside with her hand and went on filching from "Venetian Life."

"I believe I do not want it," she said.

The clerk hunted around awhile, glancing at one title and then another, but apparently not finding what he wanted. However, he succeeded at last. Said he:

"Have you ever read this, ma'm? I am sure you'll like it. It's by the author of 'The Hooligans of Hackensack.' It is full of love troubles and mysteries and all sorts of such things. The heroine strangles her own mother. Just glance at the title please,—'Gonderil the Vampire, or The Dance of Death.' And here is 'The Jokist's Own Treasury, or, The Phunny Phellow's Bosom Phriend.' The funniest thing!—I've read it four times, ma'm, and I can laugh at the very sight of it yet. And 'Gonderil,'—I assure you it is the most splendid book I ever read. I know you will like these books, ma'm, because I've read them myself and I know what they are."

"Oh, I was perplexed—but I see how it is, now. You must have thought I asked you to tell me what sort of books I wanted —for I am apt to say things which I don't really mean, when I am absent minded. I suppose I did ask you, didn't I?"

"No ma'm,—but I—"

"Yes, I must have done it, else you would not have offered your services, for fear it might be rude. But don't be troubled— it was all my fault. I ought not to have been so heedless—I ought not to have asked you."

"But you didn't ask me, ma'm. We always help customers all we can. You see our experience—living right among books all the time—that sort of thing makes us able to help a customer make a selection, you know."

"Now does it, indeed? It is part of your business, then?"

"Yes'm, we always help."

"How good it is of you. Some people would think it rather obtrusive, perhaps, but I don't—I think it is real kindness—even charity. Some people jump to conclusions without any thought —you have noticed that?"

"O yes," said the clerk, a little perplexed as to whether to feel comfortable or the reverse; "oh yes, indeed, I've often noticed that, ma'm."

"Yes, they jump to conclusions with an absurd heedlessness. Now some people would think it odd that because you, with the budding tastes and the innocent enthusiasms natural to your time of life, enjoyed the Vampires and the volume of nursery jokes, you should imagine that an older person would delight in them too—but I do not think it odd at all. I think it natural—perfectly natural—in you. And kind, too. You look like a person who not only finds a deep pleasure in any little thing in the way of literature that strikes you forcibly, but is willing and glad to share that pleasure with others—and that, I think, is noble and admirable—very noble and admirable. I think we ought all to share our pleasures with others, and do what we can to make each other happy, do not you?"

"Oh, yes. Oh, yes, indeed. Yes, you are quite right, ma'm."

But he was getting unmistakably uncomfortable, now, notwithstanding Laura's confiding sociability and almost affectionate tone.

"Yes, indeed. Many people would think that what a bookseller —or perhaps his clerk—knows about literature *as* literature, in contradistinction to its character as merchandise, would hardly be of much assistance to a person—that is, to an adult, of course —in the selection of food for the mind—except of course wrapping paper, or twine, or wafers, or something like that—but I never feel that way. I feel that whatever service you offer me, you offer with a good heart, and I am as grateful for it as if it were the greatest boon to me. And it *is* useful to me—it is bound to be so.—It cannot be otherwise. If you show me a book which you have read—not skimmed over or merely glanced at, but *read*—and you tell me that *you* enjoyed it and that *you* could read it three or four times, then I know what book I want—"

"Thank you!—th—"

—"to avoid. Yes indeed. I think that no information ever comes amiss in this world. Once or twice I have traveled in the cars —and there you know, the peanut boy always measures you with his eye, and hands you out a book of murders if you are fond of theology; or Tupper or a dictionary or T. S. Arthur if you are fond of poetry; or he hands you a volume of distressing jokes or a copy of the American Miscellany if you particularly dislike that sort of literary fatty degeneration of the heart—just for the world like a pleasant-spoken well-meaning gentleman in any book store—. But here I am running on as if business men had nothing to do but listen to women talk. You must pardon me, for I was not thinking.—And you must let me thank you again for helping me. I read a good deal, and shall be in nearly every day; and I would be sorry to have you think me a customer who talks too much and buys too little. Might I ask you to give me the time? Ah—two—twenty-two. Thank you very much. I will set mine while I have the opportunity."

But she could not get her watch open, apparently. She tried, and tried again. Then the clerk, trembling at his own audacity, begged to be allowed to assist. She allowed him. He succeeded, and was radiant under the sweet influences of her pleased face and her seductively worded acknowledgements with gratification. Then he gave her the exact time again, and anxiously watched her turn the hands slowly till they reached the precise spot without accident or loss of life, and then he looked as happy as a man who had helped a fellow being through a momentous undertaking, and was grateful to know that he had not lived in vain. Laura thanked him once more. The words were music to his ear; but what were they compared to the ravishing smile with which she flooded his whole system? When she bowed her adieu and turned away, he was no longer suffering torture in the pillory where she had had him trussed up during so many distressing moments, but he belonged to the list of her conquests and was a flattered and happy thrall, with the dawn-light of love breaking over the eastern elevations of his heart.

It was about the hour, now, for the chairman of the House Committee on Benevolent Appropriations to make his appearance, and Laura stepped to the door to reconnoitre. She glanced up the street, and sure enough—

## CHAPTER 23

That Chairman was nowhere in sight. Such disappointments seldom occur in novels, but are always happening in real life.

She was obliged to make a new plan. She sent him a note, and asked him to call in the evening—which he did.

She received the Hon. Mr. Buckstone with a sunny smile, and said:

"I don't know how I ever dared to send you a note, Mr. Buckstone, for you have the reputation of not being very partial to our sex."

"Why I am sure my reputation does me wrong, then, Miss Hawkins. I have been married once—is that nothing in my favor?"

"Oh, yes—that is, it may be and it may not be. If you have known what perfection is in woman, it is fair to argue that inferiority cannot interest you now."

"Even if that were the case it could not affect *you*, Miss Hawkins," said the chairman gallantly. "Fame does not place you in the list of ladies who rank below perfection."

This happy speech delighted Mr. Buckstone as much as it seemed to delight Laura. But it did not confuse him as much as it apparently did her.

"I wish in all sincerity that I could be worthy of such a felicitous compliment as that. But I am a woman, and so I am gratified for it just as it is, and would not have it altered."

"But it is not merely a compliment—that is, an empty compliment—it is the truth. All men will endorse that."

Laura looked pleased, and said:

"It is very kind of you to say it. It is a distinction indeed, for a country-bred girl like me to be so spoken of by people of brains and culture. You are so kind that I know you will pardon my putting you to the trouble to come this evening."

"Indeed it was no trouble. It was a pleasure. I am alone in the
world since I lost my wife, and I often long for the society of
your sex, Miss Hawkins, notwithstanding what people may say
to the contrary."

"It is pleasant to hear you say that. I am sure it must be so.
If I feel lonely at times, because of my exile from old friends, although surrounded by new ones who are already very dear to
me, how much more lonely must you feel, bereft as you are, and
with no wholesome relief from the cares of state that weigh you
down. For your own sake, as well as for the sake of others, you
ought to go into society oftener. I seldom see you at a reception,
and when I do you do not usually give me very much of your
attention."

"I never imagined that you wished it or I would have been
very glad to make myself happy in that way.—But one seldom
gets an opportunity to say more than a sentence to you in a
place like that. You are always the centre of a group—a fact
which you may have noticed yourself. But if one might come
here—"

"Indeed you would always find a hearty welcome, Mr. Buckstone. I have often wished you would come and tell me more
about Cairo and the Pyramids, as you once promised me you
would."

"Why, do you remember that yet, Miss Hawkins? I thought
ladies' memories were more fickle than that."

"Oh, they are not so fickle as gentlemen's promises. And besides, if I had been inclined to forget, I—did you not give me
something by way of a remembrancer?"

"Did I?"

"Think."

"It does seem to me that I did; but I have forgotten what it
was now."

"Never, never call a lady's memory fickle again! Do you recognize this?"

"A little spray of box! I am beaten—I surrender. But have you
kept that all this time?"

Laura's confusion was very pretty. She tried to hide it, but the more she tried the more manifest it became and withal the more captivating to look upon. Presently she threw the spray of box from her with an annoyed air, and said:

"I forgot myself. I have been very foolish. I beg that you will forget this absurd thing."

Mr. Buckstone picked up the spray, and sitting down by Laura's side on the sofa, said:

"Please let me keep it, Miss Hawkins. I set a very high value upon it now."

"Give it to me, Mr. Buckstone, and do not speak so. I have been sufficiently punished for my thoughtlessness. You cannot take pleasure in adding to my distress. Please give it to me."

"Indeed I do not wish to distress you. But do not consider the matter so gravely; you have done yourself no wrong. You probably forgot that you had it; but if you had given it to me I would have kept it—and not forgotten it."

"Do not talk so, Mr. Buckstone. Give it to me, please, and forget the matter."

"It would not be kind to refuse, since it troubles you so, and so I restore it. But if you would give me part of it and keep the rest—"

"So that you might have something to remind you of me when you wished to laugh at my foolishness?"

"Oh, by no means, no! Simply that I might remember that I had once assisted to discomfort you, and be reminded to do so no more."

Laura looked up, and scanned his face a moment. She was about to break the twig, but she hesitated and said:

"If I were sure that you—" She threw the spray away, and continued: "This is silly! We will change the subject. No, do not insist—I must have my way in this."

Then Mr. Buckstone drew off his forces and proceeded to make a wily advance upon the fortress under cover of carefully-contrived artifices and stratagems of war. But he contended with an alert and suspicious enemy; and so at the end of two hours it was manifest to him that he had made but little progress. Still, he had made some; he was sure of that.

Laura sat alone and communed with herself:

"He is fairly hooked, poor thing. I can play him at my leisure and land him when I choose. He was all ready to be caught, days and days ago—I saw that, very well. He will vote for our bill —no fear about that; and moreover he will work for it, too, before I am done with him. If he had a woman's eyes he would have noticed that the spray of box had grown three inches since he first gave it to me, but a man never sees anything and never suspects. If I had shown him a whole bush he would have thought it was the same. Well, it is a good night's work: the committee is safe. But this is a desperate game I am playing in these days—a wearing, sordid, heartless game. If I lose, I lose everything—even myself. And if I win the game, will it be worth its cost after all? I do not know. Sometimes I doubt. Sometimes I half wish I had not begun. But no matter; I *have* begun, and I will never turn back; never while I live."

Mr. Buckstone indulged in a reverie as he walked homeward:

"She is shrewd and deep, and plays her cards with considerable discretion—but she will lose, for all that. There is no hurry; I shall come out winner, all in good time. She *is* the most beautiful woman in the world; and she surpassed herself to-night. I suppose I must vote for that bill, in the end maybe; but that is not a matter of much consequence—the government can stand it. She is bent on capturing me, that is plain; but she will find by and by that what she took for a sleeping garrison was an ambuscade."

[Laura and Washington Hawkins were just about to leave a day reception when Laura's attention was caught by the sight of a man. Then she saw it was George Selby and she "put out her hand and clutched Washington's arm to prevent herself from falling." Selby had not noticed her. At home she told herself that she ought to kill Selby, that he had no right to live. She vowed that he would not escape her this time. She did not go to dinner, nor did she go to the President's reception that evening. That night was an agony for her. In the times when she did not hate Selby she wondered if he might still love her.

She kept to her room for two days. At breakfast on the third day she said that she had heard some unusual noise during the night and that she feared burglars. She said she would feel safer if Washington would lend her one of his pistols. He brought one and showed her how to load and fire it. That morning she discovered where Selby was staying and learned that he was in Washington on a cotton claim. She wrote him a note in a disguised hand. The note said: "A Lady at Senator Dilworthy's would like to see Col. George Selby, on business connected with the Cotton Claims. Can he call Wednesday at three o'clock P.M." It was a day and an hour when no one of the family was likely to be at home.

Selby went to the Senator's house and was startled to meet Laura, with whom he had a stormy interview. He told her that he was trapped in his marriage and that he still loved her. She believed him and thought that he rightfully belonged to her, and she began to consider how he could free himself from his wife.

Meanwhile Col. Sellers had become one of the best-known men in the capital. He enjoyed the capital's feverish atmosphere and was at the center of events. He even knew the President, who liked to hear him talk. The Colonel was careful to look after his own affairs—the Columbus River navigation scheme and the Tennessee Land plan. Part of the plan, it was rumored, was to build an experimental institution, a university, in Tennessee, which would help that state in the way that the Industrial School in Zurich had helped Switzerland. The benefactors would be the colored race. As for Laura, she was exposing herself increasingly to gossip but she did not care. She would have *money* soon and she and Selby could go to Europe—or anywhere. Selby promised and lied. He was afraid to break with her, and also he was unwilling to give her up. He told his wife that Laura was a lobbyist who could be useful to him in getting his cotton claim through, and that he had to tolerate her awhile.

Harry was jealous of the attentions Laura showed Selby and was "huffy" with her in response to her "lofty condescension." During one meeting with her he revealed that Selby had just won his claim and was soon going abroad. Laura was shocked by this news. Questioning Harry, she learned that Selby's wife was "a dark little woman, rather worn," and that she had three

or four children, one of them a baby. The wife and children
would accompany Selby to Europe. Laura was bitter. Afterwards
Harry wrote her a long, incoherent letter, warning of the dangers
that surrounded her. She read the letter with contempt and
thought, "They are all alike." Harry wrote to Philip about Laura's
friendship with Selby, about the town gossip and about his own
love for her. He said he wished Philip were in Washington to
advise Laura for her own good. Laura had respect for his
opinions and character, Harry said, and might listen to him.
Philip decided to go to Washington.]

## CHAPTER 24

Mr. Buckstone's campaign was brief—much briefer than he supposed it would be. He began it purposing to win Laura without being won himself; but his experience was that of all who had fought on that field before him; he diligently continued his effort to win her, but he presently found that while as yet he could not feel entirely certain of having won her, it was very manifest that she had won him. He had made an able fight, brief as it was, and that at least was to his credit. He was in good company, now; he walked in a leash of conspicuous captives. These unfortunates followed Laura helplessly, for whenever she took a prisoner he remained her slave henceforth. Sometimes they chafed in their bondage; sometimes they tore themselves free and said their serfdom was ended; but sooner or later they always came back penitent and worshiping. Laura pursued her usual course: she encouraged Mr. Buckstone by turns, and by turns she harassed him; she exalted him to the clouds at one time, and at another she dragged him down again. She constituted him chief champion of the Knobs University bill, and he accepted the position, at first reluctantly, but later as a valued means of serving her—he even came to look upon it as a piece of great good fortune, since it brought him into such frequent contact with her.

Through him she learned that the Hon. Mr. Trollop was a bitter enemy of her bill. He urged her not to attempt to influence Mr. Trollop in any way, and explained that whatever she might attempt in that direction would surely be used against her and with damaging effect.

She at first said she knew Mr. Trollop, "and was aware that he had a Blank-Blank;"* but Mr. Buckstone said that while he

* Her private figure of speech for Brother—or Son-in-law.—M.T.

was not able to conceive what so curious a phrase as Blank-Blank might mean, and had no wish to pry into the matter, since it was probably private, he "would nevertheless venture the blind assertion that *nothing* would answer in this particular case and during this particular session but to be exceedingly wary and keep clear away from Mr. Trollop; any other course would be fatal."

It seemed that nothing could be done. Laura was seriously troubled. Everything was looking well, and yet it was plain that one vigorous and determined enemy might eventually succeed in overthrowing all her plans. A suggestion came into her mind presently and she said:

"Can't you fight against his great Pension bill and bring him to terms?"

"Oh, never; he and I are sworn brothers on that measure; we work in harness and are very loving—I do everything I possibly can for him there. But I work with might and main against his Immigration bill,—as pertinaciously and as vindictively, indeed, as he works against our University. We hate each other through half a conversation and are all affection through the other half. We understand each other. He is an admirable worker outside the capitol; he will do more for the Pension bill than any other man could do; I wish he would make the great speech on it which he wants to make—and then I would make another and we would be safe."

"Well if he wants to make a great speech why doesn't he do it?"

Visitors interrupted the conversation and Mr. Buckstone took his leave. It was not of the least moment to Laura that her question had not been answered, inasmuch as it concerned a thing which did not interest her; and yet, human being like, she thought she would have liked to know. An opportunity occurring presently, she put the same question to another person and got an answer that satisfied her. She pondered a good while, that night, after she had gone to bed, and when she finally turned over to go to sleep, she had thought out a new scheme.

The next evening at Mrs. Gloverson's party, she said to Mr. Buckstone:

"I want Mr. Trollop to make his great speech on the Pension bill."

"*Do* you! But you remember I was interrupted, and did not explain to you—"

"Never mind, I know. You must make him make that speech. I very particularly desire it."

"Oh, it is easy to say make him do it, but *how* am I to make him?"

"It is perfectly easy; I have thought it all out."

She then went into the details. At length Mr. Buckstone said:

"I see now. I can manage it, I am sure. Indeed I wonder he never thought of it himself—there are no end of precedents. But how is this going to benefit you, after I *have* managed it? There is where the mystery lies."

"But I will take care of that. It will benefit me a great deal."

"I only wish I could see how; it is the oddest freak. You seem to go the furthest around to get at a thing—but you are in earnest, aren't you?"

"Yes, I am, indeed."

"Very well, I will do it—but why not tell me how you imagine it is going to help you?"

"I will, by and by.—Now there is nobody talking to him. Go straight and do it, there's a good fellow."

A moment or two later the two sworn friends of the Pension bill were talking together, earnestly, and seemingly unconscious of the moving throng about them. They talked an hour, and then Mr. Buckstone came back and said:

"He hardly fancied it at first, but he fell in love with it after a bit. And we have made a compact, too. I am to keep his secret and he is to spare me, in future, when he gets ready to denounce the supporters of the University bill—and I can easily believe he will keep his word on this occasion."

A fortnight elapsed, and the University bill had gathered to itself many friends, meantime. Senator Dilworthy began to think the harvest was ripe. He conferred with Laura privately. She was able to tell him exactly how the House would vote. There was a majority—the bill would pass, unless weak members got frightened at the last, and deserted—a thing pretty likely to occur. The Senator said:

"I wish we had one more good strong man. Now Trollop ought to be on our side, for he is a friend of the negro. But he is against us, and is our bitterest opponent. If he would simply vote No, but keep quiet and not molest us, I would feel perfectly cheerful and content. But perhaps there is no use in thinking of that."

"Why I laid a little plan for his benefit two weeks ago. I think he will be tractable, maybe. He is to come here tonight."

"Look out for him, my child! He means mischief, sure. It is said that he claims to know of improper practices having been used in the interest of this bill, and he thinks he sees a chance to make a great sensation when the bill comes up. Be wary. Be very, very careful, my dear. Do your very ablest talking, now. You can convince a man of anything, when you try. You must convince him that if anything improper has been done, you at least are ignorant of it and sorry for it. And if you *could* only persuade him out of his hostility to the bill, too—but don't overdo the thing; don't seem too anxious, dear."

"I won't; I'll be ever so careful. I'll talk as sweetly to him as if he were my own child! You may trust me—indeed you may."

The door-bell rang.

"That is the gentleman now," said Laura. Senator Dilworthy retired to his study.

Laura welcomed Mr. Trollop, a grave, carefully dressed and very respectable looking man, with a bald head, standing collar and old-fashioned watch seals.

"Promptness is a virtue, Mr. Trollop, and I perceive that you have it. You are always prompt with me."

"I always meet my engagements, of every kind, Miss Hawkins."

"It is a quality which is rarer in the world than it has been, I believe. I wished to see you on business, Mr. Trollop."

"I judged so. What can I do for you?"

"You know my bill—the Knobs University bill?"

"Ah, I believe it *is* your bill. I had forgotten. Yes, I know the bill."

"Well, would you mind telling me your opinion of it?"

"Indeed, since you seem to ask it without reserve, I am obliged to say that I do not regard it favorably. I have not seen the bill itself, but from what I can hear, it—it—well, it has a bad look about it. It—"

"Speak it out—never fear."

"Well, it—they say it contemplates a fraud upon the government."

"Well?" said Laura tranquilly.

"Well! *I* say 'Well?' too."

"Well, suppose it *were* a fraud—which I feel able to deny— would it be the first one?"

"You take a body's breath away! Would you—did you wish me to vote for it? Was that what you wanted to see me about?"

"Your instinct is correct. I *did* want you—I *do* want you to vote for it."

"Vote for a fr—for a measure which is generally believed to be at least questionable? I am afraid we cannot come to an understanding, Miss Hawkins."

"No, I am afraid not—if you have resumed your principles, Mr. Trollop."

"Did you send for me merely to insult me? It is time for me to take my leave, Miss Hawkins."

"No—wait a moment. Don't be offended at a trifle. Do not be offish and unsociable. The Steamship Subsidy bill was a fraud on the government. You voted for it, Mr. Trollop, though you always opposed the measure until after you had an interview one evening with a certain Mrs. McCarter at her house. She was my agent. She was acting for me. Ah, that is right—sit down again.

You can be sociable, easily enough if you have a mind to. Well? I am waiting. Have you nothing to say?"

"Miss Hawkins, I voted for that bill because when I came to examine into it—"

"Ah yes. When you came to examine into it. Well, I only want you to examine into *my* bill. Mr. Trollop, you would not sell your vote on that subsidy bill—which was perfectly right—but you accepted of some of the stock, with the understanding that it was to stand in your brother-in-law's name."

"There is no pr—I mean, this is utterly groundless, Miss Hawkins." But the gentleman seemed somewhat uneasy, nevertheless.

"Well, not entirely so, perhaps. I and a person whom we will call Miss Blank (never mind the real name,) were in a closet at your elbow all the while."

Mr. Trollop winced—then he said with dignity:

"Miss Hawkins is it possible that you were capable of such a thing as that?"

"It was bad; I confess that. It *was* bad. Almost as bad as selling one's vote for—but I forget; you did not sell your vote—you only accepted a little trifle, a small token of esteem, for your brother-in-law. Oh, let us come out and be frank with each other. I know you, Mr. Trollop. I have met you on business three or four times; true, I never offered to corrupt your principles—never hinted such a thing; but always when I had finished sounding you, I manipulated you through an agent. Let us be frank. Wear this comely disguise of virtue before the public—it will count there; but here it is out of place. My dear sir, by and by there is going to be an investigation into that National Internal Improvement Directors' Relief Measure of a few years ago, and you know very well that you will be a crippled man, as likely as not, when it is completed."

"It cannot be shown that a man is a knave merely for owning that stock. I am not distressed about the National Improvement Relief Measure."

"Oh indeed I am not trying to distress you. I only wished to make good my assertion that I knew you. Several of you gentle-

men bought of that stock (without paying a penny down), received dividends from it, (think of the happy idea of receiving
dividends, and very large ones, too, from stock one hasn't paid
for!) and all the while your names never appeared in the transaction; if ever you took the stock at all, you took it in other
people's names. Now you see, you had to know one of two things;
namely, you either knew that the idea of all this preposterous
generosity was to bribe you into future legislative friendship, or
you *didn't* know it. That is to say, you had to be either a knave
or a—well, a fool—there was no middle ground. *You* are not a
fool, Mr. Trollop."

"Miss Hawkins you flatter me. But seriously, you do not forget
that some of the best and purest men in Congress took that
stock in that way?"

"Did Senator Blank?"

"Well, no—I believe not."

"Of course you believe not. Do you suppose he was ever
approached, on the subject?"

"Perhaps not."

"If *you* had approached him, for instance, fortified with the
fact that some of the best men in Congress, and the purest, etc.,
etc., what would have been the result?"

"Well, what *would* have been the result?"

"He would have shown you the door! For Mr. Blank is neither
a knave *nor* a fool. There are other men in the Senate and the
House whom no one would have been hardy enough to approach
with that Relief Stock in that peculiarly generous way, but they
are not of the class that *you* regard as the best and purest. No, I
say I know you Mr. Trollop. That is to say, one may suggest a
thing to Mr. Trollop which it would not do to suggest to Mr.
Blank. Mr. Trollop, you are pledged to support the Indigent
Congressmen's Retroactive Appropriation which is to come
up, either in this or the next session. You do not deny that,
even in public. The man that will vote for that bill will break the
eighth commandment in any *other* way, sir!"

"But he will not vote for *your* corrupt measure, nevertheless,

madam!" exclaimed Mr. Trollop, rising from his seat in a
passion.

"Ah, but he will. Sit down again, and let me explain why.
Oh, come, don't behave so. It is very unpleasant. Now be good,
and you shall have the missing page of your great speech. Here
it is!"—and she displayed a sheet of manuscript.

Mr. Trollop turned immediately back from the threshold. It
might have been gladness that flashed into his face; it might
have been something else; but at any rate there was much
astonishment mixed with it.

"Good! Where did you get it? Give it me!"

"Now there is no hurry. Sit down; sit down and let us talk and
be friendly."

The gentleman wavered. Then he said:

"No, this is only a subterfuge. I will go. It is not the missing
page."

Laura tore off a couple of lines from the bottom of the sheet.

"Now," she said, "you will know whether this is the handwriting or not. You know it *is* the handwriting. Now if you will
listen, you will know that this must be the list of statistics which
was to be the 'nub' of your great effort, and the accompanying
blast the beginning of the burst of eloquence which was continued on the next page—and you will recognize that there was
where you broke down."

She read the page. Mr. Trollop said:

"This is perfectly astounding. Still, what is all this to me? It
is nothing. It does not concern me. The speech is made, and
there an end. I *did* break down for a moment, and in a rather
uncomfortable place, since I had led up to those statistics with
some grandeur; the hiatus was pleasanter to the House and the
galleries than it was to me. But it is no matter now. A week has
passed; the jests about it ceased three or four days ago. The
whole thing is a matter of indifference to me, Miss Hawkins."

"But you apologized, and promised the statistics for next day.
Why didn't you keep your promise?"

"The matter was not of sufficient consequence. The time was gone by to produce an effect with them."

"But I hear that other friends of the Soldiers' Pension Bill desire them very much. I think you ought to let them have them."

"Miss Hawkins, this silly blunder of my copyist evidently has more interest for you than it has for me. I will send my private secretary to you and let him discuss the subject with you at length."

"Did he copy your speech for you?"

"Of course he did. Why all these questions? Tell me—how did you get hold of that page of manuscript? *That* is the only thing that stirs a passing interest in my mind."

"I'm coming to that." Then she said, much as if she were talking to herself: "It does seem like taking a deal of unnecessary pains, for a body to hire another body to construct a great speech for him and then go and get still another body to copy it before it can be read in the House."

"Miss Hawkins, what do you mean by such talk as that?"

"Why I am sure I mean no harm—no harm to anybody in the world. I am certain that I overheard the Hon. Mr. Buckstone either promise to write your great speech for you or else get some other competent person to do it."

"This is perfectly absurd, madam, perfectly absurd!" and Mr. Trollop affected a laugh of derision.

"Why, the thing has occurred before now. I mean that I have heard that Congressmen have sometimes hired literary grubs to build speeches for them. Now didn't I overhear a conversation like that I spoke of?"

"Pshaw! Why of course you may have overheard some such jesting nonsense. But would one be in earnest about so farcical a thing?"

"Well if it was only a joke, why did you make a serious matter of it? Why did you get the speech written for you, and then read it in the House without ever having it copied?"

Mr. Trollop did not laugh, this time; he seemed seriously perplexed. He said:

"Come, play out your jest, Miss Hawkins. I can't understand what you are contriving—but it seems to entertain you—so please go on."

"I will, I assure you; but I hope to make the matter entertaining to you, too. Your private secretary never copied your speech."

"Indeed? Really you seem to know my affairs better than I do myself."

"I believe I do. You can't name your own amanuensis, Mr. Trollop."

"That is sad, indeed. Perhaps Miss Hawkins can?"

"Yes, I *can*. I wrote your speech myself, and you read it from my manuscript. There, now!"

Mr. Trollop did not spring to his feet and smite his brow with his hand while a cold sweat broke out all over him and the color forsook his face—no, he only said, "Good God!" and looked greatly astonished.

Laura handed him her commonplace-book and called his attention to the fact that the handwriting there and the handwriting of this speech were the same. He was shortly convinced. He laid the book aside and said, composedly:

"Well, the wonderful tragedy is done, and it transpires that I am indebted to you for my late eloquence. What of it? What was all this for, and what does it amount to, after all? What do you propose to do about it?"

"Oh nothing. It is only a bit of pleasantry. When I overheard that conversation I took an early opportunity to ask Mr. Buckstone if he knew of anybody who might want a speech written—I had a friend, and so forth and so on. *I* was the friend, myself; I thought I might do you a good turn then and depend on you to do me one by and by. I never let Mr. Buckstone have the speech till the last moment, and when you hurried off to the House with it, you did not know there was a missing page, of course, but I did."

"And now perhaps you think that if I refuse to support your bill, you will make a grand exposure?"

"Well I had not thought of that. I only kept back the page for the mere fun of the thing; but since you mention it, I don't know but I might do something if I were angry."

"My dear Miss Hawkins, if you were to give out that you composed my speech, you know very well that people would say it was only your raillery, your fondness for putting a victim in the pillory and amusing the public at his expense. It is too flimsy, Miss Hawkins, for a person of your fine inventive talent—contrive an abler device than that. Come!"

"It is easily done, Mr. Trollop. I will hire a man, and pin this page on his breast, and label it, 'The Missing Fragment of the Hon. Mr. Trollop's Great Speech—which speech was written and composed by Miss Laura Hawkins under a secret understanding for one hundred dollars—and the money has not been paid.' And I will pin round about it notes in my handwriting, which I will procure from prominent friends of mine for the occasion; also your printed speech in the *Globe*, showing the connection between its bracketed hiatus and my Fragment; and I give you my word of honor that I will stand that human bulletin board in the rotunda of the capitol and make him stay there a week! You see you are premature, Mr. Trollop, the wonderful tragedy is not done yet, by any means. Come, now, doesn't it improve?"

Mr. Trollop opened his eyes rather widely at this novel aspect of the case. He got up and walked the floor and gave himself a moment for reflection. Then he stopped and studied Laura's face a while, and ended by saying:

"Well, I am obliged to believe you *would* be reckless enough to do that."

"Then don't put me to the test, Mr. Trollop. But let's drop the matter. I have had my joke and you've borne the infliction becomingly enough. It spoils a jest to harp on it after one has had one's laugh. I would much rather talk about my bill."

"So would I, now, my clandestine amanuensis. Compared with some other subjects, even your bill is a pleasant topic to discuss."

"Very good indeed! I thought I could persuade you. Now I am

sure you will be generous to the poor negro and vote for that
bill."

"Yes, I feel more tenderly toward the oppressed colored man
than I did. Shall we bury the hatchet and be good friends and
respect each other's little secrets, on condition that I vote Aye
on the measure?"

"With all my heart, Mr. Trollop. I give you my word of that."

"It is a bargain. But isn't there something else you could give
me, too?"

Laura looked at him inquiringly a moment, and then she comprehended.

"Oh, yes! You may have it now. I haven't any more use for
it." She picked up the page of manuscript, but she reconsidered
her intention of handing it to him, and said, "But never mind; I
will keep it close; no one shall see it; you shall have it as soon
as your vote is recorded."

Mr. Trollop looked disappointed. But presently made his
adieu, and had got as far as the hall, when something occurred
to Laura. She said to herself, "I don't simply want his vote,
under compulsion—he might vote aye, but work against the bill
in secret, for revenge; that man is unscrupulous enough to do
anything. I must have his hearty co-operation as well as his
vote. There is only one way to get that."

She called him back, and said:

"I value your vote, Mr. Trollop, but I value your influence
more. You are able to help a measure along in many ways, if
you choose.—I want to ask you to work for the bill as well as
vote for it."

"It takes so much of one's time, Miss Hawkins—and time is
money, you know."

"Yes, I know it is—especially in Congress. Now there is no use
in you and I dealing in pretenses and going at matters in round-
about ways. We know each other—disguises are nonsense. Let
us be plain. I will make it an object to you to work for the
bill."

"Don't make it unnecessarily plain, please. There are little proprieties that are best preserved. What do you propose?"

"Well, this." She mentioned the names of several prominent Congressmen. "Now," said she, "these gentlemen are to vote and work for the bill, simply out of love for the negro—and out of pure generosity I have put in a relative of each as a member of the University incorporation. They will handle a million or so of money, officially, but will receive no salaries.—A larger number of statesmen are to vote and work for the bill—also out of love for the negro—gentlemen of but moderate influence, these—and out of pure generosity I am to see that relatives of theirs have positions in the University, *with* salaries, and good ones, too. You will vote and work for the bill, from mere affection for the negro, and I desire to testify my gratitude becomingly. Make free choice. Have you any friend whom you would like to present with a salaried or unsalaried position in our institution?"

"Well, I have a brother-in-law—"

"That same old brother-in-law, you good unselfish provider! I have heard of him often, through my agents. How regularly he does 'turn up,' to be sure. He could deal with those millions virtuously, and withal with ability, too—but of course you would rather he had a salaried position?"

"Oh, no," said the gentleman, facetiously, "we are very humble, very humble in our desires; we want no money; we labor solely for our country and require no reward but the luxury of an applauding conscience. Make him one of those poor hard working unsalaried corporators and let him do every body good with those millions—and go hungry himself! I will try to exert a little influence in favor of the bill."

Arrived at home, Mr. Trollop sat down and thought it all over—something after this fashion: it is about the shape it might have taken if he had spoken it aloud.

"My reputation is getting a little damaged, and I meant to clear it up brilliantly with an exposure of this bill at the supreme moment, and ride back into Congress on the éclat of it; and if I had that bit of manuscript, I would do it yet. It would be more money in my pocket, in the end, than my brother-in-law will get out of that incorporatorship, fat as it is. But that sheet of paper is out of my reach—she will never let that get out of her hands. And what a mountain it is! It blocks up *my* road, completely. She was going to hand it to me, once. Why *didn't* she! Must be a deep woman. Deep devil! That is what she is; a beautiful devil—and perfectly fearless, too. The idea of her pinning that paper on a man and standing him up in the rotunda looks absurd at a first glance. But she would do it! She is capable of doing anything. I went there hoping she would try to bribe me—good solid capital that would be in the exposure. Well, my prayer was answered; she did try to bribe me; and I made the best of a bad bargain and let her. I am check-mated. I must contrive something fresh to get back to Congress on. Very well; a bird in the hand is worth two in the bush; I will work for the bill—the incorporatorship will be a very good thing."

As soon as Mr. Trollop had taken his leave, Laura ran to Senator Dilworthy and began to speak, but he interrupted her and said distressfully, without even turning from his writing to look at her:

"Only half an hour! You gave it up early, child. However, it was best, it was best—I'm sure it was best—and safest."

"Give it up! *I!*"

The Senator sprang up, all aglow:

"My child, you can't mean that you—"

"I've made him promise on honor to think about a compromise to-night and come and tell me his decision in the morning."

"Good! There's hope yet that—"

"Nonsense, uncle. I've made him engage to let the Tennessee Land bill utterly alone!"

"*Impossible!* You—"

"I've made him promise to vote with us!"

"INCREDIBLE! Abso—"

"I've made him swear that he'll *work* for us!"

"PRE---POSTEROUS!—Utterly pre—break a window, child, before I suffocate!"

"No matter, it's true anyway. Now we can march into Congress with drums beating and colors flying!"

"Well—well—well. I'm sadly bewildered, sadly bewildered. I can't understand it at all—the most extraordinary woman that ever—it's a great day, it's a great day. There—there—let me put my hand in benediction on this precious head. Ah, my child, the poor negro will bless—"

"Oh bother the poor negro, uncle! Put it in your speech. Good-night, good-bye—we'll marshal our forces and march with the dawn!"

Laura reflected a while, when she was alone, and then fell to laughing, peacefully.

"Everybody works for me,"—so ran her thought. "It was a good idea to make Buckstone lead Mr. Trollop on to get a great speech written for him; and it was a happy part of the same idea for me to copy the speech after Mr. Buckstone had written it, and then keep back a page. Mr. B. was very complimentary to me when Trollop's break-down in the House showed him the *object* of my mysterious scheme; I think he will say still finer things when I tell him the triumph the sequel to it has gained for us.

"But what a coward the man was, to believe I would have exposed that page in the rotunda, and so exposed myself. However, I don't know—I don't know. I will think a moment. Suppose he voted no; suppose the bill failed; that is to suppose this stupendous game lost forever, that I have played so desperately for; suppose people came around pitying me—odious! And he could have saved me by his single voice. Yes, I *would* have exposed him! What would I care for the talk that that would have made about me when I was gone to Europe with Selby and all the world was busy with my history and my dishonor? It would be almost happiness to spite somebody at such a time."

## CHAPTER 25

The very next day, sure enough, the campaign opened. In due course, the Speaker of the House reached that Order of Business which is termed "Notices of Bills," and then the Hon. Mr. Buckstone rose in his place and gave notice of a bill "To Found and Incorporate the Knobs Industrial University," and then sat down without saying anything further. The busy gentlemen in the reporters' gallery jotted a line in their note-books, ran to the telegraphic desk in a room which communicated with their own writing-parlor, and then hurried back to their places in the gallery; and by the time they had resumed their seats, the line which they had delivered to the operator had been read in telegraphic offices in towns and cities hundreds of miles away. It was distinguished by frankness of language as well as by brevity:

"The child is born. Buckstone gives notice of the thieving Knobs University job. It is said the noses have been counted and enough votes have been bought to pass it."

For some time the correspondents had been posting their several journals upon the alleged disreputable nature of the bill, and furnishing daily reports of the Washington gossip concerning it. So the next morning, nearly every newspaper of character in the land assailed the measure and hurled broadsides of invective at Mr. Buckstone. The Washington papers were more respectful, as usual—and conciliatory, also, as usual. They generally supported measures, when it was possible; but when they could not they "deprecated" violent expressions of opinion in other journalistic quarters. They always deprecated, when there was trouble ahead.

However, *The Washington Daily Love-Feast* hailed the bill

with warm approbation. This was Senator Balaam's paper—or rather, "Brother" Balaam, as he was popularly called, for he had been a clergyman, in his day; and he himself and all that he did still emitted an odor of sanctity now that he had diverged into journalism and politics. He was a power in the Congressional prayer meeting, and in all movements that looked to the spread of religion and temperance. His paper supported the new bill with gushing affection; it was a noble measure; it was a just measure; it was a generous measure; it was a pure measure, and that surely should recommend it in these corrupt times; and finally, if the nature of the bill were not known at all, the *Love-Feast* would support it anyway, and unhesitatingly, for the fact that Senator Dilworthy was the originator of the measure was a guaranty that it contemplated a worthy and righteous work.

Senator Dilworthy was so anxious to know what the New York papers would say about the bill, that he had arranged to have synopses of their editorials telegraphed to him; he could not wait for the papers themselves to crawl along down to Washington by a mail train which has never run over a cow since the road was built, for the reason that it has never been able to overtake one. It carries the usual "cow-catcher" in front of the locomotive, but this is mere ostentation. It ought to be attached to the rear car, where it could do some good; but instead, no provision is made there for the protection of the traveling public, and hence it is not a matter of surprise that cows so frequently climb aboard that train and among the passengers.

The Senator read his dispatches aloud at the breakfast table. Laura was troubled beyond measure at their tone, and said that that sort of comment would defeat the bill; but the Senator said:

"Oh, not at all, not at all, my child. It is just what we want. Persecution is the one thing needful, now—all the other forces are secured. Give us newspaper persecution enough, and we are safe. Vigorous persecution will alone carry a bill sometimes, dear; and when you start with a strong vote in the first place, persecution comes in with double effect. It scares off some of the weak supporters, true, but it soon turns strong ones into stubborn ones.

And then, presently, it changes the tide of public opinion. The great public is weak-minded; the great public is sentimental; the great public always turns around and weeps for an odious murderer, and prays for him, and carries flowers to his prison and besieges the governor with appeals to his clemency, as soon as the papers begin to howl for that man's blood.—In a word, the great putty-hearted public loves to 'gush,' and there is no such darling opportunity to gush as a case of persecution affords."

"Well, uncle, dear, if your theory is right, let us go into raptures, for nobody can ask a heartier persecution than these editorials are furnishing."

"I am not so sure of that, my daughter. I don't entirely like the tone of some of these remarks. They lack vim, they lack venom. Here is one calls it a 'questionable measure.' Bah, there is no strength in that. This one is better; it calls it 'highway robbery.' That sounds something like. But now this one seems satisfied to call it an 'iniquitous scheme!'—'Iniquitous' does not exasperate anybody; it is weak—puerile. The ignorant will imagine it to be intended for a compliment. But this other one—the one I read last—has the true ring: 'This vile, dirty effort to rob the public treasury, by the kites and vultures that now infest the filthy den called Congress'—that is admirable, admirable! We must have more of that sort. But it will come—no fear of that; they're not warmed up, yet. A week from now you'll see."

"Uncle, you and Brother Balaam are bosom friends—why don't you get his paper to persecute us, too?"

"It isn't worth while, my daughter. His support doesn't hurt a bill. Nobody reads his editorials but himself. But I wish the New York papers would talk a little plainer. It is annoying to have to wait a week for them to warm up. I expected better things at their hands—and time is precious, now."

At the proper hours, according to his previous notice, Mr. Buckstone duly introduced his bill entitled "An Act to Found and Incorporate the Knobs Industrial University," moved its proper reference, and sat down.

The Speaker of the House rattled off this observation:

" 'Fnobjectionbilltakuzhlcourssoreferred!"

Habitués of the House comprehended that this long, lightning-heeled word signified that if there was no objection, the bill would take the customary course of a measure of its nature, and be referred to the Committee on Benevolent Appropriations, and that it was accordingly so referred. Strangers merely supposed that the Speaker was taking a gargle for some affection of the throat.

The reporters immediately telegraphed the introduction of the bill.—And they added:

"The assertion that the bill will pass was premature. It is said that many favorers of it will desert when the storm breaks upon them from the public press."

The storm came, and during ten days it waxed more and more violent day by day. The great "Negro University Swindle" became the one absorbing topic of conversation throughout the Union. Individuals denounced it, journals denounced it, public meetings denounced it, the pictorial papers caricatured its friends, the whole nation seemed to be growing frantic over it. Meantime the Washington correspondents were sending such telegrams as these abroad in the land: Under date of—

SATURDAY. "Congressmen Jex and Fluke are wavering; it is believed they will desert the execrable bill."
MONDAY. "Jex and Fluke *have* deserted!"
THURSDAY. "Tubbs and Huffy left the sinking ship last night."

Later on:

"Three desertions. The University thieves are getting scared, though they will not own it."

Later:

"The leaders are growing stubborn—they swear they can carry it, but it is now almost certain that they no longer have a majority!"

After a day or two of reluctant and ambiguous telegrams:

"Public sentiment seems changing, a trifle, in favor of the bill—but only a trifle."

And still later:

"It is whispered that the Hon. Mr. Trollop has gone over to the pirates. It is probably a canard. Mr. Trollop has all along been the bravest and most efficient champion of virtue and the people against the bill, and the report is without doubt a shameless invention."

Next day:

"With characteristic treachery, the truckling and pusillanimous reptile, Crippled-Speech Trollop, has gone over to the enemy. It is contended, now, that *he has been a friend to the bill, in secret, since the day it was introduced,* and has had bankable reasons for being so; but he himself declares that he has gone over because the malignant persecution of the bill by the newspapers caused him to study its provisions with more care than he had previously done, and this close examination revealed the fact that the measure is one in every way worthy of support. (Pretty thin!) It cannot be denied that this desertion has had a damaging effect. Jex and Fluke have returned to their iniquitous allegiance, with six or eight others of lesser calibre, and it is reported and believed that Tubbs and Huffy are ready to go back. It is feared that the University swindle is stronger to-day than it has ever been before."

Later—midnight:

"It is said that the committee will report the bill back to-morrow. Both sides are marshaling their forces, and the fight on this bill is evidently going to be the hottest of the session.—All Washington is boiling."

[Philip, in Washington to help Harry, found Harry despondent. Philip soon learned that Laura's intimacy with Selby was open gossip. Laura received Philip cordially and told him that Harry's love for her was a hopeless one. She asked him to tell Harry to stay away. Philip told Harry about the conversation and Harry "made up his own mind that Philip didn't know much about women." As for Laura, she determined that if Selby was deceiving her again it would be the last time. When she accused Selby of intending to abandon her he denied the charge, swearing that as soon as she succeeded with her university bill he would go with her wherever she wished.]

## CHAPTER 26

The galleries of the House were packed, on the momentous day, not because the reporting of an important bill back by a committee was a thing to be excited about, if the bill were going to take the ordinary course afterward; it would be like getting excited over the empaneling of a coroner's jury in a murder case, instead of saving up one's emotions for the grander occasion of the hanging of the accused, two years later, after all the tedious forms of law had been gone through with.

But suppose you understand that this coroner's jury is going to turn out to be a vigilance committee in disguise, who will hear testimony for an hour and then hang the murderer on the spot? That puts a different aspect upon the matter. Now it was whispered that the legitimate forms of procedure usual in the House, and which keep a bill hanging along for days and even weeks, before it is finally passed upon, were going to be overruled, in this case, and short work made of the measure; and so, what was beginning as a mere inquest might turn out to be something very different.

In the course of the day's business the Order of "Reports of Committees" was finally reached and when the weary crowds heard that glad announcement issue from the Speaker's lips they ceased to fret at the dragging delay, and plucked up spirit. The Chairman of the Committee on Benevolent Appropriations rose and made his report, and just then a blue-uniformed brass-mounted little page put a note into his hand. It was from Senator Dilworthy, who had appeared upon the floor of the House for a moment and flitted away again:

"Everybody expects a grand assault in force; no doubt you believe, as I certainly do, that it is the thing to do; we are strong, and everything is hot for the contest. Trollop's espousal of our cause has immensely helped us and we grow in power constantly. Ten of the opposition were called away from town about noon (*but*—so it is said—*only for one day*). Six others are sick, but expect to be about again *to-morrow or next day*, a friend tells me. A bold onslaught is worth trying. Go for a suspension of the rules! You will find we can swing a two-thirds vote—I am perfectly satisfied of it. The Lord's truth will prevail.

"DILWORTHY."

Mr. Buckstone had reported the bills from his committee, one by one, leaving *the* bill to the last. When the House had voted upon the acceptance or rejection of the report upon all but it, and the question now being upon *its* disposal—

Mr. Buckstone begged that the House would give its attention to a few remarks which he desired to make. His committee had instructed him to report the bill favorably; he wished to explain the nature of the measure, and thus justify the committee's action; the hostility roused by the press would then disappear, and the bill would shine forth in its true and noble character. He said that its provisions were simple. It incorporated the Knobs Industrial University, locating it in East Tennessee, declaring it open to all persons without distinction of sex, color or religion, and committing its management to a board of perpetual trustees, with power to fill vacancies in their own number. It provided for the erection of certain buildings for the University, dormitories, lecture-halls, museums, libraries, laboratories, work-shops, furnaces, and mills. It provided also for the purchase of sixty-five thousand acres of land, (fully described) for the purposes of the University, in the Knobs of East Tennessee. And it appropriated [blank] dollars for the purchase of the Land, which should be the property of the national trustees in trust for the uses named.

Every effort had been made to secure the refusal of the whole amount of the property of the Hawkins heirs in the Knobs, some seventy-five thousand acres, Mr. Buckstone said. But Mr.

Washington Hawkins (one of the heirs) objected. He was, indeed, very reluctant to sell any part of the land at any price; and indeed this reluctance was justifiable when one considers how constantly and how greatly the property is rising in value.

What the South needed, continued Mr. Buckstone, was skilled labor. Without that it would be unable to develop its mines, build its roads, work to advantage and without great waste its fruitful land, establish manufactures or enter upon a prosperous industrial career. Its laborers were almost altogether unskilled. Change them into intelligent, trained workmen, and you increased at once the capital, the resources of the entire south, which would enter upon a prosperity hitherto unknown. In five years the increase in local wealth would not only reimburse the government for the outlay in this appropriation, but pour untold wealth into the treasury.

This was the material view, and the least important in the honorable gentleman's opinion. [Here he referred to some notes furnished him by Senator Dilworthy, and then continued.] God had given us the care of these colored millions. What account should we render to Him of our stewardship? We had made them free. Should we leave them ignorant? We had cast them upon their own resources. Should we leave them without tools? We could not tell what the intentions of Providence are in regard to these peculiar people, but our duty was plain. The Knobs Industrial University would be a vast school of modern science and practice, worthy of a great nation. It would combine the advantages of Zurich, Freiburg, Creuzot and the Sheffield Scientific. Providence had apparently reserved and set apart the Knobs of East Tennessee for this purpose. What else were they for? Was it not wonderful that for more than thirty years, over a generation, the choicest portion of them had remained in one family, untouched, as if consecrated for some great use!

It might be asked why the government should buy this land, when it had millions of acres, more than the railroad companies desired, which it might devote to this purpose? He answered, that the government had no such tract of land as this. It had nothing comparable to it for the purposes of the University. This was to be a school of mining, of engineering, of the working of metals, of chemistry, zoology, botany, manufactures, agriculture, in short of all the complicated industries that make a state great. There was no place for the location of such a school like the Knobs of East Tennessee. The hills abounded in metals of all sorts, iron in all its combinations, copper, bismuth, gold and silver in small quantities, platinum he believed, tin, aluminium; it was covered with forests and strange plants; in the woods were found the coon, the opossum, the fox, the deer and many other animals who roamed in the domain of natural history; coal existed in enormous quantity and no doubt oil; it was such a place for the practice of agricultural experiments that any student who had been successful there would have an easy task in any other portion of the country.

No place offered equal facilities for experiments in mining, metallurgy, engineering. He expected to live to see the day when the youth of the south would resort to its mines, its workshops, its laboratories, its furnaces and factories for practical instruction in all the great industrial pursuits.

A noisy and rather ill-natured debate followed, now, and lasted hour after hour. The friends of the bill were instructed by the leaders to *make no effort to check this;* it was deemed better strategy to tire out the opposition; it was decided to vote down every proposition to adjourn, and so continue the sitting into the night; opponents might desert, then, one by one and weaken their party, for they had no personal stake in the bill.

Sunset came, and still the fight went on; the gas was lit, the crowd in the galleries began to thin, but the contest continued; the crowd returned, by and by, with hunger and thirst appeased, and aggravated the hungry and thirsty House by looking contented and comfortable; but still the wrangle lost nothing of its bitterness. Recesses were moved plaintively by the opposition, and invariably voted down by the University army.

At midnight the House presented a spectacle calculated to interest a stranger. The great galleries were still thronged—though only with men, now; the bright colors that had made them look like hanging gardens were gone, with the ladies. The reporters' gallery was merely occupied by one or two watchful sentinels of the quill-driving guild; the main body cared nothing for a debate that had dwindled to a mere vaporing of dull speakers and now and then a brief quarrel over a point of order; but there was an unusually large attendance of journalists in the reporters' waiting-room, chatting, smoking, and keeping on the *qui vive* for the general irruption of the Congressional volcano that must come when the time was ripe for it. Senator Dilworthy and Philip were in the Diplomatic Gallery; Washington sat in the public gallery, and Col. Sellers was not far away. The Colonel had been flying about the corridors and button-holing Congressmen all the evening, and believed that he had accomplished a world of valuable service; but fatigue was telling upon him, now, and he was quiet and speechless—for once. Below, a few Senators lounged upon the sofas set apart for visitors, and talked with idle Congressmen. A dreary member was speaking; the presiding officer was nodding; here and there little knots of members stood in the aisles, whispering together; all about the House others sat in all the various attitudes that express weariness; some, tilted back, had one or more legs disposed upon their desks; some sharpened pencils indolently; some scribbled aimlessly; some yawned and stretched; a great many lay upon their breasts upon the desks, sound asleep and gently snoring. The flooding gaslight from the fancifully wrought roof poured down upon the tranquil scene. Hardly a sound disturbed the stillness, save the monotonous eloquence of the gentleman who occupied the floor. Now and then a warrior of the opposition broke down under the pressure, gave it up and went home.

Mr. Buckstone began to think it might be safe, now, to "proceed to business." He consulted with Trollop and one or two others. Senator Dilworthy descended to the floor of the House and they went to meet him. After a brief comparison of notes, the Congressmen sought their seats and sent pages about the House with messages to friends. These latter instantly roused

up, yawned, and began to look alert. The moment the floor was
unoccupied, Mr. Buckstone rose, with an injured look, and said
it was evident that the opponents of the bill were merely talking
against time, hoping in this unbecoming way to tire out the
friends of the measure and so defeat it. Such conduct might be
respectable enough in a village debating society, but it was trivial among statesmen, it was out of place in so august an assemblage as the House of Representatives of the United States. The
friends of the bill had been not only willing that its opponents
should express their opinions, but had strongly desired it. They
courted the fullest and freest discussion; but it seemed to him
that this fairness was but illy appreciated, since gentlemen were
capable of taking advantage of it for selfish and unworthy ends.
This trifling had gone far enough. He called for the question.

The instant Mr. Buckstone sat down, the storm burst forth.
A dozen gentlemen sprang to their feet.

"Mr. Speaker!"

"Mr. Speaker!"

"Mr. Speaker!"

"Order! Order! Order! Question! Question!"

The sharp blows of the Speaker's gavel rose above the din.

The "previous question," that hated gag, was moved and carried. All debate came to a sudden end, of course. Triumph No. 1.

Then the vote was taken on the adoption of the report and it
carried by a surprising majority.

Mr. Buckstone got the floor again and moved that the rules
be suspended and the bill read a first time.

*Mr. Trollop*—"Second the motion!"

*The Speaker*—"It is moved and—"

*Clamor of Voices.* "Move we adjourn! Second the motion! Adjourn! Adjourn! Order! Order!"

*The Speaker*, (after using his gavel vigorously)—"It is moved
and seconded that the House do now adjourn. All those in favor—"

*Voices*—"Division! Division! Ayes and nays! Ayes and nays!"

It was decided to vote upon the adjournment by ayes and

nays. This was war in earnest. The excitement was furious. The galleries were in commotion in an instant, the reporters swarmed to their places, idling members of the House flocked to their seats, nervous gentlemen sprang to their feet, pages flew hither and thither, life and animation were visible everywhere, all the long ranks of faces in the building were kindled.

"This thing decides it!" thought Mr. Buckstone; "but let the fight proceed."

The voting began, and every sound ceased but the calling of the names and the "Aye!" "No!" "No!" "Aye!" of the responses. There was not a movement in the House; the people seemed to hold their breath.

The voting ceased, and then there was an interval of dead silence while the clerk made up his count. There was a two-thirds vote on the University side—and two over!

*The Speaker*—"The rules are suspended, the motion is carried—first reading of the *bill!*"

By one impulse the galleries broke forth into stormy applause, and even some of the members of the House were not wholly able to restrain their feelings. The Speaker's gavel came to the rescue and his clear voice followed:

"Order, gentlemen! The House will come to order! If spectators offend again, the Sergeant-at-Arms will clear the galleries!"

Then he cast his eyes aloft and gazed at some object attentively for a moment. All eyes followed the direction of the Speaker's, and then there was a general titter. The Speaker said:

"Let the Sergeant-at-Arms inform the gentleman that his conduct is an infringement of the dignity of the House—and one which is not warranted by the state of the weather."

Poor Sellers was the culprit. He sat in the front seat of the gallery, with his arms and his tired body overflowing the balustrade—sound asleep, dead to all excitements, all disturbances. The fluctuations of the Washington weather had influenced his dreams, perhaps, for during the recent tempest of applause he had hoisted his gingham umbrella and calmly gone on with his slumbers. Washington Hawkins had seen the act, but was not near enough at hand to save his friend, and no one who was near enough desired to spoil the effect. But a neighbor stirred up the Colonel, now that the House had its eye upon him, and the great speculator furled his tent like the Arab. He said:

"Bless my soul, I'm so absent-minded when I get to thinking! I never wear an umbrella in the house—did anybody notice it? What—asleep? Indeed? And did you wake me sir? Thank you —thank you very much indeed. It might have fallen out of my hands and been injured. Admirable article, sir—present from a friend in Hong Kong; one doesn't come across silk like that in this country—it's the real Young Hyson, I'm told."

By this time the incident was forgotten, for the House was at war again. Victory was almost in sight, now, and the friends of the bill threw themselves into their work with enthusiasm. They soon moved and carried its second reading, and after a strong, sharp fight, carried a motion to go into Committee of the whole. The Speaker left his place, of course, and a chairman was appointed.

Now the contest raged hotter than ever—for the authority that compels order when the House sits *as* a House, is greatly diminished when it sits as a Committee. The main fight came upon the filling of the blanks with the sum to be appropriated for the purchase of the land, of course.

*Mr. Buckstone*—"Mr. Chairman, I move you, sir, that the words *three millions of* be inserted."

*Mr. Hadley*—"Mr. Chairman, I move that the words *two and a half dollars* be inserted."

*Mr. Clawson*—"Mr. Chairman, I move the insertion of the words *five and twenty cents,* as representing the true value of this barren and isolated tract of desolation."

The question, according to rule, was taken upon the smallest sum first. It was lost.

Then upon the next smallest sum. Lost, also.

And then upon the three millions. After a vigorous battle that lasted a considerable time, this motion was carried.

Then, clause by clause the bill was read, discussed, and

amended in trifling particulars, and now the Committee rose and reported.

The moment the House had resumed its functions and received the report, Mr. Buckstone moved and carried the third reading of the bill.

The same bitter war over the sum to be paid was fought over again, and now that the ayes and nays could be called and placed on record, every man was compelled to vote by name on the three millions, and indeed on every paragraph of the bill from the enacting clause straight through. But as before, the friends of the measure stood firm and voted in a solid body every time, and so did its enemies.

The supreme moment was come, now, but so sure was the result that not even a voice was raised to interpose an adjournment. The enemy were totally demoralized. The bill was put upon its final passage almost without dissent, and the calling of the ayes and nays began. When it was ended the triumph was complete—the two-thirds vote held good, and a veto was impossible, as far as the House was concerned!

Mr. Buckstone resolved that now that the nail was driven home, he would clinch it on the other side and make it stay forever. He moved a reconsideration of the vote by which the bill had passed. The motion was lost, of course, and the great Industrial University act was an accomplished fact as far as it was in the power of the House of Representatives to make it so.

There was no need to move an adjournment. The instant the last motion was decided, the enemies of the University rose and flocked out of the Hall, talking angrily, and its friends flocked after them jubilant and congratulatory. The galleries disgorged their burden, and presently the House was silent and deserted.

When Col. Sellers and Washington stepped out of the building they were surprised to find that the daylight was old and the sun well up. Said the Colonel:

"Give me your hand, my boy! You're all right at last! You're a millionaire! At least you're going to be. The thing is dead sure. Don't you bother about the Senate. Leave me and Dilworthy to take care of that. Run along home, now, and tell Laura. Lord, it's magnificent news—perfectly magnificent! Run, now. I'll telegraph my wife. She must come here and help me build a house. Everything's all right now!"

Washington was so dazed by his good fortune and so bewildered by the gaudy pageant of dreams that was already trailing its long ranks through his brain, that he wandered he knew not where, and so loitered by the way that when at last he reached home he woke to a sudden annoyance in the fact that his news must be old to Laura, now, for of course Senator Dilworthy must have already been home and told her an hour before. He knocked at her door, but there was no answer.

"That is like the Duchess," said he. "Always cool. A body can't excite her—can't keep her excited, anyway. Now she has gone off to sleep again, as comfortably as if she were used to picking up a million dollars every day or two."

Then he went to bed. But he could not sleep; so he got up and wrote a long, rapturous letter to Louise, and another to his mother. And he closed both to much the same effect:

"Laura will be queen of America, now, and she will be applauded, and honored and petted by the whole nation. Her name will be in every one's mouth more than ever, and how they will court her and quote her bright speeches. And mine, too, I suppose; though they do that more already, than they really seem to deserve. Oh, the world is so bright, now, and so cheery; the clouds are all gone, our long struggle is ended, our troubles are all over. Nothing can ever make us unhappy any more. You dear faithful ones will have the reward of your patient waiting now. How father's wisdom is proven at last! And how I repent me, that there have been times when I lost faith and said the blessing he stored up for us a tedious generation ago was but a long-drawn curse, a blight upon us all. But everything is well, now—we are done with poverty, and toil, weariness and heart-breakings; all the world is filled with sunshine."

[Philip and Senator Dilworthy left the Capitol and walked up Pennsylvania Avenue. The Senator enjoyed the tranquil morning after the excitement of an all-night session. The Tennessee Land measure still had to receive the Senate's approval but the Senator felt sure of victory. At the Senator's home the two men discovered that Laura was gone and that she had not spent the night there. The Senator doubted that she had run away with Selby, for he had heard from a reliable source that Selby and his family had gone to New York yesterday morning and were to sail for Europe to-day. Philip hurried to Harry's lodgings, where he learned that Harry had gone to New York the previous day. On a table in Harry's room Philip found a note. "Dear Mr. Brierly:—Can you meet me at the six o'clock train, and be my escort to New York? I have to go about this University bill, the vote of an absent member we must have here. Senator Dilworthy cannot go. Yours &c., L. H."

Philip wrote a note to the Senator, telling him what he had learned and saying that he was hastening to New York. On the ferry boat from Jersey City to New York he read in an evening paper about the murder of Col. George Selby by Miss Laura Hawkins. At nine o'clock that morning she had accosted Selby in the lobby of the Southern Hotel and had said, "George, will you come with me?" Throwing his hand up and retreating, he had replied, "My God! I can't. Don't fire." She had shot him twice. Selby had lived for about an hour, during which he had declared that she was a Washington lobbyist, and had accused her of trying to make him desert his wife and go to Europe with her. He said that when he had avoided her she had threatened him. Her companion, Mr. Harry Brierly, "a New York dandy," had been taken into custody as a witness.

Philip went to the city prison, where Laura and Harry had been taken, but he was not admitted. The evening papers and the next morning's papers were full of the murder. It was reported that Laura, when asked why she had shot Col. Selby, had replied, "Did I shoot him? Do they say I shot him?" but would say no more. Philip, with the help of Harry's uncle, managed to get Harry released. Col. Sellers and Washington Hawkins arrived in New York and were moved by Laura's condition. Senator Dilworthy, although shocked, was full of charity for Laura and promised help. Laura's mother went to New York and lived near the prison. Her devotion to Laura was reported in the papers and helped Laura's cause. Laura declined to see either Philip or Harry. She was indicted for first-degree murder and held for trial in the summer term. The two most distinguished criminal lawyers in the city were retained to defend her. Meanwhile Congress had adjourned without Laura's bill being approved by the Senate. The bill would have to wait for the next session, a fact which greatly depressed her.]

## CHAPTER 27

December, 18—, found Washington Hawkins and Col. Sellers once more at the capitol of the nation, standing guard over the University bill. The former gentleman was despondent, the latter hopeful. Washington's distress of mind was chiefly on Laura's account. The court would soon sit to try her case, he said, and consequently a great deal of ready money would be needed in the engineering of it. The University bill was sure to pass, this time, and that would make money plenty, but might not the help come too late? Congress had only just assembled, and delays were to be feared.

"Well," said the Colonel, "I don't know but you are more or less right, there. Now let's figure up a little on the preliminaries. I think Congress always tries to do as near right as it can, according to its lights. A man can't ask any fairer than that. The first preliminary it always starts out on, is to clean itself, so to speak. It will arraign two or three dozen of its members, or maybe four or five dozen, for taking bribes to vote for this and that and the other bill last winter."

"It goes up into the dozens, does it?"

"Well, yes; in a free country like ours, where any man can run for Congress and anybody can vote for him, you can't expect immortal purity all the time—it ain't in nature.—Sixty or eighty or a hundred and fifty people are bound to get in who are not angels in disguise, as young Hicks the correspondent says; but still it is a very good average; very good indeed. As long as it averages as well as that, I think we can feel very well satisfied. Even in these days, when people growl so much and the newspapers are so out of patience, there is still a very respectable minority of honest men in Congress."

"Why a respectable *minority* of honest men can't do any good, Colonel."

"Oh, yes it can, too."

"Why, how?"

"Oh, in many ways, many ways."

"But what *are* the ways?"

"Well—I don't know—it is a question that requires time; a body can't answer every question right off-hand. But it *does* do good. I am satisfied of that."

"All right, then; grant that it does good; go on with the preliminaries."

"That is what I am coming to. First, as I said, they will try a lot of members for taking money for votes. That will take four weeks."

"Yes, that's like last year; and it is a sheer waste of the time for which the nation pays those men to *work*—that is what that is. And it pinches when a body's got a bill waiting."

"A waste of time, to purify the fountain of public law? Well, I never heard anybody express an idea like that before. But if it were, it would still be the fault of the minority, for the majority don't institute these proceedings. *There* is where that minority becomes an obstruction—but still one can't say it is on the wrong side.—Well, after they have finished the bribery cases, they will take up cases of members who have bought their seats with money. That will take another four weeks."

"Very good; go on. You have accounted for two-thirds of the session."

"Next they will try each other for various smaller irregularities, like the sale of appointments to West Point cadetships, and that sort of thing—mere trifling pocket-money enterprises that might better be passed over in silence, perhaps, but then one of our Congresses can never rest easy till it has thoroughly purified itself of all blemishes—and that is a thing to be applauded."

"How long does it take to disinfect itself of these minor impurities?"

"Well, about two weeks, generally."

"So Congress always lies helpless in quarantine ten weeks of a session. That's encouraging. Colonel, poor Laura will never get any benefit from our bill. Her trial will be over before Congress has half purified itself.—And doesn't it occur to you that by the time it has expelled all its impure members there may not be enough members left to do business legally?"

"Why I did not say Congress would expel anybody."

"Well *won't* it expel anybody?"

"Not necessarily. Did it last year? It never does. That would not be regular."

"Then why waste all the session in that tomfoolery of trying members?"

"It is usual; it is customary; the country requires it."

"Then the country is a fool, *I* think."

"Oh, no. The country *thinks* somebody is going to be expelled."

"Well, when nobody *is* expelled, what does the country think then?"

"By that time, the thing has strung out so long that the country is sick and tired of it and glad to have a change on any terms. But all that inquiry is not lost. It has a good moral effect."

"Who does it have a good moral effect on?"

"Well—I don't know. On foreign countries, I think. We have always been under the gaze of foreign countries. There is no country in the world, sir, that pursues corruption as inveterately as we do. There is no country in the world whose representatives try each other as much as ours do, or stick to it as long on a stretch. I think there is something great in being a model for the whole civilized world, Washington."

"You don't mean a model; you mean an example."

"Well, it's all the same; it's just the same thing. It shows that a man can't be corrupt in this country without sweating for it, I can tell you that."

"Hang it, Colonel, you just said we never punish anybody for villainous practices."

"But good God we *try* them, don't we! Is it nothing to show a disposition to sift things and bring people to a strict account? I tell you it has its effect."

"Oh, bother the effect!—What is it they *do* do? How do they proceed? You know perfectly well—and it is all bosh, too. Come, now, how do they proceed?"

"Why they proceed right and regular—and it ain't bosh, Washington, it ain't bosh. They appoint a committee to investigate, and that committee hears evidence three weeks, and all the witnesses on one side swear that the accused took money or stock or something for his vote. Then the accused stands up and testifies that he *may* have done it, but he was receiving and handling a good deal of money at the time and he doesn't remember this particular circumstance—at least with sufficient distinctness to enable him to grasp it tangibly. So of course the thing is not proven—and that is what they say in the verdict. They don't acquit, they don't condemn. They just say, 'Charge not proven.' It leaves the accused in a kind of a shaky condition before the country, it purifies Congress, it satisfies everybody, and it doesn't seriously hurt anybody. It has taken a long time to perfect our system, but it is the most admirable in the world, now."

"So one of those long stupid investigations always turns out in that lame silly way. Yes, you are correct. I thought maybe you viewed the matter differently from other people. Do you think a Congress of ours could convict the devil of anything if he were a member?"

"My dear boy, don't let these damaging delays prejudice you against Congress. Don't use such strong language; you talk like a newspaper. Congress has inflicted frightful punishments on its members—now you know that. When they tried Mr. Fairoaks, and a cloud of witnesses proved him to be—well, you know what they proved him to be—and his own testimony and his own confessions gave him the same character, what did Congress do then?—come!"

"Well, what *did* Congress do?"

"You know what Congress did, Washington. Congress intimated plainly enough, that they considered him almost a stain upon their body; and without waiting ten days, hardly, to think the thing over, they rose up and hurled at him a resolution declaring that they disapproved of his conduct! Now *you* know that, Washington."

"It *was* a terrific thing—there is no denying that. If he had been proven guilty of theft, arson, licentiousness, infanticide, and defiling graves, I believe they would have suspended him for two days."

"You can depend on it, Washington. Congress is vindictive, Congress is savage, sir, when it gets waked up once. It will go to any length to vindicate its honor at such a time."

"Ah well, we have talked the morning through, just as usual in these tiresome days of waiting, and we have reached the same old result; that is to say, we are no better off than when we began. The land bill is just as far away as ever, and the trial is closer at hand. Let's give up everything and die."

"Die and leave the Duchess to fight it out all alone? Oh, no, that won't do. Come, now, don't talk so. It is all going to come out right. Now you'll see."

"It never will, Colonel, never in the world. Something tells me that. I get more tired and more despondent every day. I don't see any hope; life is only just a trouble. I am so miserable these days!"

The Colonel made Washington get up and walk the floor with him, arm in arm. The good old speculator wanted to comfort him, but he hardly knew how to go about it. He made many attempts, but they were lame; they lacked spirit; the words were encouraging, but they were only words—he could not get any heart into them. He could not always warm up, now, with the old Hawkeye fervor. By and by his lips trembled and his voice got unsteady. He said:

"Don't give up the ship, my boy—don't do it. The wind's bound to fetch around and set in our favor. I *know* it."

And the prospect was so cheerful that he wept. Then he blew a trumpet-blast that started the meshes of his handkerchief, and said in almost his breezy old-time way:

"Lord bless us, this is all nonsense! Night doesn't last always; day has got to break some time or other. Every silver lining has a cloud behind it, as the poet says; and that remark has always cheered me, though I never could see any meaning to it. Everybody uses it, though, and everybody gets comfort out of it. I wish they would start something fresh. Come, now, let's cheer up; there's been as good fish in the sea as there are now. It shall never be said that Eschol Sellers—. Come in?"

It was the telegraph boy. The Colonel reached for the message and devoured its contents.

"I said it! Never give up the ship! The trial's postponed till February, and we'll save the child yet. Bless my life, what lawyers they have in New York! Give them money to fight with, and the ghost of an excuse, and they would manage to postpone anything in this world, unless it might be the millennium or something like that. Now for work again, my boy. The trial will last to the middle of March, sure; Congress ends the fourth of March. Within three days of the end of the session they will be done putting through the preliminaries, and then they will be ready for national business. Our bill will go through in forty-eight hours, then, and we'll telegraph a million dollars to the jury—to the lawyers, I mean—and the verdict of the jury will be 'Accidental murder resulting from justifiable insanity'—or something to that effect, something to that effect. Everything is dead sure, now. Come, what is the matter? What are you wilting down like that, for? You mustn't be a girl, you know."

"Oh, Colonel, I am become so used to troubles, so used to failures, disappointments, hard luck of all kinds, that a little good news breaks me right down. Everything has been so hopeless that now I can't stand good news at all. It is too good to be true, anyway. Don't you see how our bad luck has worked on me? My hair is getting gray, and many nights I don't sleep at all. I wish it was all over and we could rest. I wish we could lie down and just forget everything, and let it all be just a dream that is done and can't come back to trouble us any more. I am so tired."

"Ah, poor child, don't talk like that—cheer up—there's daylight

ahead. Don't give up. You'll have Laura again, and Louise, and
your mother, and oceans and oceans of money—and then you
can go away, ever so far away somewhere, if you want to, and
forget all about this infernal place. And by George I'll go with
you! I'll go with you—now there's my word on it. Cheer up. I'll
run out and tell the friends the news."

And he wrung Washington's hand and was about to hurry away
when his companion, in a burst of grateful admiration said:

"I think you are the best soul and the noblest I ever knew,
Colonel Sellers! and if the people only knew you as I do, you
would not be tagging around here a nameless man—you would
be in Congress."

The gladness died out of the Colonel's face, and he laid his
hand upon Washington's shoulder and said gravely:

"I have always been a friend of your family, Washington, and
I think I have always tried to do right as between man and man,
according to my lights. Now I don't think there has ever been
anything in my conduct that should make you feel justified in
saying a thing like that."

He turned, then, and walked slowly out, leaving Washington
abashed and somewhat bewildered. When Washington had
presently got his thoughts into line again, he said to himself,
"Why, honestly, I only meant to compliment him—indeed I
would not have hurt him for the world."

## CHAPTER 28

The weeks drifted by monotonously enough, now. The "preliminaries" continued to drag along in Congress, and life was a dull suspense to Sellers and Washington, a weary waiting which might have broken their hearts, maybe, but for the relieving change which they got out of an occasional visit to New York to see Laura. Standing guard in Washington or anywhere else is not an exciting business in time of peace, but standing guard was all that the two friends had to do; all that was needed of them was that they should be on hand and ready for any emergency that might come up. There was no work to do; that was all finished; this was but the second session of the last winter's Congress, and its action on the bill could have but one result—its passage. The House must do its work over again, of course, but the same membership was there to see that it did it.— The Senate was secure—Senator Dilworthy was able to put all doubts to rest on that head. Indeed it was no secret in Washington that a two-thirds vote in the Senate was ready and waiting to be cast for the University bill as soon as it should come before that body.

Washington did not take part in the gaieties of "the season," as he had done the previous winter. He had lost his interest in such things; he was oppressed with cares, now. Senator Dilworthy said to Washington that an humble deportment, under punishment, was best, and that there was but one way in which the troubled heart might find perfect repose and peace. The suggestion found a response in Washington's breast, and the Senator saw the sign of it in his face.

From that moment one could find the youth with the Senator even oftener than with Col. Sellers. When the statesman presided at great temperance meetings, he placed Washington in the

front rank of impressive dignitaries that gave tone to the occasion and pomp to the platform. His bald headed surroundings
made the youth the more conspicuous. When the statesman
made remarks in these meetings, he not infrequently alluded
with effect to the encouraging spectacle of one of the wealthiest
and most brilliant young favorites of society forsaking the light
vanities of that butterfly existence to nobly and self-sacrificingly
devote his talents and his riches to the cause of saving his hap-
less fellow creatures from shame and misery here and eternal
regret hereafter. At the prayer meetings the Senator always
brought Washington up the aisle on his arm and seated him
prominently; in his prayers he referred to him in the cant terms
which the Senator employed, perhaps unconsciously, and mis-
took, maybe, for religion, and in other ways brought him into
notice. He had him out at gatherings for the benefit of the negro,
gatherings for the benefit of the Indian, gatherings for the benefit of the heathen in distant lands. He had him out time and
again, before Sunday Schools, as an example for emulation. Upon
all these occasions the Senator made casual references to many
benevolent enterprises which his ardent young friend was planning against the day when the passage of the University bill
should make his ample means available for the amelioration of
the condition of the unfortunate among his fellow men of all
nations and all climes. Thus as the weeks rolled on Washington
grew up into an imposing lion once more, but a lion that roamed
the peaceful fields of religion and temperance, and revisited the
glittering domain of fashion no more. A great moral influence
was thus brought to bear in favor of the bill; the weightiest of
friends flocked to its standard; its most energetic enemies said
it was useless to fight longer; they had tacitly surrendered while
as yet the day of battle was not come.

## CHAPTER 29

[The session was drawing to its close and Senator Dilworthy decided to visit his constituents, the state legislators who were due to re-elect him. There was a member of the state legislature named Noble who was opposed to reform, to progress and to *him*, and it was best, therefore, that Senator Dilworthy visit his state. As for the university bill, it was safe, in the Senator's opinion.]

When he arrived on the ground he found his friends unterrified; they were standing firmly by him and were full of courage. Noble was working hard, too, but matters were against him, he was not making much progress. Mr. Dilworthy took an early opportunity to send for Mr. Noble; he had a midnight interview with him, and urged him to forsake his evil ways; he begged him to come again and again, which he did. He finally sent the man away at 3 o'clock one morning; and when he was gone, Mr. Dilworthy said to himself,

"I feel a good deal relieved, now, a great deal relieved."

[Then the Senator "turned his attention to matters touching the souls of his people." He appeared in church, at prayer meetings, at temperance societies, at sewing circles, at Bible classes, at Sunday schools.]

He even traveled a tedious thirty miles in a poor little rickety stage-coach to comply with the desire of the miserable hamlet of Cattleville that he would let its Sunday School look upon him.

All the town was assembled at the stage office when he arrived, two bonfires were burning, and a battery of anvils was popping exultant broadsides; for a United States Senator was a sort of god in the understanding of these people who never had seen any creature mightier than a county judge. To them a

United States Senator was a vast, vague colossus, an awe inspiring unreality.

Next day everybody was at the village church a full half hour before time for Sunday School to open; ranchmen and farmers had come with their families from five miles around, all eager to get a glimpse of the great man—the man who had been to Washington; the man who had seen the President of the United States, and had even talked with him; the man who had seen the actual Washington Monument—perhaps touched it with his hands.

When the Senator arrived the Church was crowded, the windows were full, the aisles were packed, so was the vestibule, and so indeed was the yard in front of the building. As he worked his way through to the pulpit on the arm of the minister and followed by the envied officials of the village, every neck was stretched and every eye twisted around intervening obstructions to get a glimpse. Elderly people directed each other's attention and said, "There! that's him, with the grand, noble forehead!" Boys nudged each other and said, "Hi, Johnny, here he is! There, that's him, with the peeled head!"

The Senator took his seat in the pulpit, with the minister on one side of him and the Superintendent of the Sunday School on the other. The town dignitaries sat in an impressive row within the altar railings below. The Sunday School children occupied ten of the front benches, dressed in their best and most uncomfortable clothes, and with hair combed and faces too clean to feel natural. So awed were they by the presence of a living United States Senator, that during three minutes not a "spit-ball" was thrown. After that they began to come to themselves by degrees, and presently the spell was wholly gone and they were reciting verses and pulling hair.

The usual Sunday School exercises were hurried through, and then the minister got up and bored the house with a speech built on the customary Sunday School plan; then the Superintendent put in his oar; then the town dignitaries had their say. They all made complimentary reference to "their friend the Senator," and

told what a great and illustrious man he was and what he had
done for his country and for religion and temperance, and ex-
horted the little boys to be good and diligent and try to become
like him some day. The speakers won the deathless hatred of
the house by these delays, but at last there was an end and
hope revived; inspiration was about to find utterance.

Senator Dilworthy rose and beamed upon the assemblage for
a full minute in silence. Then he smiled with an access of sweetness upon the children and began:

"My little friends—for I hope that all these bright-faced little
people are my friends and will let me be their friend—my little
friends, I have traveled much, I have been in many cities and
many States, everywhere in our great and noble country, and by
the blessing of Providence I have been permitted to see many
gatherings like this—but I am proud, I am truly proud to say that
I never have looked upon so much intelligence, so much grace,
such sweetness of disposition as I see in the charming young
countenances I see before me at this moment. I have been asking
myself as I sat here, Where am I? Am I in some far-off mon-
archy, looking upon little princes and princesses? No. Am I in
some populous centre of my own country, where the choicest
children of the land have been selected and brought together
as at a fair for a prize? No. Am I in some strange foreign clime
where the children are marvels that we know not of? No. Then
where am I? Yes—where am I? I am in a simple, remote, un-
pretending settlement of my own dear State, and these are the
children of the noble and virtuous men who have made me what
I am! My soul is lost in wonder at the thought! And I humbly
thank Him to whom we are but as worms of the dust, that He
has been pleased to call me to serve such men! Earth has no
higher, no grander position for me. Let kings and emperors
keep their tinsel crowns, I want them not; my heart is here!

"Again I thought, Is this a theatre? No. Is it a concert or a
gilded opera? No. Is it some other vain, brilliant, beautiful temple of soul-staining amusement and hilarity? No. Then what is
it? What did my consciousness reply? I ask you, my little friends,
What did my consciousness reply? It replied, It is the temple of

the Lord! Ah, think of that, now. I could hardly keep the tears back, I was so grateful. Oh, how beautiful it is to see these ranks of sunny little faces assembled here to learn the way of life; to learn to be good; to learn to be useful; to learn to be pious; to learn to be great and glorious men and women; to learn to be props and pillars of the State and shining lights in the councils and the households of the nation; to be bearers of the banner and soldiers of the cross in the rude campaigns of life, and ransomed souls in the happy fields of Paradise hereafter.

"Children, honor your parents and be grateful to them for providing for you the precious privileges of a Sunday School.

"Now my dear little friends, sit up straight and pretty—there, that's it—and give me your attention and let me tell you about a poor little Sunday School scholar I once knew.—He lived in the far west, and his parents were poor. They could not give him a costly education, but they were good and wise and they sent him to the Sunday School. He loved the Sunday School. I hope you love your Sunday School—ah, I see by your faces that you do! That is right.

"Well, this poor little boy was always in his place when the bell rang, and he always knew his lesson; for his teachers wanted him to learn and he loved his teachers dearly. Always love your teachers, my children, for they love you more than you can know, now. He would not let bad boys persuade him to go to play on Sunday. There was one little bad boy who was always trying to persuade him, but he never could.

"So this poor little boy grew up to be a man, and had to go out in the world, far from home and friends to earn his living. Temptations lay all about him, and sometimes he was about to yield, but he would think of some precious lesson he learned in his Sunday School a long time ago, and that would save him. By and by he was elected to the legislature. Then he did everything he could for Sunday Schools. He got laws passed for them; he got Sunday Schools established wherever he could.

"And by and by the people made him governor—and he said it was all owing to the Sunday School.

"After a while the people elected him a Representative to the Congress of the United States, and he grew very famous.—Now temptations assailed him on every hand. People tried to get him to drink wine, to dance, to go to theatres; they even tried to buy his vote; but no, the memory of his Sunday School saved him from all harm; he remembered the fate of the bad little boy who used to try to get him to play on Sunday, and who grew up and became a drunkard and was hanged. He remembered that, and was glad he never yielded and played on Sunday.

"Well, at last, what do you think happened? Why the people gave him a towering, illustrious position, a grand, imposing position. And what do you think it was? What should you say it was, children? It was Senator of the United States! That poor little boy that loved his Sunday School became that man. *That man stands before you!* All that he is, he owes to the Sunday School.

"My precious children, love your parents, love your teachers, love your Sunday School, be pious, be obedient, be honest, be diligent, and then you will succeed in life and be honored of all men. Above all things, my children, be honest. Above all things be pure-minded as the snow. Let us join in prayer."

When Senator Dilworthy departed from Cattleville, he left three dozen boys behind him arranging a campaign of life whose objective point was the United States Senate.

When he arrived at the State capital at midnight Mr. Noble came and held a three-hours' conference with him, and then as he was about leaving said:

"I've worked hard, and I've got them at last. Six of them haven't got quite back-bone enough to slew around and come right out for you on the first ballot to-morrow, but they're going to vote against you on the first for the sake of appearances, and then come out for you all in a body on the second—I've fixed all that! By supper time to-morrow you'll be re-elected. You can go to bed and sleep easy on that."

After Mr. Noble was gone, the Senator said:

"Well, to bring about a complexion of things like this was worth coming West for."

## CHAPTER 30

[Laura's trial began eleven months after she killed Selby. Philip and Harry were present. Harry testified that after shooting Selby she had aimed the pistol at her own breast but that he, Harry, had snatched it from her. Col. Selby's deposition was produced and it was revealed that the newspapers had reported only the first part of it. After Selby had accused Laura of threatening him he was told for the first time that his wound was mortal, upon which he had added, with great difficulty, "I—have—not—told—all. I must tell—put—it—down—I—wronged—her. Years—ago—I—can't—see—O—God—I—deserved—" Then he had died.

The prosecution rested and Mr. Braham opened the case for the defense. He promised to unfold a terrible drama of misfortune and to prove that the prisoner was the victim of hereditary insanity inflamed by mental torture. Laura's mother took the stand. She narrated Laura's history in detail, and Washington Hawkins corroborated her testimony regarding Laura's relations with Selby. Then Col. Sellers took the stand, and at this point the correspondence of Major Lackland with Silas Hawkins was placed in evidence. When Col. Sellers testified about Laura's supposed father and about how Laura was not informed of his existence until after the death of Silas Hawkins, the district attorney objected that these details were irrelevant. A dispute between him and Mr. Braham followed.]

The wrangle continued, waxing hotter and hotter. The Colonel seeing the attention of the counsel and Court entirely withdrawn from him, thought he perceived here his opportunity. Turning and beaming upon the jury, he began simply to talk, but as the grandeur of his position grew upon him—his talk broadened unconsciously into an oratorical vein.

"You see how she was situated, gentlemen; poor child, it might have broken her heart to let her mind get to running on such a thing as that. You see, from what we could make out her father was lame in the left leg and had a deep scar on his left forehead. And so ever since the day she found out she *had* another father, she never could run across a lame stranger without being taken all over with a shiver, and almost fainting where she stood. And the next minute she would go right after that man. Once she stumbled on a stranger with a game leg, and she was the most grateful thing in this world—but it was the wrong leg, and it was days and days before she could leave her bed. Once she found a man with a scar on his forehead, and she was just going to throw herself into his arms, but he stepped out just then, and there wasn't anything the matter with his legs. Time and time again, gentlemen of the jury, has this poor suffering orphan flung herself on her knees with all her heart's gratitude in her eyes before some scarred and crippled veteran, but always, always to be disappointed, always to be plunged into new despair—if his legs were right his scar was wrong, if his scar was right his legs were wrong. Never could find a man that would fill the bill. Gentlemen of the jury, you have hearts, you have feelings, you have warm human sympathies, you can feel for this poor suffering child. Gentlemen of the jury, if I had time, if I had the opportunity, if I might be permitted to go on and tell you the thousands and thousands and thousands of mutilated strangers this poor girl has started out of cover, and hunted from city to city, from state to state, from continent to continent, till she has run them down and found they wan't the ones, I know your hearts—"

By this time the Colonel had become so warmed up, that his voice had reached a pitch above that of the contending counsel; the lawyers suddenly stopped, and they and the Judge turned towards the Colonel and remained for several seconds too surprised at this novel exhibition to speak. In this interval of silence, an appreciation of the situation gradually stole over the audience, and an explosion of laughter followed, in which even the Court and the bar could hardly keep from joining.

*Sheriff.* "Order in the Court."

*The Judge.* "The witness will confine his remarks to answers to questions."

The Colonel turned courteously to the Judge and said,

"Certainly, your Honor, certainly. I am not well acquainted with the forms of procedure in the courts of New York, but in the West, sir, in the West—"

*The Judge.* "There, there, that will do, that will do.!"

"You see, your Honor, there were no questions asked me, and I thought I would take advantage of the lull in the proceedings to explain to the jury a very significant train of—"

*The Judge.* "That will *do*, sir! Proceed Mr. Braham."

"Col. Sellers, have you any reason to suppose that this man is still living?"

"Every reason, sir, every reason."

"State why."

"I have never heard of his death, sir. It has never come to my knowledge. In fact, sir, as I once said to Governor—"

"Will you state to the jury what has been the effect of the knowledge of this wandering and evidently unsettled being, supposed to be her father, upon the mind of Miss Hawkins for so many years?"

Question objected to. Question ruled out.

Cross-examined. "Major Sellers, what is your occupation?"

The Colonel looked about him loftily, as if casting in his mind what would be the proper occupation of a person of such multifarious interests, and then said with dignity.

"A gentleman, sir. My father used to always say, sir"—

"Capt. Sellers, did you ever see this man, this supposed father?"

"No, sir. But upon one occasion, old Senator Thompson said to me, it's my opinion, Colonel Sellers"—

"Did you ever see any body who *had* seen him?"

"No, sir. It was reported around at one time, that"—

"That is all."

[The defense spent a day examining medical experts in insanity, who testified "that sufficient causes had occurred to produce an insane mind in the prisoner." The prosecution spent a day examining experts who refuted the notion of insanity. Washington Hawkins and Col. Sellers were obliged to go to Washington in connection with the university bill. Laura's case went to the jury.]

## CHAPTER 31

The momentous day was at hand—a day that promised to make or mar the fortunes of the Hawkins family for all time. Washington Hawkins and Col. Sellers were both up early, for neither of them could sleep. Congress was expiring, and was passing bill after bill as if they were gasps and each likely to be its last. The University was on file for its third reading this day, and to-morrow Washington would be a millionaire and Sellers no longer impecunious; but this day, also, or at farthest the next, the jury in Laura's case would come to a decision of some kind or other—they would find her guilty, Washington secretly feared, and then the care and the trouble would all come back again and there would be wearing months of besieging judges for new trials; on this day, also, the re-election of Mr. Dilworthy to the Senate would take place. So Washington's mind was in a state of turmoil; there were more interests at stake than it could handle with serenity. He exulted when he thought of his millions; he was filled with dread when he thought of Laura. But Sellers was excited and happy. He said:

"Everything is going right, everything's going perfectly right. Pretty soon the telegrams will begin to rattle in, and then you'll see, my boy. Let the jury do what they please; what difference is it going to make? To-morrow we can send a million to New York and set the lawyers at work on the judges; bless your heart they will go before judge after judge and exhort and beseech and pray and shed tears. They always do; and they always win, too. And they will win this time. They will get a writ of habeas corpus, and a stay of proceedings, and a supersedeas, and a new trial and a nolle prosequi, and there you are! That's the routine, and it's no trick at all to a New York lawyer. That's the regular routine—everything's red tape and routine in the law, you see;

it's all Greek to you, of course, but to a man who is acquainted
with those things it's mere—I'll explain it to you sometime.
Everything's going to glide right along easy and comfortable now.
You'll see, Washington, you'll see how it will be. And then, let
me think . . . . . Dilworthy will be elected to-day, and by day
after to-morrow night he will be in New York ready to put in *his*
shovel—and you haven't lived in Washington all this time not to
know that the people who walk right by a Senator whose term is
up without hardly seeing him will be down at the deepo to say
'Welcome back and God bless you, Senator, I'm glad to see you,
sir!' when he comes along back re-elected, you know. Well, you
see, his influence was naturally running low when he left here,
but now he has got a new six-years' start, and his suggestions
will simply just weigh a couple of tons a-piece day after to-
morrow. Lord bless you he could rattle through that habeas corpus and supersedeas and all those things for Laura all by himself if he wanted to, when he gets back."

"I hadn't thought of that," said Washington, brightening, "but
it is so. A newly-elected Senator *is* a power, I know that."

"Yes indeed he is.—Why it is just human nature. Look at
me. When we first came here, I was *Mr.* Sellers, and *Major*
Sellers, and *Captain* Sellers, but nobody could ever get it right,
somehow; but the minute our bill went through the House, I
was *Colonel* Sellers every time. And nobody could do enough
for me; and whatever I said was wonderful, Sir, it was always
wonderful; I never seemed to say any flat things at all. It was
Colonel won't you come and dine with us; and Colonel why
*don't* we ever see you at our house; and the Colonel says
this; and the Colonel says that; and we know such-and-such is
so-and-so, because husband heard Col. Sellers *say* so. Don't
you see? Well, the Senate adjourned and left our bill high and
dry, and I'll be hanged if I warn't *Old Sellers* from that day
till our bill passed the House again last week. Now I'm the
*Colonel* again; and if I were to eat all the dinners I am invited to, I reckon I'd wear my teeth down level with my gums in
a couple of weeks."

"Well I do wonder what you will be to-morrow, Colonel, after the President signs the bill?"

"*General*, sir!—General, without a doubt. Yes, sir, to-morrow it will be General, let me congratulate you, sir; General, you've done a great work, sir;—you've done a great work for the niggro; Gentlemen, allow me the honor to introduce my friend General Sellers, the humane friend of the niggro. Lord bless me, you'll see the newspapers say, General Sellers and servants arrived in the city last night and is stopping at the Fifth Avenue; and General Sellers has accepted a reception and banquet by the Cosmopolitan Club; you'll see the General's opinions quoted, too —and what the General has to say about the propriety of a new trial and a habeas corpus for the unfortunate Miss Hawkins will not be without weight in influential quarters, I can tell you."

"And I want to be the first to shake your faithful old hand and salute you with your new honors, and I want to do it *now* —General!" said Washington, suiting the action to the word, and accompanying it with all the meaning that a cordial grasp and eloquent eyes could give it.

The Colonel was touched; he was pleased and proud, too; his face answered for that.

Not very long after breakfast the telegrams began to arrive. The first was from Braham, and ran thus:

"We feel certain that the verdict will be rendered to-day. Be it good or bad, let it find us ready to make the next move instantly, whatever it may be."

"That's the right talk," said Sellers. "That Braham's a wonderful man. He was the only man there that really understood me; he told me so himself, afterwards."

The next telegram was from Mr. Dilworthy:

"I have not only brought over the Great Invincible, but through him a dozen more of the opposition. Shall be re-elected to-day by an overwhelming majority."

"Good again!" said the Colonel. "That man's talent for organization is something marvelous. He wanted me to go out there

214 THE ADVENTURES OF COLONEL SELLERS

and engineer that thing, but I said, No, Dilworthy, I must be
on hand here, both on Laura's account and the bill's—but you've
no trifling genius for organization yourself, said I—and I was
right. You go ahead, said I—you can fix it—and so he has. But
I claim no credit for that—if I stiffened up his back-bone a little,
I simply put him in the way to make his fight—didn't make
it myself. He has captured Noble—I consider that a splendid piece
of diplomacy—Splendid, sir!"

By and by came another dispatch from New York:

"Jury still out. Laura calm and firm as a statue. The report that
the jury have brought her in guilty is false and premature."

"Premature!" gasped Washington, turning white. "Then they all
expect that sort of a verdict, when it comes."

And so did he; but he had not had courage enough to put
it into words. He had been preparing himself for the worst, but
after all his preparation the bare suggestion of the possibility of
such a verdict struck him cold as death.

The friends grew impatient, now; the telegrams did not come
fast enough; even the lightning could not keep up with their
anxieties. They walked the floor talking disjointedly and listening for the door-bell. Telegram after telegram came. Still no result. By and by there was one which contained a single line:

"Court now coming in after brief recess to hear verdict. Jury
ready."

"Oh, I wish they would finish!" said Washington. "This suspense is killing me by inches!"

Then came another telegram:

"Another hitch somewhere. Jury want a little more time and further instructions."

"Well, well, well, this is trying," said the Colonel. And after a
pause, "No dispatch from Dilworthy for two hours, now. Even
a dispatch from him would be better than nothing, just to vary
this thing."

They waited twenty minutes. It seemed twenty hours.

"Come!" said Washington. "I can't wait for the telegraph boy to come all the way up here. Let's go down to Newspaper Row —meet him on the way."

While they were passing along the Avenue, they saw some one putting up a great display-sheet on the bulletin board of a newspaper office, and an eager crowd of men was collecting about the place. Washington and the Colonel ran to the spot and read this:

"Tremendous Sensation! Startling news from Saint's Rest! On first ballot for U. S. Senator, when voting was about to begin, Mr. Noble rose in his place and drew forth a package, walked forward and laid it on the Speaker's desk, saying, 'This contains $7,000 in bank bills and was given me by Senator Dilworthy in his bed-chamber at midnight last night to buy my vote for him—I wish the Speaker to count the money and retain it to pay the expense of prosecuting this infamous traitor for bribery.' The whole legislature was stricken speechless with dismay and astonishment. Noble further said that there were fifty members present with money in their pockets, placed there by Dilworthy to buy their votes. Amidst unparalleled excitement the ballot was now taken, and J. W. Smith elected U. S. Senator; Dilworthy receiving not one vote! *Noble promises damaging exposures concerning Dilworthy and certain measures of his now pending in Congress.*"

"Good heavens and earth!" exclaimed the Colonel.

"To the Capitol!" said Washington. "Fly!"

And they did fly. Long before they got there the newsboys were running ahead of them with Extras, hot from the press, announcing the astounding news.

Arrived in the gallery of the Senate, the friends saw a curious spectacle—every Senator held an Extra in his hand and looked as interested as if it contained news of the destruction of the earth. Not a single member was paying the least attention to the business of the hour.

The Secretary, in a loud voice, was just beginning to read the title of a bill:

"House - Bill - No. - 4,231, - An - Act - to - Found - and - Incorporate - the Knobs - Industrial - University! - Read - first - and - second - time — considered - in - committee - of - the - whole - ordered - engrossed - and - passed - to - third - reading - and - final - passage!"

*The President*—"Third reading of the *bill!*"

The two friends shook in their shoes. Senators threw down their extras and snatched a word or two with each other in whispers. Then the gavel rapped to command silence while the names were called on the ayes and nays. Washington grew paler and paler, weaker and weaker while the lagging list progressed; and when it was finished, his head fell helplessly forward on his arms. The fight was fought, the long struggle was over, and he was a pauper. Not a man had voted for the bill!

Col. Sellers was bewildered and well nigh paralyzed, himself. But no man could long consider his own troubles in the presence of such suffering as Washington's. He got him up and supported him—almost carried him indeed—out of the building and into a carriage. All the way home Washington lay with his face against the Colonel's shoulder and merely groaned and wept. The Colonel tried as well as he could under the dreary circumstances to hearten him a little, but it was of no use. Washington was past all hope of cheer, now. He only said:

"Oh, it is all over—it is all over for good, Colonel. We must beg our bread, now. We never can get up again. It was our last chance, and it is gone. They will hang Laura! My God they will hang her! Nothing can save the poor girl now. Oh, I wish with all my soul they would hang me instead!"

Arrived at home, Washington fell into a chair and buried his face in his hands and gave full way to his misery. The Colonel did not know where to turn nor what to do. The servant maid knocked at the door and passed in a telegram, saying it had come while they were gone.

The Colonel tore it open and read with the voice of a man-of-war's broadside:

"VERDICT OF JURY, NOT GUILTY AND LAURA IS FREE!"

[Laura left the courtroom with her mother and went to her hotel, where she learned that the university bill had been lost and Dilworthy ruined. She was bitter. A Mr. Griller wished to speak with her. She asked that he be sent up.]

Mr. Griller entered. He was a small man, slovenly in dress, his tone confidential, his manner wholly void of animation, all his features below the forehead protruding—particularly the apple of his throat—hair without a kink in it, a hand with no grip, a meek, hang-dog countenance. He was a falsehood done in flesh and blood; for while every visible sign about him proclaimed him a poor, witless, useless weakling, the truth was that he had the brains to plan great enterprises and the pluck to carry them through. That was his reputation, and it was a deserved one.

He softly said:

"I called to see you on business, Miss Hawkins. You have my card?"

Laura bowed.

Mr. Griller continued to purr, as softly as before:

"I will proceed to business. I am a business man. I am a lecture-agent, Miss Hawkins, and as soon as I saw that you were acquitted, it occurred to me that an early interview would be mutually beneficial."

"I don't understand you, sir," said Laura coldly.

[Mr. Griller made her a lecture offer: $12,000 for thirty nights. He suggested a title for her lecture—"The Revelations of a Woman's Life." She said she would consider the offer. Meanwhile Harry went to the Pacific coast on a mission for his uncle, and Philip went to Pennsylvania on business.]

The parting between Laura and her mother was exceedingly painful to both. It was as if two friends parted on a wide plain, the one to journey towards the setting and the other towards the rising sun, each comprehending that every step henceforth must separate their lives wider and wider.

## CHAPTER 32

When Mr. Noble's bombshell fell in Senator Dilworthy's camp, the statesman was disconcerted for a moment.—For a moment; that was all. The next moment he was calmly up and doing. From the centre of our country to its circumference, nothing was talked of but Mr. Noble's terrible revelation, and the people were furious. Mind, they were not furious because bribery was uncommon in our public life, but merely because here was *another* case. Perhaps it did not occur to the nation of good and worthy people that while they continued to sit comfortably at home and leave the true source of our political power ( the "primaries,") in the hands of saloon-keepers, dog-fanciers and hod-carriers, they could go on expecting "another" case of this kind, and even dozens and hundreds of them, and never be disappointed. However, they may have thought that to sit at home and grumble would some day right the evil.

Yes, the nation was excited, but Senator Dilworthy was calm —what was left of him after the explosion of the shell. Calm, and up and doing. What did he do first? What would you do first, after you had tomahawked your mother at the breakfast table for putting too much sugar in your coffee? You would "ask for a suspension of public opinion." That is what Senator Dilworthy did. It is the custom. He got the usual amount of suspension. Far and wide he was called a thief, a briber, a promoter of steamship subsidies, railway swindles, robberies of the government in all possible forms and fashions. Newspapers and everybody else called him a pious hypocrite, a sleek, oily fraud, a reptile who manipulated temperance movements, prayer meetings, Sunday Schools, public charities, missionary enterprises, all for his private benefit. And as these charges were backed up by what seemed to be good and sufficient evidence, they were believed with national unanimity.

Then Mr. Dilworthy made another move. He moved instantly to Washington and "demanded an investigation." Even this could not pass without comment. Many papers used language to this effect:

"Senator Dilworthy's remains have demanded an investigation. This sounds fine and bold and innocent; but when we reflect that they demand it at the hands of the Senate of the United States, it simply becomes matter for derision. One might as well set the gentlemen detained in the public prisons to trying each other. This investigation is likely to be like all other Senatorial 'investigations'—amusing but not useful. Query. Why does the Senate still stick to this pompous word, 'Investigation?' One does not blindfold one's self in order to investigate an object."

Mr. Dilworthy appeared in his place in the Senate and offered a resolution appointing a committee to investigate his case. It carried, of course, and the committee was appointed. Straightway the newspapers said:

"Under the guise of appointing a committee to investigate the late Mr. Dilworthy, the Senate yesterday appointed a committee to *investigate his accuser, Mr. Noble.* This is the exact spirit and meaning of the resolution, and the committee cannot try anybody but Mr. Noble without overstepping its authority. That Mr. Dilworthy had the effrontery to offer such a resolution will surprise no one; and that the Senate could entertain it without blushing and pass it without shame will surprise no one. We are now reminded of a note which we have received from the notorious burglar Murphy, in which he finds fault with a statement of ours to the effect that he had served one term in the penitentiary and also one in the U. S. Senate. He says, 'The latter statement is untrue and does me great injustice.' After an unconscious sarcasm like that, further comment is unnecessary."

And yet the Senate was roused by the Dilworthy trouble. Many speeches were made. One Senator (who was accused in the public prints of selling his chances of re-election to his opponent for $50,000 and had not yet denied the charge) said that, "the presence in the Capital of such a creature as this man Noble, to testify against a brother member of their body, was an insult to the Senate."

Another Senator said, "Let the investigation go on; and let it make an example of this man Noble; let it teach him and men like him that they could not attack the reputation of a United States Senator with impunity."

Another said he was glad the investigation was to be had, "for it was high time that the Senate should crush some cur like this man Noble, and thus show his kind that it was able and resolved to uphold its ancient dignity."

A by-stander laughed, at this finely delivered peroration, and said,

"Why, this is the Senator who franked his baggage home through the mails last week—registered, at that. However, perhaps he was merely engaged in 'upholding the ancient dignity of the Senate,' then."

"No, the modern dignity of it," said another by-stander. "It don't resemble its ancient dignity, but it fits its modern style like a glove."

There being no law against making offensive remarks about U. S. Senators, this conversation, and others like it, continued without let or hindrance. But our business is with the investigating committee.

Mr. Noble appeared before the Committee of the Senate, and testified to the following effect:

He said that he was a member of the State legislature of the Happy-Land-of-Canaan; that on the——day of——he assembled himself together at the city of Saint's Rest, the capital of the State, along with his brother legislators; that he was known to be a political enemy of Mr. Dilworthy and bitterly opposed to his re-election; that Mr. Dilworthy came to Saint's Rest and was reported to be buying pledges of votes with money; that the said Dilworthy sent for him to come to his room in the hotel at night, and he went; was introduced to Mr. Dilworthy; called two or three times afterward at Dilworthy's request—usually after midnight; Mr. Dilworthy urged him to vote for him; Noble declined; Dilworthy argued; said he was bound to be elected, and could then ruin him (Noble) if he voted no; said he had every railway and every public office and stronghold of political power in the State under his thumb, and could set up or pull down any man he chose; gave instances showing where and how he had used this power; if Noble would vote for him he would make him a Representative in Congress; Noble still declined to vote, and said he did not believe Dilworthy was going to be elected; Dilworthy showed a list of men who would vote for him—a majority of the legislature; gave further proofs of his power by telling Noble everything the opposing party had done or said in secret caucus; claimed that his spies reported everything to him, and that——

Here a member of the Committee objected that this evidence was irrelevant and also in opposition to the spirit of the Committee's instructions, because if these things reflected upon any one it was upon Mr. Dilworthy. The chairman said, let the person proceed with his statement—the Committee could exclude evidence that did not bear upon the case.

Mr. Noble continued. He said that his party would cast him out if he voted for Mr. Dilworthy; Dilworthy said that that would inure to his benefit because he would then be a recognized friend of his (Dilworthy's) and he could consistently exalt him politically and make his fortune; Noble said he was poor, and it was hard to tempt him so; Dilworthy said he would fix that; he said, "Tell me what you want, and say you will vote for me;" Noble could not say; Dilworthy said "I will give you $5,000—"

A Committee man said, impatiently, that this stuff was all outside the case, and valuable time was being wasted; this was all a plain reflection upon a brother Senator. The Chairman said it was the quickest way to proceed, and the evidence need have no weight.

Mr. Noble continued. He said he told Dilworthy that $5,000 was not much to pay for a man's honor, character and everything that was worth having; Dilworthy said he was surprised; he considered $5,000 a fortune for some men; asked what Noble's figure was; Noble said he could not think $10,000 too little; Dilworthy said it was a great deal too much; he would not do it for any other man, but he had conceived a liking for Noble, and where he liked a man his heart yearned to help him; he was aware that Noble was poor, and had a family to support, and that he bore an unblemished reputation at home; for such a man and such a man's influence he could do much, and feel that to help such a man would be an act that would have its reward; the struggles of the poor always touched him; he believed that Noble would make a good use of this money and that it would cheer many a sad heart and needy home; he would give the $10,000; all he desired in return was that when the balloting began, Noble should cast his vote for him and should explain to the legislature that upon looking into the charges against Mr. Dilworthy of bribery, corruption, and forwarding stealing measures in Congress he had found them to be base calumnies upon a man whose motives were pure and whose character was stainless; he then took from his pocket $2,000 in bank bills and handed them to Noble, and got another package containing $5,000 out of his trunk and gave to him also. He—

A Committee man jumped up, and said:

"*At last*, Mr. Chairman, this shameless person has arrived at the point. This is sufficient and conclusive. By his own confession he has received a bribe, and did it deliberately. This is a grave offense, and cannot be passed over in silence, sir. By the terms of our instructions we can now proceed to mete out to him such punishment as is meet for one who has maliciously brought disrespect upon a Senator of the United States. We have no need to hear the rest of his evidence."

The Chairman said it would be better and more regular to proceed with the investigation according to the usual forms. A note would be made of Mr. Noble's admission.

Mr. Noble continued. He said that it was now far past mid-night; that he took his leave and went straight to certain legislators, told them everything, made them count the money, and also told them of the exposure he would make in joint convention; he made that exposure, as all the world knew. The rest of the $10,000 was to be paid the day after Dilworthy was elected.

Senator Dilworthy was now asked to take the stand and tell what he knew about the man Noble. The Senator wiped his mouth with his handkerchief, adjusted his white cravat, and said that but for the fact that public morality required an example, for the warning of future Nobles, he would beg that in Christian charity this poor misguided creature might be forgiven and set free. He said that it was but too evident that this person had approached him in the hope of obtaining a bribe; he had intruded himself time and again, and always with moving stories of his poverty. Mr. Dilworthy said that his heart had bled for him—insomuch that he had several times been on the point of trying to get some one to do something for him. Some instinct had told him from the beginning that this was a bad man, an evil-minded man, but his inexperience of such had blinded him to his real motives, and hence he had never dreamed that his object was to undermine the purity of a United States Senator. He regretted that it was plain, now, that such was the man's object and that punishment could not with safety to the Senate's honor be withheld. He grieved to say that one of those mysterious dispensations of an inscrutable Providence which are decreed from time to time by His wisdom and for His righteous purposes, had given this conspirator's tale a color of plausibility,—but this would soon disappear under the clear light of truth which would now be thrown upon the case.

It so happened, (said the Senator,) that about the time in question, a poor young friend of mine, living in a distant town of my State, wished to establish a bank; he asked me to lend him the necessary money; I said I had no money just then, but would try to borrow it. The day before the election a friend said to me that my election expenses must be very large—especially my hotel bills,—and offered to lend me some money. Remembering my young friend, I said I would like a few thousands now,

and a few more by and by; whereupon he gave me two packages of bills said to contain $2,000 and $5,000 respectively; I did
not open the packages or count the money; I did not give any
note or receipt for the same; I made no memorandum of the
transaction, and neither did my friend. That night this evil
man Noble came troubling me again. I could not rid myself of
him, though my time was very precious. He mentioned my
young friend and said he was very anxious to have $7,000 now
to begin his banking operations with, and could wait a while for
the rest. Noble wished to get the money and take it to him. I
finally gave him the two packages of bills; I took no note or receipt from him, and made no memorandum of the matter. I no
more look for duplicity and deception in another man than I
would look for it in myself. I never thought of this man again
until I was overwhelmed the next day by learning what a shameful use he had made of the confidence I had reposed in him
and the money I had entrusted to his care. This is all, gentlemen. To the absolute truth of every detail of my statement I
solemnly swear, and I call Him to witness who is the Truth and
the loving Father of all whose lips abhor false speaking; I pledge
my honor as a Senator, that I have spoken but the truth. May
God forgive this wicked man—as I do.

Mr. Noble—"Senator Dilworthy, your bank account shows that
up to that day, and even on that very day, you conducted all
your financial business through the medium of checks instead
of bills, and so kept careful record of every moneyed transaction.
Why did you deal in bank bills on this particular occasion?"

The Chairman—"The gentleman will please to remember that
the Committee is conducting this investigation."

Mr. Noble—"Then will the Committee ask the question?"

The Chairman—"The Committee will—when it desires to
know."

Mr. Noble—"Which will not be during this century perhaps."

The Chairman—"Another remark like that, sir, will procure
you the attentions of the Sergeant-at-Arms."

*Mr. Noble*—"D——n the Sergeant-at-Arms, and the Committee too!"

*Several Committeemen*—"Mr. Chairman, this is contempt!"

*Mr. Noble*—"Contempt of whom?"

"Of the Committee! Of the Senate of the United States!"

*Mr. Noble*—"Then I am become the acknowledged representative of a nation. You know as well as I do that the whole nation hold as much as three-fifths of the United States Senate in entire contempt.—Three-fifths of you are Dilworthys."

The Sergeant-at-Arms very soon put a quietus upon the observations of the representative of the nation, and convinced him that he was not in the over-free atmosphere of his Happy-Land-of-Canaan.

The statement of Senator Dilworthy naturally carried conviction to the minds of the Committee.—It was close, logical, unanswerable; it bore many internal evidences of its truth.—For instance, it is customary in all countries for business men to loan large sums of money in bank bills instead of checks. It is customary for the lender to make no memorandum of the transaction. It is customary for the borrower to receive the money without making a memorandum of it, or giving a note or a receipt for it—because the borrower is not likely to die or forget about it. It is customary to lend nearly anybody money to start a bank with, especially if you have not the money to lend him and have to borrow it for the purpose. It is customary to carry large sums of money in bank bills about your person or in your trunk. It is customary to hand a large sum in bank bills to a man you have just been introduced to (if he asks you to do it,) to be conveyed to a distant town and delivered to another party. It is not customary to make a memorandum of this transaction; it is not customary for the conveyor to give a note or a receipt for the money; it is not customary to require that he shall get a note or a receipt from the man he is to convey it to in the distant town. It would be at least singular in you to say to the proposed conveyor, "You might be robbed; I will deposit the money in bank and send a check for it to my friend through the mail."

Very well. It being plain that Senator Dilworthy's statement was rigidly true, and this fact being strengthened by his adding to it the support of "his honor as a Senator," the Committee rendered a verdict of "Not proven that a bribe had been offered and accepted." This in a manner exonerated Noble and let him escape.

The Committee made its report to the Senate, and that body proceeded to consider its acceptance. One Senator—indeed, several Senators—objected that the Committee had failed of its duty; they had proved this man Noble guilty of nothing, they had meted out no punishment to him; if the report were accepted, he would go forth free and scathless, glorying in his crime, and it would be a tacit admission that any blackguard could insult the Senate of the United States and conspire against the sacred reputation of its members with impunity; the Senate owed it to the upholding of its ancient dignity to make an example of this man Noble—he should be crushed.

An elderly Senator got up and took another view of the case. This was a Senator of the worn-out and obsolete pattern; a man still lingering among the cobwebs of the past, and behind the spirit of the age. He said that there seemed to be a curious misunderstanding of the case. Gentlemen seemed exceedingly anxious to preserve and maintain the honor and dignity of the Senate.

Was this to be done by trying an obscure adventurer for attempting to trap a Senator into bribing him? Or would not the truer way be to find out whether the Senator was capable of *being* entrapped into so shameless an act, and then try *him*? Why, of course. *Now* the whole idea of the Senate seemed to be to shield the Senator and turn inquiry away from him. The true way to uphold the honor of the Senate was to have none but honorable men in its body. If this Senator had yielded to temptation and had offered a bribe, he was a soiled man and ought to be instantly expelled; therefore he wanted the Senator tried, and not in the usual namby-pamby way, but in good earnest. He wanted to know the truth of this matter. For himself, he believed that the guilt of Senator Dilworthy was established beyond the shadow of a doubt; and he considered that in trifling with his case and shirking it the Senate was doing a shameful and cowardly thing—a thing which suggested that in its willingness to sit longer in the company of such a man, it was acknowledging that it was itself of a kind with him and was therefore not dishonored by his presence. He desired that a rigid examination be made into Senator Dilworthy's case, and that it be continued clear into the approaching extra session if need be. There was no dodging this thing with the lame excuse of want of time.

In reply, an honorable Senator said that he thought it would be as well to drop the matter and accept the Committee's report. He said with some jocularity that the more one agitated this thing, the worse it was for the agitator. He was not able to deny that he believed Senator Dilworthy to be guilty—but what then? Was it such an extraordinary case? For his part, even allowing the Senator to be guilty, he did not think his continued presence during the few remaining days of the Session would contaminate the Senate to a dreadful degree. [This humorous sally was received with smiling admiration—notwithstanding it was not wholly new, having originated with the Massachusetts General in the House a day or two before, upon the occasion of the proposed expulsion of a member for selling his vote for money.]

The Senate recognized the fact that it could not be contaminated by sitting a few days longer with Senator Dilworthy, and so it accepted the committee's report and dropped the unimportant matter.

Mr. Dilworthy occupied his seat to the last hour of the session. He said that his people had reposed a trust in him, and it was not for him to desert them. He would remain at his post till he perished, if need be.

His voice was lifted up and his vote cast for the last time, in support of an ingenious measure contrived by the General from Massachusetts whereby the President's salary was proposed to be doubled and every Congressman paid several thousand dollars extra for work previously done, under an accepted contract, and already paid for once and receipted for.

Senator Dilworthy was offered a grand ovation by his friends at home, who said that their affection for him and their confidence in him were in no wise impaired by the persecutions that had pursued him, and that he was still good enough for them. *

---

* The $7,000 left by Mr. Noble with his state legislature was placed in safe keeping to await the claim of the legitimate owner. Senator Dilworthy made one little effort through his protégé the embryo banker to recover it, but there being no notes of hand or other memoranda to support the claim, it failed. The moral of which is, that when one loans money to start a bank with, one ought to take the party's written acknowledgment of the fact.—M.T.

## CHAPTER 33

For some days Laura had been a free woman once more. During this time, she had experienced—first, two or three days of triumph, excitement, congratulations, a sort of sunburst of gladness, after a long night of gloom and anxiety; then two or three days of calming down, by degrees—a receding of tides, a quieting of the storm-wash to a murmurous surf-beat, a diminishing of devastating winds to a refrain that bore the spirit of a truce—days given to solitude, rest, self-communion, and the reasoning of herself into a realization of the fact that she was actually done with bolts and bars, prison horrors and impending death; then came a day whose hours filed slowly by her, each laden with some remnant, some remaining fragment of the dreadful time so lately ended—a day which, closing at last, left the past a fading shore behind her and turned her eyes toward the broad sea of the future. So speedily do we put the dead away and come back to our place in the ranks to march in the pilgrimage of life again!

And now the sun rose once more and ushered in the first day of what Laura comprehended and accepted as a new life.

The past had sunk below the horizon, and existed no more for her; she was done with it for all time. She was gazing out over the trackless expanses of the future, now, with troubled eyes. Life must be begun again—at eight and twenty years of age. And where to begin? The page was blank, and waiting for its first record; so this was indeed a momentous day.

Her thoughts drifted back, stage by stage, over her career. As far as the long highway receded over the plain of her life, it was lined with the gilded and pillared splendors of her ambition all crumbled to ruin and ivy-grown; every milestone marked a disaster; there was no green spot remaining anywhere in memory of a hope that had found its fruition; the unresponsive earth had uttered no voice of flowers in testimony that one who was blest had gone that road.

Her life had been a failure. That was plain, she said. No more of that. She would now look the future in the face; she would mark her course upon the chart of life, and follow it; follow it without swerving, through rocks and shoals, through storm and calm, to a haven of rest and peace—or, shipwreck. Let the end be what it might, she would mark her course now—to-day—and follow it.

On her table lay six or seven notes. They were from lovers; from some of the prominent names in the land; men whose devotion had survived even the grisly revealments of her character which the courts had uncurtained; men who knew her now, just as she was, and yet pleaded as for their lives for the dear privilege of calling the murderess wife.

As she read these passionate, these worshiping, these supplicating missives, the woman in her nature confessed itself; a strong yearning came upon her to lay her head upon a loyal breast and find rest from the conflict of life, solace for her griefs, the healing of love for her bruised heart.

With her forehead resting upon her hand, she sat thinking, thinking, while the unheeded moments winged their flight. It was one of those mornings in early spring when nature seems just stirring to a half consciousness out of a long, exhausting lethargy; when the first faint balmy airs go wandering about, whispering the secret of the coming change; when the abused brown grass, newly relieved of snow, seems considering whether it can be worth the trouble and worry of contriving its green raiment again only to fight the inevitable fight with the implacable winter and be vanquished and buried once more; when the sun shines out and a few birds venture forth and lift up a forgotten song; when a strange stillness and suspense pervades the waiting air. It is a time when one's spirit is subdued and sad, one knows not why; when the past seems a storm-swept desolation, life a vanity and a burden, and the future but a way to death. It is a time when one is filled with vague longings; when one dreams of flight to peaceful islands in the remote solitudes of the sea, or folds his hands and says, What is the use of struggling, and toiling and worrying any more? let us give it all up.

It was into such a mood as this that Laura had drifted from the musings which the letters of her lovers had called up. Now she lifted her head and noted with surprise how the day had wasted. She thrust the letters aside, rose up and went and stood at the window. But she was soon thinking again, and was only gazing into vacancy.

By and by she turned; her countenance had cleared; the dreamy look was gone out of her face, all indecision had vanished; the poise of her head and the firm set of her lips told that her resolution was formed. She moved toward the table with all the old dignity in her carriage, and all the old pride in her mien. She took up each letter in its turn, touched a match to it and watched it slowly consume to ashes. Then she said:

"I have landed upon a foreign shore, and burned my ships behind me. These letters were the last thing that held me in sympathy with any remnant or belonging of the old life. Henceforth that life and all that appertains to it are as dead to me and as far removed from me as if I were become a denizen of another world."

She said that love was not for her—the time that it could have satisfied her heart was gone by and could not return; the opportunity was lost, nothing could restore it. She said there could be no love without respect, and she would only despise a man who could content himself with a thing like her. Love, she said, was a woman's first necessity: love being forfeited, there was but one thing left that could give a passing zest to a wasted life, and that was fame, admiration, the applause of the multitude.

And so her resolution was taken. She would turn to that final resort of the disappointed of her sex, the lecture platform. She would array herself in fine attire, she would adorn herself with jewels, and stand in her isolated magnificence before massed audiences and enchant them with her eloquence and amaze them with her unapproachable beauty. She would move from city to city like a queen of romance, leaving marveling multitudes behind her and impatient multitudes awaiting her coming. Her life, during one hour of each day, upon the platform, would be a rapturous intoxication—and when the curtain fell, and the lights were out, and the people gone, to nestle in their homes and forget her, she would find in sleep oblivion of her homelessness, if she could, if not she would brave out the night in solitude and wait for the next day's hour of ecstasy.

So, to take up life and begin again was no great evil. She saw her way. She would be brave and strong; she would make the best of what was left for her among the possibilities.

She sent for the lecture agent, and matters were soon arranged.

Straightway all the papers were filled with her name, and all the dead walls flamed with it. The papers called down imprecations upon her head; they reviled her without stint; they wondered if all sense of decency was dead in this shameless murderess, this brazen lobbyist, this heartless seducer of the affections of weak and misguided men; they implored the people, for the sake of their pure wives, their sinless daughters, for the sake of decency, for the sake of public morals, to give this wretched creature such a rebuke as should be an all-sufficient evidence to her and to such as her, that there was a limit where the flaunting of their foul acts and opinions before the world must stop; certain of them, with a higher art, and to her a finer cruelty, a sharper torture, uttered no abuse, but always spoke of her in terms of mocking eulogy and ironical admiration. Everybody talked about the new wonder, canvassed the theme of her proposed discourse, and marveled how she would handle it.

Laura's few friends wrote to her or came and talked with her, and pleaded with her to retire while it was yet time, and not attempt to face the gathering storm. But it was fruitless. She was stung to the quick by the comments of the newspapers; her spirit was roused, her ambition was towering, now. She was more determined than ever. She would show these people what a hunted and persecuted woman could do.

The eventful night came. Laura arrived before the great lecture hall in a closed carriage within five minutes of the time set for the lecture to begin. When she stepped out of the vehicle her heart beat fast and her eyes flashed with exultation: the whole street was packed with people, and she could hardly force her way to the hall! She reached the ante-room, threw off her wraps and placed herself before the dressing-glass. She turned herself this way and that—everything was satisfactory, her attire was perfect. She smoothed her hair, re-arranged a jewel here and there, and all the while her heart sang within her, and her face was radiant. She had not been so happy for ages and ages, it seemed to her. Oh, no, she had never been so overwhelmingly grateful and happy in her whole life before. The lecture agent appeared at the door. She waved him away and said:

"Do not disturb me. I want no introduction. And do not fear for me; the moment the hands point to eight I will step upon the platform."

He disappeared. She held her watch before her. She was so impatient that the second-hand seemed whole tedious minutes dragging its way around the circle. At last the supreme moment came, and with head erect and the bearing of an empress she swept through the door and stood upon the stage. Her eyes fell upon—

Only a vast, brilliant emptiness—there were not forty people in the house! There were only a handful of coarse men and ten or twelve still coarser women, lolling upon the benches and scattered about singly and in couples.

Her pulses stood still, her limbs quaked, the gladness went out of her face. There was a moment of silence, and then a brutal laugh and an explosion of cat-calls and hisses saluted her from the audience. The clamor grew stronger and louder, and insulting speeches were shouted at her. A half-intoxicated man rose up and threw something, which missed her but bespattered a chair at her side, and this evoked an outburst of laughter and boisterous admiration. She was bewildered, her strength was forsaking her. She reeled away from the platform, reached the ante-room, and dropped helpless upon a sofa. The lecture agent ran in, with a hurried question upon his lips; but she put forth her hands, and with the tears raining from her eyes, said:

"Oh, do not speak! Take me away—please take me away, out of this dreadful place! Oh, this is like all my life—failure, disappointment, misery—always misery, always failure. What have I done, to be so pursued! Take me away, I beg of you, I implore you!"

Upon the pavement she was hustled by the mob, the surging masses roared her name and accompanied it with every species of insulting epithet; they thronged after the carriage, hooting, jeering, cursing, and even assailing the vehicle with missiles. A stone crushed through a blind, wounding Laura's forehead, and so stunning her that she hardly knew what further transpired during her flight.

It was long before her faculties were wholly restored, and then she found herself lying on the floor by a sofa in her own sitting-room, and alone. So she supposed she must have sat down upon the sofa and afterward fallen. She raised herself up, with difficulty, for the air was chilly and her limbs were stiff. She turned up the gas and sought the glass. She hardly knew herself, so worn and old she looked, and so marred with blood were her features. The night was far spent, and a dead stillness reigned. She sat down by her table, leaned her elbows upon it and put her face in her hands.

Her thoughts wandered back over her old life again and her tears flowed unrestrained.—Her pride was humbled, her spirit was broken. Her memory found but one resting place; it lingered about her young girlhood with a caressing regret; it dwelt upon it as the one brief interval in her life that bore no curse. She saw herself again in the budding grace of her twelve years, decked in her dainty pride of ribbons, consorting with the bees and the butterflies, believing in fairies, holding confidential converse with the flowers, busying herself all day long with airy trifles that were as weighty to her as the affairs that tax the brains of diplomats and emperors. She was without sin, then, and unacquainted with grief; the world was full of sunshine and her heart was full of music. From that—to this!

"If I could only die!" she said. "If I could only go back, and be as I was then, for one hour—and hold my father's hand in mine again, and see all the household about me, as in that old innocent time—and then die! My God, I am humbled, my pride is all gone, my stubborn heart repents—have pity!"

When the spring morning dawned, the form still sat there, the elbows resting upon the table and the face upon the hands. All day long the figure sat there, the sunshine enriching its costly raiment and flashing from its jewels; twilight came, and presently the stars, but still the figure remained; the moon found it there still, and framed the picture with the shadow of the window sash, and flooded it with mellow light; by and by the darkness swallowed it up, and later the gray dawn revealed it again; the new day grew toward its prime, and still the forlorn presence was undisturbed.

But now the keepers of the house had become uneasy; their periodical knockings still finding no response, they burst open the door.

The jury of inquest found that death had resulted from heart disease, and was instant and painless. That was all. Merely heart disease.

## CHAPTER 34

Clay Hawkins, years gone by, had yielded, after many a struggle, to the migratory and speculative instinct of our age and our people, and had wandered further and further westward upon trading ventures. Settling finally in Melbourne, Australia, he ceased to roam, became a steady-going substantial merchant, and prospered greatly. His life lay beyond the theatre of this tale.

His remittances had supported the Hawkins family, entirely, from the time of his father's death until latterly when Laura by her efforts in Washington had been able to assist in this work. Clay was away on a long absence in some of the eastward islands when Laura's troubles began, trying (and almost in vain,) to arrange certain interests which had become disordered through a dishonest agent, and consequently he knew nothing of the murder till he returned and read his letters and papers. His natural impulse was to hurry to the States and save his sister if possible, for he loved her with a deep and abiding affection.—His business was so crippled now, and so deranged, that to leave it would be ruin; therefore he sold out at a sacrifice that left him considerably reduced in worldly possessions, and began his voyage to San Francisco. Arrived there, he perceived by the newspapers that the trial was near its close. At Salt Lake later telegrams told him of the acquittal, and his gratitude was boundless—so boundless, indeed, that sleep was driven from his eyes by the pleasurable excitement almost as effectually as preceding weeks of anxiety had done it. He shaped his course straight for Hawkeye, now, and his meeting with his mother and the rest of the household was joyful—albeit he had been away so long that he seemed almost a stranger in his own home.

But the greetings and congratulations were hardly finished when all the journals in the land clamored the news of Laura's miserable death. Mrs. Hawkins was prostrated by this last blow, and it was well that Clay was at her side to stay her with comforting words and take upon himself the ordering of the household with its burden of labors and cares.

Washington Hawkins had scarcely more than entered upon that decade which carries one to the full blossom of manhood which we term the beginning of middle age, and yet a brief sojourn at the capital of the nation had made him old. His hair was already turning gray when the late session of Congress began its sittings; it grew grayer still, and rapidly, after the memorable day that saw Laura proclaimed a murderess; it waxed grayer and still grayer during the lagging suspense that succeeded it and after the crash which ruined his last hope—the failure of his bill in the Senate and the destruction of its champion, Dilworthy. A few days later, when he stood uncovered while the last prayer was pronounced over Laura's grave, his hair was whiter and his face hardly less old than the venerable minister's whose words were sounding in his ears.

A week after this, he was sitting in a double-bedded room in a cheap boarding house in Washington, with Col. Sellers. The two had been living together lately, and this mutual cavern of theirs the Colonel sometimes referred to as their "premises" and sometimes as their "apartments"—more particularly when conversing with persons outside. A canvas-covered modern trunk, marked "G. W. H." stood on end by the door, strapped and ready for a journey; on it lay a small morocco satchel, also marked "G. W. H." There was another trunk close by—a worn, and scarred, and ancient hair relic, with "E. S." wrought in brass nails on its top; on it lay a pair of saddle-bags that probably knew more about the last century than they could tell. Washington got up and walked the floor a while in a restless sort of way, and finally was about to sit down on the hair trunk.

"Stop, don't sit down on that!" exclaimed the Colonel. "There, now—that's all right—the chair's better. I couldn't get another trunk like that—not another like it in America, I reckon."

"I am afraid not," said Washington, with a faint attempt at a smile.

"No indeed; the man is dead that made that trunk and that saddle-bags."

"Are his great-grandchildren still living?" said Washington, with levity only in the words, not in the tone.

"Well, I don't know—I hadn't thought of that—but anyway they can't make trunks and saddle-bags like that, if they are—no man can," said the Colonel with honest simplicity. "Wife didn't like to see me going off with that trunk—she said it was nearly certain to be stolen."

"Why?"

"Why? Why, aren't trunks always being stolen?"

"Well, yes—some kinds of trunks are."

"Very well, then; this is some kind of a trunk—and an almighty rare kind, too."

"Yes, I believe it is."

"Well, then, why shouldn't a man want to steal it if he got a chance?"

"Indeed I don't know.—Why should he?"

"Washington, I never heard anybody talk like you. Suppose you were a thief, and that trunk was lying around and nobody watching—wouldn't you steal it? Come, now, answer fair—wouldn't you steal it?"

"Well, now, since you corner me, I don't know but I would *take* it,—but I wouldn't consider it stealing."

"You wouldn't! Well, that beats me. Now what would you call stealing?"

"Why, taking property is stealing."

"Property! Now what a way to talk that is. What do you suppose that trunk is worth?"

"Is it in good repair?"

"Perfect. Hair rubbed off a little, but the main structure is perfectly sound."

"Does it leak anywhere?"

"Leak? Do you want to carry water in it? What do you mean by does it leak?"

"Why—a—do the clothes fall out of it when it is—when it is stationary?"

"Confound it, Washington, you are trying to make fun of me. I don't know what has got into you to-day; you act mighty curious. What *is* the matter with you?"

"Well, I'll tell you, old friend. I am almost happy. I am, indeed. It wasn't Clay's telegram that hurried me up so and got me ready to start with you. It was a letter from Louise."

"Good! What is it? What does she say?"

"She says come home—her father has consented, at last."

"My boy, I want to congratulate you; I want to shake you by the hand! It's a long turn that has no lane at the end of it, as the proverb says, or somehow that way. You'll be happy yet, and Eschol Sellers will be there to see, thank God!"

"I believe it. General Boswell is pretty nearly a poor man, now. The railroad that was going to build up Hawkeye made short work of him, along with the rest. He isn't so opposed to a son-in-law without a fortune, now."

"Without a fortune, indeed! Why that Tennessee Land—"

"Never mind the Tennessee Land, Colonel. I am done with that, forever and forever—"

"Why no! You can't mean to say—"

"My father, away back yonder, years ago, bought it for a blessing for his children, and—"

"Indeed he did! Si Hawkins said to me—"

"It proved a curse to him as long as he lived, and never a curse like it was inflicted upon any man's heirs—"

"I'm bound to say there's more or less truth—"

"It began to curse me when I was a baby, and it has cursed every hour of my life to this day—"

"Lord, lord, but it's so! Time and again my wife—"

"I depended on it all through my boyhood and never tried to do an honest stroke of work for my living—"

"Right again—but then you—"

"I have chased it years and years as children chase butter-flies. We might all have been prosperous, now; we might all have been happy, all these heart-breaking years, if we had accepted our poverty at first and gone contentedly to work and built up our own weal by our own toil and sweat—"

"It's so, it's so; bless my soul, how often I've told Si Hawkins—"

"Instead of that, we have suffered more than the damned themselves suffer! I loved my father, and I honor his memory and recognize his good intentions; but I grieve for his mistaken ideas of conferring happiness upon his children. I am going to begin my life over again, and begin it and end it with good solid work! I'll leave *my* children no Tennessee Land!"

"Spoken like a man, sir, spoken like a man! Your hand, again my boy! And always remember that when a word of advice from Eschol Sellers can help, it is at your service. I'm going to begin again, too!"

"Indeed!"

"Yes, sir. I've seen enough to show me where my mistake was. The law is what I was born for. I shall begin the study of the law. Heavens and earth, but that Braham's a wonderful man—a wonderful man sir! Such a head! And such a way with him! But I could see that he was jealous of me. The little licks I got in in the course of my argument before the jury—"

"Your argument! Why, you were a witness."

"Oh, yes, to the popular eye, to the popular eye—but *I* knew when I was dropping information and when I was letting drive at the court with an insidious argument. But the court knew it, bless you, and weakened every time! And Braham knew it. I just reminded him of it in a quiet way, and its final result, and he said in a whisper, 'You did it, Colonel, you did it, sir—but keep it mum for *my* sake; and I'll tell you what *you* do,' says he, 'you go into the law, Col. Sellers—go into the law, sir; that's *your* native element!' And into the law the subscriber is going. There's worlds of money in it!—whole worlds of money! Practice first in Hawkeye, then in Jefferson, then in St. Louis, then in New York! In the metropolis of the western world! Climb, and climb, and climb—and wind up on the Supreme bench. Eschol Sellers, Chief Justice of the Supreme Court of the United States, sir! A made man for all time and eternity! That's the way I block it out, sir—and it's as clear as day—clear as the rosy morn!"

Washington had heard little of this. The first reference to Laura's trial had brought the old dejection to his face again, and he stood gazing out of the window at nothing, lost in reverie.

There was a knock—the postman handed in a letter. It was from Obedstown, East Tennessee, and was for Washington. He opened it. There was a note saying that enclosed he would please find a bill for the current year's taxes on the 75,000 acres of Tennessee Land belonging to the estate of Silas Hawkins, deceased, and added that the money must be paid within sixty days or the land would be sold at public auction for the taxes, as provided by law. The bill was for $180—something more than twice the market value of the land, perhaps.

Washington hesitated. Doubts flitted through his mind. The old instinct came upon him to cling to the land just a little longer and give it one more chance. He walked the floor feverishly, his mind tortured by indecision. Presently he stopped, took out his pocket book and counted his money. Two hundred and thirty dollars—it was all he had in the world.

"One hundred and eighty . . . . . . from two hundred and thirty," he said to himself. "Fifty left . . . . . . It is enough to get me home . . . . . . Shall I do it, or shall I not? . . . . . . . I wish I had somebody to decide for me."

The pocket book lay open in his hand, with Louise's small letter in view. His eye fell upon that, and it decided him.

"It shall go for taxes," he said, "and never tempt me or mine any more!"

He opened the window and stood there tearing the tax bill to bits and watching the breeze waft them away, till all were gone.

"The spell is broken, the life-long curse is ended!" he said. "Let us go."

The baggage wagon had arrived; five minutes later the two

friends were mounted upon their luggage in it, and rattling off toward the station, the Colonel endeavoring to sing "Homeward Bound," a song whose words he knew, but whose tune, as he rendered it, was a trial to auditors.

# NOTES

On the flyleaf of the Seaver copy of *The Gilded Age* Clemens wrote in pencil: "To friend Seaver from Mark. Hartford, July '74. Some of my errors in this book would have been simply outrageous, but Warner criticized them faithfully & so I re-wrote 200 pages of my MS & cooled the absurdities down to a reasonable temperature."

Chapter 6 of *The Gilded Age* (and of *Colonel Sellers*). The first eleven chapters of *The Gilded Age* are by Clemens, with the exception of four paragraphs of approximately 265 words which Warner contributed to Chapter 6. These are the third, fourth, fifth and seventh paragraphs of the chapter.

Chapter 18 of *The Gilded Age* (about Laura's meeting Selby in Hawkeye, "marrying" him, being deserted by him, etc.). Clemens wrote in the Seaver copy, "[The chapter mapped out by C & written by W.]"

Chapter 29 of *The Gilded Age*. At the head of this chapter in the Seaver copy Clemens wrote, referring to an incident on a train, "This incident is fact—recounted by C & written by W." Clemens supplied a passage dealing with Philip's conscience and citizenship, beginning on the bottom of page 268 of the first edition. "He confessed that neither he nor any citizen had a right to consult his own feelings or conscience in a case where a law of the land had been violated before his own eyes. He confessed that every citizen's first duty in such a case is to put aside his own business and devote his time and his best efforts to seeing that the infraction is promptly punished; and he knew that no country can be well governed unless its citizens as a body keep religiously before their minds that they are the guardians of the law, and that the law officers are only the machinery for its execution, nothing more. As a finality he was obliged to confess that he was a bad citizen, and also that the general laxity of the time, and the absence of a sense of duty toward any part of the community but the individual himself were ingrained in him, and he was no better than the rest of the people."

Chapter 35 of *The Gilded Age* (Chapter 21 of *Colonel Sellers*).
In the Seaver copy Clemens wrote, "Written first by C, but re-
written by W, who incorporated half of C's MS in it & the rest was
discarded." Clemens did not mark the passages which had been retained by Warner but it is not difficult to make a good guess at which
they are, which I have done. This is the only chapter in *The Gilded
Age* where Clemens did not specify in detail his own contribution.
I have not been able to locate the manuscript of Chapter 35 of
*The Gilded Age*.

Chapter 53 of *The Gilded Age* (Chapter 29 of *Colonel Sellers*).
In a letter to Mrs. Mary Mason Fairbanks, February 25, 1874, and in
a letter to Dr. John Brown, February 28, 1874, Clemens claimed
authorship of the whole of this chapter, but in the Seaver copy he
marked the small portion which Warner had contributed.

Chapter 56 of *The Gilded Age* (part of Chapter 30 of *Colonel
Sellers*). Clemens wrote in the Seaver copy, "This was first done in
narrative style by W & afterward broken up into dialogue by C,"
and he marked the portions which he and Warner had written respectively.

Chapter 58 of *The Gilded Age* (appended to Chapter 31 of
*Colonel Sellers*). Referring to his description of Mr. Griller, Clemens
wrote in the Seaver copy, "This is the late Mr. Brelsford."

Chapter 60 of *The Gilded Age* (Chapter 33 of *Colonel Sellers*).
At the end of this chapter Clemens wrote in the Seaver copy,
"Warner wrote a chapter, first, disposing of Laura by sending her
into Western retirement & obscurity—but I replaced it with this one."